HE'S
TO DIE FOR

HE'S
TO DIE FOR

A Novel

ERIN DUNN

MINOTAUR BOOKS
NEW YORK

First published in the United States by Minotaur Books, an imprint of St. Martin's Publishing Group

HE'S TO DIE FOR. Copyright © 2025 by Erin Dunn. All rights reserved. Printed in the United States of America. For information, address St. Martin's Publishing Group, 120 Broadway, New York, N.Y. 10271.

www.minotaurbooks.com

Design by Meryl Sussman Levavi

Phone emojis: VectorHive/Shutterstock

The Library of Congress Cataloging-in-Publication Data is available upon request.

ISBN 978-1-250-36062-5 (trade paperback)
ISBN 978-1-250-39735-5 (hardcover)
ISBN 978-1-250-36063-2 (ebook)

Our books may be purchased in bulk for promotional, educational, or business use. Please contact your local bookseller or the Macmillan Corporate and Premium Sales Department at 1-800-221-7945, extension 5442, or by email at MacmillanSpecialMarkets@macmillan.com.

First Edition: 2025

10 9 8 7 6 5 4 3 2 1

A book isn't supposed to be a mirror.
It's supposed to be a door.

—Fran Lebowitz

HE'S
TO DIE FOR

CHAPTER ONE

It's 11:45 on a Friday night, and Rav Trivedi is cranky. It's been a long day and a long week. He should be ordering dessert at his favorite restaurant, or sipping champagne at a gallery opening, or whatever it is normal people do on a Friday night in New York City, but instead he had to work late, and now he's inching his way crosstown in the back of a yellow cab that reeks of cotton candy. It's taken ten minutes to travel two blocks, and the pink air freshener swinging from the rearview is so overpowering it's making him dizzy. He tries to lower the window to vent the sickly-sweet odor, but the button doesn't respond. "Excuse me," he says, leaning forward, "the window back here won't go down."

"I don't open windows in traffic," the driver informs him. "Exhaust fumes give me a headache."

"Right." Rav fades back into the seat and considers his options. As usual, his instincts are torn between the two sides of his upbringing, as if one of his parents is perched on each shoulder. On the left sits His Lordship, English to a fault, counseling his son to bear it in dignified silence. On the right is Eva, native New Yorker and consummate diva, quoting the yellow taxi passenger bill of rights and reminding Rav that *he* is the customer here.

He tries to split the difference. "Only the trouble is . . ." He leans forward again. "This air freshener is giving *me* a headache, so we have a dilemma."

Dark eyes meet his in the rearview, sizing him up. Rav catches his own reflection in the acrylic divider: young, pretty, scrubbed and tweezed and carefully styled. Bespoke suit, high-maintenance haircut, Oxford English accent. He can guess well enough what it adds up to in the driver's mind.

"Sorry to hear it, princess. You don't like it, get a limo next time." He punches the radio and turns it up loud.

Apparently, Rav isn't the only one having a *day*.

He surrenders to his fate, tucking his fingers under his nose and letting the delicate cedar scent of his hand lotion do what it can against the smell. It's going to cling to him like a bad cologne, isn't it? Eau de Coney Island: cotton candy and grime, with subtle notes of despair.

A call comes in on his phone. It's work, because of course it is. Rav hits *decline*, but before he's even stuffed it back in his pocket, it buzzes with a message.

Pick up.

It's vibrating again. This time, Rav takes the call. "You have reached the voicemail of Detective Rav Trivedi of the New York City Police Department. I can't take your call right now, because I don't want to. If you require immediate assistance, you can contact my partner, Detective Will Shepard. Unless you *are* the aforementioned partner, in which case you can kindly sod off, because it's been a very long day and I have a date with a strapping fireman and some massage oil."

In his dreams, anyway.

There's a pause on the line. "Are you done?"

"It's nearly midnight, Will. I've spent the past four hours canvassing every bingo hall in Brooklyn and I'm in a *mood*."

"Cry me a river. I spent my day sifting through trash under the Brooklyn-Queens Expressway."

Rav grimaces. "Touché."

"Anyway, what's so bad about bingo halls? Don't tell me you're afraid of a bunch of harmless old biddies?"

"Harmless? Clearly, you haven't spent enough time in the company of old biddies. Young men in well-tailored suits are like catnip to them. You wouldn't believe the sorts of things that come out of their mouths."

"Such as?"

"One of them called me a 'sleek sports car' she'd like to take for a joyride. Another had some engaging suggestions for how I might make use of my handcuffs."

"Yikes."

"My trouser pockets are full of Werther's Originals."

"The butterscotch? That's not so—"

"*I didn't put them there.*"

"Wow," Will says, laughing. "And here I thought interviewing drug dealers was dangerous."

"More guns, less inappropriate touching."

"Where are you, anyway? Is that music I hear?"

"In a cab, and that last part is debatable." Rav sticks a finger in his ear. "The worst part is that I got absolutely nowhere. Please tell me you had more luck."

"Might have. Wanted to run it by you while it's fresh in my mind. Nobody saw our vic, but they did see his car, and a witness claims—"

"Hold on, I can hardly hear you." Rav leans forward in his seat. "I beg your pardon, but would you mind turning that down? Official police business."

The cab driver meets his eye in the rearview again. Then he hits the *up* arrow on his stereo. Twice.

Rav can just make out Will's laughter over the pounding of drums. "Saw that coming. Gotta love New York cabbies. Great tune, by the way. Nicks."

"What?"

"The Nicks. The New Knickerbockers? You know, the band?"

"Sorry, I'm not up on what the kids are listening to these days."

"You're twenty-nine years old, Rav."

"Don't remind me. I turn thirty in precisely three months, whereupon my desiccated husk will most likely disintegrate into gold glitter and blow away."

"Saves me having to buy you a birthday present."

Rav snorts appreciatively. Though they haven't worked to-gether long, the two of them have found a comfortable rhythm. Shepard is always up for a little banter, and he's got this low-key wit that Rav quite enjoys. They complement each other well, too. Rav can be a little intense, and Shepard's more slow-and-steady approach balances that out. More important, despite being ex-army and built like an NFL quarterback, Will doesn't feel the need to prove his masculinity at every turn, which is refreshing. As an openly gay cop, Rav's had to put up with a lot of alpha male bullshit over the years, so it's a relief to work with someone who's safe enough in his own skin to let Rav be safe in his.

"Hey, you still there?"

"Sorry, my mind is wandering. It's been a long one. You were saying about a witness?"

"Right. He claims to have seen a white female—"

The cab driver slams on the brakes, jerking Rav into his seat belt and sending his phone flying. "Did you see that?" The driver lays on the horn with both hands. "This woman just jumped in front of my car! Hey, lady, are you nuts?" Rav isn't paying much attention, too busy fishing his phone out of the seat well. Then a chorus of honking goes up all around them, and the driver murmurs an ominous "Shit . . ."

Rav sits up and looks out the window. The street is swarming with scared-looking people running away from something.

"Rav?" Will's voice floats up from the phone. "You there?"

He is very much there, his fatigue instantly evaporating in a jolt of adrenaline. "Something's going down near Union Square." He describes what he's looking at and gives Shepard the cross streets.

"The Concord Theater?"

"Looks like it." Rav opens an app on his NYPD-issued phone, but there's no alert yet. "You in the squad room?"

"Yeah. Hold on, I'll turn on the radio." A police radio squawks in the background. Shepard listens for a second, and then he swears softly. "It's the Concord," he confirms. "10–13."

10–13. Officer needs assistance.

Shit. Rav eyes the street. "I'm less than a block away."

"You're off duty, man."

Rav hears the warning tone, and he knows his partner is right. Responding to a situation when you're off duty can get messy.

"There'll be a hundred cops converging on the place in five minutes," Shepard says.

Already, sirens wail nearby, punctuated by the blasting horns of FDNY fire trucks, but the traffic is piled up for blocks. They'll be a while getting through that mess. "That could be any of us in there, Will."

"Yeah." Shepard curses again. "Call me back when you can. And watch your ass out there."

Rav bails out of the cab. The sidewalk is bedlam, and the street, too; nobody's watching where they're going, too busy gawking or running away or filming on their phones. "NYPD!" he shouts as he jostles his way through the crowd. "Coming through!"

He's reached the theater now. It's still emptying out, and though the faces he passes look scared, he doesn't spot any injuries. He grabs his shield and hangs it around his neck.

"Officer!" A guy in a bright yellow shirt that says EVENT SECURITY runs up to him. "Hey, Officer, there's a guy with a gun in there!"

"Are you sure?"

"Yeah, man!" He points at the doors. "I already told those other cops! I saw it sticking out of the back of his pants. He was waving this big sign around and ranting and raving."

Rav hesitates another precious second. Will is right: this place will be swarming with cops any minute, guys who are in a much better position to do some good in there. The smart thing would be to stand down. And Rav is smart, he really is, but he'd never forgive himself if something awful happened while he just stood there like a tourist, so he draws his weapon and goes in.

His mouth is dry, and there's a metallic taste on his tongue. He's trained for this, but training only goes so far. He's never fired his weapon in the real. Now he's charging after an armed suspect without backup, no vest, no tactical gear of any kind. At least his hands are steady, his sidearm pointed carefully at the floor as he rushes past the remaining trickle of concertgoers. "Hey," he calls after one of them, a girl in a New Knickerbockers shirt. "Is anyone still in there?"

She shakes her head frantically. "I don't know!"

"Did you see a—" But she's already gone.

The doors to the auditorium are open. Rav presses himself against the doorframe. "NYPD! Is anyone in there?"

No answer.

Rav speaks three languages and can swear floridly in all of them. He does so now. Then, taking a deep breath, he plunges into the auditorium. The house lights are up, the stage lights still glowing. He pauses, listening. It's eerily quiet, but he hears what sounds like a door squeaking on its hinges somewhere. Slowly, he makes his way toward the stage. The floor is sticky, littered with discarded plastic cups and reeking of spilled beer. There's definitely noise coming from back there.

He pauses at the edge of the stage to listen, then vaults himself up. It's hot under the stage lights, as if he wasn't sweating enough already.

Something shifts in the shadows. Rav inches toward it. "Police! Identify yourself!"

"NYPD." The voice sounds strained. Stepping beyond the glare of the lights, Rav sees a uniformed officer slumped on the floor, grimacing in pain.

"Are you all right? Do you need an ambulance?"

The cop shakes his head. "Just sprained my ankle or something. Wiped out chasing the guy. Watch your step, there's water all over the floor back here."

"Where did he go?"

The cop tilts his head toward the dressing rooms. "White male, definitely armed. Some kind of protester, I think. Found his sign on the floor over there." He points. Even from here, Rav can see the word in bright red letters.

MURDERED.

"Where's your partner?"

"Loading dock. We heard a noise."

"You'll be all right here?" Rav starts toward the stage door.

"Hey, man, you sure you wanna go back there on your own? Backup'll be here any minute."

By which point the suspect will probably be long gone. *You've come this far*, Rav tells himself. *Just get it done.* Swallowing, he heads backstage.

He hasn't gone far before he hears a door slamming—and then a voice, half-angry, half-scared. "Where are you?" More banging, as if someone is trying one door after another. "I know you're back here! Come on, man, I just wanna talk to you!" A figure lurches into view at the far end of the corridor. He turns full circle, seemingly at a loss.

Rav raises his weapon. "*NYPD! Get on the ground!*"

The guy bolts.

So now Rav is chasing after him, but the suspect has a thirty-foot head start and he's knocking over lighting stands and shoving wheeled equipment cases and doing everything he can to trip Rav up, and by the time Rav clears the obstacle course, the emergency exit at the end of the hall is slamming shut. He bursts out into the side street behind the theater to find it empty, and it's anybody's guess which way the guy went.

He starts left just as a trio of cops in tactical gear pour out of the emergency exit behind him. "Which way?" one of them snaps. Rav shakes his head, and two of them peel off. "Did you get a look at him?" the third cop asks.

"Not really. He's wearing a hooded sweatshirt. White guy, built like a whippet. Runs like one, too," he adds, still out of breath.

"You should've waited for us," the cop says, looking him over. "You're not even wearing a vest."

"Yeah." Rav sighs and holsters his weapon. "Well, it's all yours now, mate."

Forty minutes later, he's slumped in the passenger seat of Will Shepard's Volkswagen Golf, massaging his temples and dreaming of his queen-size bed. "Sounds like it was pretty intense in there," Shepard says, glancing him over. "You okay?"

"I'm fine, really. You didn't need to come all the way out here." Rav tried to talk him out of it, but Will insisted. He brushes it off now, too.

"That's what partners do."

"Well, I owe you one." Rav sighs. "You were right, I should never have gone in there. It was reckless."

"I get it. You were looking out for one of your own."

The anodyne music playing on the stereo fades out. *"In the news, a bizarre and frightening incident at the Concord Theater when an armed protester tried to force his way backstage during a rock concert headlined by the New Knickerbockers. Witnesses describe a chaotic scene as concertgoers evacuated the venue shortly before midnight. No serious injuries have been reported, although—"*

Will turns it off. "Can't believe the guy got away. You'd think there'd be at least a dozen witnesses who saw which way he went."

"Please don't rub it in. I should've had him."

"You did everything you could." Will pauses, brow creasing. "Hey, do you smell that? Is that . . . cotton candy?"

It's after three when Rav finally gets home, and he doesn't even bother to put his suit on the valet, leaving bits of it strewn across the hardwood on his way to the bath. He runs it extra hot, with some lavender salts, and pours himself a glass of wine. Then he sinks in up to his ears, vowing never to think of the Concord, the New Knickerbockers, or any of the rest of it ever again.

CHAPTER TWO

Two weeks later . . .

Rav is perched on the edge of his partner's desk, tossing an apple from hand to hand. It's not his apple. He avoids fruit wherever possible, unless you count fermented grapes. Will, on the other hand, nearly always has an apple or an orange on his desk, and Rav finds these to be an acceptable substitute for those little rubber balls some of the other officers bounce off the walls to blow off steam. Will finds this less acceptable, but Rav figures if it really bothered him he'd stop leaving fruit lying around where any inconsiderate arsehole can grab it.

"I'm *saying*," Will is saying, snatching the apple out of the air, "a little healthy competition is well and good, and you have every right to be proud of your clearance rate. But if you keep rubbing Jobs's nose in it, he's gonna break *your* nose. He's thought about it, trust me."

"We've all thought about it," Ayalew puts in without looking up from her paperwork.

"What?" Rav laughs. "Aida, what have I ever done to you?"

"I'm just trying to help you out. You're a little too pristine there, pretty boy. A crooked nose might give you some credibility."

Rav glances at Will. "Is she suggesting I lack gravitas?"

"In a polka-dot suit? *Nah.*"

"It's *pin dot*, you Philistine. As for credibility, may I refer you to the case board." He gestures airily at a whiteboard on the wall, where a brand-new line in erasable red ink marks the Gordon case as *closed*.

They put it to bed yesterday, and he's still high on it. The perp they locked up is a genuine menace, a serial offender who's been preying on his community for years. Victories like that are few and far between, and well worth savoring. And if it happens to put Rav at the front of the pack in terms of cases closed this year, that's a bonus. Maybe now his colleagues will start taking him seriously. He's the youngest on the squad by nearly a decade, and they never tire of reminding him of it. Boy Wonder, they call him. The Little Prince. Or his personal favorite, Doogie Howser, PD. (He had to look that last one up, because the reference is older than he is.) The ribbing he can handle, but not all of it is good-natured. The older guys, in particular, seem to think his promotion to Homicide was more about politics than merit. Rav figures the best way to prove them wrong is to keep putting cases away. So yeah, when he wins one, he's going to celebrate it.

The lieutenant sticks her head out of her door. "Trivedi. My office."

She's got a file folder open on her desk when Rav comes in. "New case?" he asks hopefully as he settles in.

"We'll get to that. First, I've completed your performance evaluation."

Ugh. It's only his second since joining the squad, and the first was . . . frank. One line in particular sticks out in his mind. *Prone to obsessive behavior and an occasionally smug attitude.*

Which, come on. Obsessive? There's nothing obsessive about him. It's obviously absurd, and he really ought to put it out of his mind, but for some reason he can't stop thinking about it.

Howard perches her reading glasses on the end of her nose and proceeds to quote from the page. "*Trivedi is a diligent and resourceful investigator. His greatest strength is his ability to strike an immediate rapport with witnesses and suspects. He is highly personable and possesses remarkable poise for someone of his youth, allowing him to command respect in challenging situations.*" She pauses and eyes him over the top of her glasses, and he feels the *but* whistling down from overhead like a cartoon anvil.

"He is also a perfectionist, and his drive for results sometimes comes at the expense of being a team player. He has a tendency to over-rely on his own instincts instead of benefitting from the experience of senior colleagues, and his attitude can occasionally be characterized as—"

"Smug," Rav finishes with a sigh.

"Smug," Howard confirms, removing her glasses. "You're a talented detective, Trivedi, but if you want to keep moving up the ladder the way you have so far, you need to learn to play well with others. That includes knowing when to step back and let someone else take charge. You can't be pulling stunts like you did at the Concord the other night."

Rav plucks some imaginary lint off his trousers. "It was a 10–13."

"In one of the most policed areas of the city. You could have trusted your colleagues to do their jobs. Maybe if you had, the suspect would be in custody right now."

Ouch.

"Part of being a team player is recognizing you are not always the best man for the job. It also requires a little diplomacy. That means not letting yourself get drawn into petty squabbles in the squad room. I know Jobs and the older guys give you a hard time, and you absolutely should not take any shit from them, but you don't need to go looking for it, either. As my kids would say, don't feed the trolls."

Rav scowls and glances away. "What's his issue with me, anyway?"

"You're the psych major. I'm sure you can come up with a few theories."

"Maybe he feels threatened by me."

"Whether he does or not, it's not your problem. You don't need his approval. Just do your job—and at the end of the day, go home and have a *life*."

This is strange advice coming from a woman who almost never leaves her office. Rav can't count the number of weekends he's come in bright and early, expecting the place to be deserted, only to find the lieutenant sitting at her desk, office door closed. If Angela Howard has a *life*, she does a damned good job disposing of the evidence.

Maybe the thought shows on his face, because she leans back in her chair and eyes him steadily. "Do you know what I do when I get home from work? After my kids have gone to bed, and Marvin has fallen asleep in front of the TV?"

"Er . . ." Is this a trap? It feels like a trap.

"I color."

"Sorry?"

She yanks open a drawer, takes out a coloring book, and drops it on her desk. *Stained Glass Sensation*, Rav reads upside down. There's a dragonfly on the cover. "It's extremely relaxing," she informs him.

Rav has a hard time imagining this. He has a hard time imagining her with *any* sort of hobby. Hobbies require a personality, and Howard doesn't have one of those. She's like a female Captain Holt from *Brooklyn Nine-Nine*, minus the sparkling sense of humor.

"Do you understand what I'm saying to you, Detective?"

"Get a life?"

"Find some balance. Because I promise you, if you keep running it into the red the way you do, you *will* burn out. This case"—she taps the folder with a beautifully manicured nail—"will be high profile. Media attention, possibly political pressure. More sensitive than anything you've handled so far, the sort of file that'll eat you alive if you let it. So." She arches an eyebrow. "Are you up for it?"

Up for it? He's only been waiting for a case like this forever. A chance to prove once and for all that he really belongs here, that he earned his place like everybody else. "Balance," he says soberly. "Diplomacy. I hear you, LT, and I'm ready."

"Good. Now get Shepard in here."

Rav motions his partner in, and they both flip open their notebooks.

"Richard Vanderford." Howard pushes the folder across the desk. "Music executive, found dead in his apartment this morning." She gives them a quick rundown of the basics. "Jobs and Jiménez are there now, along with the guys from the local precinct."

"Er . . ." Rav exchanges a glance with Will. "At the risk of sounding ungrateful, if Jobs is already there, why isn't he on lead?"

"Because you are."

Rav sighs inwardly. Jobs has been on the squad since dinosaurs roamed the Earth. He is *not* going to like taking orders from a junior detective he can hardly stand.

This must be some sort of test. Either that, or Howard is trying to make a point. Maybe both.

"That'll be all, gentlemen." They're halfway out the door when she adds, "And Trivedi. Don't let this turn into a media circus. If I catch you preening for the cameras, I will tear you a new one right through that designer suit. Understood?"

Rav's back teeth come together, hard. He turns away and closes the door behind him.

* * *

"That pissed you off," Will says once they're in the car. "That thing about preening for the cameras."

Rav just shakes his head, staring at his reflection in the passenger side window. Where is it written that if you take pride in your appearance, you must be vain and shallow? Well . . . all right, he might be a *little* vain, but that's hardly his fault. His mum is an ex-model; he's genetically programmed to be vain. But he's not shallow. He takes pride in his appearance because it's part of the image he puts out there in the world. That perfectionism Howard mentioned? That poise? Those things didn't come about by accident; they were drilled into him from birth. His Lordship had to make sure his kid was the smartest in the room. Eva wanted him to be the belle of the ball. Rav spent his entire childhood trying to live up to someone else's idea of perfect. Stand up straight. Speak clearly. *Smile*. Then he joined the force, and that came with a whole new set of expectations, ones that would be impossible to live up to even if he wanted to. You can always study more. Smile more. But you can't change who you are, and Rav is nobody's idea of a typical cop—unless he somehow missed all the other Ivy League–educated gay Brits on the force. Maybe there's a Facebook group.

Shepard peels off the BQE and heads toward the waterfront. The vic's building is one of those posh new condos in Williamsburg, the kind with glittering glass exteriors and a lobby that looks like a bomb shelter furnished by West Elm. The sidewalk outside is filled with rubberneckers snapping photos and keeping their video screens open in hopes of catching something interesting for their social media. The hashtag #DickEatsIt is already trending on Twitter (Rav *refuses* to call it X), and a camera crew from NY1 is unloading their gear from a white van parked at the curb. The LT wasn't kidding about the profile of this case.

"Our victim was not a popular man," Rav remarks as he scrolls through Twitter on the elevator. He taps a link to an article titled NO WONDER THEY CALL HIM DICK and raises his eyebrows. "Well, well. Do you remember the band that was playing at the Concord the other night, when that armed protester shut the place down?"

"The Nicks? Sure."

"It seems most of the internet vitriol directed at Mr. Vanderford comes from their fans." Before he can elaborate, the elevator *dings*, and they head down the hall to a five-thousand-square-foot penthouse with views to eternity. Will whistles softly, and even Rav is impressed. He'd kill for a place like this.

The scene is already a few hours old; he can tell by the discarded latex gloves and little numbered placards everywhere.

The victim's feet peek out from behind the sofa, and a bunch of guys from the Crime Scene Unit are clustered around him, doing their thing. A big camera on a tripod does a slow three-sixty of the room, digitizing the scene, while a fan hums near the body, sucking up trace particles from the air. Jiménez is over by the window, speaking in low tones with the detectives from the local precinct, while Jobs hovers over the CSU guys—looking, as usual, like he just stepped out of a noir film. Brimmed hat, rumpled trench coat, toothpick sticking out of his mouth in place of a cigar. Like somebody's cliché idea of a detective brought to life. "Oh look," he says as Rav and Will walk up. "His Lordship is here."

"Not a lord," Rav says, looking the victim over.

"You will be, though, when Daddy kicks it."

He won't, actually, but he has no intention of trying to explain the difference between life peers and hereditary peers to a man who looks like a character from *Who Framed Roger Rabbit*. "I assume Howard filled you in on the latest?"

"You mean the fact you're taking lead?" Jobs grins around his toothpick and thumps him on the shoulder. "You're welcome to it, junior. This case has all three Ps. I make it a policy to avoid the three Ps if I can."

Rav knows he's going to regret this, but . . . "The three Ps?"

"Politics, press, and pricks. Right up your alley." He winks, in case anyone missed the double entendre.

It's been like this since Rav joined the squad. Cops like to bust each other's balls, but with Jobs there's always an edge to it, a kidding/not kidding vibe that lets Rav know he's an outsider and always will be. He doesn't let it get to him. He's got thick skin and a sharp tongue, and if they were back at the squad room, he'd be quick with a comeback. But there's a dead man at their feet, and he's a fucking professional, so he focuses on the job at hand. "What do we have so far?"

"Double GSW," Jiménez says. "One to the head, one to the chest. Doorman saw him come in around 10 P.M. last night, so

they're estimating time of death between then and about 2 A.M.
No sign of forced entry. Haven't started canvassing the neighbors
yet, but the doorman says he saw someone in a dark hooded
sweatshirt and jeans exiting the building at around 11 P.M.,
looking"—he makes air quotes with his fingers—"shifty."

"Male or female?" Rav asks.

"Doorman couldn't tell. Swears up and down he didn't let
whoever it was in, though."

"Who found the body?"

"The PA, at around seven this morning." Jiménez gestures to
an adjoining room, where a young woman sits on a sofa, dabbing at her eyes with a tissue.

"Right. Well, let's get started knocking on doors."

"As you wish, Your Lordship." Jobs gives him a mock bow and
heads for the elevator.

"Asshole," Will mutters.

Rav considers their vic through a moving screen of CSU
bodies. It's definitely the guy from the online photos, minus the
smug grin. Midfifties, expensive clothes, flashy jewelry. "One to
the head, one to the chest," he murmurs, half to himself.

"Execution-style," Will says. "Our guy was trained."

Rav thinks back to his experience at the Concord, how shaky
he was with all that adrenaline in his veins. He'd have been
hard-pressed to make two perfectly placed shots, even at close
range. "Not just trained. He was dispassionate."

Will grunts. "Premeditated?"

"Looking that way. Plenty of people had issues with him, if
social media is anything to go by." They're interrupted by the PA
hovering nearby, looking lost. "Will, would you mind?"

"Sure." Shepard heads over to review her statement while
Rav continues his perusal of the flat.

The victim got home around 10 P.M., the doorman said.
Working late? Out for dinner, perhaps? He was still wearing his
sport jacket when he died, suggesting he hadn't been home long.
That, or . . . Rav spots a bottle of wine on the coffee table and

goes in for a closer look. It's unopened, but the foil wrap has been removed, and there's a corkscrew sitting beside it. He raises his eyebrows when he sees the label. A 2012 Petrus. Rav knows his wines, and this one's worth at least three grand. An awfully expensive bottle to be drinking alone on a Tuesday, even for a man of Vanderford's means. He turns to one of the precinct detectives. "Was he expecting company?"

"Doorman didn't know."

No sign of forced entry, Jiménez said. That, and the disposition of the body, suggests Vanderford knew his killer.

Will rejoins him, fresh from speaking with the PA. "You were right about the long list of enemies. But only one of them was seen arguing with Vanderford in his office the day before yesterday. A real barn burner, apparently. Security called and everything. You'll never guess who it was."

"Someone affiliated with the New Knickerbockers, perhaps?" When Will raises his eyebrows, Rav smiles. "Don't be too impressed, I'm just doing the maths. That article I mentioned in the elevator? Apparently, Vanderford purchased Flashpoint Records a couple of years ago. That deal included buying the master recordings of the Nicks' first two albums, right out from under the band's noses. Worth millions, apparently."

"Sure. They're one of the biggest acts of the last few years."

"Presumably, the band is unhappy about this. So, with whom was our victim burning barns? The band's manager?"

"Better. Jack Vale himself."

"Who?"

Will shakes his head. "Wow. The front man, Rav. The lead singer. You really don't . . . ? Wow."

"I told you, I'm not up on these things." His acquaintance with pop culture is pretty limited. He knows a bit about the fashion world, thanks to his mum, and he follows the occasional well-dressed celeb: Rami Malek, David Beckham, Mahershala Ali, and of course his sartorial idol, Tom Hiddleston. Musicians? Not his thing. Which is handy, because it means there's pretty much zero chance of him being starstruck while trying to do his job. He scrolls through some numbers on his phone and cradles it in the crook of his neck. "Aida, can I ask a favor? We've still got a couple of hours here, but I need to get the ball rolling on something. Can you set up an interview for Will and me? The person we need to talk to is a celebrity, and I'm guessing his people will throw up all sorts of roadblocks . . ."

✳ ✳ ✳

It takes three hours to get past all the gatekeepers, but Ayalew gets it done. She's resourceful, and failing that, downright mean. "Never doubted you for a second," Rav says on the phone, giving Will the thumbs-up as they make their way across the lobby of Vanderford's apartment building. "Seriously? How would that conversation go? *Well, Mr. Vale, you're looking quite good for this murder, but before we lock you up for life, could I trouble you for an autograph? My friend Aida down at the station is SUCH a fan. . . .* Rude. I'm hanging up."

"She asked for an autograph?"

"She did. And when I declined, she had some helpful suggestions for how I might spend some quality alone time."

Will laughs. "Sounds about right. So where to?"

"The Palace Hotel."

There's a cluster of TV crews outside, and they swoop in when they spot the detectives. Rav is good with the press, and normally he wouldn't hesitate to offer a few bland words, but he's still stinging from Howard's comment about preening for the cameras, so he keeps walking. The uniforms keep the scrum at bay, and Rav and Shepard almost make it to the car before a familiar voice hails them.

"Come on, Trivedi, are you really going to do us like that?" Rav turns to find Carrie Campbell from the *Times* smiling at him, pocket recorder in hand. They have a good rapport—she even brings him coffee sometimes—but she's still press, so he never really lets his guard down. "Just one little quote? I promise I'll make you look good in the article." Her eyes trail down the length of him, and she gives a little shake of her head. "Not that you need my help."

He smiles. "Flattery will get you nowhere, Ms. Campbell."

"That hasn't generally been my experience."

"Fair enough, but I can't give you anything right now. It's too early."

"But the NYPD is calling it a homicide?"

Rav's gaze falls meaningfully to the glowing light on her recorder.

"Fine." She flicks it off with a cherry-red thumbnail. "What's up with you? You're usually more fun to play with."

"And I hate to be a killjoy, but we're not ready to go on the record."

"How about off the record?"

"Off the record, we'll let you know as soon as we have something."

"Boring," she says, spinning on her heel and walking back toward the scrum.

Will pops the car door. "If this thing is as high-profile as Howard says, we're not going to be able to put them off for long."

"I'm aware, believe me." Rav slides into the passenger seat, his brain already racing ahead to the interview they're about to have. He types *New Knickerbockers* into the search bar on his phone and brings up the first photo he finds—an album cover, from the look of it. Terribly broody, of course, black-and-white with a vaguely distressed filter. Four twentysomethings, two men and two women, stare unsmiling at the camera. The album is called *Apple Pie*, the words wrapped in barbed wire. "Political, are we?" he murmurs.

"Very much so," Will says. "The bass player, especially. He's the angry-looking one."

They're all angry-looking. And pretty. The boys, especially, dark-haired and slight, each intense in his own way. Brothers, maybe? Rav pulls up another photo—older, from the look of it, with five members instead of four. "This third man. Did he leave the band?"

"Yeah, that's a sad story. He was the original front man, but he died in a motorcycle accident a few years ago. I think this is their first tour since it happened."

"You seem to know a lot about them. Are you a *fan*, William?"

"I guess I am," he laughs. "But it won't affect my work."

Rav keeps flicking through pictures as they head uptown. He finds one of Vale from *Hot Wax Magazine*, a full-page spread, and *oh my*. He pinches the screen out. The face looking back at him isn't just pretty; it's film-star, double-take-on-the-street pretty. Vale straddles a chair, arms draped across the back, holding the neck of an acoustic guitar posed in front of him. What Rav had taken for dark brown hair is actually black, short and wavy and tousled in a way that manages to be both casual and stylish. An understated grayscale tattoo climbs his left forearm in a flowing organic pattern. Quite beautiful, really. Pale eyes gaze into the camera. They're the color of a swimming pool, somewhere between blue and green, a striking contrast to his dark hair.

Rav pinches the photo back in. It's from a feature story called "Behind the Vale: A rare interview with rock and roll's most elusive prodigy."

Will glances at Rav's phone out of the corner of his eye. "Is that Vale? Hey, don't you think he looks a little like that guy from *Magic Mike*? Not Channing Tatum, the yoga one. Ken, I think his name was?"

Rav starts to answer, and then he snags on something. "You've seen *Magic Mike*?"

"What? Straight guys aren't allowed to watch movies about male strippers?"

"No, absolutely, you are. You *should*. Expand your horizons."

Will rolls his eyes. "Anyway, he looks more like a model than a murderer, is all I'm saying. Not that it means anything."

"Especially since he's a professional performer. He makes his living getting up in front of thousands of screaming strangers night after night. It takes a special kind of narcissist to do that, don't you think?"

"Guess we're about to find out," Will says, and he pulls into the loop at the Palace Hotel.

CHAPTER THREE

Take good care of her," Will says, depositing his car keys in the hands of the hotel valet.

"I hope the poor woman isn't too intimidated," Rav remarks as they cross the sparkling lobby. "She parks Bentleys and Ferraris all day long, but can she manage a turd-brown Golf?"

"What is it with you and my car?"

"I just don't see why you won't take a department car like everybody else."

"I like knowing where my stuff is at. If I want a tissue, there's a tissue. If I want a mint, there's a mint."

"You know Tic Tacs fit in your pocket, right?"

"If you don't like it, maybe you could drive for once."

"We both know *that's* not going to happen."

Vale is staying in the penthouse. Rav has actually been to this very suite once before, at a New Year's Eve party thrown by an extravagantly wealthy friend from London. It takes up the entire floor, with a massive terrace overlooking the park. There's a pool and everything. Rav has a vague memory of skinny-dipping and champagne . . . or does he? That might have been a different night. His college antics tend to bleed together in his memory.

A huge man in a sharp black suit stands beside the door. "You the cops?" Rav flashes his badge, and the bodyguard waves a key card in front of the panel.

They're met by a harried-looking young woman clutching a tablet to her chest. "Hi there! I'm Eloise, Mr. Vale's assistant?" She says it like it's a question. "If you'll follow me, please?" She leads them through a maze of rooms, her neon-striped trainers squeaking on the parquet floor. Things have been rearranged since Rav was last here, but it's still like walking through the pages of *Architectural Digest*. Live-edge hardwoods, pudding-soft leather, floor-to-ceiling windows. Eventually they reach a lounge area that gives out onto the terrace. "Mr. Banks thought you might enjoy mimosas by the pool?"

Rav is honestly not sure if it's a question.

"We're on duty," Will says.

"Oh, right." The PA laughs, high-pitched and nervous. "Well, anyway." She deposits them poolside with assurances it'll only be a moment, and then she flees, leaving them alone with a bucket of champagne and a pitcher of fresh-squeezed orange juice.

Will takes in their surroundings with a shake of his head. "Rock stars. You could land a helicopter on this terrace."

Rav has seen worse. Or better, depending on your point of view. He helps himself to the juice.

"Ah," says a voice, "I see you've found the mimosas." Rav and Will rise to meet their interviewee, but instead they find a middle-aged man with a graying ponytail and a fake tan. He's wearing a bright red Hawaiian shirt, unbuttoned to reveal an unconscionable amount of chest hair, and he's got a phone in each hand, one of which is pressed to his ear. "I'll look into it," he tells whoever is on the line. Then he thumbs off the call and sticks out a hand. "Charlie Banks. I'm the band's manager."

Rav shakes and flashes his badge again. "I'm Detective Trivedi and this is Detective Shepard. We're here to interview Mr. Vale."

"Sure, sure." Banks gestures for them to sit. "Why don't the three of us get started, and if you still have questions—"

"I'm sorry; Mr. Banks, was it? I was under the impression we'd already cleared the gatekeepers."

Banks chuckles and throws an arm over the back of his seat, clearly no stranger to tense conversations. "Nobody's gatekeeping, Detective. I'm just trying to be efficient. You're here about Dick Vanderford, right? You heard about the little dustup he and

Jack had on Monday, and you've read about the falling-out with Flashpoint. As the band's manager, I know more about that than anybody. If you've got questions about Flashpoint or the band's relationship with Dick Vanderford, I'm the man to ask. If after that you still wanna talk to Jack, I'm not gonna stop you."

He has a point, Rav supposes. They'll want to interview him anyway, so there's no harm in starting there.

"Champagne?"

"Thank you, Mr. Banks, but we'd rather get down to it."

"Please, call me Charlie. And shoot."

"You offered to tell us about the band's relationship with Mr. Vanderford. Why don't we start there?"

"Sure. So, look, I know you're not supposed to speak ill of the dead, but I'm just gonna give it to you straight: Dick Vanderford was a parasite. One of these trust fund kids who never had to work a day in his life." He pauses, eyes flicking over Rav. "No offense to trust fund kids," he adds.

Rav smiles thinly. Apparently, he's not the only one with a talent for sizing people up at a glance.

"I'll say this for him, Vanderford invested his assets wisely. Turned a tidy profit and used it to start gobbling up record labels."

"Including Flashpoint," Will says. "Giving him the rights to the Nicks' first two albums."

"I'm not clear on how that makes him a villain, though," Rav says. "When an investor purchases a business, they also purchase its assets, do they not?"

"Sure, of course." Banks pauses to pour himself a glass of orange juice. "It's not uncommon for new artists to sign away a lot of rights when they're just starting out. Once they find their feet, it's considered good industry etiquette to let them buy back their work—for a fair price, of course. It's also smart business. Sends a signal to up-and-coming artists that you're a label they can trust. Vanderford didn't give a shit about any of that."

"He wasn't willing to sell?"

"Not at any price. But that wasn't even the worst part. After

Tommy died in that motorcycle crash—that's Tommy Esposito, the former lead singer—after he died, there was a huge spike in demand. Vanderford started peddling Tommy's songs to anybody who asked. Commercials, political rallies, the works. He made every sleazy penny he could off Tommy's death."

"I imagine the band was upset about that," Rav says.

"Wouldn't you be? Jack, especially. He and Tommy were like brothers. They went to high school together. Started the band together. Wrote most of the songs together."

"Fair to say that Mr. Vale had a bone to pick with Mr. Vanderford, then."

"Sure, but it's not like you're implying." The manager flashes his too-white teeth and spreads his hands. "Jack Vale wouldn't hurt a fly. Trust me."

Oh, certainly. Why wouldn't they trust the unctuous manager? "What precipitated Monday's argument?"

"The lawsuit. We're suing Vanderford—well, I guess his estate now—for unauthorized uses of the band's images, music, and so on. If you're interested in the details, I can have the lawyers get in touch. But the part you should focus on is this, Detective." He leans forward, looking Rav right in the eye. "We were gonna win that suit, and it was gonna be worth millions. Vanderford knew it, and he was starting to sweat. So Jack went over there to try to reason with him. Make one last personal appeal. Sell us the masters back, and we drop the suit."

"I take it he refused."

"Categorically."

"Did he give a reason?"

"You'd have to ask Jack."

"I will. That is, if we're allowed to see him now." Rav arches an eyebrow.

Banks sighs. "You're allowed, Detective. Just . . . be gentle with him, all right? He's a sweet kid."

Rav stands, buttoning his jacket. "Shall we?"

The manager leads them back inside, pausing by a set of

French doors. "One sec," he says, and slips through. They hear him murmuring on the other side, presumably preparing his client for the big bad detectives, and then he opens the door and beckons them through.

Vale is perched on a sofa near the window, curled over a guitar as he plucks out a soft sequence of notes. He's dressed casually: simple knit shirt pushed up at the elbows, faded gray jeans. No bling, just a couple of plain silver rings and a leather bracelet. The whole vibe is effortlessly sexy, which annoys Rav for some reason. Vale looks up at their approach, and *damn*, those eyes. They're even more stunning in person. They travel over Rav, taking in his dark blue pin dot suit (Gucci) and burgundy polka-dot tie (Tom Ford), his high-maintenance haircut and neatly trimmed beard. His expression is hard to read. "You don't look like a cop," he says.

Rav tilts his head. "What does a cop look like?"

Vale's glance strays to Will and his quite acceptable but undeniably bureaucratic suit. Then his eyes meet Rav's again, and the faintest of smiles touches his mouth. *Like that.*

It's a fraction of a moment, but it's electric, as if a secret has just passed between them, and Rav is thrown enough that he just stands there, mute.

He's startled back to reality by the crisp rhythm of high heels as a stylish older woman crosses the parquet floor. She has chin-length blond hair and icy-blue eyes, and the curl of her mouth says, *Bring it on, little boy.* She's Diane Lockhart in a gray pantsuit, and Rav is feeling a little fanboy about it. "Joanne Reid, Hogan & Baker. I'm Mr. Vale's attorney." She hands him a business card, and as she does so, Rav gets a whiff of her perfume. It's spectacular.

"Detective Rav Trivedi." He offers his card in turn. "And this is—"

"Trivedi?" Belatedly, Rav realizes there's another person in the room. The bass player—Nash, was it?—eyes him coldly from by the window. "As in Lord Trivedi?"

A Londoner, from the accent. Even so, Rav is surprised the name would ping. Most people don't pay much attention to parliament. "My father," he admits grudgingly. "How nice to meet a fellow Englishman."

"We're not fellow anything, mate," Nash says.

Charming.

"Would you excuse us please, Ryan?" ~~Diane~~ Joanne says with an indulging smile.

The bass player leaves, but not before giving his bandmate an elaborate solidarity handshake that is almost certainly for the benefit of the cops.

Rav takes a seat directly across from Vale and makes steady eye contact. That moment they had before, whatever it was—he can use that. Establishing a rapport with your interviewee is just about the most important thing you can do as an investigator. A comfortable witness is more likely to share sensitive information. And a comfortable suspect? They make mistakes.

"Thank you for taking the time to meet with us," he says, his tone smooth and businesslike. "We were hoping you could help us fill in some blanks regarding Richard Vanderford's last few days."

Vale nods. His eyes are watchful. Guarded, even. Does he always look like that, or just when he's being interviewed by the police?

"I understand there was a disagreement between the two of you on Monday. Can you tell us a little more about that?"

He sighs, pushing a hand through his wavy black hair. "What do you want to know?"

"For starters, what did you argue about?"

The singer's glance cuts to Charlie Banks, as if to say, *Is he serious?*

"We spoke to your manager about this already, but we'd like to hear it in your own words."

Vale sets his guitar aside, taking his time with his answer. As he moves, Rav catches a glimpse of ink peeking out of the left side of his collar, hinting at a tattoo under there. "We argued about the same thing we always argued about. His refusal to sell our property back to us." There's nothing aggressive in his demeanor. On the contrary, he has a gentle way of speaking, in a surprisingly rich timbre for someone of his slight build. Rav finds himself wondering what his singing voice sounds like. He wasn't paying attention that night in the cab.

"Shady move," Rav says, "buying your own records out from under you."

Vale doesn't bite. "That part was fine. He bought the label, right? But refusing to sell them back, even for a profit . . ." He shakes his head and leaves it at that. He's careful, this one.

"I can see why that would be upsetting. On top of which, he was profiting from Tommy Esposito's death."

That gets a reaction. A glint of fury passes through Vale's blue-green eyes. It's gone in an instant, but Rav was watching him closely. *There it is*, he thinks, and maybe the thought shows on his face, because Vale says, "Have you ever lost someone close to you, Detective?"

"I don't think that's relevant, Mr. Vale."

He nods slowly. "Fair enough. Either way, I doubt you would know what it's like to have a personal tragedy exploited for profit. So yeah, I was angry. But I didn't kill him."

"Is that why you think we're here?"

"Isn't it?"

"We're just getting started in our investigation," Rav says with a bland smile. "So, you went down there to try one last time to convince Mr. Vanderford to sell your recordings back. I gather he refused?"

Vale's jaw tenses, and he looks away, hoisting the ink at his collarbone back into view. "He told me he'd decided to sell them to someone else. Lupin Media."

"The movie studio?"

"Apparently, 'Let it Burn' is going to be the official song of *Pyrophantom.*"

Rav can't help wincing. He doesn't know the song, but he does know a little about the Pyrophantom franchise. The hero is a wisecracking dude-bro who solves his problems by setting things on fire. His catchphrase is "get crispy."

"Ouch," Will says, succinctly.

"Did he say why?" Rav asks, grimly fascinated despite himself. "If he was willing to part with them, why not sell them to you?"

"Because he was a vindictive son of a bitch," Charlie Banks puts in.

"Mr. Banks, please. If you have something to add—"

"He's right, though," Vale says. "Vanderford straight-up told me it was payback. Maybe if we hadn't weaponized our fans and dragged him on social media, blah blah. He was so smug about it, too. Going on about how this was just the beginning. Like he was holding all the cards, and he couldn't wait to make his play. He literally waved the paperwork in my face. So yes, we argued. But he was very much alive when I left, and I haven't seen him since."

Rav eyes him closely. "Where were you last night between 9 P.M. and 2 A.M.?"

"Here." Vale inclines his head at the floor. "Right here, on this sofa, writing music."

"Can anyone verify that?"

He shakes his head. "I always write alone, at least since Tommy . . ." His glance falls. "No," he finishes quietly.

Joanne Reid rises from the sofa. "Now, Detectives, I believe my client has answered enough questions."

"Actually," Rav says, "we have several more. If you'd prefer, we can continue this conversation at the station."

She just smiles, as if to say, *nice try*. "Mr. Vale has a train to catch. Please feel free to submit a request for a follow-up interview. You have my contact details."

"I'll do that. But I'd advise you to honor that request, Ms. Reid, so that when the press asks me whether Mr. Vale has cooperated with the investigation, I'm in a position to say yes."

The lawyer starts to answer, but Vale beats her to it. "We'll be back in town on Saturday. We can talk then, if need be. But I really do have a train to catch."

Rav studies him for a long moment, as if maybe, if he stares hard enough, he'll find an answer in those guarded eyes. Not that it matters. Short of arresting the singer, there's nothing he can do and everyone in this room knows it. "I hope I can count on that, Mr. Vale," he says, rising. "I look forward to our next meeting."

"Lawyers," Shepard mutters as the harried PA escorts them back to the elevators. "What are the odds she's gonna let us within fifty feet of her client without a warrant?"

"I'm hoping he'll overrule her. Him, or the manager, or his publicist. Avoiding us won't play well for him in the media."

The bodyguard hails them as they walk by. "Hey, Officers, if you catch the guy who offed Vanderford . . ." He lets that dangle, and Rav glances back over his shoulder. "Tell him I'd like to buy him a drink."

The elevator *pings*. Shaking his head, Rav steps in.

CHAPTER FOUR

The New Knickerbockers

The New Knickerbockers are an American indie rock band formed in Brooklyn, New York, in 2014. The band consists of Jack Vale (vocals, guitar, piano), Claudia Baldwin (guitar, keyboards), Ryan Nash (bass, vocals), and Sarah Creed (drums, percussion). The band's original lead singer, Tommy Esposito (vocals, guitar), died in a motorcycle accident in 2021. The Nicks, as they are known by their fans, are renowned for their diverse influences and styles.

History and early years (2014–2017)

The founding members of the band, Esposito, Vale, and Creed, met while attending Fiorello H. LaGuardia High School of Music & Art and Performing Arts on the Upper West Side of Manhattan, New York. The trio rehearsed in an auto garage owned by Esposito's father in Bushwick, Brooklyn. The band took its name from Knickerbocker Avenue, a main street running through the neighborhood. Baldwin and Nash joined the group in 2016.

The group's 2017 demo garnered interest from several record labels. They eventually signed a two-album recording contract with Flashpoint Records. Vale would later describe signing with Flashpoint as "the biggest mistake of my life."

✷ ✷ ✷

It's late evening. Rav and Shepard are in the squad room, eating greasy takeout from soggy cartons while they search for a needle in a haystack. Rav is scanning the internet—interviews, magazine profiles, anything that might offer a glimmer of insight into their suspect—while Will sifts through security camera footage from the vic's apartment building.

Just now, Rav is reading a review of the New Knickerbockers' latest album. "*By turns hopeful, exhilarating, and beautifully melancholy,* Background, *the group's fourth studio album and its finest to date, charts a course through grief. Songwriter Vale is at his most painfully personal here, setting raw, evocative lyrics against an ever-shifting canvas of slick indie-pop, pop-punk emo, and gritty alt-rock. Whether it's the frenetic energy of 'Sound Off' or the achingly melodic 'Soar'* . . . blah blah fawning." Rav shakes his head. "Who writes this rubbish? *Achingly melodic?* And what in the bloody hell is *pop-punk emo?*"

"No idea, but I dare you to listen in the car and not sing along."

Rav pauses, momentarily distracted by the image of his two-hundred-pound partner singing *pop-punk emo* in his turd-brown Golf. "Anything on your side?"

Will shakes his head, pushing a hand through his sandy blond hair. "Nothing new."

So far, all they have is a few frames of the "shifty" figure the doorman saw, first from the elevator camera and then from the lobby, showing them exiting Vanderford's building at 11:07 P.M. They show up again a few minutes later on a traffic cam on Wythe Avenue, but that's it. Rav rolls his chair over to Will's desk. "Let's see it again?"

Shepard punches it up, and for the dozenth time, they watch a slight figure in a hooded jumper and dark jeans cross the lobby. The person is obviously conscious of the cameras, hood up, head bowed, hands jammed in pockets. "The doorman wasn't wrong," Will says. "It's hard to say whether that's a man or a woman."

"No curves," Rav notes, unwrapping a Werther's.

"That doesn't prove anything. Women come in all shapes and sizes."

"True, though there's something about that gait that says *man* to me. And the shoulders . . ." Rav pauses, leaning forward abruptly. "Sorry, can you zoom in on the shoulders? Go back a few frames. There, do you see it?" He points at the screen. There's a flash on the shoulder as the figure passes under a light.

"Huh." Will runs it back again. "Some sort of reflective fabric, looks like."

"Pretty distinctive. We could canvass the street again, see if anyone noticed a hooded jumper with reflective piping on the shoulders."

"Long odds." Will chews meditatively on a ballpoint pen, eyes on the screen. "Weird that we have footage of them coming out of the lobby, but not going in. Unless the guy's Spider-Man, he's not climbing up to the thirtieth floor. So how did he get in?"

"Good point. There's an underground car park, isn't there? Did you check the cameras there?"

Will starts punching keys, bringing up the time of the murder and running back from there. "Bingo. 10:52 P.M. Wasn't there long, was he?" The footage is from just outside the elevator, and it shows what they've already seen—namely, a slender figure in a hoodie. The suspect is turned away from the camera, hunched over their phone. "Looking up the code for the elevator?"

"Or texting someone to get the code. Vanderford himself, maybe."

"Let's see if he shows up on any of the other cameras down there." He does, at the vehicle entrance, darting in behind a car. "Figures," Will says. "But hold on—if Vanderford is expecting him, why does he need to sneak into the building?"

"So he can avoid the doorman. Which you'd definitely want to do, especially if there was a chance you'd be recognized. Say, if you've got a famous face."

"You're liking Vale for this, then?"

Rav tilts his head from side to side. "He has a strong motive, and he's the right build for Mr. Hoodie here."

"Why would Vanderford let him in?"

"Maybe he was expecting someone else, or . . ." Rav pauses, crunching what's left of his butterscotch. "You said Vanderford was bisexual?"

"According to his Tinder profile. Why?"

"I'm thinking about the wine he started to open. The Petrus. That's a bottle you use to romance someone. Maybe *that's* what he wanted from Vale all along. Sleep with me, and I'll sell you your precious recordings. Vale relents, or so Vanderford thinks. Vale goes over, and then . . ." He makes a gun out of his thumb and forefinger.

"It works, but it's pure speculation. Besides." Will leans back in his chair and knits his fingers behind his head. "Did he strike you as the type? I thought he was going to be some arrogant prick of a rock star, but he actually seems . . . I don't know, sensitive?"

"He's a professional performer."

"So, you do like him for this."

"I don't know. Vale's motive is one of anger, but our shooter was dispassionate. Not to mention trained."

"So, you *don't* like him for this."

Rav gives his partner a sour look. "I told you, I don't know. I do think it's quite a coincidence that Vale finds himself mixed up in two gun-related incidents within weeks of each other."

"You mean the Concord thing? Do we know where that investigation is at?"

The FBI is running point on that one. Rav isn't sure why, and he doesn't mind having an excuse to find out. It feels like unfinished business. "We can check in with the Bureau tomorrow."

Will scrubs a hand down his face. "It's late. We should clock out."

"Soon," Rav says distractedly, reaching for the mouse.

"Dude." Will flicks the mouse away. "We've been at it for twelve hours straight. Go home. You look like shit."

"That's hurtful, William." The words are barely out of his

mouth before a yawn catches him. "*Humm*, but you may be right. Give me a ride?"

It's a ridiculous ask. They live on opposite sides of the city. "Dream on, buddy. You can take the subway like a normal person."

Rav takes an Uber.

He's stepping out of the elevator when his phone *pings*. It's a text from his mum. No message, just a link to a Bloomberg article about how much attorneys in New York are making these days. It's vintage Eva. You have to hand it to her; she's efficient. With a single link, she says everything she wants to. *Hello, darling, just your quarterly reminder that you are a disappointment to your parents. Hugs, Mum.*

He unlocks his door and heads inside, kicking off his shoes and flicking on the lights. He divests himself of his gear—badge, cuffs, shoulder holster—and then he pours himself a glass of red. This is typically the part where he puts on some classical music, but tonight he finds himself typing *New Knickerbockers* into his phone. He's not sure what to expect, even after reading about them online. He really isn't into popular music. Even as a kid, he never listened to it much. He couldn't name a single Top 40 song, and the last time he watched a music video he was still an awkward ten-year-old grappling with complicated feelings about Justin Timberlake.

He cues up a random song on his wireless speakers and starts loosening his tie. Then the opening strains of "Soar" fill his apartment, and his fingers go still. Whatever he was expecting, it wasn't this. The shimmering guitar, the quiet urgency of the drums—and then Vale's rich tenor, barely a murmur but thrumming with tension. Rav finds himself sinking onto the couch, his wine forgotten. The guitars build, layering over each other in cascading arpeggios, a glittering waterfall of sound, and when Vale goes up the octave and smoothly over the break, reaching until his voice scatters like smoke . . . "Achingly melodic," Rav murmurs, recalling the words he'd read in the review. He gets it now.

An hour later, he's sprawled on the sofa, still in his shirt and tie, swiping through pictures of Vale on his phone as the Nicks play in the background. He tells himself this is research, but the tug of guilt at the bottom of his belly says otherwise.

He should stop. No good can come of this, but . . . Wait, is this one at the beach? Ugh. Rav pinches out, and of course Vale is perfection, lean and fit and actually smiling for once, apparently oblivious to the photographer lurking somewhere in the shrubbery. The photo is a few years old, from the look of it. No tattoos, and his hair is shorter. Mostly, though, it's the expression on his face—the lightness of it, as if he doesn't have a care in the world. As Rav looks at him, his traitor brain conjures a brief but vivid fantasy in which he's there with Vale, standing just out of frame. He's the one Vale is smiling at, sharing a secret with just a glance.

Bloody hell, Trivedi. He tosses his phone onto the sofa, piling cushions on top of it for good measure. He will *not* let this suspect mess with his head.

He goes to bed, but it takes him forever to fall asleep. "Soar" is stuck in his head, relentless and hauntingly beautiful.

He drifts off with Jack Vale crooning softly in his ears.

* * *

Flashpoint Records occupies the third floor of a nondescript office building on the Lower East Side. The corner office is Vanderford's, but Rav can tell from the moment they walk in that the victim spent very little time here. The desk is virtually barren. No photos or knickknacks, generic modern art on the walls. Even the framed platinum albums feel impersonal, more like trophies than genuine mementos.

Someone else's trophies at that. What must it have felt like for Vale, standing here surrounded by his own music while Vanderford told him about his plans to sell it to someone else? Even Rav is irritated. *It wasn't enough for you to steal his music, you had to rub his nose in it?*

"Makes you wonder if he even liked the music business," Will muses. "Looks to me like this was just a prestige asset for him."

Rav starts going through the desk and is pleasantly surprised when he hits pay dirt almost immediately, in the form of an intriguing business card. "Look here." He shows the card to Will.

"A private investigator?" Will grunts. "Something to do with the ex-wife, maybe?"

"Let's pay him a visit when we're done here."

Their interviews take most of the morning. No one overheard much of the argument between the victim and Jack Vale, but security confirms that the singer didn't offer any resistance when they were called to escort him from the office. "Sounds like Vanderford just did it to be a prick," Will says in an undertone on their way out. "I know we're supposed to remain objective and all that, but it's really hard to like this guy."

The PI's office is only a few blocks away, in a dingy walk-up on Henry Street. Rav scans the buzzer and finds the one he's looking for.

CHRIS NOVAK, PRIVATE INVESTIGATIONS
GRACE KIM, PRIVATE INVESTIGATIONS

They buzz in and head up to a small office on the third floor, where they find a young woman working alone at a desk. "Excuse me," Rav says, "we're looking for Chris Novak."

"You and me both," she says without glancing up. "If you'd like to leave a note, there's some stickies and a pen on his desk there."

"Are you Ms. Kim?"

"That's right."

Rav shows his badge, and he's definitely got her attention now. "Do you know how we might be able to reach him?"

A troubled look crosses her face. "I don't, actually. He hasn't been in for days, and his phone goes straight to voicemail."

"Is it unusual for him to be away like this?"

"Without giving me a heads-up? Yes. Especially when the rent is due."

Rav exchanges a glance with Will. "Did he ever mention a Richard Vanderford?"

"The name sounds familiar. Is that a client of Chris's?"

"We were hoping you could tell us."

"Sorry, we just share office space."

Rav scans Novak's desk. There's a wide-screen monitor and a USB dock, but that's about it. No laptop, no paper files. "What sort of investigative work does Mr. Novak do?"

"Just the usual. Insurance fraud, background checks, missing persons." Her glance shifts between Rav and Will. "You guys are freaking me out. Is this Vanderford guy bad news or something?"

"He's been murdered."

"Oh." She swallows.

Rav gives her his card. "If Mr. Novak turns up, or if you think of anything else that might be useful, please let us know."

He's halfway to the door when she says, "Detective? Should I file a missing persons report?"

"I think that would be a good idea, Ms. Kim."

Will waits until they're out of earshot before saying what's on both their minds. "Hell of a coincidence that he vanishes around the same time as the murder."

"For all we know, he's just skipping out on his rent, but . . ."

"Yeah," Will says. "*But.*"

They spend the afternoon trawling the victim's social media and his finances, sifting through Richard Vanderford's life like raccoons going through his trash. They get the IT guys to work on his laptop and have his car towed to the lab, but it'll be a while before anything comes of that. The whole day is pretty fruitless and Rav goes home to have quite a lot of wine about it—while listening to the Nicks and cruising the internet for tidbits about Jack Vale.

For research, obviously.

Will catches him humming in the car the next morning, on their way into the city to meet the FBI. "Is that 'Soar'?"

"Sorry, what?" Rav sits up a little straighter.

"It is! You're humming a Nicks song!" Shepard grins. "Oh, this is priceless. Please tell me you don't have a crush on our suspect."

"Hilarious. I'm in a chipper mood, that's all. I have a good feeling about this meeting. They're going to give us something useful, I know it."

"I suppose there's a first time for everything," Will mutters. "By the way, the lawyers got back to me this morning about the Lupin Media deal. You were right, the papers hadn't been signed yet. The whole thing's on hold until further notice."

"How convenient."

"Right? With Vanderford out of the way, the deal gets trashed."

"A deal Vale very much doesn't want." As if he needed even more of a motive. How could this guy *not* be their perp?

They pull up outside a federal building downtown and submit to the ignominious screening, after which they're shown to a bleak conference room that smells of old coffee. The agents keep them waiting just long enough to demonstrate that their dicks are longer, and then they settle in across a chipped faux-wood table. They're a matched set, Thing One and Thing Two, a man and a woman in ill-fitting pantsuits. "I'm Agent Rice," the woman says, "and this is Agent Keller. How can we help you?"

They know perfectly well what this meeting is about. It's just more flexing, but Rav plays along. *Diplomacy*, right? "We're hoping you might have turned up something in your investigation that could shed light on ours."

Her expression stays closed. "Such as?"

"I'm not sure. It would help if we knew the nature of the investigation. The media made it sound like the incident at the Concord was a political stunt gone wrong, but there must be more to it if the Bureau is involved."

"For the moment, we're treating the matter as an attempted homicide."

Rav's eyebrows go up. For one thing, murder is usually the NYPD's patch; there's only a handful of circumstances that would warrant FBI involvement. "Who was the presumed target?"

"Jack Vale. We believe the suspect traveled from out of state with the express purpose of killing him, possibly as part of a broader conspiracy."

"What kind of conspiracy?" Will asks.

"We're still gathering the facts," she says evasively. "What we do know is that the suspect, Joseph Miller, is a dyed-in-the-wool conspiracy theorist. Frequents all the usual sites, posting about all the usual subjects—tracking chips in vaccines, chemical trails from secret government aircraft, that sort of thing. He was put on a federal watch list a few months ago after he made some threatening statements about a congressman in Georgia, but until now it's been small-time stuff."

"What's his issue with Vale?" Rav asks.

"Another conspiracy theory. Are you familiar with the band's original lead singer, Tommy Esposito? There's a fringe group of fans who claim the motorcycle crash that killed him wasn't an accident. Miller has been writing to the Bureau about it since it happened, asking us to investigate."

That explains the sign Rav saw at the theater. In full, it probably said, *Tommy was murdered.*

"Who's supposed to have done it?" Will asks.

Agent Keller hitches a shoulder indifferently. "There's at least a dozen different versions, in all the usual flavors. The government did it, or the CIA, or the record label. You see it every time one of these music gods meets a sudden end. John Lennon, Tupac, Notorious B.I.G. We still get letters about Kurt Cobain. Miller has been trying to get close to Vale for a couple of years now, to 'show him the evidence.'"

"So he's a stalker," Rav says. "But what makes you think he wants to *kill* Vale?"

"We got a tip—"

Agent Rice cuts across her partner smoothly. "We received some information that inclines us in that direction. But as I said, we're still gathering the facts."

Why does Rav get the feeling they're holding something back?

"Is he in custody?" Will asks.

"Not yet."

Rav squirms. What if Lieutenant Howard was right, and it's his fault Miller got away? "Is Vale aware of the threat?"

"Sure," Keller says. "That's why he's got Morillo."

"Who?"

"Ángel Morillo, the body man? He's no joke, either. Former CIA."

"The bodyguard used to be CIA?" Will glances at Rav. "The kind of guy who'd be packing a .40 S&W and know how to use it?"

"What's the significance of that?" Rice asks.

"Vanderford was killed with a .40 caliber," Rav explains. "One to the head, one to the chest."

"Sounds like a pro," Rice says, and she slides her partner a look.

They're holding something back, no doubt about it. *So much for interdepartmental collaboration*, Rav thinks sourly.

"Well, gentlemen," Rice says, "it sounds as if you have an interview to arrange. Don't let us keep you."

Rav rises and buttons his jacket. "If you turn up anything connected to Vanderford . . ."

"You'll be the first to know," Agent Rice assures him as they shake hands. "And likewise. You come across anything linked to our stalker, you be sure to pass it along."

"They're playing it pretty close to the vest," Will observes as they head to the car.

"They're being territorial wankers. But at least we came out of it with a solid tip. We'll need to pull up everything we can on this Morillo."

"Vale's PA confirmed they're back in town late tomorrow afternoon. I've already made appointments to interview the other band members on Monday, but maybe we can squeeze in the bodyguard before then."

"We'll want his phone records as well. Are Vale's back yet?"

"Anytime now."

"Good," Rav says, popping open the door of Will's Golf. "I think we're finally getting somewhere."

There are still plenty of unanswered questions. If the bodyguard was the trigger man, where does the guy in the hooded jumper come into it? What does any of it have to do with Vale's stalker?

The answers are out there, and he's going to find them. In the meantime, he tells himself that flutter in his belly is excitement about the case and nothing more.

He almost manages to believe it.

CHAPTER FIVE

I swear, man, half the file was redacted. Does that mean he used to be a field agent?"

"No idea. You're the veteran, you'd know more about this sort of thing than me."

It's late Saturday afternoon. Rav and Will are on the way to the Palace Hotel, where Ángel Morillo is expecting them. They'd considered asking him to come down to the station, but they're still in "friendly chat" territory, and besides, given what the feds told them about the threats against Vale, Rav is reluctant to pull the bodyguard from his post if he can avoid it.

Will has "Lights Out" playing on the car stereo, and Rav turns it up. "Listen to this. They start playing with the time signature here. It's really quite complicated."

"Time signature?"

"You know, how many beats in a measure, which note gets the beat."

"Sorry, we didn't cover that in football practice."

"You were on the football team? I'm shocked." He is not shocked. Will looks like an off-brand Tom Brady.

"I suppose you were in the school band?"

"If only. His Lordship didn't approve of extracurricular activities."

Will grunts. "One of those, huh? A buddy of mine had a dad like yours."

Rav seriously doubts it.

"What about your mom? Was she strict too?"

"On the contrary, she prided herself on being the *fun* parent. Mainly because she knew it would piss my father off."

"I guess it's easy to be the fun parent when your kid lives on the other side of the ocean."

"Quite. Especially when you lead a glamorous lifestyle. Film premieres, fashion shows, celebrity weekends in the Hamptons. I lived for those summers in New York. In London, the closest thing I had to a life outside school was piano lessons, and that certainly wasn't *my* choice. More of a box to be ticked in the toff's guide to modern parenting."

"Were you any good?"

"At the piano? God, no. The entire experience was torture for all concerned, but for some reason I retained the theory. Probably why I enjoy classical music as much as I do."

"That, and you're a huge snob."

"There is that."

They arrive at the hotel—the valet deadpans her assurance that she'll take very good care of Will's Golf—and take the elevator to the penthouse. The bodyguard is waiting for them, and he escorts them to the sunroom, where they'll be doing the interview. They walk in just as Jack Vale is crossing the room, barefoot and drinking a sparkling water; he pauses, visibly surprised to see them. "Um," he says. "Do we have an appointment?"

Rav tries not to stare, but it's hard. Seeing someone in the flesh after days of reading about them online tends to result in staring. Especially when they look that good in jeans and a plain crewneck. In a disorienting blend of his two current obsessions, Rav finds himself studying Vale's shoulders, trying to decide if they're square enough to belong to the suspect in the hoodie.

"Sorry, boss," the bodyguard says. "It's actually me they're here to see."

"Oh." There's an awkward pause. Vale's glance strays to Rav. "I like your suit."

Rav looks down at himself, as though he's only just now realizing he happens to be wearing his most killer ensemble, an impeccably tailored cobalt-blue number with a crisp white shirt and spanky white trainers. It's so on point even Tom Hiddleston would be envious. "Thank you," he says offhandedly.

"Didn't your people tell you we were coming?" Will asks.

"They never tell me anything," Vale says with a strained laugh.

On cue, the harried assistant rushes into the room. "Oh, you're here? I'm so sorry, Jack, I was just coming to tell you? Mo said you wouldn't mind? You're early!" This last is directed accusingly at Rav. He consults his watch, which confirms that they are not, in fact, early.

"They operate on showbiz time around here," Morillo says in an undertone, and Will snorts.

"Apologies for intruding on your space, Mr. Vale," Rav says. "We wanted to minimize the impact on your security arrangements in these tense times."

Vale's smile vanishes. "I appreciate it."

"On that note, you'll have to excuse us. If you and I exchange another word your lawyer is liable to come after us with something sharp."

He can feel Vale's gaze following them as they arrange themselves around the coffee table. He'll be wondering why the police want to speak to his bodyguard, but that's between the two of them.

Morillo unbuttons his suit jacket as he sits down, offering a glimpse of his sidearm. They've pulled the paperwork on it already, and it is indeed a .40 caliber, a Glock 22. All aboveboard, of course. He's got another firearm registered to him as well, a 9mm Sig Sauer. Rav hopes he's confident with it, since it's about to be his only option. "I won't beat about the bush, Mr. Morillo. We'll be needing the Glock."

The bodyguard gives him a long, calculating look. "You got a warrant?"

"We don't need one if we suspect the weapon was involved in a crime."

There's the sound of Velcro tearing as the bodyguard takes out his sidearm. "So Vanderford was offed with a .40 cal, huh? Interesting." He ejects the cartridge, snaps the round out of the chamber, and sets it on the table between them.

"We thought so." Will puts on a latex glove and carefully places the weapon, the magazine, and the loose round in a plastic evidence bag.

"How long's it gonna take for ballistics to come back?"

"Are you in a hurry, Mr. Morillo?" Rav says.

"It's Mo, and yes. I can use my Siggie in the meantime, but I'm more comfortable with the Glock. I don't like being without it, given everything that's going down."

"Fair enough. We'll do our best to get it back to you as soon as possible. Presuming it's clean, of course."

"It will be." Morillo studies him with that shrewd gaze again. "The media keep using the words 'execution-style' to describe the murder, so I guess you're thinking a pro. Maybe the close protection guy, acting on the orders of his boss, who had a beef with the victim. And oh, look, he just happens to carry a Glock 22. Am I warm?"

"You're red-hot," Rav says flatly.

If the bodyguard is worried, he doesn't let on. "Couple of problems with your theory, though. Do I look like the kind of guy who can waltz into a fancy apartment building unnoticed?" It's a rhetorical question. The bodyguard is about six-four, 250 pounds, and bald as a cue ball. He wouldn't blend in anywhere. It makes Rav wonder what he did for the CIA. Tough to go undercover when you look like Dwayne Johnson's stunt double. "Is there security or traffic cam footage of a guy fitting my description anywhere near the building that night? Oh, and I assume you've checked the hotel's CCTV, too. Do you see me leave at any point that night?"

He's entirely too patronizing for Rav's liking. "We've already determined it's possible to leave the hotel without being caught by the cameras. I imagine a man in your line of work makes a point of knowing where the security cameras are."

"True. And maybe there's an unidentified Latino man in the mix somewhere. But he ain't me. That gun's gonna come back clean, and it's officially gonna be a dead end." He shrugs. "I'm not trying to be a dick about it. In your shoes, I'd be going through the same motions. But I'd hate to see you waste too much time chasing your tails."

"Would you?" Will snaps. He's irritated by the bodyguard's attitude, too. "The other day, you didn't seem all that interested in us catching the guy who did this. As I recall, you said you'd like to buy him a drink."

Morillo at least has the grace to squirm. "Yeah, that was a dumb thing to say. Vanderford was an asshole, but nobody wins when there's a murderer on the loose. Especially when he's in the orbit of the guy you're protecting. Jack's got enough on his plate."

Rav hesitates. It's not *strictly* relevant, but . . . "How worried are you about this stalker?"

"Which one? The Concord guy?"

Bloody hell, there's more than one?

"On a scale of one to ten? If you asked me before the Concord thing, I'd have said maybe three. People spew all sorts of crap on social media. I could show you hundreds of posts from dozens of different accounts with threatening statements about the Nicks, especially the women. Jack and Sarah have both had their places broken into, and Claudia gets the creepiest letters I've ever seen. Then there's the guy who threatened to cut out Jack's tongue."

"*Jesus*," Will says.

"Sick, right? And the really messed up thing is, it's not even that unusual. I mean, one of Bieber's stalkers hired a couple of guys to cut his balls off. Point being, when you reach a certain level of fame, it comes with the territory, and it's hard to know who's all talk and who's actually dangerous. But this Concord business is a whole other level. Showing up at a concert with a gun? That's serious shit. So yeah, I'm plenty worried about Joe Miller."

"Do you think he actually means Vale harm?" Rav asks.

"Hard to say. Guy like that, who knows how his mind works? But I'm not taking any chances. As of next week, we'll have dedicated CPOs for each band member. We'd have done that anyway—the band always takes on additional security when they go on tour—but I made sure to bring in people I trust. Former colleagues, mostly, plus an ex-marine."

"You're monitoring Miller's social media, obviously. Have you seen anything relating to Richard Vanderford?"

Will slides Rav a look, wondering where he's going with this. There's no reason to suspect any connection between Joseph Miller and Dick Vanderford. Except Rav still thinks it's a hell of a coincidence that the New Knickerbockers find themselves embroiled in two gun-related incidents less than three weeks apart.

"Not that I've noticed," Morillo says, "but I wasn't on the lookout for that specifically. Wanna check?"

Rav fishes out his phone. "What's his thing? TikTok? Truth Social?"

"Nah, if you want the really spicy stuff, it's the online forums you keep an eye on." He grabs a laptop on the coffee table and flips it open. "I'll ask Erika about it, too," he says as he types. "She'll be joining us next week as Ryan's CPO. She's the one who set up the algo we use to flag content on social media. My team keeps a database of known stalkers, threats against the band, all that stuff."

"Sounds like a sophisticated operation," Rav says, grudgingly impressed.

"Hey, man, you want top-notch security, you can't do better than ex-intelligence."

They start with Reddit. Rav goes to write down the name of the sub, only for his fancy cartridge pen to explode, getting ink all over his hands. So much for getting what you pay for.

"Bathroom's down that way," Morillo says, pointing. "Second door on the right."

It takes forever to scrub the ink off. As if that weren't embarrassing enough, Rav gets turned around on his way back, unexpectedly finding himself in the lounge. How the hell do you get lost in a hotel room? He's standing there like an idiot when Jack Vale bursts through the French doors, making a beeline for the terrace—and he does *not* look well. He's white as a sheet and moving fast, disappearing through the sliding doors without so much as a glance in Rav's direction.

It's probably nothing, and almost certainly none of his business, but . . .

Rav follows him out onto the terrace. Vale is halfway to the rail already, pausing long enough to throw back some pills. He tosses the plastic container onto a chaise as he passes, and Rav can't help stealing a look at the little orange bottle. Xanax.

Rav hesitates, glancing back over his shoulder. He's not quite sure what to do here. The lawyer will have his arse if she catches him trying to talk to her client alone. But Vale is clearly on the verge of a panic attack, his PA is nowhere in sight, and Rav *really* doesn't like the way he's leaning over the glass railing. "Are you all right?" he calls from a respectful distance. "Can I get someone out here for you?"

Vale doesn't respond. He's gripping that glass as if his life depends on it, knuckles white.

"Mr. Vale?" Still no response. "*Jack.*"

He turns. For a second he doesn't seem to recognize Rav. Then he blinks and says, "Hi."

"Are you all right? How's your breathing?"

"It's fine," he says mechanically, turning back toward the park. "I'm fine."

"You're not, and that's okay. Just tell me what you need."

"I need . . ." He draws a shuddering breath. "I need it all to go away for *five fucking seconds.*" He shakes his head. "Sorry," he whispers.

Rav joins him at the rail. He looks out over the park as if he's just taking in the sights, but he's listening carefully to Vale's breathing, alert for any sign of real distress. His mum used to get panic attacks, and he knows the symptoms themselves aren't dangerous, but he's not taking any chances with Vale standing so close to the railing. "It's beautiful up here, isn't it?" he says casually. "Peaceful. Even the air smells better." He takes a long, deep breath, hoping to entice Vale to do the same.

Vale flashes a tight smile. "Not your first time dealing with this, then."

"And here I thought I was being very clever and subtle."

"Not sure a guy in a bright blue suit can do subtle."

"Fair," Rav says with a startled laugh.

Vale jams his fingers under his jaw like he's trying to take a pulse, but his hands are shaking, and he gives up after a second.

"May I?" Rav reaches out, and after a moment's hesitation, Vale offers his wrist. Rav presses down until he feels the throb beneath his fingertips, racing but steady. He checks his watch, but he doesn't really need the count. This is about reassuring the patient. "You're okay. Just keep taking deep breaths."

Vale grips the glass again and drops his head between his arms. "Talk to me? About anything. Whatever, just . . . I need to be anywhere but inside my head right now."

If there's one thing Rav Trivedi specializes in, it's breezy bull-shit.

"It really is beautiful up here," he says, turning back toward the park. "Especially when you can actually see the view. I've been in this suite before, but it was at night, at a party. I've been trying to remember if we went skinny-dipping in that pool. I'm about eighty percent sure we did, but there was a lot of champagne. You're a musician, you know how that goes. This was years ago, of course. I'd just moved here from London. Hadn't quite outgrown my rebellious phase."

"You have now?" The question sounds forced, but the fact that he's able to engage at all is a good sign.

"Sadly, yes. One is obliged when one decides on a career in law enforcement. On top of which, I'm twenty-nine, which means that in three months I'll officially be old. Now, I know what you're thinking. *He doesn't look a day over twenty-five.* All I can say is that I take my moisturizing regimen very seriously. How am I doing, by the way? Distracting you, I mean. The moisturizing is clearly a triumph."

A shaky laugh. "I get the feeling you could do this all day."

"Which proves you're an excellent judge of character."

Vale straightens, and then he stares out over the park for a while, the breeze tugging at his dark hair. "I like it up here, too," he says eventually. "It helps. I get a little claustrophobic sometimes. That's why they always set me up in this ridiculous room. They're afraid if they put me someplace more closed in, I'll lose my mind."

"Ah, I see. You're medically required to live in luxury."

"Stop," he says, wrestling a smile. "I feel weird enough about it as it is." The smile fades, and he shakes his head. "I keep hoping I'll get better at this."

"The anxiety?"

"All of it. This whole . . ." He gestures behind him at the glittering penthouse suite. "But yeah, mostly that."

"Have you been dealing with it long?"

"A few years now. Basically since . . ." *Since Tommy died.* He doesn't say it, but he doesn't need to. "It's just a lot right now. Even before you showed up."

Rav feels guilty. Guilty for contributing to the anxiety of a *murder suspect.* It's absurd.

And yet there's something disarmingly genuine about this man. Not at all what you'd expect from a pampered celebrity. What he's dealing with *is* a lot. The pressure of fame. The death of his best friend. A stalker with a gun. And now, finding himself a suspect in a murder investigation.

"On a good day, it's barely controlled chaos. Always someone telling you where to go and what to do, hustling you through a schedule you have no control over."

"Like a dog on a leash," Rav blurts—and instantly regrets it, but Vale doesn't miss a beat.

"Like a dog on ten leashes, and they're all being pulled in different directions." He shakes his head again. "I'm sure that sounds dramatic, but I feel like I should explain why I'm pounding Xanax in a five-star hotel."

"You don't owe anyone any explanations about your health."

He snorts softly. "Tell that to the media."

"Horrible, aren't they? I know a little of what it's like to have them poking around your life, and it's not pleasant."

Vale glances at him out of the corner of his eye. "Seems like politicians get a pretty rough time in the British press."

"They do, yes. Though in our case, they were usually more interested in my mother."

"She used to be a model, right?" Vale freezes like a rabbit as soon as he says it.

Rav's mum never changed her name. She goes by Eva Small. There's no way Vale could possibly make the connection, unless . . . "Did you Google me?"

A hint of color touches Vale's cheeks. "It's not every day you get investigated in a murder case. I wanted to know who I was dealing with."

"And?" Rav's skin is warming too. He doesn't know how to feel about this. The fact that Jack Vale would take an interest in him is quietly thrilling, but he shudders to think what the internet might have coughed up. Lord Trivedi's son was in the spotlight a fair bit during the aforementioned rebellious phase, for all the wrong reasons.

Vale meets his eye for the first time since they got out here, and it sends a jolt of dopamine through his veins. "You seem like an interesting person. It's too bad we had to meet like this."

What if we hadn't?

Rav wants to ask that and a hundred other things. He wants those incredible eyes on him for as long as possible.

He needs to leave. Right now.

"I should see how my partner is getting on," he says, stepping away from the rail.

It's abrupt to the point of being awkward, and Vale looks a little taken aback. "I thought you wanted to do a follow-up interview?"

"Now is not the appropriate time. I'll make an appointment with your attorney if I need to. I'm glad you're feeling better, Mr. Vale."

Before Vale can even finish thanking him, Rav turns and walks away.

CHAPTER SIX

He spends Sunday morning at the gym and then heads to the office, even though there's very little for him to do. They're waiting on the ballistics, waiting on the phone records, waiting on forensics, and he's climbing the walls with impatience. There's a gnawing in his belly that he doesn't know what to do with. He can feel the time slipping through his fingers, and he's already dreading the 9 A.M. briefing on Monday. He can see Danny Jobs sitting in the front row, smirking as Rav updates them on his so-called progress on the Vanderford case. *Told you the little prince was a lightweight*, that smirk says. Then there's Lieutenant Howard. Her face won't give anything away, but she'll be wondering if she made a mistake giving him lead on this case. *Maybe he wasn't ready*, she'll be thinking, and maybe she'll be right.

"You're worrying way too much," Ana tells him as they stroll along the waterfront later that afternoon, sipping frozen margaritas in to-go cups and watching shirtless guys play beach volleyball in the shadow of the Williamsburg Bridge. "Who gives a damn what Danny Jobs thinks?"

"It's not just him. Half the squad is convinced I'm only there to fill some unspoken quota. I'm the token queer hire."

Ana snorts. "Is that the same quota system that gave you *one* lady detective on the whole squad?" She shakes her head. "Quotas. Por favor. Anyway, what do you care what they think? What counts is that you know, and Howard knows, you're nobody's token anything. You busted your ass to get where you are. Shit, you've only been talking about making Homicide since we met."

This is true. Rav and Ana go back to their academy days,

when they were both young and bright-eyed and fresh out of college. They bonded over their mutual outsider status—queer people of color being in short supply among that year's crop of recruits—and they've been each other's biggest cheerleaders ever since. Ana wants to be captain of her own precinct someday, but she's not in a hurry, moving up the ranks at her own pace and giving herself time to have a life outside of work. Rav, meanwhile, has been in a flat-out sprint since college. He had it all planned out. Make detective in five years—check. Get promoted to Homicide—check. Show everyone how it's done—in progress, anyway. This Vanderford thing was supposed to be *the one*, the case that got the dinosaurs like Jobs off his back and proved he could handle even the hot potatoes with poise and efficiency. Instead . . . "I feel like this one's slipping through my fingers."

"It won't. And look, even if it does, there'll be a next time. Nobody expects you to be perfect. Nobody but you, anyway." She claps his shoulder and gives him a serious look. "There's a fine line between perfectionism and narcissism, and you are dangerously close to crossing it. So do yourself a favor and get your head out of your ass, *hermano*." She pauses to slurp noisily at her margarita. "Speaking of asses, that boy in the blue shorts . . ."

She's trying to distract him, and it almost works. The volleyball game going on a few feet away is straight out of *Top Gun*, but Rav can't even properly enjoy it. He chews the end of his straw, his gaze going right through the toned bodies leaping up to spike the ball in each other's faces.

"The Nicks," Ana says. "Man, I was obsessed with those guys a couple of years back."

"*Mmm*," Rav murmurs distractedly.

"Hey, what's going on with you? Ignoring me is one thing, but there are four total hotties flexing their abs right in front of you and you're not even looking." There's a pause; Rav senses her eyes on him. "Bumped into Devon at the gym the other day.

Straight-up asked me, *Is your boy ever gonna call me back?* I told him Rav doesn't do callbacks. It's one and done."

Rav *tsks* into his drink. "That's not true."

"No? When was the last time you went on a second date?" She doesn't wait for an answer. "It's been forever, because second dates say *maybe there's something here*, and you don't have time for that. You're too busy being a workaholic so you can prove something to Danny Jobs and your dad and a bunch of other assholes who aren't worth it."

"Wow," Rav laughs. "Now who's overthinking it? I didn't feel a connection with Devon, that's all."

"Because you won't let yourself. Seriously, when's the last time you felt a connection with anyone?"

Well, actually . . . Rav sips his margarita.

"Hold up, I saw that." She narrows her eyes. "You got a crush you're not telling me about?"

Rav's drink goes down the wrong pipe, and he coughs until his eyes water.

"I'll take that as a *yes*," she says wryly, pounding his back. "Why're you being so cagey, Trivedi? Wait, oh my god! It's not Will, is it?"

His cough morphs into a gasping laugh. Granted, his romantic judgment isn't always top-notch, but even he isn't masochistic enough to go crushing on straight boys. "Don't be insane," he rasps.

"Good. You know he's mine."

It's a favorite joke of hers. At least, he hopes it's a joke. The idea of his wholesome, corn-fed Midwesterner partner with his tough-as-nails, no-fucks-to-give best mate is legitimately terrifying. "You would eat him *alive*, Rodriguez."

"Yeah," she says with a wicked grin. "Come on, I need ice cream."

Evening finds Rav back online, trawling Vale's social media. It's something he would do with any suspect, but this feels different. For one thing, he concluded long ago that most of Vale's social media is handled by someone else, so it's not likely to provide much insight into the man himself. On top of which, there are some angles he's actively avoiding. Like, say, romantic history. If he finds out Jack Vale is into guys he's going to spontaneously combust.

He turns in early, vowing to redouble his efforts tomorrow. *Eyes on the prize*, he reminds himself. He has a murderer to catch, and that's all that matters.

✳ ✳ ✳

"This place is starting to feel like home," Will remarks dryly as they walk through the doors of the Palace Hotel on Monday morning. "I spend more time here than at my own apartment."

"Hopefully, this is the last time." They're here to interview Ryan Nash and Claudia Baldwin. The fourth member of the New Knickerbockers, Sarah Creed, is upstate, so they'll have to interview her remotely. If they need to speak to any of the band members again after that, it'll mean they're on to something.

"How do you wanna do this?" Will asks. "Nash seems to have a chip on his shoulder about your father, so I'm thinking I do that one, and you can interview Baldwin."

"And let Nash think he's gotten under my skin? Not bloody likely. I'll take that one."

"Fair enough." Will jabs the elevator button, and they head up to Vale's suite on the thirtieth floor. The door is ajar, and voices tumble into the hallway.

It's chaos in there.

It almost looks like a crime scene, with all the people milling about. Joanne Reid and a posse of lawyers stand stiffly to one side as a trio of desperately stylish young people sets up for a photo shoot in the lounge. In the sunroom, Ángel Morillo is briefing the newly beefed-up security team; Rav counts almost two dozen people in there. Eloise flits back and forth, clutching her tablet, while Charlie Banks and the band's publicist go over ground rules for an upcoming interview.

In the eye of the storm is Jack Vale, doing his best to juggle all the people demanding his attention. There are schedules to look over, questions to approve, makeup to dodge, leather trousers to politely decline—all while trying to absorb legal advice from Joanne Reid and her team. From the chatter, Rav gathers they're doing a feature for *Variety*. And they *really* want him to wear those leather trousers. A Tan France look-alike with gravity-defying hair keeps holding them up hopefully, as if Jack will change his mind, until the publicist finally loses her patience. "It's a *no* on the leather pants, okay? He's not Harry fucking Styles."

Like a dog on ten leashes, Rav thinks, recalling Vale's words from the other day. How on earth does he cope? Not happily, judging from his body language. He's putting on a brave face, but there are tells: the tense set of his shoulders, the way he keeps pushing his hand through his hair. He spots Rav through the crowd, and his eyes spark—with what, Rav can't tell. For a second, he almost looked happy to see Rav, but that can't be right. Why would anyone be happy to see the cops?

"This is ridiculous," Will growls. "How are we supposed to do interviews like this?"

Rav tries to catch Joanne Reid's eye, only to find himself being hustled toward the door by the grumpy publicist. "What are you doing in here?" she hisses. "God, I hope nobody from the magazine saw you!"

"We have an appointment," Rav says, too surprised to resist as she herds him into the hallway.

"On the twenty-ninth floor," she says, pointing at the stairwell. "In *private*." She makes a shooing motion and closes the door behind her, the lock clicking noisily.

"Wow," Will says.

Rav just shakes his head and makes for the stairwell.

There are two suites on the twenty-ninth floor, but only one of them has a bodyguard standing outside. At least, Rav assumes she's a bodyguard, though she could pass for a model: six feet and svelte, stylish three-piece suit, wearing a Cartier ring of all things. She introduces herself as Erika Strauss, the new CPO on Nash's detail. "I gather you guys went upstairs first," she says with a look of wry amusement. "Bet they loved that."

"If there was a message about the meeting being down here," Rav says coolly, "we didn't get it."

"Doesn't surprise me. It's a mess up there today." She swipes them in and leads them to a lounge, where they find a pair of lawyers flanking a petite young woman with close-cropped platinum hair and Zoë Kravitz cheekbones. Rav recognizes her from the photos. This is Claudia Baldwin, guitarist/keyboardist for the New Knickerbockers, and she looks nervous enough to throw up.

The bodyguard notices, too. "Do you want someone in the room with you, Claud? I can ask Mo if he has a few minutes." Glancing at Rav, she explains, "Claudia's new CPO doesn't start until later this week."

"That's okay," Baldwin says, stuffing her hands deeper into the pockets of her cargo pants. "He should stay with Jack."

"We want you to feel comfortable, Ms. Baldwin," Will says. "If you'd rather reschedule . . ."

The offer alone seems to relax her a little. "Thanks, but I'd rather just get this over with."

"You're in good hands," Rav assures her. "Now, where will I find Mr. Nash?"

Strauss leads him to a second lounge, where the bass player and his attorney are waiting. Nash sits hunched on the sofa, elbows propped on his knees, glaring. His look is edgier than Vale's: work boots, torn jeans, leather jacket over a graphic T-shirt. His black hair is unwashed—and, unless Rav is much mistaken, dyed. It seems like an odd choice, given that the lead singer's hair is also black. As if he's Vale's adoring kid brother or something. It works on him, at any rate. Brings out the blue of his eyes, in all their ice-cold intensity.

"Thank you for taking time out of your morning," Rav says. "It looks as though it's a busy day."

Nash shrugs. "For Jack. Rest of us don't really count."

"I'm sure that's not true."

"I'm sure you don't know shit about it," Nash returns mildly.

Rav smiles, clicking the end of his brand-new (cheap) pen. "You don't like cops very much, do you, Mr. Nash?"

"Does anyone?" His eyes flick over Rav dismissively. "Don't much fancy trust fund brats, either. Or politicians' sons."

"The trifecta! Lucky me." Rav sits back and crosses his perfectly pressed Armani trousers. "We don't have to be friends, but I have a job to do, so perhaps we can shelve the baggage for now. I'll treat you with respect if you'll do the same. Fair?"

The lawyer leans in and whispers something in Nash's ear. He rolls his eyes. "Whatever. Can we just get on with it?"

"Happily. To start with, how would you describe your relationship with Richard Vanderford?"

"He was a prick."

"So you didn't get on?"

The lawyer leans in again. "Yeah, all right," Nash growls, waving her off impatiently. "Look, I barely spoke to the guy. That was Charlie's job, and Jack's. The rest of us didn't interact with him much. He didn't even show his face at our album release party. He knew what we all thought of him."

"Which was?"

"I didn't like him. I didn't like his politics, his business practices, his shiny fucking suits. I didn't like the way he cashed in on Tommy's death, and I *really* didn't like what he was doing to Jack."

"Tell me more about that. What was he doing to Mr. Vale?"

"*Killing him*," Nash says with feeling. "I saw it every day. Every time we heard a Nicks tune on a commercial, flogging online betting or a fucking pickup truck. Our music, Tommy's voice, pumping up the crowd at some right-wing political rally. Claudia and Sarah and me, we'd hear it and be pissed, but Jack . . . he'd die a little inside. Tommy was his brother. And Jack is *my* brother. Seeing him go through that . . ." Nash shakes his head and looks away. "Can't even describe it. And now here's you lot, trying to jam him up."

"What makes you think we're trying to jam him up?"

"You're here, aren't you?"

"Interviewing the victim's acquaintances is standard procedure."

"And taking Mo's gun? Is that standard procedure?"

Rav spreads his hands. "There's nothing malicious here, Mr. Nash. We're just trying to find out who killed Richard Vanderford."

"Yeah, well, it wasn't Jack. You'd see that if you were any good at your job."

Rav will say this for Nash: he's a loyal friend. Most people in his shoes would be trying to stay off the cops' radar, not antagonizing them out of misplaced protectiveness. "Where were you on the night of the sixteenth?"

"At a mate's, shooting pool. There were four of us."

"I'll get you their details, Detective," his bodyguard puts in from by the door.

"Look." Nash sits back with a sigh. "I get that you've got a job to do, all right? I'm not trying to crawl up your arse. I just hate what this is doing to Jack. He knows you're looking at him, and for what? Because he had a beef with Vanderford? There's dozens of people who could say the same, and I promise you, not one of them is a better human being than Jack Vale."

The interview doesn't last long after that. Nash doesn't recall the last time he saw Vanderford, but he reckons it was at least six months ago. And while he can't vouch for Vale's whereabouts on the night in question, he confirms that it's not unusual for the singer to write alone, late into the night.

"Baldwin said the same," Will says when the two of them compare notes in the hallway afterward. "So, what do you wanna do? Should we ask for a follow-up with Vale?"

Rav glances at the ceiling, imagining the scene up there. Is Vale out on the terrace again, gulping Xanax and wishing someone would distract him? He pictures the look in those blue-green eyes—and he remembers what it did to him, how close he came to forgetting himself.

There's what Rav wants, and then there's what's best for the investigation. "No need," he says, punching the elevator button. "Let's go."

$$* * *$$

The phone records come back later that afternoon, and Rav has the satisfaction of confirming a hunch.

"Vanderford *was* expecting company that night." They're sitting in Lieutenant Howard's office, filling her in on the latest. "He sent a text to a prepaid number at 9:12 P.M. with the address to his building."

"A burner phone?" Howard grunts thoughtfully. "His dealer, maybe?"

It's possible. They did find a small amount of cocaine in the apartment. "But wouldn't his dealer already have the address? Besides, I'm still hung up on that bottle of Petrus. I'm inclined to think the rendezvous was romantic in nature, or at least sexual. The doorman says he brought one-night stands home on a regular basis. Women, mostly, but occasionally men."

Howard flicks a glance at the ceiling. "Of course. Heaven forbid we should be able to narrow it down to only *half* the population."

"There's a hole in the timeline as well. According to his colleagues, Vanderford left a label function a little before 7 P.M. Security footage has him entering the lobby of his building at 10:13 P.M. We can't account for his whereabouts in between, except that cell phone towers place him on the Lower East Side until just before ten. No activity on his credit cards. Whatever he got up to, he paid in cash, or someone else paid. Which is dodgy, right? Who even *uses* cash anymore?"

Howard nods. "Whoever did this was either very meticulous or very lucky. What about the security footage from his building?"

"Not much help," Will says. "Too many unidentifieds."

"You can actually avoid some of the cameras altogether," Rav adds, "if you scoped it out beforehand. It's one of the reasons we liked the bodyguard for it."

"Where are we with that?"

"Cell towers place his phone, and Vale's, in the vicinity of the Palace Hotel, nowhere near Vanderford's place." That doesn't prove anything, of course. Either or both of them could have left their phones behind while they killed Vanderford. But if Morillo's Glock does come back clean, they're back to square one. On top of which, having spent a little more time with Vale, Rav is skeptical he would have what it takes to gun someone down in cold blood.

He tells them about the incident on the terrace.

"Panic attacks?" Will gnaws at his pen. "Interesting. How come you didn't mention it?"

Because we had a moment out there and I was kind of spinning out about it. Probably best to keep that to himself.

"It's neither here nor there," Howard says. "Panic attacks don't speak to who he is or what he's capable of."

"And his motive is pretty compelling," Rav points out.

"Don't the other band members have the same motive?" Howard asks.

"Up to a point. But Vale is the principal songwriter, and he was closest to Tommy Esposito. Financially and personally, he's more invested than the others. Also, he's the only one without an alibi."

"But you have nothing on him."

"There's the person in the security video. Vale is the right build."

"Assuming that person is even involved. It's thin."

It's worse than thin; it's translucent. Ordinarily, Rav would start looking elsewhere, but he doesn't entirely trust his own judgment right now. What if he's only seeing—or not seeing— what he wants to?

"We need progress, gentlemen. I've already got the higher-ups breathing down my neck. If the Vale angle isn't working, find a new one."

"Just find a new one, shall I?" Rav mutters as he slinks back to his desk with his tail between his legs, pretending not to notice the smirk Danny Jobs is directing his way. *Fuck you, Jobs. As if you ever had to work a file with burner phones and cash payments and goddamned professional assassins.* How does he get stuck with *this* as his first big case? The universe obviously hates him.

"Well, whaddya know?" Will is scrolling through something on his phone as he drops into his chair. "Our boy will be in your neck of the woods tomorrow night."

"Vale? What for?"

"Charity thing. Some youth organization is throwing an event at that skate park near your place."

"Where are you reading this?"

"I set up a Google alert when we decided Vale was a suspect."

"So you do know how to use the internet."

"Shut up." Will tosses his phone on his desk. "So what now?"

"We get in touch with Vanderford's PA again, I guess. Ask about her boss's favorite restaurants on the Lower East Side. Maybe we get lucky and find the one he went to that night."

"Blind canvassing?" Will groans. "It's official, we're grasping at straws."

"Keep it down, will you?" Rav glances in the direction of the Jobs–Jiménez axis. "I really don't need the commentary from the peanut gallery today."

"Guess we'd better get on with it," Will sighs, grabbing his keys.

On their way out, Rav feels something bounce off his arm.

It's a straw.

CHAPTER SEVEN

Rav clocks out at around six on Tuesday, and though he's spent the day telling himself he's not going to lurk Vale's charity event, he knows it's a lie. The Pier 62 skate park is only a few blocks from his flat. He can't *not* go.

On the way, he puts in his earbuds, and his phone automatically cues up the latest episode of Ana's podcast, *Graphic Girl*. Rav is not into comics or graphic novels, but he wants to support Ana, and besides, he loves listening to her geek out over the latest installment of *Deadpool* or *The Me You Love in the Dark*.

"*You know I love me some queer shape-shifters,*" Ana is saying. "*And this one is just so deliciously dark . . .*"

But it's not Ana he plans to listen to just now. "Sorry, baby," he murmurs, switching to a podcast called *The Sound Board*, which Spotify was thoughtful enough to recommend given his recent obsession with the New Knickerbockers. This week's episode is devoted to dissecting the Nicks' latest album.

"*Personally, I was skeptical they could even keep going after Tommy Esposito died. He was just so insanely charismatic, and Jack—look, he was always a great singer, but as far as being front man goes—*"

"*He seems kind of reserved.*"

"*Reserved and unassuming, a bit of a wallflower, and I couldn't see him filling Tommy's shoes. But he's proven me and all the other naysayers wrong . . .*"

The skate park is full of music and press and that rarest of creatures, happy teenagers. Skateboards roar up and down a deep bowl while an *extremely* enthusiastic fellow on a PA makes jokes and encourages the skaters. Rav scans the crowd, and he immediately spots Ángel Morillo's bulky frame near some event security guys. From there it's easy to pick out Jack Vale, in faded jeans and a knit hat, chatting with a couple of girls wearing T-shirts from the youth organization. Vale is wearing one too, over his long-sleeved shirt, and he somehow manages to make it look cool despite the alarming shade of orange.

Mo nods at the security guys to let Rav through. He looks surprised to see Rav, maybe a little wary. "You here in a professional capacity, Detective?"

Is he? Even Rav isn't sure. "I live close by. Thought I'd drop by and see what the kids are up to these days."

"Too bad you missed the boss."

Rav glances back at the bowl, his eyebrows hiking. "He went on *that* thing? On a skateboard?"

"Right? He's actually not bad. Did a grab and everything. Thought the kid he borrowed the helmet from was gonna pass out." He crooks his chin in the direction of a group of teenagers clustered around an autographed helmet. The kid holding it wears a dazed little smile, as if this is the greatest moment of his life.

"You get the ballistics back yet?"

Rav sighs. No point in being coy. "I did. And yes, it's clean. You'll have it back soon."

"Appreciate it."

They're playing a Nicks tune over the PA now. It's from their first album, *Alien Nation*, one of the few songs Vale sang lead on. He sounds younger, edgier.

> *Fact that is fiction / Feeds your addiction / Opium for the masses / Covering their asses / Keep you high, keep you taking / Bloodshot and shaking / Too strung out to ask how much money they're making*

The sound is edgy too, gritty guitars and belligerent drums. Is *this* pop-punk emo?

Rav starts to ask, but Mo is distracted by something on the far side of the skate bowl. Three white males are getting in the faces of a couple of the event organizers. One of them, a tattooed guy with a bushy blond beard, shoves one of the orange shirts. Security is on them in an instant, ejecting them from the park; the whole thing happens so fast most people don't even notice.

"Time to go," Mo says, already shouldering his way through the security clustered around his client. He murmurs in Vale's ear. The singer shakes hands with the organizers and waves to his adoring fans, and then Mo is herding him along the path toward a shiny black car parked in the street. "You coming, Detective?" the bodyguard calls over his shoulder.

"—need a walk," Vale is saying as Rav jogs up. "Just a couple of minutes, to burn off some of this energy."

"I don't know, boss. I didn't like the look of that scuffle. They were too far away to see their faces, but I thought maybe . . . Anyways, it looked like trouble brewing. That's why I asked the detective here to walk us back to the gate."

"Once around the block. Come on, Mo, this is the first time I've been out in ages. Hi, Detective," he adds with an awkward smile.

Before Rav can reply, a skinny white guy cuts them off on the path. Rav recognizes him as one of the three who were harassing the event organizers. Vale stiffens, and Mo steps in front of him.

"I need to talk to you," the guy says, trying to peer around Mo's huge frame.

"You need to step back," Mo counters, raising a hand.

"It'll only take a minute. Please, Jack, you can fix this. You can make it right."

Something about his demeanor puts Rav on his guard. He unbuttons his jacket in case he needs to reach for his sidearm.

"I got this, Detective." Mo's voice is low and soothing. Trying to de-escalate. "Everybody take it easy."

"Just hear me out," the skinny guy says.

"I've heard enough from you," Vale replies grimly. "I know what you think."

The guy shakes his head. He looks scared. Desperate, even. "No, that's just it. If you'll just listen—"

Mo advances a step, hand still raised. "Write it in the sky, Joe. Just *step back.*"

Joe? Joseph Miller, the gunman from the Concord? Rav didn't get a good look at him that night, but this guy is the right build, and there's a warrant out for his arrest. He reaches for his sidearm.

It goes down in the blink of an eye. Miller lunges at Vale. Mo tackles him to the sidewalk. There's a glint of metal and a grunt, and then Miller is on his feet and scrambling away.

"*Stop!*" Rav raises his weapon, but he doesn't dare open fire in a crowded street. Mo is down, and that leaves Vale unprotected with two accomplices nearby. The car is just a few feet away, and in a split-second decision Rav is hustling Vale toward it, gaze raking the street for any sign of Miller's friends. By the time he's bundled Vale into the car, Mo is on his feet, hunched over a wound in his side.

"Little prick stabbed me," the bodyguard growls.

"How bad is it?"

"Not sure." He grimaces, drawing bloodied fingers away from his side.

"Did you see which way he went?" Rav is already calling it in, phone perched on his shoulder as he holsters his sidearm.

"Toward the High Line."

"Let's get you to a hospital." Rav helps Mo into the back before jumping into the passenger seat. "Trivedi," he says into his phone as the driver puts the car in gear. "Shield number 8–5–5 . . ."

"Just breathe, man," Mo is saying in the back seat. "You got your meds?"

Rav looks in the rearview. Vale is chalk white, his eyes squeezed shut. "I need to get out. I can't breathe in here."

Mo puts a hand on his shoulder. "It'll just be a few—"

"*I need to get out right now.*"

Rav hesitates. "My flat is just up the street. Will that—"

"Yes." Vale gives a desperate little nod. "Yes, please. Pull over." He's already reaching for the car door.

Mo grabs his wrist. "You're not *walking*, Jack."

"I'll go with him," Rav says. "You head on to the hospital."

Mo checks the wound in his side. "I'm fine for a few minutes. We'll go together."

Five minutes later, Rav is unlocking his door and escorting Jack Vale out onto the balcony. Vale takes huge gulps of air, gripping the rail and dropping his head between his arms. Rav stays with him while Mo crashes around his half bath in search of something to patch himself up with. "Coat closet," Rav calls, on hold with the NYPD. "Beside the fire extinguisher."

Mo does what he can with the first aid kit, but he needs stitches, maybe an ultrasound to make sure nothing serious is going on. He clearly doesn't want to leave his client unprotected, but Erika Strauss is in Philly with Ryan Nash, and the other CPOs aren't on board yet, so there's no one to step in.

"Get yourself sorted," Rav says. "As soon as he's feeling better, I'll put him in a car."

"I don't want him going anywhere without protection. It's too hot right now. I *told* him that skate park thing was a bad idea." Mo swears under his breath. "Can I leave him with you for a bit?"

"Er," Rav says, startled. "I'm not sure that's a good idea."

"A couple of hours. I wouldn't ask if I had options."

Rav glances over his shoulder. Vale is still on the balcony, head between his arms, but his breathing seems to have leveled out.

"You okay with that, boss?" Mo calls. "If I leave you with the detective for a bit?"

Vale waves an arm. *Go.*

"I'll see you in a couple of hours, all right?"

And then he's gone, and Rav has a rock star in his flat.

A rock star who is still technically a person of interest in a homicide. This particular situation is decidedly *not* covered in the manual, and Rav is at a bit of a loss as to how to deal with it. He waits until Vale has a little color back in his cheeks, and then he says, "I think maybe we should call your lawyer. I don't want there to be any suggestion that I've violated your rights."

"It's okay, we just won't talk about the case."

"With all due respect, Mr. Vale, even the appearance of impropriety could be enough to damage any eventual case." *Not to mention my career*, he doesn't add, already scrolling through his contacts.

The next thing he knows, Vale has grabbed the phone and is taking a video of himself. "I hereby waive my right to have my attorney present while I recover from an anxiety attack on Detective Trivedi's balcony." He hands the phone back.

Rav feels like an arse. This guy has just been through a traumatic incident, and here he is acting like a robot, worrying more about the integrity of his case than the flesh-and-blood human in front of him. "I'm sorry, I don't mean to be insensitive. You're welcome to stay for as long as you need. Is there someone else I can call for you? Claudia, or . . . ?"

He shakes his head. "I just need a little space."

"Of course. I'll be inside if you need anything."

Rav rattles around the kitchen for a bit, restless and frustrated. That's twice now he's let Joe Miller slip through his fingers. The feds will be pissed. No way he was going to open fire on a crowded street, but there must have been *something* he could have done. He wishes Mo had ID'd the guy sooner, but he understands why he didn't. Mo's priority was to protect his client, and the best way to do that was to de-escalate. Arresting the guy was Rav's job.

Belatedly, he realizes Vale has drifted back inside and is hovering awkwardly in his living room. It's not big, but it's airy and stylish, and Rav quietly congratulates himself on being a fastidious housekeeper. You never know when you're going to have a celebrity in your flat. "How are you feeling?"

"Like I just ran the hundred-yard dash, but I'm okay. Thanks for this." He gestures at the balcony. "I'm sure it's weird for you."

Weird is finding out you're dating your ex's ex. Rav can't even begin to describe what *this* is. Is there a word for celebrity murder suspect you secretly want to unwrap like a birthday present? The Germans probably have one. "It's no trouble," he says smoothly. "Can I get you anything? Water, or . . . ?"

"Water is great, thanks."

Rav's brain is still going a mile a minute. Should he call his CO? Charlie Banks, maybe?

"This is amazing."

He turns to find his guest admiring a musical instrument hanging on the wall. It's a lovely piece, resembling a cross between a banjo and a cello, elaborately decorated with a gilded floral pattern.

"It's a sarod, right? Do you play?"

"Alas, I do not. To be honest, I'm not sure it does, either. I picked it up at an antique shop a few years back. I just thought it was beautiful."

"Where is it from? Where in India, I mean?"

"No idea. I wish I knew more about it, actually." He could say the same about a lot of things to do with his father's heritage. His Lordship never talks about his childhood, or anything else that might be deemed *sentimental*. The only piece of family history Ajay Trivedi ever passed down to his son was a medal his great-grandfather earned in the First World War. Rav pawned it in a fit of adolescent spite and has hated himself for it ever since.

"I could look into it, if you like." Vale takes out his phone and snaps a photo. "I know some people who are really into this kind of thing."

"Thanks." It's a gracious gesture; once again, Rav is struck by how little this man resembles the pampered celebrity he'd imagined.

There's a second instrument hanging beside the sarod, an antique banjo with mother-of-pearl inlay. Vale smiles up at it. "What about this old girl?"

"It seemed only fair to have something from my mother's heritage as well." It feels silly when he says it out loud. Like he's still twelve years old, trying not to show favoritism to one parent over the other. As if they cared. As if anything Rav felt or did ever factored into the ridiculous melodrama that is the Eva and Lord Trivedi show.

Vale glances over his shoulder. "May I?"

"Please. Not sure it plays either, mind you."

Gingerly, Vale takes the banjo down and turns it over in his hands. "She's a beauty." He plucks a string. It's wildly out of tune, of course, but as he turns a peg, the note bends into something resembling a G. He settles onto the couch and adjusts another peg, plucking the string until it lands on D. Rav finds himself watching Vale's hands, the gentle but confident movements as he coaxes the instrument back into tune. "Tommy had one of these," he says, his voice distant with memory. "He played it on a couple of tracks on *Alien Nation*."

Rav sets a glass of water in front of his guest. "I'm sorry for your loss. It must have been very difficult."

Vale nods, but he doesn't say anything. He withdraws into his task, turning the pegs until he arrives at a decent-sounding chord. He picks out a few experimental notes, and then he starts playing a gentle folk tune. Something old, by the sound of it, that wouldn't be out of place on the soundtrack for *O Brother, Where Art Thou?* He's curled over the instrument, in a world of his own, and gradually, Rav feels himself being drawn into its orbit. As if the gravity in the room is shifting, pulling him forward in his seat. The grace of those fingers, the intensity of his expression as he plays . . . It's mesmerizing.

He's not starstruck. Well. Maybe a *little*. Mostly he's in awe of Vale's talent, the ease with which he coaxes beautiful music out of something that hangs on Rav's wall. He's acutely aware that something special is happening here, and he tries to silence his whirring brain for once, to be present in the moment and just appreciate it.

Vale's been playing for around twenty minutes when he gets a text from Mo. "The waiting room at the ER is totally packed," he reports with a sigh. "Do you need me out of your hair, or is it okay if I hang for a bit?"

Rav hesitates, but the damage is already done. He's well in it anyway. "You're fine. Can I offer you a proper drink? Or, actually . . ." Actually, that's a *terrible* idea. The situation is delicate enough without introducing alcohol into the equation. He feels creepy for even suggesting it.

Vale smiles awkwardly. "That's okay, thanks, I'm fine with water."

"Sorry, I'm . . ." He doesn't know what he is. He's not Rav Trivedi, that's for sure. Rav Trivedi is smooth. This mumbling dork can't even finish a sentence.

Vale smiles again, a real one this time, and it's *dazzling*. "It's okay, man, I get it. It's a weird situation."

It's a fucking minefield, is what it is. Rav could use a Xanax himself right now.

Vale rises from the sofa and peels off the orange youth group shirt. It clings to the long-sleeved shirt underneath, hiking it up, and Rav gets a glimpse of inked abs. Is that the same tattoo as the one that keeps peeking out of his collar? *Inquiring minds want to know.*

He looks up to find Vale's eyes on him. Did he just catch Rav checking him out? Fuck. Rav reaches for the empty water glass, and as he straightens, a pair of blue-green eyes flick away hastily. Wait, was Vale just checking *him* out?

This isn't a minefield, it's hell.

Rav is in hell.

Thank god for the bloody banjo. Vale settles in with it again, pausing to push a few strands of black hair out of his eyes. Then he starts strumming—a strong, up-tempo rhythm this time. His whole body moves with it, shoulders jerking, foot tapping. Rav knows this tune. Led Zeppelin? No, that's not right. Vale glances up and sees Rav struggling to identify it, and he sings, "*Hope you guessed my name . . .*"

Rolling Stones, then.

Vale abandons it mid-go. A cheeky grin curls his mouth, and he starts plucking out the unmistakable opening of that classic Who song, the one Rav can never remember the name of. He's clearly amusing himself, turning classic rock into plinky banjo ditties on the fly, and seeing him like this—relaxed and happy, free of the white-knuckled grip of his panic attack—makes Rav a little melty.

By this point it's past dinner, so they order some takeout and settle in to watch TV. Rav's PVR comes up automatically, and he cringes when it outs his addiction to *Top Chef*. "Sorry," he says, frantically mashing the *exit* button. "We, er, don't have to watch that."

"I don't mind. I've only seen a couple of episodes, but it seems cool. I actually have a bit of a weakness for reality TV." Laughing, he adds, "Not the respectable stuff, either. The trashy kind."

"What, are we talking *Real Housewives*, or . . . ?" He glances over, and Vale is wearing the most deliciously embarrassed grin.

"*Love Island.*"

"Seriously?" Rav feels his own grin widening. "I mean, I've never seen it so I shouldn't judge, but it seems pretty ridiculous."

"Exactly. It makes *my* life feel half-normal, and that's . . ." He trails off, his smile fading. "Normal is hard to come by these days. To the point where, as messed up as this day has been, it's actually a relief to be here right now. Getting the chance to just chill—it's *air*." His gaze falls. "I'm sure that sounds weird."

"No, I get it. I'd say you're welcome anytime, but . . ." Rav smiles awkwardly. "Like you said the other day, it's too bad about the circumstances."

"Yeah." Their eyes connect, and there it is again—that current running between them.

They look away at the same moment. Rav clears his throat. "Right, shall we?" Without waiting for an answer, he presses *play.*

"*Tonight, on* Top Chef . . ."

They're three episodes in when Rav gets a text from Mo. **How's he doing?**

He looks over, and Vale is sound asleep, arms folded, chin resting against his chest. **Passed out on the sofa**, he replies. **How are you?**

Still at the ER. They want to do an ultrasound.

Rav sighs. **Okay. I need to get some sleep, but I'll set him up with a blanket. Call me when you're here and I'll buzz you in.**

Mo gives him a thumbs-up. **Thanks.**

Rav grabs a blanket from the hall closet, drapes it over Vale, and heads off to bed.

He stares at the ceiling for a while. Then he picks up his phone and pulls up the video Vale recorded of himself. He watches it on mute, over and over, as if he's studying a suspect on an interview video. If there's guilt in those eyes, he doesn't see it. All he sees is fear, exhaustion, and the unmistakable shadow of grief.

When he finally drifts off, it's with those blue-green eyes burned into his brain.

CHAPTER EIGHT

Rav wakes to an empty apartment. The blanket is folded neatly on the sofa, and the empty water glass has been placed in the sink. Mo was supposed to call, but he must have phoned his client instead. Rav is surprised Vale didn't wake him, but maybe he couldn't wait to be out of there. Or maybe he was just half asleep. Trace evidence would seem to support the latter theory: he finds Vale's knit hat on the kitchen counter, and the youth organization T-shirt hanging from the back of the bathroom door. Most intriguing, he finds a little black notebook jammed between the cushions of the sofa. It's dog-eared and worn, held together with a hot-pink rubber band. Rav is burning with curiosity, but he leaves the elastic where it is. Instead he opens his laptop and pulls up the email containing Vale's phone records. He finds the number, enters it into his contacts, and sends off a text.

> **You left some things here.**
>
> **Guessing you're not too worried about the orange T-shirt but you also left your hat. And a little black notebook.**
>
> **This is Rav by the way.**

He hits *send* on that last one before he catches himself, and he cringes. That's what he gets for texting before his first cup of coffee. *This is Rav.* Not *Detective Trivedi* but just *Rav*, as if they're friends or something. "Idiot," he mutters, tossing his phone onto the sofa while he gets ready for work.

He spends the next two hours trying not to check his phone every five seconds.

Will wanders into the office sometime after 8:30 (Rav is *not looking* at his phone) with a thermos-sized coffee and a poppy seed bagel. Rav gives the latter some serious side-eye. He does not approve of poppy seed bagels in the workplace. He himself never eats them—what if he were to meet the love of his life with a little black seed stuck in his teeth?—and he hates the mess they make. He's explained all this to Will, but admittedly Rav has hundreds of pet peeves and it would be superhuman to keep track of them all.

"Damn," Shepard says around a mouthful of bagel when Rav fills him in on the events of the previous evening. "Good thing we'd pretty much crossed him off our suspect list, or you'd be in hot water."

"To put it mildly." Rav frowns and flicks an errant seed off his keyboard. "As it is, I'm guessing the LT won't be pleased."

"You're gonna tell her?"

"I think I'm obliged."

The look on Will's face says *it's your funeral.* Rav is inclined to agree, which is why he's putting it off. He buries his nose in work, *not looking* at his phone until a little after noon, at which point he caves, refreshing his home screen in case he somehow missed a notification.

He fires off another message. **Fair warning, if I don't hear from you soon I'm putting these things on eBay.**

He's just hit *send* when his desk phone rings. "Trivedi."

"Hi, this is Grace Kim. Not sure if you remember me . . ."

The private investigator. "Of course," Rav says, motioning Will over and putting her on speaker. "Has your colleague turned up?"

"No. That's actually why I'm calling. I filed a missing persons report like you said, but that was a week ago, and I haven't heard anything."

"I'm sorry, but missing persons isn't my beat. Would you like me to check in with the case officer?"

"That's okay. I just thought maybe something had come up in your murder case that might provide some closure."

Rav glances at Will. "How do you mean, closure?"

"I've got Chris's family calling me, and his clients. Nobody's heard from him, and . . ." There's a wet-sounding sniffle. "I guess I'm pretty well braced for the worst."

Shit. "I'm sorry to hear that, Ms. Kim. I wish there was something I could do. If anything comes up on our side, we'll certainly let you know." He hangs up with a sigh. "I fear that's not going to turn out well."

"Speaking of things that aren't gonna turn out well." Will tilts his chin in the direction of the lieutenant's office. She's standing in the doorway, motioning Rav in.

"Wish me luck," he says, rising and buttoning his jacket like a man about to receive a death sentence.

As usual, Howard doesn't beat about the bush. "I've just had a call from the mayor's office, looking for an update."

"On the Vanderford case?" Rav squirms a little. "I didn't realize they were following this one."

"The Vanderfords are old money, and they've got friends in high places. City Hall's been on my ass since this thing started."

"I'm sorry. I didn't realize you were dealing with that."

"It's part of the job. I deal with the political bullshit so my detectives don't have to." She sits back and folds her hands on her desk. "So. Anything new?"

"Nothing promising." He goes through some dry details about the estate, plus a couple of other business-related angles they're looking at. "We're still waiting on forensics. In the meantime, the strongest motive we can find is that business with the Nicks and their master recordings. Jack Vale is the only band member without an alibi, but we have nothing on him or the bodyguard, and—"

"Why are we still talking about Vale? I thought we'd put him aside."

"We have, but that's not quite the same as exonerating him."

She frowns. "What's with the dance? Do you think he's our guy or not?"

Rav hesitates, but his gut is firm on this one. "No. Frankly, I'm not sure I ever did."

"Then *move on*."

"I will. I have." He squirms some more. "Look, there's something you should know." Bracing himself, he tells her about yesterday.

There's a full fifteen seconds of silence. Howard stares at him, fingers laced on her desk, her expression on freeze-frame. "Well," she says. "That was stupid. If he files a complaint, it'll be your ass."

"I didn't say or do anything inappropriate."

"You're not that naïve, Trivedi. The optics alone could be enough to sink you. But"—she raises a hand to forestall another protest—"I understand why you did it. It was a compassionate decision made under pressure."

"Thank you."

"Don't breathe a sigh of relief just yet. This could still come back to bite us both. You'll need to file a note for the record, attaching the video Vale made. In case there are questions later."

"I'll do that right away."

"Good." She pauses, eying him. "And make this a teaching moment, Trivedi. Don't go thinking that just because you're clever and charming you can talk your way out of anything."

Rav nods solemnly. And then, because he can't help himself: "But you do think I'm clever and charming?"

"Get out of my office."

He's walking back to his desk when he hears his phone *ping*, and he practically does a flying pancake for it.

MESSAGES

Jack Vale   1m
Haha. Sorry crazy day

Rav types, **Admit it, you just woke up.**

The response is immediate. **I wish. I've been with Mo all day talking to the police and the FBI about yesterday. Kind of feels like I'm cheating on you haha**

Rav has to read that twice. *Don't flirt*, he tells himself. *Don't flirt, don't flirt . . .* But his thumbs are arseholes and they have other ideas. **I'm heartbroken. Never took you for the cheating type.**

. . .

. . .

Vale is typing, but it's slow. Distracted or just considering his reply?

Srsly though thanks for finding the notebook. That thing is my life

> **Shall I have it couriered over to the hotel?**

It's OK it's my fault it's there. I'll send someone to pick it up

> **It's good to have minions.**
>
> **What else do they do? Wait, let me guess.**
>
> **They're the ones who sign those autographed photos you send to your fans.**

Busted

> **What else? I promise not to tell a soul.**

Pretty much everything. To be honest I'm not even a real musician

It's all a sham

> Aha. So you're just a pretty face
> for the album cover.

And the photo shoots. It pays well
and I get to keep the clothes

Rav laughs. He can feel Will's eyes on him, wondering who he's texting. They're packed like sardines in that room, a dozen detectives sitting elbow to elbow. Rav shifts subtly, angling his phone away.

> How's Mo?

OK. Lots of stitches but nothing too
serious

> Please give him my best.

I will

Thank you. For everything. Really
Rav

. . .

. . .

He stares at those little blinking dots until they disappear.

✳ ✳ ✳

Inevitably, evening finds Rav strewn across his sofa, staring at his phone. He's graduated to YouTube now. Interviews, streamed concerts, music videos. He's watching one for a song called "Need," and *sweet Jesus*. It's a slow, smoldering track. Ominous bass line, brooding vocals in a minor key. The video is black-and-white, arty, with layered speeds and flickering light, as if a thunderstorm is building nearby. Vale is lying on a beach, soaking wet jeans slung low around his hips as the surf washes gently over him, swirling around his body before retreating down the glistening sand. The camera hovers over him like a lover, gazing down while he croons about being the creeping sensation along your spine, the gnawing need you try to ignore. His eyes are closed, face turned slightly away; with each surge of the waves, his body stirs in the sand. The song builds to a climax, a slow-motion kaleidoscope of glittering raindrops and frothing sea. The waves are up to his chin now; he tips his head back, arching up out of the water, and Rav . . .

Well, Rav breaks a promise to himself.

He's in a filthy mood about it the next day. He gets up early and goes for a run—he *never* goes for a run—as if that's going to curb the anxiety clawing at him. Nothing is happening the way it should. The case is going nowhere. They used to have a suspect and now they don't, and all the while the one suspect they *did* have is burrowing deeper under his skin, the creeping sensation along his spine, the gnawing need he's trying to ignore.

It's not the first time he's been attracted to someone he shouldn't be. Attraction is a primal thing; you can't control it. You can only control your actions, and he's always been pretty disciplined about that. He's never cheated, or knowingly been with a cheater. Never stepped over the line at work. But this business with Vale is new territory. Dangerous territory. And that's just it, isn't it? Vale is forbidden fruit wrapped up in an intellectual puzzle. In other words, Rav's own personal kryptonite.

He needs to talk about this with someone or he's going to lose his mind. The logical choice would be Ana, but she's a cop; he doesn't want to put her in an awkward position. He thinks about it for a second, and then he drops onto a bench and dials.

There's a *click* on the line. Then: "Are you in jail?"

"What?"

"That's the only reason I can think of that you would be calling me in the middle of the day, when you know I'm trying to sleep."

Rav winces. He didn't even consider the time difference. Mags has kept vampire hours for as long as he's known her, even before she bought the club—hence her nom de guerre, Margaret Moon. It's 12:30 in London; of course she would be asleep. "Sorry, but it's an emergency."

"Does this emergency perchance involve a boy?" There's no need to answer. They've been friends for too long. "Go on, then. Tell Auntie Mags everything."

He does.

"A *suspect*? Have you lost your mind?" There's a shrill whistle in the background; she's making tea. He wishes he were there, in her adorable little kitchen in Chelsea, with its floral-patterned tiles and antique Shaker cabinets. How many afternoons did he spend in that breakfast nook as a teenager, dishing about his latest crush while Mags—ten years older and infinitely wiser—dispensed strong tea and sage advice? He doesn't miss much about London, but he does miss that. Mags and her little kitchen were there for him when no one else was.

"You always did have a thing for bad boys," she muses.

"Slander and nonsense." It's neither, but that's all behind him now. Mostly. "Technically, he's not a suspect anymore. I'm not even sure he's a person of interest. But it's definitely a gray area, and if I were to act on it, it might cost me my job." Frankly, he's not sure. Do the rules even cover a situation like this?

"What band did you say he was with? The New Knickerbockers?" He hears her typing into her phone. "Oh. Oh, I *see*." There's a pause as she studies whatever photo she's pulled up. "Well, really, how much do you actually like that job?"

Rav laughs ruefully.

"Because honestly, given the choice—"

"This is serious."

"Oh, don't be dramatic. So you have a crush. Who could blame you? He's very crushable. Just rub one out and be done with it."

There's a silence.

"Ah, we're past that, are we? Dear me, you really are pining, aren't you?"

"But that's just it!" Rav springs to his feet and starts pacing. "I haven't *pined* since I was sixteen! It isn't my style. I'm remote and unattainable. I drive *them* to distraction, not the other way around. The whole thing is so thoroughly off-brand I don't know what to do with myself!"

"Hold on, I need to deal with a rogue eyebrow hair."

"*Mags.*"

"If you're going to call me in the middle of the day, you're going to have to accept a few interruptions. You know how little time I get away from the club." Mags's club, The Rainbow Room, has been the hottest thing in London ever since she took it over a few years ago. Even before, it was one of the top spots for London's LGBTQ community. Rav used to love it there, even though he was underage back then. It was the first place he really felt *seen*. Using a fake ID and a fake name somehow felt more authentic than the life he led under His Lordship's roof. Mags was the DJ back then, and she knew a lost soul when she saw one. She took him under her wing—hence those therapy sessions in the kitchen.

God, talking to her is making him nostalgic.

"Look," she says in the vague tones of someone peering closely in the mirror, "he'll leave town soon, right? Out of sight, out of mind. Unless . . . this *is* unrequited, isn't it?"

"I mean, I assume so."

"You don't sound so sure."

"There's a vibe. I thought maybe it was all in my head, but then there was this text exchange yesterday." He reads it to her. "Is it my imagination, or is that flirting?"

"Mild flirting, perhaps, but flirting nonetheless. Hold on."

Rav hears her typing again. "What are you doing?"

"Looking to see if he's one of ours." By which she means queer. Rav doesn't want to know. He doesn't stop her, either.

"*Hmm.* If he's seeing anyone, he's very discreet about it.

I can't find anything on his love life. Surprising, considering how much coverage he . . . Wait. Oh dear." She starts laughing. "Type TMZ into your search bar."

"What?"

"The gossip website, TMZ. Take a look."

Rav does as he's told, fully expecting to land on an article about Vale. Instead he finds . . .

Oh. Oh *no*.

It's a picture of Rav, gun drawn, looking over his shoulder as he hustles Jack Vale into the car outside the skate park. It looks like it was taken from a long way off, probably by one of the photographers at the charity event.

My Hero! Mystery Man Identified!

Yesterday, TMZ brought you photos of this swoon-worthy savior whisking New Knickerbockers front man Jack Vale to safety following a terrifying attack outside a charity event in New York. We identified him as Vale's bodyguard, but an unnamed source has since confirmed exclusively to TMZ that he is an officer with the NYPD, Detective Rav Trivedi. Talk about New York's finest! A dishy detective in a Gucci suit? Yes, please!

"Swoon-worthy!" Mags crows. "What a triumph! And *dishy* as well. Is that suit really Gucci?"

Rav is only half listening, still staring at the image on his screen. A picture of *him*. On a *gossip website*. That hasn't happened since he was a teenager, and it was a minor blog in London, not bloody TMZ.

Howard is going to be furious. If the media start asking questions about what a homicide detective is doing in the company of Jack Vale, they'll connect the dots, and then there'll be no stopping it. They'll be *everywhere*, hounding, speculating.

"Your father is going to shit himself," Mags says gleefully.

"His Lordship is the least of my worries." Rav rubs his eyes.

"I've got to go, Mags. This has been no help at all, but I adore you for trying."

"Kisses," she says airily, and hangs up.

Rav's phone *pings*. It's a text from Will, with a link to the TMZ article.

You're famous

He sighs and braces himself for a very long day.

CHAPTER NINE

It starts as soon as he walks into the office.

"Looky here," Jobs calls from his desk. "If it ain't the dishy detective."

Rav gives a mock salute but otherwise ignores him. He goes straight to the lieutenant's office, but she's not at her desk. *Don't panic*, he tells himself. *She's probably in the loo. Or getting a coffee.* No reason at all to assume she's been summoned before the chief of detectives to explain why one of her team is on the landing page of a bloody tabloid.

Jiménez picks it up again as soon as Rav walks back into the squad room. He's perched on the edge of his desk, phone in hand. "The face you're making in this photo. Did you practice it in the mirror? It's *fierce*, bro. Real action hero stuff. You almost look like the real deal."

"You should get that picture framed," Jobs suggests. "Hang it up on the wall next to all the other pictures of yourself."

"*Detectives*." Lieutenant Howard darkens the doorway, wearing a scowl that could stop traffic. "You are not being paid to chitchat. Trivedi, my office. You too, Shepard."

They haven't even sat down before Rav starts trying to explain. "Listen, about this TMZ business—"

"That's not why I called you in here. You're off the Vanderford case."

Rav stares. "Because of the other night? What was I supposed to—"

"Let me rephrase. *We* are off the Vanderford case. The FBI has assumed jurisdiction."

"Since when?" Will demands.

"Since this morning. I just got off a conference call in the chief's office. Apparently, the Bureau has evidence linking Vanderford to Joseph Miller and the incident at the Concord. They think his murder was an attempt to cover up his role, or at least silence him."

Rav scowls. "If they had something on Vanderford, why didn't they share it?"

"They are not obliged to explain themselves to us, as they made abundantly clear on the call. All I know is that they're treating the Concord incident as a federal crime, and they believe Vanderford was involved. I would have liked for our teams to work together on this, but the Bureau wasn't interested, and the chief seemed just as happy to let it go." Her tone is cool, but Rav isn't buying it. She's just as pissed as they are. "Let's look on the bright side. At least now this tabloid mess won't matter. When the *New York Post* comes calling, we can truthfully tell them we are not investigating Jack Vale. Let the FBI deal with the media and city hall and the rest of the baggage this case brings along with it."

Rav knows he should be relieved. This case gave every indication of going nowhere. At least now, nobody can say he failed. Nobody but him, that is. Handing it over to someone else feels like admitting defeat.

His morning doesn't improve after that. Word of the TMZ piece spreads through the department like wildfire, and soon his inbox is overflowing with delightful witticisms. He has four missed calls from Carrie Campbell at the *Times* and about a million texts from Ana. His social media blows up too, his mentions an odd ratio of mockery and that GIF of the three Disney princesses swooning. By noon, his followers have gone from the hundreds to the thousands. His phone *pings* so often that he puts it on vibrate, and even then the constant buzzing is getting on his nerves. Just as he goes to shut the damn thing off altogether—

MESSAGES

Jack Vale   Now
Shit man I'm sorry

Rav taps the notification and finds those agonizing little dots blinking away. Happily, he doesn't have to wait long.

Photographers

Like oh hey don't worry about us getting shivved over here, just make sure you get the shot

Sorry for dragging you into the relentless shitshow that is my life

Hope you're not in trouble

> **It's not your fault.**
>
> **You still haven't picked up your notebook, by the way.**
>
> **Cruel of you, leaving it here to tempt me. I'm dying of curiosity.**
>
> **It just sits there beckoning me with its sexy little hot-pink elastic.**

Haha. Sorry got caught up in band drama yesterday

I can send someone by your place this evening if that works?

> **That's fine.**
>
> **I'll be home on time for once, since apparently I don't have a case anymore.**

?

The FBI has assumed jurisdiction on the Vanderford case.

. . .

. . .

His phone rings. Rav counts to ten before answering. It wouldn't do to come off as *too* eager. "Good afternoon."

"The FBI?"

That voice. It thrums in his chest, but somehow Rav manages to keep his own voice casual. "Indeed. It might be a good idea to inform your attorney, just so she's in the loop."

"I will, but . . . why?"

"I'm afraid I can't discuss it."

"Right, of course." Rav hears the low rumble of the sliding glass doors being opened, and a moment later a distant honk from the street below. He can picture Vale out on the terrace, barefoot in his faded jeans, wind tugging at his hair. "I just . . . putting two and two together . . . No, you know what? I don't want to know. So, what does this mean for you?"

Rav shrugs and leans back in his chair, instinctively telegraphing nonchalance even though Vale can't see it. "On to the next thing, whenever that comes around. As for you, you're officially free of me forevermore." He doesn't know what he expects Vale to say to that, but he's met with silence, and he finds himself talking to fill it. "Once you pick up your little black book, that is. Now that I put it like that, I wonder . . . is this a little black book in the traditional sense? Would TMZ be interested in it?"

The pause on the other end is a little too long to be comfortable. "It's song lyrics," Vale says quietly. "And yes, you would probably get a lot of money for it."

"I'm joking. I would never . . ." He winces. "I'm an idiot."

"You're fine. I should run, though. We were supposed to do a set at the Uncharted festival tomorrow night. We canceled because of all this, but maybe it's not too late to slot us back in. I should get a hold of our manager."

Rav hesitates. This is probably the last time they'll speak. Should he acknowledge that somehow? *Take care of yourself, it was nice meeting you*—something?

Before he can decide, Jack says, "Bye," and hangs up.

Ten minutes later, he gets a call from Ángel Morillo. "Hey, you're on speaker with Erika."

"I take it Jack told you about the Bureau taking over?"

"Just now. Anything you can share?"

"I'm sorry, but not really."

"Can you at least tell us who's running point? Is it Rice and Keller?" Rav confirms that it is, and Mo hums thoughtfully. "They're on the Concord thing, so I guess they think Vanderford's mixed up in that."

Rav plucks an orange from Shepard's desk and tosses it from hand to hand. "What is this, Mo? A fishing expedition?"

"Just thinking out loud. But you can confirm the NYPD is done with Jack?"

"Barring new evidence, which we would be obliged to transmit to the FBI."

"Okay. That's good to hear."

"Yeah, but . . ." It's Strauss's voice now, sounding baffled. "Do you buy it, though? Vanderford teaming up with Miller?"

"Hypothetically, if that *were* the angle the FBI was taking, I would have questions. How does a New York record executive get mixed up with a conspiracy theorist from Georgia?"

"Are you going to tell them that?" Strauss asks.

"I'm not sure they care what I think." This is a lie; Rav is quite sure they don't.

The bodyguards are quiet, and Rav can't help reading disappointment into their silence. Maybe they think he's being overly deferential to the feds, or just plain lazy.

"Look," he says, "the truth is, I don't like having a case yanked out from under me. There's a few loose ends I plan to look into, for my own peace of mind if nothing else. If I find anything, I'll give the FBI a frank assessment."

"Appreciate it, Detective," Mo says. "Until next time."

* * *

Rav doesn't really expect there to be a next time, not with Mo and not with Jack Vale, and he's already had quite a lot of wine over it when his phone *pings* a little after 9 P.M. It's from Vale.

**Congratulations you're officially a
meme**

There's a link; tapping it, Rav finds himself on a Twitter thread with the hashtag #DetectiveMcDreamy. It's photo after photo of him, gun in hand, glancing over his shoulder (he *does* look rather fierce, doesn't he?) as he hustles Vale into the car. Only the images have been photoshopped, the background swapped out to make it look like an action movie poster. Rav is rescuing Vale from the walking dead, or invading aliens; they're running from a T-Rex, or the Terminator, or the monster from *Stranger Things*. Rav scrolls through dozens of them, ranging from crude to professional-looking. He types, **Who are these people and how do they have so much time on their hands? Your fans are strange.**

They're your fans now baby

Vale is clearly enjoying this.

It's mad.

Yeah but you're kind of here for it

I do look rather dashing.

**Imagine if you'd been wearing the
blue suit. You would have melted the
internet**

He thinks Rav looked hot in the blue suit! Rav is *dyyyying.*

These hashtags, though.

McDreamy?

That's how you're entered in my
contacts btw. Detective McDreamy

By this point, Rav has his laptop open on the kitchen counter so he can text and scroll through social media at the same time. One of the comments freezes his fingers above the touch pad.

Beatrice @WrKrbee

SO, AM I THE ONLY ONE SHIPPING THESE TWO
LOL

Judging from the replies, @WrKrbee is not, in fact, the only one. Rav feels heat on the back of his neck and is thankful there are no witnesses. After a moment's hesitation, he types, **So, look, are you sending someone to pick up this notebook, or . . . ?**

. . .

He sips his wine and watches those infernal blinking dots. "Why, yes," he murmurs to himself as he paces about the room. "I thought I would see to it personally. I'm coming by just now."
As if that would *ever* happen.
"You sad creature, Trivedi," he mutters into his glass.

Ugh sorry. I completely forgot and
now we're on the road

Well . . . on a train.

I swear i'm not usually this scattered
but we were in a scramble to pull
this festival thing off

We'll be back the day after tomorrow
so i can pick it up then

I didn't realize rock stars travelled
by train. Do you at least have a
private car?

Yeah. It's pretty comfortable actually
but i can't sleep on trains

Or planes

Or buses

Tight spaces aren't really my thing
haha

Sorry.

I guess your options are limited,
aren't they?

Yeah

It's one of the reasons we didn't tour
our last album

I'm getting better but it's still not
great

Well, if you need to take your mind
off things, I'm here.

. . .

. . .

The dots. They're fucking *agony*. And then . . .

Jack Vale

Mobile

Decline

Accept

Butterflies swirl in Rav's stomach as he picks up. "You have reached the Rav Trivedi hotline, your twenty-four-hour source for frivolous fluff and distracting drivel."

Jack's laugh sends those butterflies into a frenzy. "Twenty-four hours? Wow."

"No one ever accused me of being low energy."

There's an awkward pause. "So, uh, what are you up to?"

"No, no, it's *what are you wearing?* Are you new at this?"

"I didn't realize this was *that* sort of hotline. Do you need a credit card number?"

Rav laughs. He's quick.

"Besides, I know what you're wearing. Something way too fancy to be doing whatever you're doing in it."

"Actually, I'm in jeans." Rav stretches out on the sofa and considers his faded Ralph Laurens. "I've been trying to crib your look, but I just can't pull it off."

"Pretty sure you'd pull it off better than I'd pull off your look."

"Oh, I don't know. I bet you'd crush a bespoke suit." There's a pause. Rav consults his watch. "What time does the train get in?"

"Three in the morning."

"Ugh. I thought my work hours were bad."

Another pause, a long one. Rav can hear the low rattle of the train.

"Is something wrong?"

"No. Sorry, I just . . ." He hesitates. "I wish I knew if I was being stupid here," he says quietly. "You're not investigating me anymore, right?"

"No," Rav says, instantly serious. "If I were, this conversation would be inappropriate. As it is, it's still strange. For both of us."

"Yeah."

Several seconds go by. The train rattles along. Rav struggles to think of the right thing to say, but he's so far out to sea on this. Maybe he should just be honest. *I like you, but I don't know if I'm allowed to like you, and it's driving me mad.* "Look, the last thing I want is for you to feel uncomfortable. This is supposed to be taking your mind off things, not adding to your stress. We can call it an evening and no hard feelings."

"The thing is, you're easy to talk to. Too easy, and I . . ." He trails off; Rav can practically hear him shaking his head.

"You can trust me, Jack." He blurts it out without meaning to. It's presumptuous. A little scary. It feels like a shot of whiskey in his chest.

"Okay," Jack says quietly. "Yeah, I think I can."

They talk for hours.

Jack is curious about Rav's job, and Rav is fascinated by his. They trade war stories over drinks (wine for Rav and gin for Jack) and marvel at the sheer strangeness of each other's lives. They bond over single malt whiskey and a mutual dislike for jazz (so naturally, when Rav has to take a pee break, he leaves jazz playing as holding music). They agree that cricket is the most bizarre sport ever devised and that electric scooters are a menace to society. They place a modest wager on the outcome of *Top Chef.*

It's a little after one when Jack says, "I should probably try to sleep."

"What time do you go on tomorrow?"

"You mean today?" He yawns. "Eight-ish. Won't be on time. These things never are. We should be back in the city by six, seven tomorrow night."

"Well, break a leg, or whatever it is you rock stars say."

"Thanks. 'Night, Rav."

"Sleep well."

He thumbs off the call and scrubs a hand down his face. Did that just happen? He feels buzzed and jittery and exhausted all at once.

One thing's for sure: that conversation wouldn't have been possible if he were still on the case. He's going to have to send the FBI a goddamned fruit basket.

Bananas and peaches, maybe.

He snorts a laugh into his wineglass, downs the last sip, and goes to bed.

CHAPTER TEN

Rav is still feeling buzzed on Saturday, so he goes for another run (!), listening to music on his earbuds. First the Nicks, and then—marking a historic first in the life of Rav Trivedi—some classic rock. It turns out the Who and the Stones are actually pretty good for running. He even finds himself breathlessly singing along. *Hope you guessed myyyyy name . . .*

He's so engrossed that he doesn't immediately spot the crowd of people gathered on the sidewalk outside his building—but they spot him, and they get between him and the door. There's about a dozen of them, mostly in their teens and early twenties. A few wear New Knickerbockers shirts. Rav is confused. Did they hear about Jack coming back here after the attack? Is this some sort of weird fan pilgrimage? Then he takes in their expressions: flushed faces, accusing eyes. These people are *pissed*. Rav's warning lights are going off now. He tries to slip past, but one of them, a meaty kid with ginger hair, cuts him off. "You piece of shit!"

Rav blinks. "Sorry?"

"You should be sorry." The kid gets right in Rav's face. "You should be fucking *ashamed*."

"You'll want to step back," Rav says, taking a page out of Mo's book.

"Or what? Or you'll harass me like you did Jack Vale? Or hey, maybe you wanna arrest me on some bullshit charges." He offers Rav his wrists.

A familiar face appears in the crowd. It's Carrie Campbell

from the *Times*, and for half a second Rav is relieved to see her. Then he spies the pocket recorder in her hand, light flashing. "Detective Trivedi, can you comment on the allegations contained in Jack Vale's social media?"

Rav's stomach drops. "What allegations?"

"Maybe you should check your phone, Detective," she says coolly. "I'll be here when you're ready to talk."

The ginger-haired kid is still in his face. He jabs a finger at Rav's chest. "We *see* you, cop. Do you hear me?" They're crowding around him now, cursing him out, and all Rav can do is shoulder his way through the scrum. Nobody grabs him or takes a swing, but even so, his heart is pounding by the time he gets to the elevator.

What the *fuck* is going on?

He waits until he's in his apartment to pull up Vale's Twitter feed, and what he finds makes his blood run cold.

Post after post about the Vanderford case, and Jack's treatment at the hands of the NYPD. Retweets, mostly, from some blogger claiming to have inside information about the investigation. About how the NYPD, under pressure from the powerful Vanderford family, latched onto Vale as a suspect and tried every dirty trick in the book to get him to incriminate himself.

Instagram is even worse. There's a reel of Jack speaking directly to his fans, urging them to check out the blog. He looks tired and sad, staring grimly into the camera as he explains why he had to speak out. *"I just feel sick, in the pit of my stomach. It's a betrayal, there's no other word for it. If they can do this to me, imagine what it's like for someone more vulnerable. Somebody's gotta hold them accountable."*

Rav makes the mistake of following the link to the full article, and it's horrifying. Not only does it mention him by name, it all but accuses him of trying to entrap Vale, using himself as bait.

Detective Trivedi did everything he could to catch me with my guard down, Vale is quoted as saying. *And I almost fell for it.*

Does he really believe that?

Rav's mentions are blowing up with threats and abuse. He turns his phone off.

He goes to the window and looks out. They're still down there, staking him out. How the hell did they find out where he lives? He considers calling it in, but bringing cops out here would just throw gasoline on the fire.

It takes a few hours, but they finally disperse. Rav had plans this evening, but he's in no shape to go out. He's in no shape to do much of anything but drink and seethe, so that's what he does.

His head is a million miles away when the intercom buzzes. Warily, he thumbs the button. "Yes?"

"Rav?"

"Who's this?"

"Um." A pause. Then, quietly, "It's Jack?"

For a second Rav is stunned. Then he sees red. All he can think in that moment is how badly he wants to give this bastard a piece of his mind. "Jack," he says coldly. "By all means, please come up." He stabs the intercom button and unlocks the door. Then he props himself against the sofa, facing the door like he's covering it. Distantly, he hears the elevator *ping*, followed by a soft knock. "It's open."

Vale walks in, anonymous in an oversized gray sweatshirt with the hood pulled up. The rush of warmth Rav gets at the sight of him is infuriating, a humiliating reminder of just how far he's let this man get under his skin. "Hey," Jack greets him casually, too focused on kicking off his trainers to notice the look on Rav's face. "Have you heard the news?"

"I'm not sure." Rav's tone is icy, but Vale doesn't notice that, either. Too wrapped up in himself. They always are, these celebrities.

"We're getting our masters back. The trustees of Vanderford's estate have agreed to . . ." He pauses, taking in Rav's body language at last. "Are you okay?"

"No, I am very much *not* okay. I am racking my brain trying to understand why you would show up here."

"I . . ." Vale blinks. "Didn't Eloise text you? I thought we agreed I would come by to pick up the notebook."

"Right. The notebook." Rav walks over to the kitchen counter, picks it up, and tosses it at him. It lands with a loud *slap* at his feet.

Vale flinches as it hits the floor. He stares at it for a second. "Wow. Okay." He gives his head a little shake and picks it up. Then he turns for the door, but not before Rav catches the look on his face, angry and confused and maybe even a little hurt, and it's such a perfect mirror of what he's feeling that he can't hold his tongue.

"Is that really what you think happened?"

Vale's glance skips over him coldly. "What?"

Rav pulls out his phone, as though the words aren't seared into his brain. "*Detective Trivedi did everything he could to catch me with my guard down.*"

Vale shakes his head. "What is that?"

"An article by someone called Hayden Beck."

"I don't know who that is."

"Odd, since he's quoting you. Then, of course, there's your Instagram post, in which you urge the entire world to read his article. The tale he spun for you must have been very convincing. Just wondering, did it occur to you at any point that he might be *completely* full of shit? That maybe you should try getting my side of the story before you blew up my life?"

"I have no idea what you're talking about," Vale says, reaching for his back pocket. "My phone has been off all day. I haven't looked at it since . . ." He trails off, staring at his screen for a long, tense beat. "What the fuck?" He taps his screen, and his voice pipes up, mid-sentence.

"*—in the pit of my stomach. It's a betrayal, there's no other word for it.*"

"What. The. *Fuck.*"

The look of blank horror on his face is enough to pierce the haze of Rav's anger. "They're your posts," he says, but he hears the doubt in his own voice.

"This isn't me," Vale says. "I mean, it is, but . . . it's not real."

"Not real? Are you saying—"

"I'm saying I didn't make this video, and I never gave this interview. I have to go." He's halfway out the door already, wedging his feet into his shoes and furiously texting someone.

"Seriously?" Heat flashes over Rav's face. "That's it? You're out?"

"You've made it pretty clear you don't want me here," Vale says impatiently.

"I *want* an explanation. I think I deserve that, don't you?"

"You're pissed. I get it. But did it occur to *you* that *this* might be completely full of shit?" He waggles his phone. "My accounts have obviously been hacked."

Rav processes that. "Why would someone do that?"

"No idea, but you could've given me the benefit of the doubt before you bit my head off."

"Right, because you're showing so much consideration for my situation."

Vale scowls at his phone, still texting. "What do you want me to say, Rav? I don't know what this is, but I'm sorry you got mixed up in it."

"Caught in the crosshairs, more like! I've been trapped in this apartment for hours. There have been death threats!"

Vale looks up, startled. "Wait, are you serious?"

"Haven't you looked at the replies?"

He does now, paling visibly as he scrolls. "Shit. Rav, I . . . *Shit.*" He shoves a hand through his hair.

Rav needs to dial it back. "Can you just . . . sit for a minute?" he growls, rubbing his eyes. "I need to understand what's going on here. If you didn't do this—"

"I didn't do this." Jack looks him right in the eye.

Rav decides he believes him. After all, would he really come here after publicly accusing Rav of harassment? He would have seen that from the start if he hadn't been so worked up. "Sit," he sighs. "Please?"

"Mo is in the car outside . . ." Jack glances at the door, and then he shakes his head. "No, you're right. We need to sort this out." He shoots off another text, and then he perches on the edge of the sofa.

Rav fills him in on the altercation with his fans. "You really had no idea this was going on?"

"My phone was off, and Mo was driving." Jack sags over his knees and blows into his steepled hands. "This is so messed up. Why would someone do this? A deepfake video, seriously?"

"You're sure that's what it is? I mean, of course you are, it's just . . ." Rav is watching it again. "It looks so real."

"Some of it might be. That bit about betrayal—it sounds familiar. Something I said about Vanderford, maybe? Whatever. We'll put out a press release, but for now I can at least delete this crap from my accounts."

He spends the next several minutes doing that, while Rav pours a couple of gin and tonics and does his best to level out. He's still pissed, but he doesn't know where to point it anymore. Was this even about him, or was he just collateral damage?

"Okay," Jack says, "I've posted about the hack on all my social feeds and asked people to leave you alone. Maybe let's grab a shot of the two of us together?" They move to the kitchen, where the light is better. Jack throws an arm around Rav and snaps a photo, and then he uploads it to Twitter and Instagram. "There. That should keep the wolves at bay until we sort this out."

"I appreciate it."

"It's the least I can do." Blue-green eyes skim Rav's features. "I'm so sorry about all this."

They're still standing shoulder to shoulder, neither of them moving away; with each second that ticks past, it feels a little weightier, a little more deliberate. "It's not your fault," Rav says, trying to ignore the heat spreading at the back of his neck.

"Maybe, but you were right before. I was so busy worrying about damage control that I didn't even process what was happening to you. I'm a dick."

"You're not a dick." Rav's mouth curls just short of a smile. "Surprisingly."

Jack arches an eyebrow. "Surprisingly?"

"Well, you *are* a celebrity. I expected you to be a self-absorbed prick, but it turns out you're a pretty decent guy. For a rock star."

"You're a pretty decent guy, too. For a cop." Those eyes. At this range, they have their own gravitational pull. They're like a bloody tractor beam, and Rav is caught in it; he can't pull away. "Seriously, you've been nothing but professional and amazing." His gaze falls to Rav's mouth, where it lingers.

This can't be happening. Is this happening?

Jack leans in. "Can I kiss you?" he murmurs.

Dear god, YES.

The thought hits Rav so forcefully that for a second he doesn't trust himself to speak. Jack takes the silence for ambivalence, and he backs away immediately. "Sorry, have I misread this? I thought . . ."

"You haven't." Rav clears his throat. "You very much haven't. But I don't know if it's appropriate."

"Okay." Jack digests that for a second. "But . . . I'm not a suspect anymore, right?"

"No."

"And you're off the case. So if I'm not part of the case, and *you're* not part of the case . . ." He lets that dangle, and maybe it's those tractor beam eyes, but Rav is having a hard time finding fault with his logic.

"It's just, those rules exist for a reason, and it's not just to protect the integrity of an investigation. There are power dynamics at play, and—"

"Rav." He blows out a breath and rubs his forehead. "Man, this is wild. I'm usually the one stressing about this stuff. Look, *I* asked to kiss *you*, and not because I'm feeling some sort of pressure about an investigation that doesn't even involve me anymore." He catches Rav's gaze again, holding it very deliberately. "I consent." He's so close now that Rav feels the whisper of his breath when he adds, "I completely, *totally* consent. Do you?"

"I want to." He completely, *totally* wants to . . .

Jack shakes his head. "It has to be one hundred per—"

"Yes." Rav is already reaching for him, and the word gets lost against Jack's mouth.

He kind of freezes there for a second, and when he finally moves his lips, it's a little tentative. His brain is still scrolling through all the reasons this is a bad idea in big, bold letters, like a Star Wars prologue on fast-forward. But he can feel his discipline melting away as the mouth against his parts, a soft tongue darting out to meet his, and now he's leaning into it, cradling Jack's head and deepening the kiss. Callused fingers glide up the back of his neck, bringing a shiver to his skin; they dive into his hair and curl tightly, tugging so hard it almost hurts, and it's . . . *god*, it's good. Then Jack's hand slides over his arse, and that's it: the last thread of control snaps. Suddenly Rav is backing him into the counter, hoisting him onto it, releasing all that pent-up frustration. His mouth is greedy, his hands are greedy, he can hardly think straight for the wash of heat over his skin. Jack is here for all of it, and things are about to get properly out of hand when there's a knock at the door. They come apart, breathless.

"Jack?" Mo's baritone sounds from the other side of the door. "You all right in there?"

Rav is so worked up he can't even speak. He's going to die if he can't kiss that mouth again.

Jack beats him to it, cupping his face and kissing him softly. "Too bad we didn't video this," he murmurs. "Show them what the real thing looks like."

Rav lets out a helpless little groan. Because he wasn't hard enough already.

"Be right there, Mo," Jack calls over his shoulder. His hands still frame Rav's face, thumbs stroking absently. "God, these cheekbones." He sighs, hands falling away. "I should go. My publicist must be losing her mind."

"I should make some calls as well." Rav steps back as Jack hops down from the counter. He feels a little lightheaded. "I must say, this is not how I pictured my day ending. You?"

"Honestly, kind of." The shy smile when he says that makes Rav want to pin him up against that counter again. He contents himself with staring shamelessly at Jack's arse as he crosses the room to let his bodyguard in. "Sorry, man," Jack says as he opens the door. "Didn't mean to keep you waiting."

Mo looks at him. He looks at Rav. "Shirt's crooked, big guy," he observes mildly.

Rav glances down. It's hanging slightly off his shoulder, showing a lot more chest than it should. He tries to pretend he's not blushing like a teenager while he straightens it. He's only grateful he's strategically positioned behind the kitchen counter, or Mo might have noticed something more embarrassing than a crooked shirt.

"I'll call you tomorrow," Jack says.

"Sure," Rav says. "Yep." He gives Jack a thumbs-up.

For fuck's sake.

"Night night," Mo says, and the cheeky bastard winks.

Rav closes the door and locks up. Then, as he's walking past the sideboard, he sees it. The bloody notebook.

He laughs like a fool all the way to the bedroom.

CHAPTER ELEVEN

Rav dreads the prospect of going into the office on Monday. Water cooler chitchat makes him want to hang himself at the best of times, but tomorrow's session promises to be especially delightful. *How was your weekend? Oh, you know. Angry mobs, death threats. Made out with a rock star. You?*

Then there's Howard. He's not sure what to expect there. Their conversation last night was economical even by the lieutenant's standards. She asked if he was safe and instructed him not to speak to the media or post anything online. The rest, she said, could wait until Monday.

The New Knickerbockers issue a press release late Sunday morning denouncing the hack and the video as a vicious prank. It doesn't go as far as Rav would like—it doesn't mention him personally or address any of the specific allegations contained in the bogus interview—but he supposes Jack's lawyers have their reasons. Carrie Campbell posts an article in the *Times* describing the scene outside Rav's building, in which "a visibly confused Detective Trivedi was nearly assaulted by a crowd of angry fans taken in by the hoax." The internet promptly rounds on Hayden Beck, and by Sunday afternoon, the blogger's social media accounts have been deleted and his website taken down.

"It's not clear whether he even exists," Howard tells Rav when they meet first thing on Monday. "Computer Crimes has said they'll look into it, but I wouldn't get my hopes up. A low-priority matter like this—"

He scowls. "Someone orchestrated a *mob* outside my apartment building."

"*Orchestrated* is a strong word. This was probably just a prank that got out of hand."

"So that's it, then? Case closed?"

"You're entitled to mental health leave, and counseling is available if you need it." She pauses, her dark eyes holding Rav's. "In your place, Detective, I'd be grateful if that proves to be the limit of the department's interest in the matter. So far, no one has bothered to ask how Jack Vale came to have a photo of the two of you together. A photo in which you appear to be on very friendly terms."

He clears his throat awkwardly. "That was the point, of course. As to the first part—"

"Your personal life is not my concern." Lifting an eyebrow, she adds, "For both our sakes, I hope it stays that way."

The message is loud and clear. *On your head be it.* The Vanderford case is still open. If Rav is wrong about Jack, it'll be the end of his career. At least she's leaving it up to him. That shows a lot of confidence in his judgment, and he appreciates that. "I hear you, LT," Rav assures her. "It won't be a problem."

Will is scrolling through Twitter when Rav gets back to his desk. "It's bizarre. First they love you, then they're baying for your blood, then they love you again. They're even turning on each other now, just to prove they're on the right side. Do any of these people actually care about Jack Vale? Seems like they're more interested in racking up likes than finding out what really happened."

"Social media in a nutshell," Rav says sourly.

"It was good of Vale to call off the dogs. Most people would hold a grudge after being investigated for murder. You look like you legitimately like each other in this photo." Will frowns, peering more closely at his screen. "Wait, is this your apart—"

"What I'd like to know," Rav says, a little too loudly, "is who's behind it. Howard thinks it was a prank, but if so, it's a pretty elaborate one."

"Maybe someone has a grudge against you. Somebody

you arrested or something." He shrugs. "We'll probably never know."

"I'm not so sure about that. Up for a little drive?"

Half an hour later, they're standing outside a four-story walk-up in the East Village, one of those old tenement buildings that might have been charming if it had been pressure washed sometime in the last thirty years. The trash bins out front are overflowing, to the delight of the local rat population, and the windows on the top floor are boarded up. "What is this place?" Will asks, looking it over with a dubious expression.

The intercom panel is filthy. No way Rav is touching that with his bare hands. He reaches into his breast pocket and pulls out a square of stylish patterned cloth.

"Is that a handkerchief?"

"It is." A real one, too, not the disposable kind. He likes the old-school feel of them. Also, they're terribly posh.

"Do you actually use it to blow your nose?"

"Don't be ridiculous. It's Paul Smith." Rav uses it to press the intercom button.

Will shakes his head. "You're a weird guy, Trivedi."

"Well, I could be a walking beige flag, but I wouldn't want to steal your thunder."

The lock buzzes. Rav grabs the door (with the handkerchief, obviously) and they head inside. "Nobody answered," Will notes as they start up the stairs. "How do they know who it is?"

"Oh, she'll have a sneaky camera installed around here somewhere." In fact, he'd be surprised if there was just the one. She's probably tapped into every security and traffic cam for blocks.

Rav finds the door he wants and knocks, and there's another loud buzz as the lock gives. "Like a prison," Shepard mutters.

They head inside, and if Will looked bemused before, he's properly gobsmacked now. Rav probably looked much the same the first time he walked through this door, stepping from a rundown tenement hallway into a high-tech wonderland full of random bits of finery. The sitting room looks like someone robbed a

Best Buy and then hit an estate sale on the way home. A massive server sits beside a century-old horsehair settee, throwing blinking green lights over the silk upholstery. A panel of flatscreens showing everything from code to security footage to stock markets competes for wall space with an ornate gilt mirror. Half the devices in here are probably some shade of illegal. Happily, Rav doesn't know much about these things, and Will even less, so they have plausible deniability.

"Um," says Will, glancing around uncomfortably. "What are we doing here?"

"That's what I'd like to know," says a voice, and Rav turns to find Aisha Khan standing in the doorway to her kitchen, glaring at him from under a fringe of frosted bangs. She's wearing leopard-print overalls and Hello Kitty high-tops, which is confusing and also very Aisha. Her look, like her décor, speaks volumes—though what it says, Rav hasn't quite worked out. "I thought I was very clear that I didn't want you bringing strangers around here," she says. "And now you show up with a *cop?*"

"I'm a cop, Aisha."

"And I try not to hold it against you, but that doesn't mean you get a free pass to bring more of them in here. Have you got any idea how many clients I'd lose if anybody found out I was having tea with the NYPD?"

"There's tea? Fantastic, I could use a cuppa."

She scowls. "How about a kick in the—"

"Look, there's nothing to worry about. Shepard is my partner. You can trust him."

"I don't trust *you.*"

"Let's not be dramatic. If you were that worried about it, you wouldn't have buzzed us in. Will Shepard, meet Aisha Khan. She's . . . what's the euphemism? A cybersecurity engineer?"

"You mean a hacker," Will says.

"I do mean that, yes."

"Since when do you know hackers?"

Since last year, when he met Aisha at a cocktail party hosted by some Wall Street types. Rav scored an invite through friends, but he was on the job that night, discreetly tailing a man he suspected of murdering his business partner to cover up an insider trading scheme. Aisha looked the part, dressed in a little black dress and strappy sandals, but Rav clocked her as an imposter right away. For one thing, she'd teetered uncertainly on those heels, and the tattoos and pierced septum didn't quite fit the scene. Also, she kept peeking inside her handbag, where Rav subsequently discovered a clever little device capable of nicking data from nearby smartphones. It turned out they were tailing the same guy. Aisha had been hired to find proof of his insider trading. Rav agreed to look the other way on the smartphone hacking if she gave him everything she had on his suspect, and while he couldn't use her intel in court, it pointed him in the right direction. Rav got his man, Aisha got paid, and they've had a mutually beneficial, if not entirely trusting, relationship ever since.

"It's a long story," Rav says. "But don't worry, it's all aboveboard." On his side, anyway. "I scratch her back, she . . . Well, now, come to think of it, I've been doing most of the back-scratching lately."

Aisha rolls her eyes. "As if running a few names through a database is such a huge favor. So you're here to collect, is that it?"

"I wouldn't put it quite so transactionally, but I do need your help. This past weekend—"

"Yeah, yeah, I know. The Jack Vale thing, right? You wanna know who set you up."

That throws Rav off a little. Aisha has her fingers in a lot of pies, but even so, he's surprised the Vale story would ping on her radar. Is she keeping tabs on him? It's a disconcerting thought. "You think someone was trying to set me up?"

"Trying to set the NYPD up, anyway. Whether you were the target or collateral damage, I couldn't say."

"Can you find the source of the hack?"

She settles into a chair in front of a bank of keyboards and screens that wouldn't look out of place in the NYPD situation center. "The most I can get you is an IP address, and that's not much help. You're better off looking into the fake blogger. If I can track down what's left of his website, there might be some fingerprints in the metadata."

"We were told it's all been deleted," Will says.

She shrugs. "You can dispose of a body, right? Wash the blood off the floor, throw the gun in the East River. But there's always something left behind for your forensics guys. Same principle here. You have your trace evidence, I have mine. Probably won't lead us to a specific individual, but hopefully it narrows things down."

"How long will it take?" Rav asks.

"That depends." She plucks a lollipop from a pencil holder and starts unwrapping it. "This could be a big project. No way I'm that far in the red with you. How will you make this worth my while?"

"How is this any different from our usual arrangement?"

"Because it's personal, like you said. Helping you hunt down a murderer—that's for the greater good. This is for you. So if I help you, will you owe me *personally*?"

"What does that even mean?"

"Say things were to get a little hot for me here, and I decided to relocate to London. Would I have the gratitude of a certain well-connected member of parliament?"

Rav can't recall ever having mentioned his father to Aisha Khan.

That settles it: she's definitely keeping tabs on him. "My father doesn't do favors," he says coolly. "Especially for me. But if it's connections you're looking for, I'd remind you that there's another party with skin in the game."

"You mean Vale?" She hums thoughtfully around her lollipop. "Interesting."

"His head of security is former intelligence, and he's invested heavily in their digital operations. I'll wager you could help them level up even more, starting with how to protect their social media accounts."

"You think they'd hire me to consult?"

He looks her over—animal-print overalls, eccentric haircut, pencil holder full of lollipops. *If I can persuade them you're not completely mad.* "I can't promise anything, but I'll certainly put in a word, and this is a chance to show them what you can do."

She thinks about it for a beat. "Throw in His Lordship's personal number, and it's a deal."

"Pass."

"Worth a try," she mutters, spinning her chair around and reaching for her mouse.

Worth a try is exactly how Rav would describe this entire enterprise. He's not sure what he expects her to find. Only he can't quite shake the nagging feeling there's something here, something bigger than a prank. It's adjacent to the twinge in his gut that tells him the FBI is barking up the wrong tree on the Vanderford case. It's as if his subconscious is trying to tell him something, but what?

What is he missing?

* * *

Rav sips his beer, grimaces, and puts it back down. An IPA, seriously? This is what he gets for letting Will order for him. He pushes it away.

They're at a cop bar in Bed-Stuy, a place called Hardy's. Rav makes it a policy to avoid cop bars—they appeal to dinosaurs like Danny Jobs, and he gets enough of that toxicity in the squad room—but they're having a working drink. Working, because they're looking into the Vanderford case; on their personal time, because technically, they're not supposed to be. They face each other across dueling laptops. Will is going through Vanderford's emails—again—while Rav trawls through the social media profiles of users who've made threatening statements about him.

"This is painful," Will grumbles. "I've got zilch over here."

Rav has the opposite problem. "The entire internet hated this man. Even if I narrow it down to profiles that follow the Nicks, it's overwhelming."

"A needle in a hate-stack." He pauses, waiting for Rav to laugh. This does not happen. "Come on, really? That was good."

Rav keeps scrolling. "I wish we had access to the algorithm Erika Strauss uses for this. I'll bet it's leagues better than ours."

"Maybe we should be thankful. In a couple of years, Homicide won't even need grunts like us. AI will be doing it all."

"Uh-oh, is AI taking over the world again?" Rav looks up to find Ana standing over them. She's come straight from work: shoulder-length hair pulled back into a severe ponytail, no makeup, no earrings.

Rav glances at his watch. "I thought we said seven?" They're supposed to be grabbing dinner after this.

"Yeah, but I got my paperwork done faster than I thought." Her eyes shift to Will, giving him a discreet once-over. "How you doing, Shepard? Listen, if you guys are still working—"

Will nudges a chair out with his foot. "Take a seat. I'm going cross-eyed anyway, and Rav is getting cranky."

"I'm not," Rav says.

He is.

Ana settles in and eyes Rav's untouched pint. She drags it over, sniffs it, and takes a swig. "What?" she says when Rav gives her a look. "We both know you weren't gonna drink it."

"Why not?" Will asks.

"Rav hates IPAs."

"Of course he does." Will rolls his eyes. "Why didn't you say something? I could have got you a glass of wine."

"Here?" Rav snorts. "I think not."

Ana fake-whispers behind her hand, "In case you haven't noticed, our boy here is a little *bougie*."

Will laughs, and Ana flashes him a winning smile—a bit *too* winning, in Rav's estimation. "Tell me about it," Will says. "Dude carries a handkerchief. A real one."

"I'll go you one better. He gets them dry-cleaned."

Okay, whatever *this* is, Rav is not up for it. "Do you mind?" he says, gesturing at his laptop.

"You're right, he is cranky. Looks like it's just you and me, Shepard." There it is again—that flirty smile. Is it possible she really does have a thing for Will? Rav has always assumed that was a joke. "Okay, sorry, you guys are trying to work." She smooths her expression. "Can I help? What're we doing?"

"Looking for a needle in a hate-stack." Will pauses significantly.

"Give him a pity laugh," Rav advises. "That's twice now he's launched that lead balloon."

Ana shrugs. "I can get with dad jokes."

Since when? Rav shakes his head. Ana's taste in romantic partners is all over the place, but he would never have guessed she'd be into Classic Ken.

"So you guys caught a new case?" she asks, sipping her pilfered beer.

"Nope," Will says. "This is still Vanderford."

"Am I missing something? I thought the feds took over that one."

"They did," Rav says, "but I've come up with a new angle, and I think it's got some real merit, so I'm looking into it."

"And because I'm a sap," Will adds, "I'm helping."

"Aren't you sweet? I hope you appreciate this one, Trivedi." She eyes Will over the rim of her pint glass, doing some appreciating of her own. "You still have access to the case file?"

"For now." Also, he had Aisha make him a cheeky offline copy, but he doesn't mention that part.

"So, what's this promising new angle?"

Rav leans forward, energized. "As many possible motives as there are for this thing, the one I keep coming back to is that business I was telling you about before, with the Nicks and their master recordings. We've looked into the band and their inner circle already, but what happened on Saturday got me thinking.

Those fans outside my apartment had been whipped into a frenzy on social media. Some nineteen-year-old kid almost assaulted a cop at his home, in front of dozens of witnesses, because of a phony interview. How much worse must it have been for Vanderford? He was Enemy Number One to Nicks fans. This list?" He shows her the spreadsheet on his screen. "Usernames of people who've made threatening statements about him on Twitter. Over a hundred of them, and that's just one platform. These fans are so obsessed, so emotionally invested, that there's no such thing as going too far."

"To the point of murder? That sounds totally ridiculous." Shaking her head, she adds, "And *totally* possible."

"So possible that I hardly know where to start. It's like Vale's bodyguard says: most of it is just talk, but how do you tell?"

Ana sips her beer, thinking. "Are there cameras outside your building? I've never paid attention."

"There are. Why?"

"You said those fans were out there for hours, right? Run them through facial, look up their social profiles, and cross-reference it with your spreadsheet. If you get a match, you're ticking a bunch of boxes. Angry, committed, living in the area. It's a start, anyway."

Will rocks his chair back. "That's not bad, actually."

"It's bloody brilliant, in point of fact." Rav pulls up his email and starts composing a message to his building's management company. "Remind me why they haven't made you detective yet?"

"I'm wondering the same," Will says. "Or is that not what you want?"

She shrugs. "At some point, but I'm taking my time. Doing some courses at CUNY, you know. Figuring out what I like."

"Smart," Will says. "You *should* take your time, especially at your age."

"My age? What, are you an old man all of a sudden?"

"Older than you, anyway. By a fair bit, I'd say."

There's a glint in Ana's eye now, one Rav has learned to dread. "You flirting with me, Shepard? I gotta say, you wanna be careful about that. I'm a junior officer, remember."

Will laughs, but it's awkward. He can't tell if she's serious. "I'm not flirting."

"Just commenting on a female colleague's appearance?"

Ana. This, right here, is what Rav meant the other day when he said she'd eat Will alive. The poor guy looks like he's standing on the subway tracks watching a train bearing down on him. On any other day, Rav might find this entertaining, but he's trying to work here. "She's fucking with you, Shepard."

Ana grins.

"Shit," Will breathes, relieved. "You're convincing. And *mean.*"

"Sorry, I couldn't resist. You Midwestern boys are just so earnest!"

He shakes his head. "I'm getting another drink. Rav, you want something?" Rav declines, and his partner retreats to nurse his dignity by the bar.

"You're evil, Rodriguez," Rav says as he types.

"Yeah, but he's so cute when he blushes." She's still grinning, eying Will like he's a tasty bar snack. "So, how much longer you need?"

"Give me half an hour." He sends off the email to the management company and opens a new tab. It'll take a while to get the footage, and even longer to run it through the NYPD's facial recognition software. In the meantime, there's always social media. Maybe he gets lucky, and one of these names turns out to be the ginger-haired kid, or someone else he recognizes from the mob.

God, he would love to nail this guy before the FBI does. And if that were to earn him some points with a certain someone, well . . . that would be a definite bonus.

CHAPTER TWELVE

av is still a little cranky when he gets home from dinner. He was planning to tell Ana about what happened with Jack, but he chickened out. Which suggests he's feeling guilty about it, but why should he? He's done nothing wrong. If he had, Howard would have said something. Well . . . something more definitive, anyway. Right?

Before he can start spiraling, his phone buzzes with a message that melts it all away.

MESSAGES

Jack Vale   Now
Got something for you

It's a link to a museum exhibition in the UK. Tapping it, Rav finds a photo of a sarod almost identical to the one hanging on his wall, with the same gilded floral pattern.

Mid-19th century, Uttar Pradesh.
Some cool history in the description
there, if you're interested

Rav's chest thrums. He hadn't really expected Jack to follow through on his offer. It's sweet of him, especially with everything he has going on right now. That has to mean something, doesn't it?

Extremely interested, thank you.

Call you in an hour?

It ends up being two hours and twelve minutes, not that Rav is counting. He grabs his AirPods; he wants Jack's voice in his ear. "I wasn't sure I'd hear from you before you left for Miami," he says, congratulating himself on how breezy he sounds.

"You didn't. I'm in the air."

Rav closes his eyes, letting that rich tenor drip like warm honey down his spine. "I take it you're flying private?"

"Yeah." He sounds embarrassed. "We take trains whenever we can, but sometimes it's just not possible."

"Don't worry, we all have our dirty little climate secrets." Rav stretches his six-foot frame out on the sofa, arm tucked behind his head. "Now that I've salved your conscience, tell me honestly: Is it divine?"

"It's comfortable, but it's still a plane. Not my favorite thing." Rav hears it in his voice, slightly tighter than it should be. "What about you, how are you holding up after Saturday?"

"Ten out of ten, would definitely kiss you again."

He laughs. "Good to know, but I was talking about the other thing."

"You mean the vicious mob? Fine, thanks. Apparently, I'm popular again."

"Seriously, though. I saw the article in the *Times*. That must have been pretty scary."

"It was disconcerting. But I don't think I was in any real danger. It certainly doesn't compare to what happened at the skate park, to say nothing of the Concord."

Jack's voice goes quiet. "Yeah, that was . . . I mean, it could have been so much worse, obviously, but in that moment, when we didn't really know what was happening . . ."

"I can imagine. I was actually there that night, you know. Responding to the call."

"Really? How come you never mentioned it?"

The bigger question is why he's mentioning it now. It must be the last thing Jack wants to talk about. "I'm sorry you had to go through that. But at least it's over."

"Is it? He's still out there."

The words send a stab of guilt through Rav's chest. Miller was right in front of him, and he blew it.

"It's not just him, either," Jack goes on. "There's the guy who broke into my place, and the tongue guy . . . It's so messed up. There have always been stalkers, but it's just too easy now. Like, I'm pretty sure the details of this flight are already on social media."

"We were talking about that today, actually. I'm wondering if social media might hold some clues to the Vanderford murder."

There's a pause. "I thought you were done with that," Jack says.

"Officially, yes. But I've got a couple of new ideas that I'm looking into."

"Okay."

Another silence. Jack doesn't seem too thrilled to hear Rav is still involved with the case. "Anyway, you're right," Rav says, pivoting back hastily. "About the dark side of social media, I mean."

"It's hard to feel safe anywhere these days. I've even thought about carrying a gun, but Mo says it's not a good idea."

"I understand the impulse, but I'm with Mo on this one. Using a firearm safely and effectively takes a lot of practice."

"Well, that part I've actually got covered. My last bodyguard took me to the firing range a bunch last year, with the idea that I'd start carrying my own when I was ready. But Mo feels differently, and I get that. The neighborhood I grew up in was pretty rough back in the day, and I've seen what the streets look like when everybody's carrying."

"You're originally from Atlanta, right?" As if Rav hasn't memorized every line of Jack's Wikipedia page, but it seems like a good way of changing the subject. Jack called him to relax, not rehash all the awful things going on in his life. "I have to say, you don't *sound* like you're from the South."

"Do I not say *y'all* enough?"

"Do you ever say it?"

"Sometimes. What about you, how come you still sound like you just walked off the set of *Downton Abbey*?"

"*Lies*," Rav says with a startled laugh.

"When Ryan mentioned your dad was a lord, I thought, of course he is."

"Ugh, please . . ."

"And when I found out your mom was an ex-model, I thought, of course she is."

"That one I'll take, thank you. But I reject the idea that I sound anything like His Lordship. My father has such a stick up the arse you can actually hear it in his voice."

"Up the arse, huh?"

"I can't bring myself to say *ass*," Rav says, exaggerating the nasal quality of the American pronunciation. "It's far too flat. *Arse* has a proper curve to it, as a good arse should."

"Seems like you've thought about this a lot." Rav hears a *clink* of ice shifting in a glass, and he reaches for his own whiskey. If he closes his eyes, he can almost pretend Jack is here in the flesh, sharing a quiet drink. "But you've been in the States for a while, right?"

Rav hums assent through a sip of scotch. "I was actually born here. We lived in New York until I was two, which is when my parents split the first time."

"The first time?"

"It's a Greek play, Jack. Don't even ask."

"Sounds like it," he says, laughing. "It would make great reality TV. The lord, the model, and their hot playboy son."

"Playboy? I'm a little offended."

"You're the one telling strangers about skinny-dipping in penthouse pools." He sounds more relaxed, and Rav flatters himself that it isn't just the alcohol. "Besides, I'm talking about your pitch here. You'd want to play up the bad boy angle for TV, right?"

"You'd have me sell my soul and become part of the machine churning out . . . what did you call it? Opium for the masses?"

"So you've been listening to my music." Rav hears the grin in his voice. He wonders if there's anyone nearby to see it; whether Jack's bandmates are wondering who he's talking to. *Remember that cop who almost arrested me for murder? I know, right?*

"I may have heard a few snippets here and there," Rav says archly. "Entirely in passing, of course."

"Of course."

"I'm sorry I won't be able to catch your show."

"You can come see us play MSG next month."

"You're coming back through?" To play Madison Square Garden, no less. Rav knew the Nicks were big, but bloody hell. "I thought you'd already done your New York dates."

"Not yet. The Miami show is the official start of the tour. We always do a handful of smaller venues before we officially kick off, just to fine-tune things. Even then, it takes a while to really get into the groove, so the timing of the MSG show is perfect. That's a place you want to get it right."

"Because it's New York?"

"In part. But that venue especially, it's iconic. When Tommy and I used to daydream about making it big, it was always, 'One day we're gonna play Madison Square Garden.'" His tone turns wistful, and Rav knows he's back in that auto body shop on Knickerbocker Avenue, a skinny high school kid with big dreams and a best friend who shared them.

"It must be hard," Rav says. "Playing there without him."

"Bittersweet, for sure. *Hard* is hearing his voice on an ad for a sports drink."

Rav has seen that commercial. The song is from their first album, a tune called "Animal." It's about structural inequality and society reaping what it sows, and they're using it to flog a bright green syrupy drink. Charlie Banks wasn't kidding: Vanderford licensed those recordings to anyone and everyone. It's not hard to understand why Jack despised the man.

"Thanks for that, *Dick*," Jack says bitterly. "At least it's over now. We got our masters back, and Vanderford is . . ." The pause is just long enough to be uncomfortable. "Out of our lives," he finishes. "Wherever Tommy is now, I hope that brings him some peace."

"Tell me about him."

"Tommy?"

"Only if you want to. I can hear how much he meant to you, and I honestly don't know that I've ever had someone like that in my life. Were the two of you . . . ?"

"More than friends?"

Fuck, why did he ask that? "Never mind, it's none of my business."

"It's okay. And no, it wasn't like that. For one thing, Tommy was straight. Plus, I just never thought of him like that. When I first met him, I was seeing someone, and by the time that was over, he was already like a brother."

"You met at LaGuardia, right?"

"Someone's been reading *Wikipedia*," Jack says, the grin back in his voice.

Rav feels his skin warming, as if he just got busted with a poster of Jack Vale in his locker. "I take it that's not accurate?"

"Tommy is the reason I ended up in New York in the first place. You asked what he was like. I'll tell you how we met, and that kind of says it all." He pauses to sip his drink, or maybe he just needs a moment. "So, Tommy's mom and his stepdad lived down the street from us in Atlanta, and he'd visit now and then. I'd see him around, shooting hoops or whatever, but we never talked. Then one day, I'm playing a show with this band my brother put together."

"Hold on, I need context. How old were you?"

"Fifteen, I guess?"

"You were in a band at fifteen?"

"Just with some kids from school. The rest of the guys were seniors, but they wanted someone on keys, and I was the only kid they knew who could play. It was my first show, and I remember being really nervous. Then after, as we're putting our gear away, this kid I'd seen around the neighborhood comes up to me and says, *You should be in a band with me.*"

"Just like that?"

"Just like that. Not even a *Hey, what's up.*" Jack laughs. "So I say, *I'm already in a band.* And he says, *Yeah, but they suck.*"

"Wow."

"*Not you, though,* he says. *You were the only one up there who knew what he was doing.* And I'm this shy kid, and this is my big brother's band, so I just stand there like a deer in the headlights while this super-cool kid with a Brooklyn accent tells me about this amazing school he goes to in New York, and how I should transfer there and start a band with him, because he's going places."

"He was confident."

"He was a force of nature. He had this incredible, in-your-face charisma. I didn't doubt for a second he was going places, and I wanted to be there. I was already pretty serious about music by then, but I was playing classical piano. The band was just something I did to hang out with the older guys. If you'd told me the day before I met Tommy that I'd end up here, I'd have laughed."

"And the day after?"

There's a long, long silence.

"You would have liked him, Rav." Jack's voice is a little wobbly.

"I'm sure I would have."

Jack clears his throat. "You remind me of him a little, actually. The way you instantly own a room."

Rav's heart skips, but he keeps it light. "I hope that doesn't mean you think of me as a brother."

"Don't worry, my thoughts are appropriately carnal."

"I look forward to hearing more about that when you can speak freely," Rav says, silently congratulating himself on the rescue. *Breezy bullshit for the win.*

"Yeah, *private plane* is kind of a misnomer. I've got a bit of space back here, but Sarah is looking at me right now with this

smirk on her face like she knows I'm thinking about phone sex."
Ice shifts in a glass. "What about you, any brothers or sisters?"

"Oh no. My parents didn't particularly want their first child;
they definitely weren't going to have another. Which is fine,
by the way," he adds hastily, before it can become awkward. "I
never really pined for siblings. Family life was messy enough as
it was."

"I take it you're not close?"

"My father and I barely speak, and my mum has always lived
on the other side of the ocean. When I was in London, she was
in New York, and vice versa. So." He takes a swallow of scotch.

"They got back together, you said."

"A few years ago. Out of the clear blue, or so it seemed to me. I
didn't even realize they were still speaking. She's back in London
now. I've no idea what she does there. She's never taken much
of an interest in my life, so I don't feel obliged to take an interest
in hers." Rav swirls his drink in the bottom of his glass. "But
enough about that. It's terribly dull." And embarrassing, and
painful, and not what he wants to talk about right now.

"If it's any consolation, I don't really get along with my dad,
either. It's one of the reasons I took Tommy up on his offer and
moved to New York. After that, Mr. Esposito was kind of my sur-
rogate dad. I even moved in with them for a little while—Tommy's
dad and his three brothers."

"Goodness. That is a *lot* of male energy under one roof."

"It was a lot of male everything. That whole house smelled
like a jockstrap."

Rav almost does a spit-take. "What?"

"I'm not even kidding. Tommy's brothers were all into sports,
and his dad was always at the garage, so there was no one to
clean up after them. They'd leave their gym bags lying around
for weeks, and—"

"Stop, you're making me ill . . ."

It ends up being another marathon session. Even longer than
the first call, and a lot more personal. Rav is acutely aware of

how intimate this is. More intimate than a kiss, or even casual sex.

Which is *terrifying*. There's a thousand reasons he shouldn't let himself get in too deep, but he can't make himself stop. He hangs up feeling high but anxious, like an addict already worrying about his next fix. Jack gets back into town at the weekend, and they've agreed to meet up.

It's going to be the longest four days of his life.

CHAPTER THIRTEEN

Aisha Khan gets in touch later that week, and the news is . . . unexpected. "Russians."

"Come again?"

"Our disappearing blogger, Hayden Beck? I managed to track down traces of his website, and from the metadata, it looks like it was designed by a Russian speaker."

Rav takes a moment to digest this. Hacking is a cottage industry in Russia, but even so . . . "Why would a Russian hacker fabricate a story about the NYPD harassing Jack Vale? Complete with deepfake video, no less."

"Couldn't tell you. Arrest any Russian mobsters recently?"

"Not that I'm aware of. Is there any way you can find out more?"

"I'll keep digging, but this isn't exactly top of my priority list. You'll just have to be patient."

Patience is not Rav's forte. Things have been quiet on the homicide beat lately, and since the Vanderford case is no longer active, Rav's request to run facial recognition on the mob of Nicks fans has been punted to the back of the queue. On the plus side, that gives him extra time to do some digging on the missing PI, only he's turned up nothing. Which is suspicious. Missing persons do not tend to leave squeaky-clean scenes behind, unless they don't *want* to be found. So either Chris Novak has gone into hiding, or someone went to a lot of trouble to make him disappear without a trace.

Then there's the whole *Jack* situation. Rav hasn't heard from him in days. Which, fine, it's not like they're dating, but still. How long does it take to send a text? *Hi, Rav, how are you?* Or even just *Thinking of u, xo.* Though admittedly, Jack does not seem like the *xo* type. Heart emoji? Kiss emoji? No, Rav decides, Jack is not an emoji man.

This is the state of him—irritable, sexually frustrated, and speculating about emoji preferences—when he gets the text. Only it's not from Jack, it's from his PA. She sends a handful of them in rapid succession; Rav can practically hear the invisible question mark at the end of each one.

Hi this is Eloise

Mr. Vale's assistant

**He was wondering if you would be
interested in meeting up tonight**

RSVP

RSVP? To a text? From a personal assistant?

Then, about an hour later, he gets another one advising him that someone will meet him at the bar of the Palace Hotel. *Someone.* Not Jack, apparently. One of his minions. Someone for whom Rav will be just another task that needs doing, in between walking the boss's dog and picking up his vitamin supplements.

He has half a mind to cancel, but of course he doesn't. Pride only goes so far. Instead he dons a pair of dark blue trousers and his best Alexander McQueen button-down, telling himself it's impossible to feel insecure when you look (and smell) this amazing.

He arrives at the hotel half an hour past the appointed time (he does have *some* pride) and orders a scotch at the bar. The place is full of beautiful people drinking eye-wateringly expensive cocktails with egg whites and little sprigs of thyme. The lighting is low, the tables impractically small, and the servers all have high-maintenance haircuts. Rav feels right at home.

He's halfway through his drink when Eloise appears at his elbow, looking even more nervous than usual. An aversion to cops, or does she just find this whole situation painfully awkward? If so, that makes two of them. "Mr. Vale asked me to give this to you?" She hands him a key card. "He's in the penthouse suite again, but um, he thought maybe you'd want to take the service elevator?"

"The service elevator," Rav echoes dumbly.

Eloise gives him directions and flees, and a moment later Rav gets a text.

MESSAGES

Jack Vale   Now
I'll be out on the terrace

Rav stares at his screen. Is this a booty call? A booty *text*? He looks at the key card in his hand, and the longer he stares at it, the stupider he feels. Is this what Vale does? Does he have a Rav in every port, some hot boy (or girl?) with just enough ego to imagine they're special?

His glance strays to the lobby. It's not too late to cut bait, to gather up the tatters of his dignity and leave.

You're overreacting, he tells himself. He'll go upstairs and see what's what. If he's not into it, he can always turn around and leave. *He doesn't own this moment, and he doesn't own you. You're Rav fucking Trivedi, and you bring men to their knees.*

Literally.

No one gives him a second look as he cuts through the kitchen and presses the button for the service elevator. Apparently, this is a *thing*. The thought is not reassuring. He flips the key card over and over in his hand, resisting the urge to check his hair in the warped reflection of the scarred elevator doors.

He hesitates outside Jack's door, giving himself one last chance to back out. Then he waves the card in front of the panel. "Hello?" he calls as he steps into the entryway. No answer, but there's music beckoning from the terrace, so he heads out. He'd forgotten how beautiful it is out here after dark: low, romantic lighting, pool glowing invitingly. He finds Jack propped against the rail, gazing out over the city lights. "Quite a view."

Jack turns, and the sight of him is like whiskey in Rav's veins. He looks just like he did that first day: jeans and a plain knit shirt pushed up at the elbows, breeze toying with his hair. Effortlessly sexy. "Does it bring back memories?" he asks, smiling.

"It does, actually."

"Sorry about the spy routine downstairs. I don't know if you noticed the woman with the pink hair in the lobby, but she's paparazzi. She's been loitering down there for hours. There's no camera in the service elevator, so she won't be able to bribe someone for footage of you coming up to my room. Figured you'd had enough publicity for one week."

Rav relaxes a little, but he keeps his distance. He still doesn't know what this is.

Jack's gaze sweeps him, and he shifts on his feet, as if he's not sure whether to go in for a hug. He heads for the poolside bar instead. "Can I offer you a drink?" Rav tries not to stare at his backside as he follows, but it's hard. Those jeans are perfection on him, slouching where they should slouch, hugging where they should hug. Jack is barefoot again, which is a turn-on for reasons Rav can't understand, and if he springs a boner like a fucking teenager he is officially going to *die*. He tucks himself up close to the bar, just in case. It's stocked with everything you'd need for craft cocktails, but Jack passes it all by in favor of a single malt scotch. Not just any single malt, mind, but Rav's favorite. "You said you liked Macallan, right?"

He did say that, on that first marathon call. He's impressed Jack remembers.

Jack opens it and pours out a generous measure. "Ice?"

"No, thank you."

Jack pours himself a glass as well, and they make their way over to the lounge suite, where a veritable buffet awaits. Charcuterie. Cheese. Carefully tweezed canapés and darling little jars of terrine. "It's a lot, I know," Jack says with an embarrassed laugh. "I wasn't sure what you liked. Or if you were vegan, or gluten-intolerant, or . . ." His eyes meet Rav's, and there's a flicker of uncertainty there. "Anyway, don't feel obliged if you're not hungry. You probably already ate." He smiles awkwardly.

He's on the back foot. Good. It levels the playing field. Rav feels more sure of himself now, maybe more than he has since that first meeting. He sets his drink down and closes the distance between them, but he doesn't lean in—not yet. Instead he holds Jack's gaze while he lifts the glass from his hands. He takes a sip of Jack's scotch and sets that aside, too. Then he slips a hand around Jack's waist and draws him into a kiss.

Jack sighs into it, as if he's been waiting all week for this. Rav definitely has, but he takes his time. He prides himself on being a great kisser, holding back just enough to leave them wanting more. Jack wants more. He presses his body in close. Rav wants more too, and he knows he can only restrain himself for so long. His blood is already rushing south, but he savors the illusion of control while it lasts, forcing Jack to chase his kiss, to seek, to catch what he can.

They come up for air, and the slightly glazed look in those blue-green eyes is extremely satisfying. "Damn," Jack whispers. "That *is* good scotch." And now he's backing Rav onto the chaise, straddling him; they're all over each other, and it occurs to Rav, even as his fingers dive under the waistband of Jack's jeans, that there might be decent sight lines to this terrace from some of the surrounding buildings and while he wouldn't mind a video of this for his own *personal* use, he'd rather not see it on TikTok. He breaks off, but Jack just redirects, his mouth going to Rav's throat instead. Rav can't help tipping his head back, and he's almost ready to forget the bloody sight lines, but he keeps it together just enough to manage a breathy "Wait."

Jack sits back immediately. "Is this too fast? Do you want to stop?"

"It's not that. I just feel like we're a bit exposed out here."

"Okay. We can go inside if you're more comfortable." They head into the sunroom. "If you'd rather just hang, that's cool, too. No pressure, really." Rav realizes the next move needs to be his, so he makes it, steering Jack toward the sofa. They kiss for a while, and Rav means to keep things on a low simmer, he really does, but his body has other ideas, and the next thing he knows he's pulling Jack's shirt over his head and guiding him back against the cushions, and there it is, the tattoo he's been obsessing over. It covers the left side of that tight little torso, climbing from his hip to his collarbone, and Rav has a sudden and powerful need to kiss the entire length of it.

He does.

He's drunk on the scent of Jack's skin, the taste of it, the feel of those inked abs stirring beneath his lips. He bites softly, feeling the vibrations as Jack growls in response, but it's not enough. He needs to feel Jack's skin against his. He goes to take his own shirt off, but Jack isn't having it; he sits up and dusts Rav's hands away. "Don't you dare. I've been fantasizing about doing this since we first met." He starts unbuttoning Rav's shirt, but *slowly*, careful not to crease the crisp fabric as one button after another slips free. He likes what he finds under there, and he pushes Rav onto his back to admire the view. His hands follow his eyes, and his mouth follows his hands. He leaves the shirt open as he kisses Rav's chest, his throat, the tender spot beneath his ear. Any sense Rav had of being in control is burning away, leaving him in free fall. Jack is trailing open-mouthed kisses down his body now, and there's a *clink* of belt buckle. "Yes?" Jack murmurs, pressing a kiss to his stomach.

Rav knows he should call time. He should have called time ages ago. But there's a half-naked rock star on top of him, who also happens to be the most beautiful man he's ever seen, and this magical creature wants to suck his dick and Rav would quite like that also and it's almost impossible to think let alone make a rational decision. So he makes an irrational one, surrendering to the riptide, and he tries not to think about . . . to think about . . . *god*, he's good at this . . . Rav's fingers are twined in the dark waves of Jack Vale's hair, and he's staring at the ceiling of the penthouse suite of the Palace Hotel, and somehow this is actually his life, and Rav is . . . Rav is . . . he's . . . *shit* . . .

It takes a solid two minutes for Rav to regain his faculties—and about five seconds to get Jack's pants off.

As much as he enjoyed being on the receiving end, he gets off on this even more. Being back in control. Being the one that has Jack Vale gasping, arching, breathing a plaintive little "*fuck*" in the heartbeat before he comes.

Afterward, they head back out to the terrace and dangle their feet in the pool while they sip their whiskey. Jack's playlist is still going; a moody voice croons about letting your fear fall away. "I like this," Rav says. "Who is it?"

"Lana Del Rey." He's quiet for a minute, and when he looks at Rav again, there's uncertainty in his eyes. "I hope this isn't too weird for you."

"The celebrity thing, or the fact that I was investigating you?"

"I was mostly thinking about the second part, but I guess the first part is pretty weird too, from your perspective."

"It is strange," Rav admits. "But I don't think we're doing anything wrong. Technically."

"Uh-oh." Jack laughs awkwardly. "Are we reduced to technicalities?"

If there was a time for this conversation, it's passed. What's done is done and there's no going back. "What about you? Does this qualify as normal, as far as hookups go?"

"I don't have a normal. Honestly, it feels like I hit pause on my love life when *Alien Nation* came out. It's just so complicated. Between the media and the lawyers, it's hard to find any privacy, and when you do, it doesn't last." His glance falls to the pool, and he swishes his feet in the water. "I'll understand if this is too much for you. It's too much for me sometimes."

"I'm not sure what *this* is," Rav answers honestly. "I realize it's all very new, and you're incredibly busy, but getting a text from your PA after days of radio silence . . ."

He winces. "I didn't tell you, did I? They took my phone in Miami."

"Who?"

"Mo and Erika. They wanted to make sure it wasn't compromised. I only got it back a couple of hours ago. I haven't even looked at all my missed messages. There's too many."

"They didn't get you a replacement in the meantime?"

"I didn't want one. It was kind of a relief to tune out for a bit. I ditch my phone a lot, actually. I don't like the idea that someone can trace my movements with it."

"Ditching phones and avoiding security cameras." Rav lifts an eyebrow. "Are you secretly—"

"The point is . . ." Jack puts a hand over Rav's. "This isn't just some throwaway thing for me. I like you. A lot."

Rav's chest flutters. "I like you, too."

Too much. He knew that already, but tonight sealed it. He's in way over his head. Which, *fuck*. But how could he not be? How could anyone sit next to this gorgeous, insanely talented, beautiful human and not be completely, totally . . . He doesn't even realize he's leaning in until Jack meets him halfway, and they kiss to the echoing strains of dreamy watercolor guitars, the glimmer of the pool dancing along their skin. It's so cinematic Rav is drowning in it; the music is taking over, bass drum thudding softly like a heartbeat; he's shifting closer now, deepening the kiss, and Jack's hand is sliding up his thigh, and Lana Del Rey is telling them to say yes to Heaven . . .

"Can you stay?" Jack murmurs.

"*Say yes to me . . .*"

Rav's whole body is begging him to say yes. But he knows, with a terrifying sort of clarity, that if he spends the night, he's going to fall in love, and that can't happen. "I shouldn't."

Jack nods, as if he was expecting that answer. "Can I see you before we leave?"

"Definitely," Rav says, kissing him one last time.

He's still humming "Say Yes to Heaven" when he walks through the door of his apartment, so caught up he doesn't check his phone until he sees Jack's little black notebook sitting there on the sideboard. He forgot to bring it. He goes to text Jack and finds that he has three missed calls from Will. There's a text, too, from twenty minutes ago, a decidedly irritable-looking **CALL ME**. It's almost two in the morning, so it must be important. Rav taps the missed call and puts it on speaker.

"Where are you?" his partner demands without preamble.

Something in his tone sinks like a stone to the bottom of Rav's stomach. "At home. My phone was on silent. What—"

"We've got the sweatshirt. And a witness."

"The sweatshirt?"

"From the security footage in Vanderford's building. The one the shifty guy was wearing. You know, our probable perp?"

"Right, of course." Rav is alert now, and pacing. "You have it? How?"

"A patrol spotted a homeless woman wearing it. She fished it out of the trash a block from Vanderford's building."

"Did she see who put it there?"

"That's what I'm trying to tell you. She's already identified him." There's a pause. Will's voice is subdued as he adds, "I really hope you weren't where I think you were tonight, Rav."

"Why?" He knows the answer, knows with sickening certainty what his partner is about to say.

"It's him," Will says. "The guy in the security video is Jack Vale."

CHAPTER FOURTEEN

There's a full twenty seconds of silence on the line.

Rav doesn't trust himself to speak. Doesn't trust himself to do anything but stand there, keys in one hand and phone in the other, staring at that little black notebook with the hot-pink rubber band.

"Rav? Are you still—"

"Is she sure?" His voice sounds like it belongs to someone else. "Is she absolutely certain?"

"Yes. She identified him without being prompted."

"She mentioned him by name?"

"No, but she described him to a T, and she picked him out of a photo lineup."

An image flashes into Rav's mind: Jack Vale standing on this very spot, gray hood pulled up over his head as he kicks off his shoes.

"There's blood on it, too, on the sleeve. It'll have to be sent to the lab, but I think we both know what they're gonna find."

Rav drops his keys in the bowl and grips the edge of the sideboard until it hurts. "Who did the interview?"

"Ayalew. I was there for the last half hour or so. She was good, Rav. Kept the witness on track without rattling her. No prompting or leading questions. You can watch the video for yourself. The witness doesn't have a doubt in her mind that it was Vale she saw."

That's when it all crashes together, one shuddering blow after another, like the cars of a freight train linking up on the tracks. All the little things that passed him by, that meant nothing on their own but added up to something he should have seen, *would* have seen if he'd been thinking with something other than his dick. Jack using a hooded sweatshirt to go incognito in Rav's building. *Have you heard the news? We're getting our masters back.* Jack being trained to use a gun. *My last bodyguard took me to the firing range a bunch last year.* Jack telling him how to bypass the security cameras in the hotel. Even the so-called deepfake video on his social media accounts.

"I'll call you back." Rav thumbs off the call, walks into the bathroom, and throws up.

He stays there awhile, sitting on the floor with his head between his knees. He sees it so clearly now. Ángel Morillo and Erika Strauss called him up that day to feel him out, see whether he was buying the FBI's theory. Vale had already got what he wanted: control over his precious master recordings, revenge on the man who'd cashed in on his best friend's death. The FBI was looking at someone else for the murder. Vale was almost home free; they just needed to make sure Rav was willing to let it go. Instead he kept sniffing around, which made him a problem. He had to be taken out of the equation, and what better way than a cooked-up allegation of misconduct?

It's a clever play. Leak a sensational story on social media, putting the NYPD on the defensive and making sure the DA won't move unless the case is airtight. Deflect responsibility by claiming your account was hacked, then issue a watered-down statement that falls short of denying that the police acted inappropriately, leaving yourself enough wiggle room to revive those allegations should the need arise. It's the perfect insurance policy—not that they need it. Rav gave them all the leverage they needed the moment he got onto that elevator at the Palace Hotel.

He can't help thinking about those sight lines he worried about on the terrace. Was that his intuition trying to break through the haze? *Hey, Rav, remember me? Your brain? Not the one the rock star is straddling, the other one.* Was Mo stationed somewhere nearby with a zoom lens? Is there a photo of them kissing on that terrace? Or . . . oh god . . . on the sofa . . . It doesn't matter that it was consensual. Rav is compromised, and that means the investigation is compromised, too.

He can hear his phone buzzing in the hallway. Shepard is not done with this conversation. Rav drags himself to his feet and answers.

"Tell me you're not sleeping with him."

Rav braces a hand against the wall as another wave of nausea washes over him.

"Tell me you're not fucking our suspect, Rav."

He can't even muster a response.

"Stay where you are," Shepard says coldly, and the line goes dead.

He must bomb his way across the bridge, because he's there in less than half an hour, bursting through Rav's unlocked door and pacing furiously in front of the sofa. "How long?"

It would be humiliating, being interrogated by your partner like this, if Rav could feel anything past the numbness. "Strictly professional until after we'd cleared him as a suspect. Not that anyone will care."

"You're right, they won't. Assuming they even believe you. Why would you put yourself in this position, Rav? Your career, this case—totally fucked. The DA is gonna side-eye every bit of evidence we've got. Federal prosecutors, too. Even if they want to charge him, they're gonna have to weigh it against the shitstorm he could cause."

Rav just nods. He can't deny it.

"You knew there was a chance this investigation could boomerang. Until it was put to bed, there was always a chance. Why would you roll the dice like that?"

"I don't know what you want me to say, Will. I fucked up."

"You're damned right you fucked up!" They're gonna think I covered for you, of course. And don't even get me started on how this plays out for you. Everything you've worked for down the drain, and for what? So you could fuck a celebrity?"

"He wasn't a suspect anymore. It wasn't my case anymore."
It sounds like a pathetic excuse, which it is.

"Yeah, you go ahead and cling to that technicality. Maybe you'll keep your badge, but you'll be damaged goods forevermore." Will rubs a hand roughly over his jaw, already bristling with stubble at two-thirty in the morning. "Did he do this on purpose? Did he set you up?"

This.

This is the part that makes him sick to his stomach. The thought that what happened between them was nothing more than a performance, and he fell for it. He fell for it *so hard*.

"I guess it doesn't matter. Either way, you've basically handed him a get-out-of-jail-free card."

It matters, Rav wants to say. *It fucking matters.*

"Here's what we're gonna do. First thing in the morning, we're gonna meet with Lieutenant Howard. Then we're gonna turn this evidence over to the FBI, you and me. Maybe if we're the ones who do it . . ."

It's as good a plan as any. Whether it will be enough to save his job is anyone's guess. *Everything I've worked for.* Ten years of doing everything just right, of giving up anything resembling a personal life, and now this.

He pours himself another drink after Shepard leaves, even though he can barely taste it. He can still taste the Macallan, though. He can still taste Jack's skin.

How could he have got it so wrong?

The next thing he knows, his phone is in his hand.

Are you awake

I need to talk to you right now

I'm coming to you

And now he's in a car heading uptown, and this is probably the stupidest thing he's ever done in his life, but he's on autopilot.

He has to know. His career is already torched. At least this way, he can look Jack in the eye and ask the question.

The hotel is quiet at this hour. A couple of die-hard fans loiter on the sidewalk outside with vinyl copies of *Background*, hoping for autographs. Rav scans the lobby for any sign of paparazzi, and then he heads for the elevator. He's still got the key card— they'd planned to get together again later—and it gets him to the top floor. There's no answer to his knock, so he calls Jack's phone. When that doesn't work, he knocks again, and then he uses the key, pausing in the entryway to listen. He can just make out the sound of an acoustic guitar coming from some-where nearby.

"Jack."

The music stops. There's a pause, followed by the sound of the doors in the sunroom being opened. "Hello? Is someone there?"

"It's Rav."

Jack appears in the entryway, looking just as he always does in Rav's dreams: barefoot, faded jeans, T-shirt. It fucking *hurts*. "Hi," he says, a little warily. He's understandably taken aback by Rav just showing up at three in the morning. "Is everything okay?"

Rav can't imagine how *he* must look right now, half-drunk and desperate, still wearing the same clothes Jack peeled off him a couple of hours ago. "Tell me you weren't there."

"Where?"

"Dick Vanderford's flat, the night he was killed. I need you to tell me it wasn't you."

For a second Jack just stares. Confusion flickers through his eyes—followed swiftly by anger. "Are you serious?"

"I need to hear you say it."

"You already have. You asked me where I was that night and I gave you my answer. If you didn't believe me, why did you come here? Why did any of this happen?" He gestures at the sofa, where they'd been tangled around each other just hours ago. "Or were you just saving this conversation until after I'd sucked your dick?"

Heat floods Rav's face. *Is that really what you think of me*, he starts to say—and then he realizes how ironic that response would be. He's the one accusing Jack of murder, after all.

He pulls up an image on his phone and holds it out wordlessly. It's a screenshot of the security footage from Vanderford's building, showing the mysterious figure in the hooded sweatshirt as he slinks out of the lobby. Jack frowns and takes it—and then his brow clears. He stares at the screen for several long seconds, and his whole body tightens up: his spine, his shoulders, the line of his mouth. He hands the phone back. "That's not me."

"A witness ID'd you. She's positive it was you she saw."

"It's not me," he says again, grimly.

"You have no alibi. You say you were here writing music—"

"That's right. Just like I was doing five minutes ago, when you showed up here. It's what I do late at night."

"But you can't prove it, and no one is going to take your word for it."

"Not even you, apparently."

"I'm trying to help you, Jack."

Something passes through Jack's eyes that might be regret. Then he says, "I think you'd better leave."

Rav nods slowly. Whatever else is going on here, Jack is lying to him, and that's enough. "You should call your lawyer," he says as he turns away. "The FBI will be here in the morning."

* * *

Three hours later, Rav is sitting at his desk watching the video of the interview with the witness. Will was right, Ayalew does a great job. She's patient. Methodical. The witness rambles a bit, and there are times when she seems a little confused, but she never wavers about where she got the jumper or who she saw stuffing it in the trash. Ayalew circles back again and again, and each time the answers are the same. It's a textbook interview. Nothing for the defense to grab hold of, nothing for the prosecution to trip over.

Danny Jobs drifts in around seven, and he smirks when he sees Rav sitting there, rumpled and unshaven, head slumped in his hand. "You look like shit, buddy." Then he sees what's on Rav's screen, and the smirk widens. "The Vanderford witness, huh? Too bad you didn't snag her back when it was your case."

"Fuck off, Danny." It sounds so weary and defeated that Jobs actually pauses, his expression softening.

"Take some advice, kid. Don't obsess over the ones that got away. Especially not for shitbags like Dick Vanderford. He ain't worth losing sleep over."

Jiménez arrives a few minutes later. He and Jobs are working a new case, so they're pulling long hours right now. He glances at Rav's screen as he walks past, and he grunts. "Ain't that a kick in the ass? I was sure that sweatshirt thing was a dead end."

Rav doesn't answer, too absorbed in the video. He clicks the *back* button and replays something.

"He was a looker, I remember that," the witness says. She's an older lady, around sixty-five, with laugh lines framing her eyes. She could be anybody's slightly addled grandmother.

"You thought he was good-looking?" says Ayalew's voice, off-screen.

"Well, he was too young for *me*," the witness says with a rough, two-packs-a-day laugh. "But he had movie-star looks. Shame about the tattoo, though. Why do young people all have tattoos these days?"

"Where was the tattoo?"

The witness touches her forearm absently. "I suppose it's because they're all so *angry*."

"Was the young man in the sweatshirt angry?"

"Sure looked it. Guess you'd have to be, to rip the shirt from your back and stuff it in the trash." She laughs for a second before a worried look comes over her. "When will I get it back? The nights are still chilly, and warm clothes are hard to come by."

Rav hits pause. Watches that last bit again.

"Hey, man." Jiménez rolls his chair over, curious. "What're you looking for, anyway?"

If only Rav knew. Something is nagging at him, but he can't put his finger on it.

"Seems pretty straightforward to me," Jiménez says. "She ID'd Vale as the guy she saw throwing the sweatshirt in the trash. End of story. Why're you obsessing over this interview?"

"Because it's not him," Rav blurts.

"Not him? Bro, are you listening to this lady? It's definitely him."

"He has a famous face," Rav says weakly.

"Yeah? You think she watches MTV at the shelter?"

"It's not him. I *know* it's not, I just can't . . ." Rav shakes his head. He's so tired he can barely finish a sentence.

"Listen, man, every cop likes to think he's got superhuman instincts. Like he just *knows* shit, down here." Jiménez points to his gut. "But take my word for it. I've been doing this a long time, and if it looks like a duck and quacks like a duck . . ." He taps Rav's screen. "That, my friend, is a duck."

"He's right," Jobs puts in. "Vale has motive, means, and opportunity. A witness ID'd him at the scene. It's a slam dunk."

Rav's eyes are still glued to the screen. He jumps back another five minutes.

Jiménez shakes his head. "You should listen to your elders, bro," he says, and rolls his chair away.

Well, that certainly sounds familiar. Lieutenant Howard said something almost identical in his performance evaluation. *Has a tendency to over-rely on his own instincts instead of benefitting from the experience of senior colleagues.* Maybe she's right. Maybe Jiménez is right, and instincts are just bullshit, stories we tell ourselves when we don't want to accept the evidence in front of us. The evidence in front of him says Jack Vale is a killer. A slam dunk, everything pointing to the same conclusion.

Everything except Jack standing in the entryway of his hotel room, barefoot and broken, looking Rav right in the eye. *It's not me.*

Rav clicks play.

"Was the young man in the sweatshirt angry?"

"Sure looked it. Guess you'd have to be, to rip the shirt from your back and stuff it in the trash."

Rav picks up his keys and his phone. He walks to the Foot Locker on Pitkin and buys a nice warm hoodie.

Then, for the second time that day, he calls an Uber and gets ready to do something incredibly stupid.

CHAPTER FIFTEEN

The witness's name is Gemma, and she's lovely.

The staff at the shelter clearly adore her, and they run a little interference until Rav assures them she's not in any trouble. Gemma, for her part, is happy to have a visitor, and receives her new jumper with wet eyes and a hug.

Rav invites her for a bagel and a stroll in the park. She shares half her breakfast with the local pigeons, which is fine. It's her bagel to do with as she pleases, and the birds obviously bring her joy. "They've got so much personality, if you really watch them," she says.

She's a little older than Rav originally thought. Other than that, his impression from the video was spot on: she's warm and personable, and she'll be devastating on the stand if it goes to trial. She's easily distracted, but a wise attorney would think twice about going after her too hard on cross. Bullying sweet old ladies is not a good look.

Rav gets her permission to record the conversation, and then he cues up the camera on his smartwatch. He doesn't use many of the apps on his watch—doesn't even get push notifications—but every now and then it comes in handy. "I'd like to show you a picture, if that's all right." He holds his phone out to her, making sure his watch picks up what's on the screen. "I thought maybe you could tell me if you recognize this person."

She holds the phone at arm's length and squints. "Nice photo. Did you take it?"

"Not personally. I'm not much for taking photos, to be honest."

"Really? Man, I'd be taking pictures all day long if I had one of these things. I'd be like those kids making pouty lips in front of the Brooklyn Bridge. 'Specially if I had looks like yours." She winks.

Rav plays along, arching an eyebrow coyly. "Are you flirting with me, Gemma?"

"Something tells me I'm not your type, darlin'." She laughs her two-packs-a-day laugh, then peers more closely at the photo. "This your man? He's a looker, too."

Rav needs to be careful here. It can't seem like he's leading her. "Do you recognize him? Here, let's zoom in a little."

"Oh wait, yeah. That's the guy who threw his sweatshirt in the trash."

Rav's pulse spikes, but he keeps his voice perfectly level. "You saw this man throw his sweatshirt in the trash?"

"I already told the police. They took it from me. The sweatshirt, I mean." Her brow creases, and she runs a hand down the sleeve of her new jumper. "Isn't that why you came? To replace it?"

"Yes. And to ask you one more time if you're absolutely certain this is the man you saw." He points at the image again.

"Yeah, that's him. Like a young Rob Lowe, circa 1983."

"Thank you, Gemma. I appreciate you speaking with me. Can I escort you somewhere? Back to the shelter, perhaps?"

"Nah, they kick you out in the morning anyway. Figure I'll head over to Williamsburg again today. It's nice by the water."

Rav thanks her again and takes his leave. He can't give her any money—it might look like he was trying to influence her account—but he vows to check in on her when this is all over. He owes her that, after coming to her under slightly dodgy pretenses.

He digs out his wallet, yanks a business card from its sleeve, and dials the number.

"Charlie Banks."

"Mr. Banks, it's Detective Trivedi."

"Yeah, I'm gonna stop you right there, Detective. I'm just

coming out of an emergency meeting at the hotel, and it doesn't sound like you and I should be talking."

"We shouldn't, and it might well mean the end of my career that we are." Saying the words out loud makes him feel light-headed, but there's no turning back now. "May I continue?"

Voices murmur in the background. Rav can only imagine the war council going on in that room. A door clicks, and the voices go quiet. "All right," Banks says, "go ahead."

"I need you to arrange a meeting."

He explains.

The manager is understandably reluctant. "Even if you're right—which I'm *not* saying you are—why in God's name would I put my guy in a room with the police?"

"It's not an interview. Just some friendly advice from some-one who's trying to help."

Another pause. Banks is thinking.

"None of the scenarios you're looking at are good, Mr. Banks. However this plays out, it's going to be messy."

"So your pitch is, 'Hey, Charlie, this is the least shitty of your menu of shitty options.'" He sighs. "I just saw my entire career flash before my eyes."

"That makes two of us."

Rav is walking into the hotel lobby twenty minutes later when his phone rings. "Where the hell are you?" Shepard snaps.

"The Palace Hotel."

A gust of breath, and then silence. "What the *fuck*, Rav?" He sounds exhausted. "This is it for you. You know that, right?"

"I'm just trying to do the right thing. I hope I am. Either way, I'm sorry." He hangs up and punches the elevator button, al-ready feeling the first pang of grief. He's most likely just lost a friend. The first of many things he'll be losing today.

Charlie Banks is waiting for him outside the appointed room. "They are *really* not happy in there. I'd buckle up for a rough ride, Detective."

"It won't be my first."

It's another huge suite, not quite as impressive as the penthouse, but close. Ryan Nash prowls the lounge like a caged tiger. His bodyguard, Erika Strauss, stands near the wall, and the look she's giving Rav could curdle milk. "This is a bad idea," she says coldly.

"Five minutes," Nash says. "If this is anything but what he said—"

"You can address me directly, Mr. Nash," Rav says. "I'm right here."

"Yeah, I see you. In your designer fucking suit."

Says the man living out of five-star hotels. "I'll cut straight to it then. Someone will be here in a few hours to arrest Jack Vale for the murder of Richard Vanderford. They have evidence that puts Vale at the scene. Security footage from the victim's building shows a man wearing a distinctive item of clothing—clothing that was later recovered and is at the lab right now."

The bass player stiffens.

"There's blood on the sleeve," Rav goes on. "Probably Vanderford's. And they have a witness who identified Vale as the man disposing of it in a dustbin not far from Vanderford's building at the approximate time of the murder. It will be more than enough for them to indict. But you and I both know it's not Jack in that security video." His gaze travels over Nash as he says it—dark hair, slender frame, tattooed arms. He doesn't get Rob Lowe, but he certainly sees Jack Vale.

"Don't say *anything*, Ryan," his bodyguard growls.

"I should get my lawyer in here," Nash says.

"By all means, though if you're referring to Joanne Reid or one of her colleagues, I'd consider whether they are your best advocates. Ms. Reid is currently acting as Mr. Vale's attorney. Your interests may not be aligned."

Nash scowls. "Of course they're aligned. Jack is my brother."

"That's good to hear. Because I will tell you candidly that I don't give a damn about you, Ryan." He looks the bass player right in the eye as he says it. "I'm here for Jack. He's protecting you, and if he continues to do so, there's a very good chance he'll take the fall for this. For *you*."

"I don't know what you're on about. I have an alibi for that night, remember?"

"I do. You were at a friend's shooting pool. Your mates are obviously lying for you, but that's neither here nor there. Jack is the one on the hook for this murder, and he doesn't have an alibi."

Nash's jaw twitches. "He'll be cleared."

"Really? You must have a lot of faith in the criminal justice system."

"It's not the cops I have faith in, it's the lawyers."

Frustration surges in Rav's belly, but he tamps it down. "Here's the thing. I watched Jack's reaction when he looked at that photo, and there was no question in my mind he knew who he was looking at. That distinctive item of clothing I mentioned? He's seen it before. Which means you've worn it before. If Jack has ever come into contact with it, or you came into contact with anything of his while wearing it—a guitar strap, say, or a hat you borrowed. Maybe you sat beside him on the plane. All it takes is a single hair. Some dried saliva, or a flake of dandruff."

He's exaggerating, but most people are only too willing to believe in the magical forensics they see on TV.

"If they find his DNA on that jumper, the witness is just gravy. Vale has a strong motive, and he was seen arguing with the victim two days before the murder. With due respect to Ms. Reid, she's going to have a very hard time keeping her client out of prison."

"You've decided it wasn't Jack," Erika Strauss puts in coolly. She's texting someone—the lawyers, Rav suspects. "Who's to say the FBI won't do the same?"

"True. Something about the witness's description stuck with me. She described a dark-haired man with a slight build and movie-star good looks, with a tattoo on his forearm. If she'd left it there, I might have assumed the same as everyone else, that she was talking about Jack Vale." His glance shifts back to Nash. "Then she described the man she saw as *angry*, and it clicked. I remembered looking at an album cover and thinking how very angry you looked, and also how much you and Jack looked alike. In the right circumstances—a dark street, say, from half a block away—it would be easy to mistake one of you for the other. So I spoke to the witness again. I showed her *your* photo, and this time, it was you she ID'd." He shrugs. "Which version of the story should we believe? I believe this version because I want to, but I wouldn't count on my colleagues doing the same."

"They might," Nash says defiantly.

"Then what? They come after you instead. By which point the New Knickerbockers have been in the news for months, maybe even years if it goes to trial. Jack has been put through hell, the Nicks brand is fatally damaged, and you're on the hook for Vanderford's murder. Is that really your best-case scenario? Taking the longest, most painful route to the same destination?"

There's an uncomfortable silence. Charlie Banks clears his throat. "I think this is the part where you offer us a better alternative, Detective."

"The better alternative is that Ryan turns himself in."

Nash shakes his head, but there's a desperation to it now. "I didn't kill him."

"Even if that's true—"

The door opens and Joanne Reid strides into the room, Jack hot on her heels. "Detective Trivedi," she says coldly. "I am extremely disappointed to find this interview taking place without my knowledge."

Rav rubs his stinging eyes. He's fucking exhausted. "I'll add you to the list of people who are extremely disappointed in me. It's rather long, I'm afraid." Inevitably, his glance strays to Jack as he says that.

Jack looks exhausted too, pale and drawn, with dark circles under his eyes. "What are you doing here, Rav?"

"Trying to keep you out of prison." He turns back to Ryan

Nash. "Whether you killed him or not, you need to turn yourself in. It'll be better for you in the long run, and it will certainly be better for Jack. You say he's your brother, so act like it. Don't let him take a bullet for you."

Joanne Reid glances sharply at Jack. This is obviously news to her, but she recovers quickly. "Detective—"

"I'm not here as a detective. By the end of the day, there's a good chance I won't even be a detective anymore."

There's a beat of silence as the room processes that. "Shit," Banks says.

"Talk some sense into your client, Ms. Reid. Both of them. It would be absurd to let Jack to take the fall for this. If Ryan truly is innocent, he's better off working with the authorities. Depending on what happened, there may even be a way forward that doesn't result in felony charges. But I promise you that path will be closed if you make them hunt you."

Nash looks at Jack.

Jack looks at the floor.

Nash nods slowly, as if coming to a decision. "He was dead when I got there."

Everyone starts talking at once.

"Ryan, don't—"

"I strongly recommend—"

"*Stop.*"

He ignores them all. "Whoever did it was already gone. I checked for a pulse, and then I got out of there. When I realized there was blood on the jumper, I threw it out. That's it."

Rav sighs. "This isn't my case anymore, Ryan. I'm not the one you need to tell."

"I didn't kill him. I just went there to shake him up. Maybe hurt him a little, but—"

"*Ryan,*" Joanne Reid snaps. "If you don't stop talking, I can't help you."

"You should listen to your lawyer," Rav says. "There's nothing to be gained by telling me this."

"There is." Nash looks at his bandmate. "Now you know for sure. Jack wasn't there."

Rav nods at his feet. "Thank you, but I came to that conclusion on my own. I wouldn't be here otherwise." He resists the urge to glance at Jack. He doesn't expect forgiveness. "I'll leave you to talk it over. Good luck."

He's waiting for the elevator when he hears his name. Jack stands in the hallway, foot jammed in the door to keep it from locking him out. "Did you mean what you said in there?" he asks quietly. "Are they going to fire you?"

"Maybe. They'll start by suspending me."

"That's such bullshit." He sounds as tired as Rav feels. "You don't deserve that."

As if that matters. If people got what they deserved, the world wouldn't need homicide detectives. Besides, maybe he does deserve it. He knew he was playing with fire. Can he really complain if he got burned?

"What will you do?"

"If they fire me?" Rav shrugs. "Travel for a spell, maybe. Or I could go back to school."

Jack's eyes meet his, clouded with regret. "I'm sorry."

"I'm sorry, too." The elevator *dings*. Rav glances inside and is relieved to find it empty. He doesn't want to deal with anyone right now. "I still have your notebook."

"Keep it. Something to remember me by."

The elevator starts to close. Rav sticks his arm between the doors, as if the extra few seconds that buys him will be enough. Later, he'll remember that image: Jack with his foot in the doorway, Rav with his arm blocking the elevator, both of them trying to keep the doors open just a little longer. "Take care of yourself, Jack."

"You, too."

Rav steps into the elevator, and the doors close behind him.

CHAPTER SIXTEEN

nd you believe him?" Agent Rice asks.

"We do," says Lieutenant Howard. "The witness appears to have identified Vale in error. My team is partly to blame. We provided her with a photo lineup on the basis of her description, but that lineup did not include Ryan Nash. There's every reason to suppose she would have identified him the first time had she been given the opportunity."

Rav has to give it to the LT, she's handling this meeting brilliantly. Especially considering she only had a few minutes to sit with all this before the three of them—Howard, Rav, and Will—headed into the city to brief the FBI. Howard was keen to get it over with. The discussion around Rav's disciplinary situation, meanwhile, has been deferred until after they've dealt with the feds.

"We understand Ryan Nash plans to come forward later today," Howard goes on.

"Sounds like you've been in touch with him," says Agent Keller. "First a witness and now a suspect. Do we have a jurisdiction problem?"

"My guys were following a hunch," Howard says, frost bristling on every word. "Once we confirmed the evidence, we brought it to you, and we now leave the matter in the capable hands of the Bureau."

"We're grateful," Rice says. "The truth is, we haven't spent much time on the Vanderford side of the investigation. We've been too focused on Miller."

"Any progress there?" Howard asks.

"He knows we're looking, and he's gone to ground. Even deleted his social media profiles. Fortunately, our digital forensics team was able to recover bits and pieces, and they turned up some solid evidence of his connection to Vanderford."

"So you said on our call last week." Howard's tone is still cool. "May I ask what kind of evidence?"

"Photos," Keller says. "Miller posted a selfie from the pier near Vanderford's building, with Vanderford himself in the background."

"Could be a coincidence," Will points out. "Great view of Manhattan from there. People take selfies in that spot all the time."

"Maybe," says Keller, "but how many have Dick Vanderford in them? Plus, we've got a shot of the two of them sitting together in a café five blocks away, time-stamped the same day. Two photos, different sources. They corroborate each other."

Rav is having a hard time digesting this. Miller and Vanderford together? What, just grabbing lunch? "Where did the second photo come from?"

"Mailed in anonymously," Keller says. "Someone from the label, we think, who saw them together and wondered what the head of the label was doing meeting with a known stalker."

"What *was* he doing?" Howard asks. "Presumably you have a theory."

"We believe the Concord incident was an attempted murder for hire," Rice informs them.

"A contract killing?" Rav blurts. "Seriously?"

Rice hears the doubt in his voice, and she doesn't appreciate it. "We were as surprised as you," she says coolly, "but evidence from the victim's laptop points in that direction. We found messages from Vanderford to an email address linked to Miller giving inside details on how to evade security at the Concord show."

Howard looks sharply at Rav. "How did we miss that? Who was responsible for looking through his emails?"

"I was." If they're going to put him on administrative leave anyway, he might as well take one for the team.

But Will isn't having it. "No, *I* was. The initial report from the analyst came up empty, so I went through his emails personally. I don't know how I missed it. Sorry, LT."

"If it makes you feel any better," Rice says, "we almost missed it ourselves. The messages were carefully worded. If we hadn't received a tip about links between Vanderford and Miller, we might not have realized what we were looking at."

Howard doesn't look mollified, but she lets it go. "I take it you think Vanderford ordered the hit?"

"Correct."

Rav knows he should keep his mouth shut, but he just doesn't see it. Dick Vanderford, record executive, calls up a stalker from out of state and asks if he would mind murdering the label's top talent? And Miller just agrees? "Why?"

Rice looks at him. "Why what, Detective?"

"For starters, why would Dick Vanderford want Jack Vale dead?"

"Vale was making his life hell," Keller says. "That whole business with the master recordings was a PR nightmare. Now here's this stalker making *Vale's* life hell. How convenient is that? He's the perfect fall guy. Nobody would connect the dots to Vanderford. Plus, Vanderford cashes in big-time when sales of the Nicks' back catalogue go wild."

It's possible, Rav supposes. Vanderford had already had a taste of how lucrative tragedy can be, having profited handsomely from Tommy Esposito's death. But would he really stoop to murder? On top of which . . . "How does he end up dead?"

"Maybe Miller panicked when things didn't go to plan. Or maybe he realized Vanderford was playing him." Keller shrugs.

"It just seems awfully elaborate," Rav says. "There are easier ways to hire a killer. Professionals who aren't going to endanger innocents or do something unpredictable that might lead back to the person who hired them."

"Who says Miller isn't a professional? You said yourself you thought Vanderford's murder looked like the work of a pro."

"Because the killer was trained and dispassionate. The man I met at the skate park was neither of those things."

"We'll take that under advisement," Rice says.

In other words, *fuck you.*

"Do you have any leads on Miller's whereabouts?" Howard asks.

"We're trying to get into his cloud account, but Fuse is stonewalling us."

No surprise there. Of all the tech giants, Fuse is the fussiest on matters of privacy. They've slammed the door in Rav's face more times than he can count—but that was before he met Aisha. "There may be another way. I have an asset who's highly effective at getting around technological barriers."

"A hacker?" Rice shakes her head. "We can't use anything gained through illegal means."

"Of course, but she may be able to point us in the direction of evidence we *can* use—"

Thing One and Thing Two rise in unison and button their jackets. "Always a pleasure to speak with our friends in the NYPD," Rice says. "We'll interview Nash and Vale, and if it looks like this is a routine homicide after all, we'll kick it back to you. You all have a good day now."

And that's that.

There's an icy silence in the elevator on the way down. Howard waits until they're outside, and then she lets Rav have it. "It is a curiosity to me, Detective, that you would presume to tell the FBI how to do their jobs given the position you're in."

Rav is too frustrated to hold his tongue. "Don't tell me you buy that bullshit theory? Dick Vanderford hired a stalker to assassinate Jack Vale?"

"No one is asking you to buy it. But you could trust your fellow professionals to do their jobs. We've talked about this. Sometimes you need to step back and let others take charge, and this is one of those times."

"Is it, though? Because it sounds to me like they don't give a damn who actually killed Vanderford as long as they can put somebody in prison for it."

"Gotta say, LT, I agree," Will puts in quietly. "Feels like they're phoning this one in."

Howard sighs and resumes walking toward the car. "They do seem quite happy to shoehorn the facts into their theory."

"I'm not even sure I believe Miller is out to kill Jack Vale," Rav says. "Seems to me he worships Vale."

"Both things can be true," Howard says. "More to the point, it doesn't matter what we think. It's not our case."

Will's glance cuts between them. "What happens now?"

"Detective Trivedi will be placed on administrative leave pending an investigation."

Rav expected as much, but it still lands like a body blow. Amazing how quickly everything you've worked for can turn to ash. "How long do you think it will take?"

"I wouldn't care to speculate. The circumstances in this case are unusual, if not unprecedented." She waits for Will to get in the car before adding, "I'm disappointed in you, Trivedi. I thought we had an understanding. Now your career is on life support, your working relationships are in tatters, and I'm short a detective. If you'd just *waited* until the investigation was concluded . . ."

She doesn't get it. He's been *waiting* since college. Putting everyone and everything aside for his career. And that was okay. He never worried about what it cost him, *who* it cost him, until he met Jack. "If I'd waited . . ." He swallows and looks away. "If I'd waited, I might have missed my chance."

"So you seized the day. And how'd that turn out?"

Rav recalls his own words from earlier this morning. *Is that really your best-case scenario? Taking the longest, most painful route to the same destination?* "Touché," he says, and he gets in the car.

* * *

Rav spends his first day of administrative leave sprawled on the sofa flipping through Jack's little black notebook, hot-pink elastic wrapped around his wrist like a bracelet, "Say Yes to Heaven" playing on repeat at max volume. He's painfully aware that he's living out the Sad Breakup Scene of some terrible rom-com. All he's missing is a gallon of ice cream and an ugly-cry with his besties. Only there's no dramatic makeup scene just around the corner. No Jack on the street below his window holding a boom box over his head. No Rav barging into Jack's place and making a grand romantic speech in front of everyone. Those things don't happen in real life, and besides, this wasn't even a relationship. It was *one night*, for god's sake. He has more extensive intimate histories with people whose names he can't remember.

The notebook isn't helping. Now that he's finally seen what's inside, he realizes just how precious a gift it is. The words on these pages are raw, unfiltered. The prose veers from angry to hopeful to reflective, circling around the central theme of grief. Some pages contain just a few stray lines; others fully formed songs. Sometimes it's possible to trace the evolution of an idea from a handful of words to a song from the Nicks' latest album. It's a chronicle of Jack's journey over the past couple of years, emotional and artistic. Why would he part with this? How can he possibly think Rav deserves to have it?

There's one lyric he keeps coming back to, from a song called "Prism."

All those little moments I recall
Hang like pictures on my wall
The truth just out of frame
Gallery of my shame
And I can't go back
Can't take it back

It resonates. Dwelling on specific moments, wishing you could go back and do things differently . . .

Bloody hell, Trivedi. Are we brooding over song lyrics like a teen-

ager now? Meanwhile, he's barely given a thought to the fact that his career is going down in flames. When did he become this person?

Ana calls him up that evening to give him shit. Not for getting involved with a former suspect, mind, but for not telling her about it. "You could have trusted me with this, Rav."

"I didn't want to put you in an awkward position."

"What's awkward? You didn't do anything wrong. Of course they're looking into it, as they should, but all they're gonna find is a couple of dudes who wanted to get it on and saw no reason they shouldn't."

"I knew there was a chance it could blow up in my face." He slumps against the kitchen counter in his Thom Browne sweats. "I was just so caught up."

"No doubt. *Jack Vale.* I knew you had rizz, Trivedi, but *daaaamn.*"

"You're not helping."

"You're laughing, aren't you?" Sirens wail in the background. Ana sounds a little out of breath, walking at the speed of New York. "Man, I cannot *wait* to hear how you go from liking him for murder to . . . how far did you get, anyhow?" He can hear that wicked grin in her voice.

"Ah, I see. You're not calling to commiserate. You want the dirt."

"Of course I want the dirt!"

"Well, there's not much to tell. It was a one-time thing, and it's done now."

"I'm sorry, baby. That sucks."

"I just wish I could go back and do things differently, you know?" Before he can finish the thought, his door buzzes. "Hold on, there's someone downstairs."

"Yeah, it's me. Hurry up and buzz me in, this ice cream is melting."

Half a pint of double fudge and two stiff whiskeys later, Ana says, "What would you do different?" She's curled up on the leather armchair, tiny feet tucked up beneath her, licking her spoon. Rav, meanwhile, is stretched out on the sofa like he's seeing his therapist. Which he kind of is.

"What do you mean?"

"Before, you said you wished you could go back and change things. Is it that you wish you'd acted differently, or you wish things were different?"

"I guess I'm not sure," he admits. "All I know is that I feel like an idiot."

"We are all fools in love."

Rav frowns at the ceiling. "Did you just Jane Austen me?"

"Look, I know you, Rav. If there was a way to keep Jack in your life without risking your career, you would have found it. You took a chance, actually went for it for once. I'm proud of you."

"Because it turned out so well."

"Just because it didn't work out doesn't mean it was the wrong call."

"Even if I lose my job?"

"You're not gonna lose your job. I'll bet you a hundred bucks you're back on duty by the end of the month."

"Even if you're right, it won't be the same. I let the squad down. Will and Howard and everybody, not to mention every gay cop who already deals with enough bullshit without me giving us all a bad name."

Ana groans. "*Por favor.* As if the entire department is looking to *you* to represent. I hate to break it to you, Trivedi, but you might not be the queer law enforcement icon you think you are."

"Narcissism?"

"So much." Her voice softens. "You're not an avatar for gay cops, okay? You're a flesh-and-blood person, and you gotta do what's right for *you*, in *your* heart. Forget about other people's bullshit."

Rav carves out another spoonful of double fudge. "You know, I should pay you for this," he says, circling his spoon to indicate his therapeutically positioned self.

"You don't have to tell me."

Later that evening, his mother calls. He lets it go to voicemail. If she finds out he's on admin leave, he'll never hear the end of it. *Maybe now you'll go to law school like you should have in the first place.* Then there's His Lordship. What will *he* say? Just imagining it makes Rav's heart beat faster, as if he's about to sit an exam he's not ready for.

The worst part is that he can't help wondering if they're right. If he should have just followed in his father's footsteps, done the whole lawyer/judge/politician thing like they wanted. It's not too late. Maybe this is a sign.

There's just one problem: Rav loves being a cop. Not everything about it, of course, not by a long shot. But that burning inside him, that *need* to solve the case . . . He feels it right now, an anxiety that has him pacing around his apartment like a caged animal. The FBI is wrong about Miller and Vanderford, he's sure of it. But there's *something* there. A connection, just not the one they're seeing.

It's not your problem, he tells himself. *Let. It. Go.*

And maybe he could, if he hadn't failed Jack that day in the skate park. He let Miller slip through his fingers for a second time. There won't be a third. The FBI might not want his help, but they're going to get it.

Picking up his phone, he calls Aisha Khan.

CHAPTER SEVENTEEN

W hat's with the civvies?" Aisha looks Rav over, taking in his chinos and polo shirt with a raised eyebrow. "Don't tell me standards are slipping in Homicide."

Didn't I mention? I've been suspended. Yeah, he's not explaining this to her. "I'm here in a personal capacity. Bearing gifts." He hoists a bag of bagels and a cup carrier.

"Is that bubble tea? Gross."

He can't disagree. He has no idea why he bought it, except that he's already had way too much coffee.

"I'll take a bagel, though." Without waiting for an invitation, she grabs the bag and starts rooting around inside, which feels very on-brand for a hacker. "What, no cream cheese? Hold on, I think I have some in the fridge." She starts for the kitchen. "So, you were pretty vague on the phone last night. Is this about the Russian hackers? Because I told you, you're gonna have to be patient."

"It's not about the Russians. I need you to locate a cell phone."

"Pass," she says from behind the fridge door. "I don't spy on ordinary citizens."

"There's nothing ordinary about this guy. He's wanted by the FBI."

"And?" She returns with a tub of cream cheese and some napkins. "Haven't we all been wanted by the federal government at some point?"

"Uh, no?" *Jesus Christ.* "Look, the bigger question is whether you can actually do it."

"If you've got access to their credentials, it's just a matter of logging in. And it so happens I have photos of a certain Fuse executive in a very compromising—"

"*La-la-la!*" Rav jams his fingers in his ears. "Still a cop, remember?" Barely, but he doesn't need to add *accessory to blackmail* to his list of sins.

"Hey, is that the new Marquesse smartwatch?" She grabs his wrist and ogles it. "Man, that is one sexy wearable. Analog beauty, digital brains. Can I see it?"

Bloody hell, she's got the attention span of the dog from *Up*. "Aisha, if you help me out here, I'll let you play with my watch all day long. Can we please *focus?*"

She rolls her eyes and licks cream cheese off her fingers. "My thing is exposing oppressive institutions, not helping them. Why would I hack some dude's phone on behalf of the NYPD?"

"Because he might be a murderer, and he's threatening someone I care about."

She plucks a finger noisily from her mouth. "Could've opened with that," she mutters, dropping into a chair and rolling it over to her desk. "Name?"

"Joseph Miller."

"The stalker guy? Ah, I get it. The someone you care about is Jack Vale. I *thought* you two looked awfully friendly in that photo. Kind of ironic, isn't it?"

"What?"

"That bogus interview implied there was something going on between you two, and it turns out—"

"It turns out that was a complete fabrication," Rav says coolly, "and anything that may have happened subsequently is neither here nor there."

"*Touchy.*" Her fingers fly over the keyboard, composing an email. "Let's say we do find his phone, then what?"

"I'll pass the information to the FBI. *Anonymously,*" he adds when she gives him a horrified look. "The feds can't act on it if they think the evidence was obtained illegally, so it's best for everyone if they get an anonymous tip."

She's attaching files to the email now, a series of JPEGs Rav is grateful he can't see. "Gotta say, this is way more interesting than insider trading. Russian hackers? Rock stars and homicidal stalkers? Keep bringing me the good stuff, Trivedi, and this could turn into a beautiful relationship."

"As long as you're in it for the right reasons," he says dryly.

"Pretty sure you're in no position to be getting all sanctimonious, there, Detective No-Badge." She waggles a finger in the general direction of his belt, where his shield would normally sit.

Damn, she's observant.

She fires off the email, and they settle in to wait. Rav lets her play around with his smartwatch while he scrolls restlessly through his phone, trying to ignore the deluge of Nicks-related content his dash is pushing at him. They're all over his social media feeds, his mentions, even the headlines. He clicks his screen off and grabs the bubble tea, sullenly sucking globs of tapioca and stewing in FML until a message arrives in Aisha's inbox. The Fuse executive will play ball. Whatever she's got on him, it must be good. "Please tell me he deserves this," Rav says uncomfortably.

"Trust me, he does."

Thirty minutes later, Aisha has everything she needs to run *Find My Phone* on Joe Miller's device. "There," she says, pointing at a flashing dot on her screen. "Looks like he's in the East Village. Or at least, he was."

"What do you mean?"

"See this black icon? That means the battery is dead. Technically, we're looking at this phone's last known location."

"Meaning it might not be there anymore." Rav swears under his breath, but it's all he has. He borrows one of Aisha's burner phones and calls the FBI tipline, leaving a detailed message with GPS coordinates.

"So," Aisha says after he hangs up. "What now?"

What indeed? Rav knows what he *should* do: go home and wait. "The thing is, it's not my case anymore."

"Uh-huh." Aisha's dark eyes hold his.

"The Bureau wouldn't thank me for interfering."

"More than you already have, you mean."

"More than that, yeah." He rubs a hand over his neatly trimmed beard. "But it couldn't hurt to keep an eye on the building, right? That way, if he leaves, I could tail him. See where he went."

"Just a concerned citizen."

"Exactly. A concerned citizen."

"Sounds reasonable to me."

"Yeah," Rav says, grabbing his jacket. "Totally reasonable."

"Totally," Aisha says, and she grabs hers, too.

Twenty minutes later, they're standing across the street from a narrow brick apartment building with a pizza place on the ground floor. "This is it," Aisha says, consulting the tablet in her hands. "We'll have to get closer before I can tell what floor he's on, though."

Now that his caffeine buzz is wearing off, Rav is having second thoughts. As badly as he wants to see Miller in custody, he's acutely aware that any fuckup on his part could make a conviction less likely. There's not much point in bringing the guy in only to see him cut loose on a technicality. "Maybe this wasn't such a bright idea."

"Getting cold feet already?" Aisha *tsks*. "See, this is why it's better to be a private contractor."

"Why are you even here?"

"On a police stakeout? Why wouldn't I be? This is *awesome*." She yanks a pair of binoculars out of her messenger bag and scans the building.

"Okay, one, it's not a police stakeout. Two, stakeouts are not awesome, they are incredibly tedious and boring. *Please* put those away. People are staring."

She ignores him. "What we need is to figure out if he's actually in there."

"And how do you propose we do that?"

"Hold on, I think someone's coming out." She thrusts the binoculars at Rav, and the next thing he knows she's darting across the street, heading for a cluster of food delivery scooters parked on the sidewalk. The delivery guys loiter under a tree, chatting and listening to music, and they don't even notice when she nicks an oven bag from the back of one of their bikes. She hurries up to the door of Miller's building just as a guy and his dog are on their way out; she smiles, flourishes the oven bag, and she's in.

Rav swears under his breath. He waits until the guy with the dog turns a corner before scurrying across the street. "This is a bad idea," he hisses as Aisha opens the door for him.

"Quit whining and follow me." She's got her tablet out again, eyes glued to the screen. "Ugh, this place reeks. Take out the garbage once in a while, why don't you?"

It does reek, badly. Rav is careful not to touch any surfaces, shouldering open the door to the stairwell.

The app leads them to an apartment on the third floor. "Looks like this is it," Aisha whispers. "Make yourself scarce." She poses the oven bag like she's delivering a pizza and gets ready to knock.

Rav is about to duck back into the stairwell when a familiar odor pricks his nose, barely discernible beneath the stench of rubbish. "Aisha. Do you smell that?"

"Yeah," she says grimly. "I do."

Not garbage. Decomposing flesh.

Rav's brain whirrs for a second. If he were on duty, he might be able to argue probable cause, but as it stands, he'd be breaking and entering. Besides, the feds will be here any minute. "We should get out of here."

"Hang on." Aisha taps at her tablet. "I've got the Wi-Fi password from Miller's phone. I'm just checking to see if there are any devices in there I can—here we go. Webcam. Give me one second . . ."

Rav watches over her shoulder as an image fills her screen.

It's a bookshelf, but as Aisha moves her fingers, the view starts to shift. She scans left and right, and then she tilts the camera at the floor.

"Damn," she says.

It's a body, all right. A man, from the look of it, but he's hidden from the shoulders up. "We need to go," Rav says. "Right now."

Aisha doesn't argue. She stuffs her tablet back in her bag, and they hustle down the stairs.

* * *

It's just after eight that evening when Rav's phone rings, and he's a little surprised to see the name on the screen. "Will. Hi."

"Hey." An awkward pause. "How're you holding up?"

"Okay, I guess. You?"

"Yeah, I'm good. So listen, I thought you'd wanna know that the FBI raided an apartment in the East Village this afternoon, looking for Joseph Miller."

Rav is on his feet in an instant. "And?"

"He'd already skipped out, but they found a body in the apartment. Looks like it'd been there for a few days. One to the head, one to the chest, probably a .40 caliber."

Just like Richard Vanderford. Holy shit. "Have they ID'd him?"

"A known associate of Miller's, guy by the name of Greg Watson. They used to be roommates."

He killed his own roommate? This keeps getting weirder. "What about Miller's phone? Was it still there?" Rav's brain is running so far ahead that it takes him a moment to realize his mistake.

"Guess I don't need to ask where the anonymous tip came from," Shepard says dryly. "Can't say I blame you. The feds were sitting on their asses."

It feels like a thaw, however modest, and it gives Rav the courage to say what he needs to. "Listen, you should know . . . This thing with Jack. It wasn't just some fling, at least not for me. I had feelings for him. I don't know if that makes a difference."

"It does."

There's a long silence. Rav doesn't know what else to say. Part of him wants to keep apologizing, but he suspects that comes from a selfish place. A need for absolution, or at least forgiveness. It wouldn't be fair to push for that. If Will decides to forgive him, it needs to be on his own terms.

"I should go," Will says, "but there's something else you should know. It won't be official until ballistics comes back, but Agent Rice is confident they're looking at the same perp for the two murders—Vanderford and the roommate. They figure it happened on Saturday, probably late in the day."

"Jack was with the FBI on Saturday afternoon. Nash, too."

"Exactly. As alibis go, being in an interview room with the investigating officers at the time of the murder ain't bad. Plus, they've got no motive for the roommate. Bottom line, they're off the hook."

Rav sinks onto the sofa. *It's finally over.*

"I don't know if it'll change anything with your disciplinary situation, but at least you know Vale is in the clear, for good this time. Thought maybe that would make you feel a little better."

"It does. Thanks, Will."

"Hang in there, man." And then he's gone.

Rav pulls up his contacts and scrolls down to V, but he changes his mind. Hearing Jack's voice will just make him feel worse. He calls Charlie Banks instead.

"Shit, that's a load off my mind," the manager says after Rav fills him in. "It's awful about the roommate, but I can't pretend it doesn't help us out to have an ironclad alibi. We might even have a shot at keeping this whole mess out of the headlines. Ryan's gonna plead to misdemeanor obstruction, but I'd be surprised if that gets much attention."

Misdemeanor obstruction. Wow. Rav underestimated Joanne Reid.

"And they were acting on your tip?" Banks says.

"They were acting on an *anonymous* tip."

"Gotcha. But how did this *anonymous* person find Miller's hidey-hole?"

"They were able to track his phone. It looks like he ditched it several days ago, but hopefully the FBI will find something on the device that leads to him."

"So Vanderford was in bed with Joe Miller." Banks grunts. "Gotta say, I did not see that one coming."

Rav still doesn't see it, but he keeps that to himself. Let the band have this moment.

"Thanks, Detective. We owe you one."

"Someone would have called the police eventually, when the smell got bad enough."

"Yeah, but I've watched enough TV to know that time counts in these things. And it'll help my guys sleep at night, knowing they're in the clear for good, so thank you. I know you stuck your neck out for this." Banks pauses. "I'll make sure he knows it, too," he adds quietly before signing off.

About half an hour later, Rav gets a text from Jack.

Just heard the news

I don't know how to thank you

I don't know what to say at all

There's no point in drawing this out. Better to rip it off like a Band-Aid. Rav types:

We've already said it.

Goodnight, Jack.

He lets out a long, slow breath. Then he powers off his phone and goes to bed.

CHAPTER EIGHTEEN

Three weeks later . . .

R av stares out over the river, watching the long line of aircraft
on approach to LaGuardia and trying not to wonder if one
of them is carrying the Nicks. The band plays Madison Square
Garden this weekend, their first performance in New York since
the incident at the Concord Theater. It's the talk of the town—
which makes it *extremely* difficult to put a certain someone out
of his mind. "It's the worst," he grumbles, adjusting his Prada
aviators against the bright June sunshine. "Just when I was finally starting to get over it."

He is *so over* not being over it.

"Give yourself time," Mags says in his earbuds.

"I think the problem is that I've had too much time on my
hands. Admin leave is torture. I'm climbing the walls."

She hums sympathetically. "It must be hard, not having closure on your last case. They won't let you keep looking into it,
even on your own time?"

"Strictly off-limits. Aside from the jurisdictional issues, I have
too much personal baggage. So instead I mope around like a
bloody teenager. Honestly, what is happening to me? All this
drama over a guy I hooked up with *once*."

"Physically, maybe, but you spent hours talking on the
phone. *More than kisses, letters mingle souls.*"

"What?"

"It's John Donne, darling. The point is, physical intimacy

is not the only kind of intimacy. Take Jason and me. We spent hours online before we ever met in person, and by then, I was head over heels." Rav hears the *click* of a makeup compact. He pictures her seated at her antique boudoir table, running a contouring brush under her cheekbones. "If you like him that much, maybe it's worth fighting for. When are they going to make a decision on your case?"

"Any day now, but it won't change anything. I basically accused him of murder. You don't come back from something like that."

"Shouldn't you let him be the judge of that? So you doubted him for a moment. Can he really blame you? After all, he didn't trust you enough to tell you about the bass player."

"Exactly. Mutual distrust is hardly an auspicious way to begin a relationship."

There's a long silence. Faintly, Rav hears Edith Piaf on scratchy vinyl in the background.

"Something you want to say?"

"I'm just trying to recall the last time I heard you talk about a *relationship*. Frankly, I'm drawing a blank, and I have to ask—"

"Please don't."

The question hangs in the air. *Are you in love?*

There's a beep in his ear. Rav looks at his screen. "That's the union. Love to Jason, and break a leg tonight."

The news is more or less what he was told to expect: as long as the relationship was consensual and Jack wasn't involved in anything criminal, nothing in the rules prohibited them from seeing each other. The rep informs Rav that the investigators are now satisfied on both fronts, and he can expect to be cleared for active duty within the week. "It took a little longer than we hoped, but they wanted to be thorough, which is in your best interests as well."

"Of course. Thank you."

There must be something in his voice, because the rep says, "This is good news, Detective."

It's great news. So why doesn't he feel like celebrating?

He's just stuffing his phone back in his pocket when it buzzes with a Twitter mention. He still gets tagged in posts about Jack now and then, and though he tries to resist reading them, he never can.

Jenna Zhang @JenZee
NOOOOOOO! WHERE WAS @RavT WHEN WE
NEEDED HIM???

When we needed him to what? Rav pulls up the thread—and his heart stops.

Breaking:
New Knickerbockers' Jack Vale
in Shooting Incident

The singer and his bodyguard have been taken to a hospital in New York City following a shooting outside the Palace Hotel.

Rav scrolls frantically through the timeline. The report is less than half an hour old, so there's virtually no information. It's not even clear who's been shot, let alone what condition they're in. Without thinking, he fires off a text.

Are you OK?

It's absurd, of course. There will be a thousand people trying to get ahold of Jack right now, and nine hundred and ninety-nine of them will be more entitled to hear from him than the cop he hooked up with that one time. Rav knows this, but he can't stop himself. **Please let me know if you can.**

He texts Eloise next, though he's not sure she'll recognize the number. He tries to reach Charlie Banks, too, but it goes straight to voicemail. He must look like a maniac, stalking up and down the waterfront, feverishly texting and refreshing Twitter every few seconds. This goes on for about twenty minutes until he can't take it anymore; he jumps in a cab and heads uptown, reasoning that they'll be at Manhattan General. He figures maybe he can flash his badge and get some proper information, and he's halfway there before he remembers he doesn't have a badge right now.

A small crowd of fans has already gathered outside the emergency entrance when he arrives. Hospital security is willing to let him through, but the woman at the admissions desk is not so accommodating. "I'll need to see a badge," she tells him. "Otherwise, family only."

He loiters in the admissions area for a bit, scrolling through the NYPD alerts on his phone, but there's even less information than on Twitter. Then his screen lights up with a text. It's from Eloise.

**Hi just to say that Mr. Vale is OK so
not to worry**

Rav drops onto a chair and lets out the breath he's been holding. He goes to compose a reply, but then he spies the PA in the flesh not twenty feet away, hurrying toward the admissions desk. She's got her nose buried in her phone when Rav walks up, and she jumps when he says her name. "Oh! I didn't realize you were here."

"I wasn't sure if I'd hear anything by text." As if that's a legitimate explanation for him showing up here. It probably looks pathetic, if not downright creepy, but he's too worried to care. "Is Mo all right?"

"He's been shot," Eloise replies, and she bursts into tears. Rav grabs a tissue from the desk. "Thanks," she sniffles.

"Have they said how serious it is?"

She shakes her head, dabbing delicately around her false eyelashes. "They've barely said two words to Jack at all."

"He's not by himself in there, is he?"

"Mr. Banks is on his way, but Jack didn't want the others coming around, with all the fans and the media and everything. He asked me to bring his medication."

"Is he having an attack?"

"I don't think so, but he wanted it just in case. I'd better hurry up and get it to him."

"Of course." Rav swallows the rest of his questions. He'll just have to wait for answers like everybody else. "Thanks for the update, and tell him if he needs anything . . ."

He leaves her at the desk, his head swimming. Was this Miller? It must have been. *You were wrong about him. You were wrong and you let him get away and this is on you.*

"Detective?" He turns to find Eloise hurrying over, brandishing her phone. "Jack says if you want to come back . . ."

Rav experiences the strangest swirl of emotion, a mixture of relief and butterflies and *dread*. "Sure. Of course."

They find Jack sitting alone in an auxiliary waiting room, head between his knees, phone buzzing away on the seat beside him. At first he has eyes only for Eloise—more specifically for the orange plastic bottle in her hand. He tosses back a pill and gulps down half a bottle of water. "Sorry," he says as he catches his breath. "I should have had them on me. The nurses won't give me anything without talking to one of the doctors, and I didn't want to bother them." His phone buzzes again, and he looks at it dully. "It hasn't stopped since I got here."

"I'll take care of it," Eloise says, picking it up and unlocking it with a practiced motion. She uses a code rather than biometrics, and Rav catches himself being annoyed about it. *Really, Mo? Is that your idea of security?* What's that saying: How you do anything is how you do everything?

It's a stupid reflex. Whatever happened out there, it isn't Mo's fault.

Eloise walks away, texting, and it's just the two of them. "Do you want to sit?" Jack asks.

Rav perches on the seat beside him. "How are you holding up?"

"Okay." His body language tells a different story. He's almost doubled over, hands knitted in front of him.

"I hope I'm not intruding. If you'd rather be alone . . ."

"I wouldn't have invited you back here if I wanted to be alone."

"Can I get you anything?"

Jack just stares at the sparkling vinyl floor. "It happened so fast," he murmurs. "I was signing autographs outside the hotel, and he stepped out of the crowd. I didn't even see the gun until . . ."

"Miller?"

Jack nods. "But it was different this time. *He* was different. Before, he seemed . . . I don't know, scared, I guess. But this time, he just looked blank. Like he was past scared. Mo stepped in front of me, and . . ." He shudders. Rav's reflex is to put an arm around him, but he's not sure it would be welcome.

"Has someone taken your statement?"

"A preliminary one." His glance falls to Rav's belt, where his badge should be. "Are you here officially?"

"I came on my own," Rav says awkwardly. "I'm sorry for just showing up like this."

"No, it's just . . . You got here so fast."

"Twitter. I still get the occasional mention after that whole TMZ circus."

"Right, the skate park memes." Jack shakes his head. "First the Concord, then the skate park, now this. It's like we're destined to keep colliding."

Colliding is the right word for it. Ricocheting off one another in the margins of violent incidents. If it's fate, it's a strange kind.

"How did it turn out with your job?" Jack asks.

"I just heard today. They're putting me back on active duty."

"That's great." A faint smile flickers across his face. "That's really great, Rav."

A doctor arrives with an update, informing them that Mo is being prepped for surgery but is expected to make a full recovery. "The bullet lodged in his shoulder, but we don't anticipate complications removing it. If you leave your number at the desk, someone can text you when he's ready to receive visitors."

Jack thanks her, and then he's on his feet, shoving his hands through his hair, and this time Rav follows his instincts. He touches Jack's shoulder—*I'm here if you need me*—and Jack throws his arms around Rav. "Thanks," he whispers into Rav's neck. "Thanks for being here."

They're just drawing apart when Charlie Banks and Ryan Nash show up, along with Nash's bodyguard. Jack fills them in on the latest.

"How the *fuck* did this happen?" Erika Strauss growls. "In what parallel universe does some ninety-pound tinfoil hat get the drop on a seasoned field agent?" She composes herself quickly, her tone turning coolly professional. "I'm going to need you to stay in this room," she tells Jack. "If you have to use the bathroom, I'll escort you. If you want something to eat or drink, we'll have Eloise get it. Just give me a minute to secure the room." She corners one of the hospital security guards and starts talking to him. Rav has to hand it to her: she takes charge of a scene like a pro. It's a comfort knowing there's someone capable to step in while Mo recovers.

"I thought we agreed you weren't coming," Jack is saying to his bandmate.

"*You* agreed I wasn't coming," Nash returns. "No way I was letting you go through this alone."

"I'm not alone."

"I see that." Nash's gaze flits over Rav, not especially friendly.

Eloise reappears, and as soon as she sees Ryan, she rushes into his arms. "It's so *awful*." She sniffles. "Isn't it *awful?*" Nash pats her back awkwardly and agrees that it's awful.

Charlie Banks fishes a bottle of scotch out of his messenger bag. "Compliments of Sarah Creed," he tells Jack, grabbing a paper cup from the water cooler. "She figured you could use some chill-out juice. How 'bout you, Detective?"

"Thanks, but I should get going." Jack's real friends are here now; he doesn't need a stand-in anymore. "I'm glad you're safe,"

Rav says, squeezing Jack's shoulder in farewell. "Please give Mo my best."

By the time he passes through the automatic doors, the crowd outside has swelled to perhaps fifty. Rav hails the first cab he sees and ducks in before anyone notices him. Then, because he's learned from his mistakes, he calls his CO. Howard is up on the news, both of Rav's reinstatement and the shooting. "Have you heard anything from Vale's people?" she asks, not unkindly.

He fills her in on the latest. "What are they saying on the radio? Is Miller in custody?"

"Unfortunately not. He was last seen fleeing into the park on foot."

He won't get far, Rav tells himself.

"Is that what you were calling to find out?"

"That, and to let you know that I'd seen Jack. I wasn't sure if that was allowed."

There's a pause. He can't tell if she's pissed or just thinking.

"Your relationship with Jack Vale has already been the subject of a thorough review, and the investigators found nothing inappropriate. That being the case, I see no reason why the department should have any further interest in the matter."

"Okay. That's . . ."

Great news? Too little, too late? He really doesn't know how to feel about it.

Maybe she hears it in his voice, because her own is surprisingly gentle. "We'll expect you in the squad room tomorrow, Detective," she says, and hangs up.

CHAPTER NINETEEN

Rav visits Mo in hospital two days later and finds the bodyguard sitting up in bed, his arm bound in a sling. They chat for a while, and Mo seems to be in good spirits, so Rav asks if he feels up to talking about the shooting.

"This an interview, Detective?" Mo eyes the newly restored badge on Rav's belt.

"Not officially, but Miller is still out there."

Somehow. It's hard to understand. By now, half of New York must have seen his face in the news. How does a guy like that stay hidden? How does he get away in the first place, especially in a park full of cops—cops on foot, cops on bikes, cops on horseback and in bloody golf carts? Central Park is big, but it's not *that* big.

"I'm not just going to sit around while this maniac runs free," Rav says, "especially with you laid up like this."

"I won't be laid up for long. Security is mostly about this anyway." Mo taps his head. "As for the physical stuff, Erika reached out to an ex-colleague from Langley to take over Ryan's detail for a few days, and she'll look after Jack personally. Unless you're interested in taking it on?"

"Tempting, but I'm not on the off-duty protection roster. Besides, I'm not sure it's the best idea for Jack and me to be spending that much time together."

Mo studies him with that unnervingly keen gaze of his. "I'm not usually one to offer hot takes on my clients' relationships, but it looked to me like you guys were on to something."

"Is that so." Rav's tone says *drop it*, but Mo has other ideas.

"For a while there, it seemed like every time I stuck my head in to check on Jack, he was on the phone. Laughing, shooting the shit. That got my attention. Jack doesn't say much. Seeing him unwind like that is pretty rare. Wasn't hard to work out who was on the other end, especially when it was over all of a sudden. I was sorry for that. It was good for him."

"What's done is done. There's too much water under that bridge."

"I get it. You've had the rug yanked out from under you once already, and it sucked. You'd rather not put yourself in that position again."

"Did you learn that fortune cookie psychology in spy school?" Rav says irritably.

Mo shrugs. "Okay."

"Sorry, I'm just . . . trying to put it behind me, that's all."

"So that's why you're here, asking questions about Joe Miller?"

"This isn't just about Jack. I don't like loose ends, especially when I'm partly responsible for them. If I'd done my job, maybe you wouldn't be lying here right now."

"Don't do that to yourself, man. The only person responsible for this is Joe Miller."

"Bottom line, he's still out there."

"True, but every cop in town is looking for him, not to mention half of TikTok. If he has two brain cells to rub together, he'll find a deep hole and never come out."

The cop in Rav agrees, but it doesn't make him feel any better. "I didn't really believe it, you know. That he actually wanted Jack dead. I'm usually pretty good at reading people, but not this time."

"Wouldn't be too hard on yourself there, either. You might not have been totally off base."

"Oh?" Rav frowns. "What makes you say that?"

"Couple of things." Mo sits up straighter, the hospital bed rattling under his bulk. Rav helps him reposition some pillows behind his back. "For one, Miller spouted some stuff before he pulled the gun. *We* know who you are. *We* know what you did. So I'm wondering, who's *we?*"

Rav takes out his notepad to write that down; too late, he realizes the hot-pink elastic from Jack's notebook is wrapped around it. Of course it draws Mo's eye, and there's precisely zero chance he doesn't know what he's looking at. Rav feels as exposed as if he just inadvertently flashed a pair of hot-pink knickers.

"Second," Mo says smoothly, as if he's not fully aware that Rav is *dying,* "I've been keeping an eye on the conspiracy theory forums. Miller's back to posting again. Under a new username, but it's definitely him. Mostly the same old stuff—details about Tommy's accident, the mystery car following him the night he died, blah blah. Until a couple weeks ago. Now all of a sudden, he's ranting about yours truly. How I offed his roommate and tried to kill him, too."

Rav glances up from his notes. "Come again?"

"He thinks I murdered his roommate. And Dick Vanderford, and Tommy Esposito. Never mind that I wasn't even in the picture at the time of Tommy's death."

"He mentioned you by name?"

"Knows about my intelligence background and everything. Which fits his conspiracy theory nicely. The CIA is everyone's favorite bogeyman. First I took out Tommy, then Vanderford, and now I'm coming for Miller. I broke into Greg Watson's place looking for him, and when he wasn't there, I shot Watson."

"*We know what you did,*" Rav murmurs. "Hold on, does that mean *you* were the target?"

"Kinda looks that way, doesn't it? So maybe your instincts were right, and he wasn't gunning for Jack after all."

Rav swears softly. "You say he mentioned Vanderford as well? I wonder what the FBI makes of that."

"That he's blaming me for killing a guy he supposedly murdered?" Mo shrugs. "They probably think he's just trying to pin it on someone else."

"Is that what you think? Because the way you're describing it, it sounds like he genuinely believes the things he's saying."

"Oh, he definitely believes them."

"But you're still planning to go through with the show this weekend?" It's none of Rav's business, but he had to say it.

"We had the conversation, including with the NYPD and the FBI. The consensus is that the show itself is low risk. Big venue like MSG, security will be crazy tight. Metal detectors, facial recognition, the works. Ironically, Jack's probably safer there than just about anywhere else in the city. It's the rest of the time I'm worried about. If I had my way, Jack wouldn't be in New York at all."

"Then why not just get on a plane? Head to Europe a few days early?"

"We had that conversation, too. The band is against it. They don't want to disappoint their fans."

"That's worth risking Jack's life over? And yours?"

"Trust me, I tried. But I get where they're coming from. Jack, especially, doesn't want his life to be defined by some QAnon crank."

Rav understands it too, but he doesn't like it any better than Mo. "These usernames you're tracking, the ones Miller posts under. Can you give them to me?"

Mo rattles off the ones he can remember and promises to have his digital team forward the rest. "Surprised you don't use your phone for that," he remarks, watching Rav scribble them down on his notepad.

"I find I remember things better if I've written them down."

"Plus, that pink elastic wouldn't look as good wrapped around a phone."

Rav glances up to find the bodyguard grinning at him. "Having fun?"

"Wouldn't have pegged you for the sentimental type, Detective."

"It keeps the pages from getting dog-eared," Rav says tartly. "Reuse and recycle, right?"

"Totally. We all gotta do our part for the planet."

"You know, I think that's my cue." Rav snaps the notepad shut and rises.

"I'll tell the boss you dropped by. Guessing you don't want me to mention the rubber band, though."

Rav flips him off on the way out.

∗ ∗ ∗

He's just walking into his flat when he gets a text.

MESSAGES

Jack Vale   1m

Thanks for going to see Mo today
I wish I could go myself but it's hard to get out right now

Rav is surprised to be hearing from him like this. He figured the hospital was a one-off, and they'd go back to their regularly scheduled program of not talking. He types:

Of course. He seemed to be in good spirits.

And he wouldn't want you putting yourself at risk.

You have nothing to feel guilty about.

Except almost getting him killed

That's his job, Jack.

He's doing just fine.

Yeah but it's not over. Tell me you really think it's over

This doesn't sound good. Rav wonders if he's alone.

Are you OK?

. . .

. . .

. . .

Fuck it. Rav hits the call icon.

Jack picks up straightaway. "I'm okay. Sorry, I didn't mean to worry you. I just needed a second."

"You don't sound okay. Are you alone?"

"Erika's around here somewhere. She's trying to give me space. But I'm not having a panic attack, I promise." Rav hears a set of sliding glass doors being opened, a rustle of wind against the phone's mic. "This is just a run-of-the-mill freakout," Jack says with a rueful laugh. "So, you know, no cause for alarm."

Someone took a shot at you two days ago. There's nothing run-of-the-mill about it. Rav doesn't say it aloud; it's not like Jack needs the reminder. "What about one of your bandmates? You shouldn't be alone right now."

"We've seen enough of each other today. Besides, I'm not alone, I'm talking to you. You're my hotline, remember?" A pause. "Sorry, that's not fair. I should let you go."

"What's not fair?"

"Me, leaning on you again. I know we're . . . you know, supposed to go our separate ways or whatever. You've already gotten into enough trouble on my account. You and everybody else." He blows out a breath. "Really, Rav, I'm sorry. I'll let you go."

"Please don't hang up. I'm worried about you, Jack."

"I know. I know you are, and it's not fair. This isn't your problem, and I have no idea why I'm making it your problem, except . . ." He trails off. He's clearly climbing the walls, and Rav isn't about to let him sign off in this state. He thinks back to that day on the terrace at the Palace Hotel, when he distracted Jack with talk of champagne and skinny-dipping. If it worked once . . .

"Except my velvety voice is practically a sedative in its own right, and you just can't help yourself. I can't blame you, really. It's one of my finer qualities."

He doesn't quite get a laugh, but he can hear the smile in Jack's voice. "You seem very aware of your own fine qualities."

"The unavoidable result of being raised by a pair of raging narcissists. One learns to be one's own cheerleader." He goes on like that for a while, babbling lighthearted nonsense, and inevitably he finds himself out on the balcony, gazing in the direction of the Palace Hotel. He imagines Jack out there on the terrace, pant legs rolled up, feet dangling in the glowing blue water. "You're sitting by the pool, aren't you?"

"I am, actually, but not where you think. The security team decided to move me someplace quieter. I'm in Brooklyn now."

Smart. Rav doesn't ask for details; the fewer people who know where he's staying, the better. "Still medically luxurious, I trust?"

"The pool isn't as big, but it's still pretty great. You could come over. Perfect weather for skinny-dipping."

Rav squeezes his eyes shut and tries *very hard* not to picture this.

"Sorry," Jack says, "that was inappropriate. For a second there, it felt like old times, you know?"

He really does.

"Are you even allowed to talk to me? The last thing I want is to get you in trouble again."

"I got myself into trouble, Jack. It's not on you."

"I pushed you."

"You didn't push me anywhere I didn't want to go."

Jack is quiet for a while. Then he says, "Did you believe it?"

Rav winces. He was afraid this question was coming.

"When you came over that night. Did you think I killed him?"

"No." Rav sighs. "And yes."

There's a long pause. "I'm trying to understand that answer."

"In my heart, I didn't believe it. But I also knew that didn't matter."

"How could it not matter?"

Rav's not sure he can explain this to a civilian, but he tries. "Because I've seen it too many times. The wife. The best friend. The brother. People who've known a suspect their entire lives, who believe with their whole hearts their loved one couldn't possibly be a murderer, and they're wrong. No matter what my gut was telling me, I know from experience that anyone can be deceived. How could I not entertain the notion that this man I barely knew, this man I was so infatuated with, was deceiving me?" He shakes his head, wandering over to the bar cart to fix himself a drink. "I don't expect you to understand, and I certainly don't expect you to forgive me. It's not the sort of thing you can just get past."

"How do you know?"

Rav pauses, gin bottle poised over the shaker. "Sorry?"

"How do you know whether it's the sort of thing you can get past?"

"How could you possibly? Why would you even try?"

"The second part's easy. I like you. Pretty sure I told you that."

"That was before I accused you of being a *murderer*. I rather thought that would put a damper on things."

"Do you want it to? If you're looking for a reason, Rav, you have plenty to choose from. In your place, I'd probably be looking for something a lot less complicated."

It's similar to what Mo said earlier—so much so that Rav wonders if there's some truth in it. Maybe he's the one pumping the brakes here, however subconsciously. Jack's life is a *lot*, even without the homicidal stalker. Tabloids. Fans. The ghost of Tommy Esposito. He's a walking land mine, and the closer Rav gets, the worse the fallout will be. Is that what he's really afraid of?

He puts the gin bottle back down, drink forgotten. "How would you ever be able to look at me and not see someone who believed, even for a second, that you might be a cold-blooded killer?"

A thoughtful silence. Then: "Ryan, when he found out we hooked up—he couldn't understand it. *A cop, seriously?*"

It's not the first time Rav has heard this. It feels like shit, every time. "What did you say?"

"I told him about you. How amazing you'd been, right from the start. How you were there for me even when it made things complicated for you. I wasn't the only one who saw it, either. That day at the hotel, when you confronted Ryan about the video . . . After you left, Charlie really let us have it. *Do you all realize what just happened here? That guy just blew up his life for you, and all he got in return was an earful of shit.*"

"Really?" Rav is touched.

"That's when Ryan got it, I think. He apologized for messing things up for me. He figured the same as you, that there was no way back from that. And I guess I thought that too, right up until the other day, at the hospital. You walked in, and I didn't think about the way we left things, or any of the shit that happened before. All I thought was how good it was to have you there, and how much I wanted to see you again.

"Maybe you're right, and we can't get past this. Or maybe we do, and it takes us to another level. I guess there's only one way to find out. I'm up for it if you are." There's a swish of water; Rav was right about him dangling his feet in the pool. "In the meantime, I'd love for you to come to the show this weekend, if you're interested. No pressure. I'll talk to you later."

"Jack, wait."

"Still here."

"I'm still here, too. If you need a hotline."

"Thanks. Really, I appreciate it. Goodnight, Rav."

CHAPTER TWENTY

Rav is still churning over the conversation from last night. He just can't get his head around it. That Jack is somehow willing to put everything behind him, just pick up where they left off. *I like you*, he says. As if meeting someone you like is so very extraordinary that it's worth overlooking that one time they accused you of being a murderer. It wouldn't make sense for anybody, let alone a bloody rock star. Jack could have anyone he wants. He could have *everyone* he wants, all at the same time. And he wants Rav? It's mad.

The good kind of mad, obviously. The kind that might, just possibly, be worth putting your heart on the butcher's block for. Part of him just wants to say sod it, jump in a cab and go over there. He pictures it: Fantasy Rav striding slow-motion out of the elevator, nodding at Mo as the bodyguard opens the door for him. Jack is surprised to see him, barefoot with a sparkling water in his hand, but he's good to go, his mouth already seeking Rav's as Rav hoists him off the floor and carries him bodily out onto the terrace. They tumble into the pool fully clothed, and Rav's suit is plastered to his body and Jack is all over him like a wild animal and maybe the neighbors are watching from a nearby window and Rav doesn't *care*, he lights Jack up like a pinball machine until he begs for release and then he fucks him right there in the pool, gazing into those magnificent eyes, the same aquamarine as the water, until they start to flutter closed and Jack throws his head back and—

"*Rav.*"

"Sorry, what?" Rav scoots his chair forward until his lap is hidden by the desk.

Will frowns at him across a stack of paperwork. "Dude, where *are* you today?"

Fucking in the pool. Please do not disturb. "Could you repeat the question?"

"I asked whether you'd heard the news about Novak. You remember, the missing PI?"

It's like a bucket of ice water in the face. "Don't tell me."

"Afraid so. They found him three days ago, in a shallow grave upstate."

Rav swears under his breath. "Have they released a cause of death?"

"Not yet. You were in touch with missing persons before you went on leave, right? Were they getting anywhere?"

"Last I heard, they were still trying to convince Fuse to release his data so they could put together a list of his clients." He wonders if Aisha could help. It seems like she's given up on the Russian hacker thing, or he'd have heard something by now. On the other hand, he's officially spent all his chits with her. "Apparently, phone records had him upstate quite a bit, so I guess he was working something up there."

"Something that got him killed." Will sighs and tosses the pen he's been chewing onto his desk. "You called it."

"Not much of a leap, unfortunately. The real question is whether his death has anything to do with Vanderford."

"Should we flag it with the Bureau?"

Rav considers that. "The only evidence we have of a connection between Novak and Vanderford is a business card."

"Yeah, but if it turns out he was shot, the feds would probably be faster on the ballistics. If the gun matches the one that killed Vanderford and Miller's roommate, we'd know for sure."

"So it's confirmed? The gun that killed Greg Watson is a match?"

"Yup. Rice called up the LT to let her know."

So the Bureau is playing nice, sort of. In which case, it behooves the NYPD to do the same. "All right, let's fill them in on Novak. I'll reach out this afternoon."

He gives Jack a call on his way out of the office that evening. He's not ready to put his cards on the table, but he can't deny he's craving the connection, and besides, Jack needs him right now. The call goes to a generic voicemail, but he gets a text a few minutes later.

Sorry in studio. Call you in a bit?

"Oh, just in the studio, making another platinum record." As though he needs the reminder that this isn't Jack Random, gorgeous and slightly neurotic musician, but *Jack Vale*, award-winning, chart-topping, stadium-filling rock god, as seen on the cover of *Hot Wax Magazine*. It's *mad*.

He can feel the doubt creeping in again. Does he really want to be pulled back into Jack's orbit, knowing he's just going to end up burning up in the atmosphere?

He needs a distraction, so he decides to take it out on the MMA bag hanging in his spare room. He jabs and hooks and crosses until his shoulders ache, and by the time his phone rings, he's so winded he has to let it go for several seconds before picking up.

"Sorry I couldn't take your call before," Jack says. "We're recording some new material for a special edition of *Background*. Couple of bonus tracks, remixes, that sort of thing."

"Ho hum. Just another Thursday."

He laughs. "How are you? You sound out of breath."

"I've just spent the past half hour pummeling an innocent boxing bag, so that probably tells you everything you need to know."

"Rough day at work?"

"Not especially," Rav says, ripping the Velcro on his gloves. "I'm just rammed rather thoroughly up my own arse at the moment."

"Been there. You should try writing songs. Extremely cathartic."

"That sounds like something that requires talent. Though I did attempt a love poem or two as a teenager."

"Oh yeah? Were they any good?"

"Awful. I did the world a favor and burned them in the most melodramatic bonfire. Nearly set His Lordship's favorite gazebo on fire. The gardener came after me with a weed-whacker, howling profanities in Turkish."

He can hear the grin in Jack's voice. "I don't even care if that story is true, it's amazing. Who were the poems about?"

"Oh no. We are not even close to the stage where I start discussing my romantic history." He grabs a coconut water from the fridge and downs a couple of big gulps from the carton. "Besides, if you're that curious, you can probably find some of it online."

"I may have come across a photo or two."

Rav feels a blush creeping up his neck. "What about you? How do you manage to keep your love life out of the tabloids?"

"What love life?"

"Seriously. The whole time I was investigating you, I didn't come across a thing about it. Granted, I wasn't expressly looking . . ."

"I don't give many interviews, and I've made it clear that my personal life is off-limits. Most journalists respect that. The real ones, anyway. I'm sure it's only a matter of time before some trash tabloid runs something."

Rav is still too sweaty for the couch, so he stretches out on the rug by the coffee table, phone resting on his chest. "Does that worry you?"

"Kind of? It's not like I have anything to hide, but like you said, having the media poking around your life is pretty unpleasant. I can't imagine having to go through that as a teenager, like you did."

"It's my own fault. I leaked the most outrageous photos myself."

"Really? Why?"

"Part of the war of escalation between my father and me. His Lordship had a very clear idea of who he wanted me to be, and I didn't exactly conform. That was true even before I came out to him, and you can imagine how that went."

"He wasn't cool with it?"

"He claimed to be, and I think he wanted to believe it. But he's the kind of stodgy traditionalist that would make most Tories blush, and if there's one thing he has in common with my mother, it's a pathological need for the approval of others. What I did in private was my own affair, but he asked that I not, quote unquote, rub people's noses in it. Be careful what you say on social media, no public displays of affection, that sort of thing. For a while I did my best to indulge him. Then a mildly compromising photo started doing the rounds on the local gossip blogs, and my father lost it. Accused me of doing it on purpose just to undermine him. As if my entire existence revolved around him. So I decided to show him what some *really* shocking photos looked like. Boys, drugs, the lot. I set my own life on fire just so I could flip him off by its pretty orange glow. Speaking of melodramatic."

"Wow." Jack's voice is subdued. "That's shit, Rav. I'm sorry."

"It was eons ago. I'm over it, though *we're* not. I don't know that I'll ever truly forgive him for that period in my life. Or myself, for that matter. I did some things I'm not proud of." For reasons he can't fathom, he finds himself telling Jack about the medal he pawned, the one his great-great-grandfather earned in the First World War. "It was stupid and spiteful, and I regretted it almost immediately, but by then it was too late. That's when I knew I needed to leave London for good. Get out of my father's space before we made each other any more toxic."

"So you moved to New York and became a cop." A pause. "Can I ask you something?"

"Why did I decide to become a cop?"

"Sorry, is that rude? It's just . . . you could have done

anything you wanted. Or nothing at all. You could have just lived off your trust fund, like Dick Vanderford."

"Well, we're not talking *that* kind of money. Four years at Columbia pretty much drained the tank. But it's a fair question." Rav takes a moment to consider his answer, but it's a comfortable silence. He can't imagine why he felt nervous about this call. It feels so good to talk to him like this again. Like coming home. "Honestly, I just thought I'd be good at it. Maybe there was a bit of rebellion in it, too, knowing my parents would hate it." He pauses. "No, there's no *maybe* about it. I was a very angry eighteen-year-old when I started college. My choices were definitely filtered through that. And back then I had a pretty romanticized view of law enforcement. A privileged kid's view."

"What about now?"

"Now, it's complicated. You have the opportunity to do a lot of good in this job. Helping people get justice, getting dangerous criminals off the streets. You're a part of something important, but that's the double-edged sword. You can't pick and choose which bits you're associated with. There are times when I'm incredibly proud of this department, and times when I'm so angry and ashamed I can hardly drag myself into work. It's hard to reconcile that, and there are days when I get very, very tired of trying. I struggle with it. Lots of us do. The answer I keep coming back to is that the world needs good cops. If all the good cops walked away, who would be left? Maybe doing some good in the world isn't just about getting terrible people off the streets, but about getting them off the force, too. Maybe it's about getting the right people into the right positions who are actually serious about reform."

"Is that what you want? To be top brass someday?"

"Maybe? Part of me wants to zoom out even farther. The problems with our criminal justice system go way beyond the police." And now he's babbling about politicized judges and mandatory minimums and the prison-industrial complex, as if he's back in college solving the world's problems over cheap wine and weed. "Sorry, I'm rambling. My friend Ana would call me a narcissist about now."

"I think it's amazing, Rav."

"Really?"

"I've been trying to imagine what your job is like. The things you must have seen, things nobody should have to see. On a good day, you put the people responsible away, but even then, you can't really fix it, because somebody's already dead. The toll that must take . . . I think it would make most people really cynical and depressed. But I hear all this optimism and passion from you, and it's amazing."

Rav's heart thrums. "I wasn't sure you'd . . . A lot of people feel the way Ryan does. About cops."

"Ryan plays bass for a living," Jack says flatly. "I sing songs about how sad I am. We're not exactly slogging it out in the trenches."

"You bring joy into the lives of thousands of people. And you shine a light on the world through music. *That's* amazing."

"I don't know if I'm shining a light so much as having a very public rant, but yeah, a lot of our songs are calling out the problems I see around me. Actually, what you said a minute ago really resonated. About the double-edged sword. I love this country, but it is deeply fucked up sometimes. I look at some of my fellow citizens and think, how can we be part of the same journey? It's hard to reconcile, like you said. So I guess I don't personally see any contradiction between being pissed with the NYPD as an institution and having warm fuzzy feelings about Detective Rav Trivedi."

Rav is blushing again. It's a good thing no one can see him, or his rep as a smooth operator would take a serious hit. "I've been thinking a lot about this since I was put on admin leave. I had this master plan, or at least I thought so. But I'm starting to realize that it was incomplete. I'm racing up this ladder, but to what?"

"I get that." A rueful laugh. "I *so* get that. Back when we started the band, all I wanted was to make it, but I never really stopped to think about what that would do to our lives."

"You wanted to be famous?"

"I wanted people to love our music as much as I did. I still want that, but I have a better idea what it costs now."

"In terms of your personal life?"

"In every way. It almost cost us the band."

"Really? I never knew that."

"It's not like we advertised it. But yeah, we had a really rough time after *Alien Nation* came out. It turned out we weren't all on the same page about what the Nicks should be. Ryan wanted us to be really activist, offstage as well as on. Tommy wanted to let the music speak for itself. They butted heads about it a lot. Sarah thought we were going too mainstream, and Claudia was just tired of all the conflict. Plus, Tommy didn't like being the center of attention as much as he thought he would. Before we even signed our first deal, he tried to get me to take over as front man, and I wasn't having it. He had so much charisma, it just didn't make sense to me that I would be the one in the spotlight. I just kept saying, *It's gotta be you, man, it's gotta be you.* If I could take that back . . ."

Later, Rav will wonder where the thought comes from. "Tommy's accident . . . *was* an accident, wasn't it?"

There's a long silence.

"I'm sorry, I don't know why I said that. It's none of my business."

When Jack speaks again, his voice is so quiet Rav can hardly hear him. "The police think he drove off that ledge on purpose. His family doesn't believe that, but I do. Looking back on it now, how unhappy he was . . ."

"I'm so sorry. I had no idea."

"No one does. Just the band and his family. They're the ones who asked the police to withhold the details. It's not some shady cover-up. They just want privacy."

"Of course." And then it hits him, the lyrics he's been mulling over for weeks. "That song in your notebook, 'Prism.' That's what it's about, isn't it?"

Another long silence.

Rav sits up a little. "That's none of my business, either. I can't seem to keep my questions to myself today. Bad detective habit."

"It's okay. I should run, though. We're just on a break, and I should get something to eat before we go back in."

"Jack, wait."

"It's okay, Rav, really, I just have to go." And before Rav can say anything else, he hangs up.

"*Fuck.*" Rav flings his phone into the sofa. What was he thinking? He knew what a sensitive subject it was.

Inevitably, he finds himself reaching for the little black notebook of song lyrics.

All those little moments I recall
Hang like pictures on my wall
The truth just out of frame
Gallery of my shame
And I can't go back
Can't take it back

A gilded mask, a siren song
I heard the lie, I felt the wrong
But still I didn't see
And now I can't get free
Can't take it back
Just wanna get it back

He aches for Jack, for the guilt he's obviously putting himself through. Raking his memory for the signs he missed, like a beaten-down detective going over the evidence again and again. *In the shattered glass I see you / In the shattered glass I see . . .*

His phone rings. He has to dig it out from between the sofa cushions.

"Hey," Jack says. "We're about to go back in, but I just wanted to make sure *you're* okay. I have a feeling you're beating yourself up right now, and you shouldn't. You caught me off guard, that's all. Those lyrics are . . ."

"Incredibly personal, and none of my business."

"I gave them to you, Rav. I wanted you to have them. I just felt a bit exposed there for a second."

"I'm sorry."

"It's not on you. I just forget what it's like to feel safe sometimes. It's okay, though, because you're reminding me."

Rav melts into a puddle on the sofa.

"Look, I really do have to go, but would you be interested in dropping by the studio tomorrow after work? I could show you around."

"I'd love that."

"Great. I'll text you the address. See you tomorrow."

"See you tomorrow," Rav echoes, and the flutter of nervousness that accompanies those words seals it. His heart—his stupid, reckless, masochistic heart—is ready to give this a second chance.

That doesn't make it a good idea. His heart hasn't exactly been making great decisions lately, and his head . . . He doesn't know where his head is at.

He supposes he'll find out tomorrow.

CHAPTER TWENTY-ONE

R av stands outside a nondescript building on the Lower East Side, checking his phone to make sure he hasn't made a mistake. He doesn't know what he expected a recording studio to look like, but it isn't this. There's no signage, nothing at all to indicate what's going on behind that seedy brick facade.

There's an intercom panel on the wall, a single button with a DIY embossed label. FARLIGHT STUDIOS. Definitely the right place. Rav presses the button and a bored voice says, "Yeah?"

"Er, Rav Trivedi? I'm here to see—"

The door buzzes, admitting him into a short corridor. There's an office on the left; a uniformed security guard hunches over a desk, watching the Yankees and eating a messy deli sandwich. Erika Strauss sits by the door, laptop balanced on her knees, while a sofa at the back is occupied by a slight woman scrolling absently on her phone. Rav spots a sidearm on her; one of the other CPOs, presumably.

He greets Erika with a nod. "I take it you're still on Jack's detail?"

"For now. Mo is hoping to be discharged later today." She looks him over. "You carrying?"

He touches his shoulder holster. "I've come straight from work. Is it an issue?"

"On the contrary. The more pros we have around Jack, the better. Just do me a favor and watch your back. Miller's a lot more dangerous than we realized." Rav eyes her laptop screen; it's covered in photos of Miller, most of them from security cameras. "For the MSG guys," she explains. "I'm making sure their facial

recognition software has him from as many angles as possible."
Glaring at her screen, she growls, "I'm gonna get this fucker if
it's the last thing I do."

"By which you mean turn him over to the proper authorities, of course." He's trying to make light, but it falls flat. Strauss
gives him a serious look.

"My number one priority is protecting my client. If all that
stands between Jack and a bullet is me, I won't hesitate to put
Miller down." She arches an eyebrow, as if to say, *What about
you, Detective?*

Does she know about the skate park? How he let Miller slip
through his fingers? Rav clears his throat uncomfortably. "Let's
hope it doesn't come to that."

Her eyes fall back to her screen. "You can head on in, he's
expecting you."

There's a door at the end of the corridor; walking through,
Rav finds himself in a room that looks like someone's flat. A kid
with elaborate sleeve tattoos perches on the edge of a sofa, playing *Halo* on a massive wall-mounted TV. The whole place smells
of weed.

"Hey, man," the kid says without taking his eyes off the screen.

"Rav." Jack walks in and embraces him—one of those bro
hugs with an extra bit of backslapping. Rav half expects to receive some sort of bewildering fist-bump hand-clasping gesture
and is considerably relieved when this does not occur. Jack is
wearing a knit hat, torn jeans, and a faded Red Hot Chili Peppers
T-shirt, Converse trainers that look like they've been salvaged
from a telephone wire. Until this moment, Rav has always believed there's no such thing as being overdressed, but he realizes
now that he was wrong. He can't recall ever feeling so out of
place, so very *uncool*. "Let me show you around," Jack says.

He leads Rav down a corridor with vintage guitars mounted
on the walls. There's a smaller break room on the right, and a
voice hails them. "Hey, Vale, aren't you gonna introduce us?"

Jack shoots Rav an apologetic glance and veers into the break room. The band's drummer, Sarah Creed, is perched on the kitchen counter. She's dyed her hair again—it's a different color in every photo Rav's seen of her—bright pink with white-blond tips, cut short at the back and long and raggedy at the front. Sarah was upstate during the Vanderford thing, so Rav interviewed her remotely. This is the first time they've met in person, and she gives him the full once-over. He's wearing his second most killer outfit, a slim-cut claret suit and crisp white shirt with the collar unbuttoned. Fresh haircut, fresh shave—the kind with a straight razor. His socks have raspberries on them. "Fancy, isn't he?" she says, as if he's not standing right there. "Not buying clothes like that on a cop's salary. Oh, wait, I forgot. Trust fund kid, right? Born with a silver spoon in his mouth."

"In my arse, actually," Rav returns mildly. "Had to have it surgically removed. Couldn't walk for days."

She grins. "Not sure they got all of it, there, Bridgerton."

Rav fully expected some hazing from Jack's bandmates. It's nothing he can't handle.

Jack, on the other hand, is already looking for a parachute. "Can I get you something to drink? There's beer in the fridge, or sparkling water . . ."

"He doesn't look like a beer guy to me," Sarah opines.

"Accurate," Rav says. "I'm not much into flavored water, either. The cherry tastes like cough syrup, and the lemon-lime is like drinking a gas station restroom."

Sarah's laugh is high-pitched and braying, but endearing nonetheless. "It's so true!"

Jack pulls a face and puts the can of lemon-lime he'd just grabbed back in the fridge. "Come on, I'll show you where we're set up."

"What's the hurry?" Sarah says. "We're just getting acquainted here. What's your zodiac, Bridgerton?"

"Cancer."

"Myers–Briggs?"

"ENTJ."

She looks him over again, assessing. "Slytherin or Ravenclaw?"

Rav rolls his eyes. "House Lannister."

"Oh my god, you *totally* are. Okay, lightning round. Connery or Craig?"

"Connery."

"Chunky or smooth?"

"Smooth."

"Stones or Beatles?"

"This is obviously a trap."

"Okay, we're done here." Jack grabs Rav's arm and drags him out of the break room. "Sorry. Sarah's great, but she likes to take the piss, as Ryan would say. It can rub people the wrong way, but you handled it well."

Rav tries not to look pleased. "Establishing rapport is my detective superpower."

"Yeah, that tracks. You had me eating out of your hand from day one."

"Is that so?"

Jack snorts softly. "Like you don't know. I was spilling my guts to you five seconds after we met. I felt safe with you even when you were investigating me for murder. If that's not a superpower, I don't know what is."

Their eyes meet, and for a second they just stand there on freeze-frame, the air between them thrumming with electricity.

Jack clears his throat and starts back down the hall. "Is that because you were a psych major?"

"I think it's mostly intuitive. I'm pretty good at reading people."

"Yeah? Well, I'll be interested to hear your take on *this* one." He ushers Rav into the control room, a cramped space dominated by a massive console of dials, knobs, switches, and sliders, plus a trio of computer screens. Behind this electronic behemoth sits an emo kid with black and purple hair, a lip piercing, and heavy purple eye makeup. He looks about eighteen. "Who do we have here?" he says, violet-tinted contacts trailing over Rav.

"This is the friend I was telling you about. Rav, this is Kid Kyle, our mixing engineer for this project. He's the wunderkind on everyone's lips right now. A certified genius."

"Certified and certifiable," Kid Kyle intones in a singsong voice, spinning his chair in a lazy three-sixty. There's something a little unsettling about him, like a dummy without the ventriloquist. "Ready to go?"

"We're re-recording the drum track and some of the vocals on 'Immortal,'" Jack explains.

"The drums are angry," Kid Kyle says, "but they should be sad. The beat of a broken heart, you know?"

Rav nods sagely.

"Kyle's incredibly intuitive," Jack says. "I can't wait to hear what it sounds like after he's worked his magic." His eyes are glued to Rav's, bright with enthusiasm.

"It's fascinating," Rav murmurs, and he means it, but what he's really caught up in at that moment is Jack's passion, and his obvious desire for Rav to share it.

The kid's violet-tinted eyes shift from Jack to Rav and back. "Oh, shit. This energy is *amazing*. Take it in there with you. Right now, while you're feeling it!"

Jack turns toward the booth—and without consciously deciding to, without thinking at all, Rav tugs him close and kisses him. Jack is surprised, but he kisses Rav back.

"*Yessss*," the kid says.

Which is a little weird, but Rav can go with it.

Jack heads into the booth and puts on a set of headphones. He paces around the mic for a second, eyes closed, and then he says, "Ready."

Kid Kyle punches a button, and "Immortal" comes on, filling the control room with sound. He offers Rav Molly, which Rav politely declines, and then Jack starts singing.

"*Do you remember that night / Sleeping under the stars / You asked me which of them was ours . . .*"

Rav knows this one well. It's not a love song, exactly; it's about legacy, about leaving your mark on the world through love and loss and all the things that make us human. But in that moment, watching Jack through the glass in the control room, it *feels* like a love song, and Rav can almost believe Jack is singing to him.

"*Deep underground / Where the bones make no sound / That's where it lies / Love never dies.*"

Kid Kyle drapes himself over the back of his chair in Molly-induced bliss. "Dude, I am so hard right now."

O-kay. Vibe over.

It's done in a single take, and when Jack walks out of the booth, he's high on it. He stirs restlessly on his feet as he listens to the playback, nodding excitedly. "Yeah, man, that's it. That's exactly it."

The kid is already engrossed in his work, headphones on, clicking away with his mouse. They leave him to it. "That was amazing," Rav says as they walk out of the control room.

"Thanks for helping me get into the right headspace."

"Sorry for jumping you like that. I got caught up in the moment."

"No, you're good. You read me right." His eyes meet Rav's, and there's a challenge in them. "How about now? What's your read?"

A surge of doubt spikes Rav's pulse, but he put his cards on the table the moment he kissed Jack in the control room. All that's left now is to play it out. "Right now . . ." He leans in close, lips grazing Jack's ear. "I'm getting that you want me to push you into the nearest broom closet and do terrible things to you."

Downy hairs rise on the back of Jack's neck. "You *are* good at this. Too bad there's no broom closets around here." He turns away, a teasing smile on his lips.

They find Sarah more or less where they left her, reclining with her Doc Martens propped on the table. "Your turn," Jack tells her.

She blows an enormous purple bubble and snaps it, and for a

second the whole room smells like fake grape. "That was quick."
Her glance slides to Rav, and she smirks. "Must've been inspired."

"Kyle is a genius," Jack says.

"Kyle is weird as fuck."

Jack shrugs. "Not mutually exclusive."

Sarah blows another bubble and snaps it. "Right," she says,
swinging her boots off the table. "Sad drums coming up."

As soon as she's gone, Jack backs Rav into the counter, and
they spend the next ten minutes making out to the muffled
pounding of drums and the lingering smell of weed and grape
bubble gum. At some point, the *Halo* kid comes in, grabs a beer,
and leaves. Rav and Jack don't miss a beat. They only come apart
when Jack's wandering hand accidentally bumps Rav's gun.
"Sorry!" He snatches it back. "Kind of feels like I just brushed
your dick," he says with an awkward smile.

"I would be fine with that," Rav murmurs, gaze drifting over
Jack's features. He feels lightheaded, overwhelmed by the beautiful improbability of them finding their way back here. He's
never wanted to get anyone naked so badly in his life. "Can I
steal you away?"

Jack gives a frustrated little growl. "I wish. But we've got a few
hours of work left, and I need to get some sleep tonight. We've
got sound check at one, and then the show, and somewhere in
between I need to find time to give an interview."

Rav sighs. "The universe keeps cock-blocking us."

"Do you think so?" Jack's eyes are earnest. "I feel like the
waves keep tossing us back into each other. Like the universe
won't take *no* for an answer."

God, what do you even say to that? Rav kisses him, hard. It
is a wave, and he's the adrenaline junkie trying to surf it, even
though he knows it's only going to spike him headfirst into the
beach. So fine, fuck it, bring it on. If there was ever a shore worth
breaking yourself on, this is it.

"You're coming to the show tomorrow, right?" Jack asks.
"Come find me backstage, after."

"I will."

The tattooed kid is still playing *Halo* when Rav passes him on the way out. "Later, man," he says without looking up.

Rav makes a peace sign and drifts out into the night with a big, dumb smile on his face.

CHAPTER TWENTY-TWO

In the news tonight, police are asking anyone with information on the shooting outside the Palace Hotel on Monday to contact the NYPD tipline. The suspect in the incident, Joseph Miller, remains at large and is considered—"

Rav's phone buzzes. It's Will. At 7 P.M. on a Friday night. This can't be good.

"How far are you from work?" Shepard asks.

"Not too far. Why?"

"We just got a walk-in. Tyler Higgs."

"Doesn't ring a bell."

"Right, you were on leave. You remember that apartment the FBI raided, where they found Greg Watson? There were two of them living there, Watson and a guy named Tyler Higgs. The feds have been looking for him ever since the raid."

"So he's turning himself in?"

"All I know is he's asking for you personally."

"Me? How does he even know my . . . ?" Right, the skate park memes.

"If you wanna talk to him, you'd better hustle. Won't be long before the feds show up to claim him."

"I'll be there in twenty minutes."

Howard and Will are waiting for him outside the interview room. "I'll be observing," the lieutenant informs him, "since Higgs is a person of interest in a federal case." *And because I don't trust you not to let your personal issues interfere with this interview.* She doesn't say it, but she doesn't have to; Rav knows he's on unofficial probation. "Stay focused in there, both of you."

The man seated at the table is about thirty, with darting blue eyes and a bushy blond beard. Rav has seen that beard before, if only from a distance. "I hear you've been asking for me."

Higgs doesn't respond. He slouches in his chair, knee bobbing, trying to telegraph cool indifference and doing a shit job.

"I remember you from the skate park," Rav goes on. "You were with Joe Miller and Greg Watson. The three of you were ejected for assaulting a pair of NGO workers."

"Assaulting." Higgs snorts. "I barely touched the guy."

Where is Joe Miller?

The question is practically burning a hole in Rav's tongue, but he needs to be patient. If he tries to interrogate this guy, he'll shut down; better to let Higgs think he's in the driver's seat. "You came here to tell me something. I'm listening."

Higgs glances at the door, as if he's having second thoughts.

"How about I get you started? Your mate Joe Miller is in some pretty deep shit. You're facing charges of your own, as an accessory. But you didn't come here to cut a deal. You would have gone straight to the FBI with that. You're here because you know something, or think you do, that might help him out. You're worried the feds won't listen, but I'm friends with Jack Vale, at least according to social media, so maybe whatever you tell me will make its way back to him. How am I doing, Tyler?"

Higgs shakes his head. "Cops. Always think you know everything, but you don't."

"What don't I know?"

"For starters, Joe Miller may be a *fucking idiot*." He sighs. "But he's no killer."

"He didn't try to kill Jack Vale?"

"Never. No way."

"We have security footage of him forcing his way backstage at the Concord."

"Yeah, but he was just trying to get the word out about

Tommy. The gun—that was for protection. A lot of people don't wanna hear the truth. Joe's had death threats, you know."

The irony is thick, but Rav stays on script. "And the shooting at the Palace Hotel?"

"I don't know nothing about that. But if Joe shot that guy, it's 'cause he's not himself."

"How do you mean?"

"Joe may not be the brightest bulb, but he's harmless. He talks a lot of shit online, but who doesn't? It never meant nothing."

"Until he threatened a congressman in Georgia," Will puts in.

"See, that's what I'm talking about," Higgs snaps. "You think you *know* things, but you don't. Those threats didn't come from Joe. His account was hacked."

"Hacked." Will nods. "Okay."

If Higgs notices the sarcasm, he ignores it. "Wasn't the first time, neither. Every time Joe posts something they don't like, his account gets hacked and they do something to make him look bad."

"Who is *they?*" Rav asks.

"I dunno, man, the government?"

Rav's heart sinks. *This is a waste of time.*

"Yeah, I see that look on your face," Higgs says with a scowl. "That's why people like me don't go to the cops."

"I'm just a bit confused. Whatever happened back in Georgia, there's no disputing what he's done here. There are multiple eyewitness accounts, not to mention security footage from several locations."

"Look, the Concord thing . . . Joe fucked up there, no question. But it's not like they're saying in the papers."

"Why don't you tell us how it is?"

Higgs leans forward, animated now. *This* is why he came: to set the record straight, at least in his own mind. "So he goes down there, right, and he's got this big sign, and he's hoping people will video him and take pictures and stuff, so it'll go viral.

The gun was just for protection. But some kid sees it and freaks, and suddenly everybody's losing their minds, and the whole thing goes to shit. Now he's wanted by the cops, so he comes to Greg 'n me, asking if he can lie low at our place."

"This is Greg Watson, your deceased roommate," Rav says for the benefit of the recording.

"Right. Then, couple weeks later, he finds out Jack Vale is doing this charity thing, and he figures this is his chance to get close to Jack and say his piece. Like, maybe if he explains about the Concord, how it all got out of hand and he wasn't there to hurt nobody, Jack will get the charges dropped." Rav's eyebrows jump at that, and Higgs laughs darkly. "I know, man, trust me. Greg 'n me told him it was nuts. But he says he's going, and he's still our boy, so like idiots, we go with him. We try to get those smug college pricks organizing the thing to get us five minutes with Jack, but they won't. Things get a little heated, so we bounce—only when we turn around, Joe's gone. We figured the cops must've got him. Then he turns up back at our place saying he stabbed some guy." Higgs throws up his hands. "On top of which, now they're saying he murdered this record executive. That's when he *really* starts losing it. Spending 24/7 online, posting on his little forums about how he's being set up. Which, don't get me wrong, he definitely is. He never even met that Vanderford guy."

Rav studies him closely. "What if I told you the FBI has photos of Miller and Vanderford together?"

"I'd tell you that shit's *fake*. Just like those threats in Georgia."

Will leans back in his chair until it creaks. He thinks this is bullshit.

Higgs jabs a tobacco-stained finger on the table. "If you wanna know who killed that record executive, you should be looking at Jack's bodyguard. Did you know he used to be CIA?"

"I'm aware of that, yes. How did you come to know about it?"

"From those online forums Joe is always on. There's this user, goes by the name of Overwatch. He's the one who told Joe about the bodyguard being CIA. He said Vale and Vanderford were beefing, and Vale got his bodyguard to take care of it. Just like he took care of Tommy, so he could be lead singer."

Rav forces himself to take a breath. God, he hopes Jack never hears that rumor. "Sounds like a conspiracy theory to me," he says coolly.

"If you say so, man. Point is, Joe believes it. That's why he's so scared. He legit thinks the CIA is out to get him. He even left the apartment 'cause he didn't want Greg 'n me to get caught in the cross fire. Look how that turned out." His voice frays, a shimmer coming into his eyes. "You tell me, if this is all some conspiracy theory, how come Greg is dead? They're saying Joe did it, but that's bullshit. He's not a murderer."

"He shot Vale's bodyguard."

"Like I said, I don't know nothing about that. But if he did, it was self-defense, at least in *his* mind. This Overwatch guy is in his head. He's just scared, man. Scared to death and flailing."

There's a knock at the door. The FBI must be here. Rav is out of time. "Do you know where Miller is now?"

Higgs shakes his head. "If I did, I'd tell you. 'Cause at this rate, he's gonna get himself killed."

A uniformed officer comes in to collect the witness, and then he's gone, scooped up by Thing One and Thing Two, and all Rav is left with is a bizarre tale about a serial screwup who got himself in way over his head and ended up shooting someone.

Howard finds her detectives debriefing by the coffee machine. "You did well in there, Trivedi. I wasn't sure you could keep your personal issues out of it, but you handled it like a pro." She pours herself a cup of stale coffee. "So, what do you make of it?"

"Assuming any of it's true, it puts Miller's actions in a different light."

"Does it?" Will makes a face. "Sounded like a bunch of half-assed excuses to me. The guy on the internet made me do it? Come on."

Howard grunts into her coffee. "At a minimum, it's pretty clear Joseph Miller craves attention and makes bad decisions, which means he won't be too hard to catch. He's been lucky so far, but luck runs out eventually."

"I hope you're right," Rav says.

"Whether I am or not, Miller isn't your case. You need to hear me on that, Detective." She eyes him pointedly. "I let you talk to Tyler Higgs because he asked for you personally. What you do with that information on your own time is your business, but in here, you work for the NYPD, and Joe Miller is not our fish to land. Copy?"

"But I can keep digging on my personal time?"

"Provided you don't cross the line and interfere with a federal investigation. You do know where that line is, don't you?"

He does.

More or less.

He grabs a cab back to the city, mind whirring. Will isn't wrong: on the face of it, most of what Higgs said sounds like bullshit. And yet it tracks with what Mo told him the other day. *We know who you are*, Miller supposedly shouted before he pulled the trigger. *We know what you did.* The *we* in question must be Miller and his fellow conspiracy theorists. Then there's Higgs's insistence that Miller wasn't trying to kill Jack. *Never. No way.* So maybe Mo was the target after all. But what has any of that got to do with Dick Vanderford?

Rav can't shake the feeling that all the pieces are right in front of him, if he can just figure out how they fit together.

He fishes out his phone and calls Mo. The bodyguard picks up right away; Rav hears traffic noise in the background. "Does that mean you've been discharged from hospital?"

"On my way to the studio now. Heard you dropped by."

Rav's stomach does a pleasant little flip at the memory. It already seems like ages ago. "Listen, does the username Overwatch mean anything to you?"

The bodyguard grunts. "Been trawling the online forums, Detective?"

"That, and I've just had an interesting conversation with a witness. I take it the name rings a bell?"

"You could say that. Listen, I can't really talk right now, but can we meet on Sunday?"

"Sure, but can it wait that long?"

"It'll have to. I'm up to my eyeballs with security arrangements for the show."

"I thought you said it was low risk?"

"Doesn't mean I'm letting my guard down. I plan to have all the bases covered and then some."

"That makes me feel a little better, at least."

"Don't worry, we got this. You're coming to the show, right? You ever seen the Nicks before?"

"I have not."

"Well, then," Mo says, "you're in for a treat."

CHAPTER TWENTY-THREE

A na arrives at Rav's flat half an hour early, bouncing with excitement. "Loving the smoky eye," Rav says, indicating her makeup with a swirl of his finger. "The shirt is a surprise."

It's merch from the Nicks' first tour, a black sleeveless number with the logo from *Alien Nation* printed in gold on the front. Rav can't recall ever having seen Ana in a T-shirt, let alone a concert tee.

"Do you have any idea how rare this is?" She hugs herself. "Trust me, people are going to be *so jealous* of this shirt. Important people. VIPs!" She seizes Rav's shoulders, grinning from ear to ear. "We're *VIPs*! At a *Nicks* concert!"

He's never seen her this worked up. "Who are you and what have you done with Ana Rodriguez?"

She swats his arm. "So I'm a little excited. I've seen every Nicks tour that's come through town, but this? VIP tickets?"

"Ah, so you *owe* me."

"Please. You're so far in the hole you'll never climb out. Now pour me a drink."

They walk to the show. Ana's already got her VIP and backstage passes around her neck, big glossy cards dangling from a bright yellow lanyard. Rav asks her if she's going to keep it for always, and she flips him off.

The mood outside the venue is jubilant. Fans converge on Madison Square Garden from every direction, pouring out of Penn Station and piling out of cabs, clogging sidewalks and stairs, all smiles and selfies and excited chatter. A few pockets of bright light mark the TV cameras in the crowd. Tonight's event was a big story even before the shooting, billed as the long-delayed encore to the Concord show. Rav wonders what's going through Jack's mind backstage—whether he's as jubilant as the fans, or in a darker place. Either way, Rav suspects this show will be incredibly emotional for him, and for the rest of the band, too.

He and Ana pass through a special VIP entrance, where they're scanned and searched and scanned again. The heightened security is comforting. He'd feel even better if he had his service weapon, but it would have been a huge hassle to get authorization, and besides, he's no bodyguard. Better to leave the close protection to the professionals.

There's a little hospitality bar in the VIP area, and Ana makes straight for it. "G and T?"

"Perfect."

Rav scans the small crowd of VIPs. He recognizes a couple of television stars, along with an ancient-looking creature he's fairly sure is a famous musician from eons past. The guy is wearing leather trousers and blue-tinted glasses, and he's so desiccated he looks like he could blow away in a stiff wind. "Hey, is that Richard Rock?" a girl murmurs conspiratorially to Rav. "I thought he was dead."

"I'm not entirely sure he isn't."

"Right?" She snort-giggles before hurrying over to get a selfie.

Ana returns with their drinks, plus an autograph on a cocktail napkin. Rav opens his mouth to tease her about it—and then he spots *Robert fucking Pattinson* across the room. "Oh my god," he hisses, clamping his hand around Ana's elbow.

She looks momentarily surprised, and then she grins. "Oh, right. You were a *Twilight* kid, weren't you? Should we ask for a selfie?"

"No. Yes. Oh god, he's looking this way. *Don't look.*"

She's loving this. "Who are you and what have you done with Rav Trivedi? Wait, does Jack know you're a Robert Pattinson stan? Is he gonna be jealous?"

"I beg you to stop talking immediately."

"Are you sure you don't want me to—" The rest is cut off as Rav yanks her toward the tunnel leading to the arena floor.

An usher directs them to a cordoned-off area near the sound-board. There's a fair bit of distance between them and the stage, and Rav is a little disappointed until a helpful bystander explains that the sound is always best near the mixing desk.

"Holy crap," Ana whispers as the guy walks away. "Do you know who that was?"

"Someone terribly famous?"

"Timothée Chalamet! He's only been in *everything* for the past few years. Man, you're hopeless!"

Rav scans the arena, turning full circle to take it all in. It feels strangely small down here, surrounded by the stands. Small and exposed, and he can't help feeling a flutter of anxiety, but he knows it's irrational. Whatever else he may be, Joe Miller is no master criminal. His photos have been fed into MSG's facial recognition system, and every cop in town—not to mention every Nicks fan—is on the lookout. He wouldn't even make it through the doors.

The stadium is only half-full when the warm-up act goes on, an indie rock group Rav has of course never heard of, but who Ana assures him is going to be huge any day now. The crowd gives them a warm send-off when their set is over, but it's not until the house lights go down twenty minutes later that the real noise begins, a swell of cheers that lasts for several minutes before fading into hushed anticipation. A few stray whistles sound, and then a recording fades in, a slow, pulsing hum, ambient music rising and falling softly like a distant surf. Phones wink on in the darkness, thousands of pinpricks of blue-white light. It's eerily beautiful; Rav has the strange impression of floating in water, gazing up at the stars. And then, in a *whoosh* of sound, the bass comes in, and the kick drum. The crowd claps along as music builds in the darkness, a ringing guitar folding in—until the beat drops and the stage lights flare, golden and blinding.

The place goes *apeshit*.

The band appears in silhouette against the glare, and there's Jack, striding up to the mic, guitar slung low at his hips as he belts out the first notes of "Sound Off."

The next ninety minutes are surreal.

There are twenty thousand people in that building, and each and every one of them is riveted on Jack. They scream for him. Cry for him. Sing along with him. They surge toward the stage like iron filings drawn by a magnet every time he comes near, reaching, straining, calling his name. He's like a priest up there, or a god. It's a religious experience for these people—and for Jack, too. Rav sees it on his face, the way he closes his eyes and tips his head back when twenty thousand voices sing his words back to him. There's no other word for it but *ecstasy*, and Rav can't begin to imagine what it feels like. He can't even sort out what *he's* feeling, the staggering dissonance of trying to reconcile this glowing deity with the flesh-and-blood person he knows. A teasing lover in a kitchenette. A shaken friend in a hospital waiting room. Faded jeans and bare feet, white knuckles on a railing, a whispered *fuck* in the heartbeat before he comes.

"I can't believe that's your *boyfriend*!" Ana screams in his ear at one point.

He's not my boyfriend, Rav starts to say, but it feels stupid and meaningless. She's not listening anyway, too busy singing along with "New World Order"—her and everyone else in the building.

No I / I won't cry / Not for a lie / That was never mine
And I / I won't die / Not for a lie / That was never mine

Jack talks to the crowd now and then. Engages in a bit of banter with his bandmates. It's not until the first encore, though, that he mentions the elephant in the room, the reason this show is such a big media story. The crowd senses it coming, quieting down instinctively as he steps up to the mic after the last notes of "Green Screen" fade away. "We want to thank you all for coming. It's been a hard road these past few weeks. Out there."

He points toward the exits. "In here." He taps his chest. "But we're still standing."

For the next several minutes he speaks—eloquently, like the poet he is—about the fans coming together after the Concord show. About their love and support after the shooting, and how much it meant to him. He talks about Mo—"I know you're watching backstage right now, man, and we love you"—eliciting a full minute of cheers for the bodyguard.

He pauses, gaze on the floor. He's sweating under the hot lights, and Rav is absolutely not fantasizing about tasting the salt on his lips as he trails kisses down that tattooed torso, because that would be inappropriate in this solemn moment, like making out at a movie about D-Day, which he has certainly never done.

"Hate has its moments in the spotlight," Jack says. "But all of us standing here tonight are proof that it never wins. Whatever they break, we rebuild. Whatever they take, we take back." He raises a hand in signal to the band. "Because we're stronger than hate. Stronger than fear. We live. We love. We rise."

Sarah cracks her drumsticks and they kick into "Rise," and it's bedlam. The crowd is heaving, leaping up and down with their hands in the air; Ana is doing it, and Robert Pattinson and Timothy whatshisname, and Rav manages to hold out for a moment or two until the whole thing breaks over him like a wave, and whatever happens after that will be strenuously denied at the office on Monday.

The vibe backstage is almost as electric as it was out there, celebs and other VIPs milling about, booze and music and a few controlled substances Rav and Ana pretend not to notice as they grab drinks of their own. Ryan Nash is first to emerge from the dressing rooms, in torn jeans and a leather jacket, every inch the rock star. His bodyguard, meanwhile, looks like she's on the red carpet, clad in a sleek ivory pantsuit so formfitting Rav wonders where she could possibly stash her sidearm. Then again, maybe she doesn't need one: those heels could definitely take a man out, and that chunky Cartier ring is basically a brass knuckle.

"Detective," says a familiar voice, and Rav turns to find Charlie Banks, beer in one hand, phone in the other, chest hair billowing proudly between the lapels of his printed silk shirt. He *clinks* the neck of his beer bottle against Rav's champagne glass. "Hell of a show, wasn't it? It's been a long time since I've seen a band vibe with a crowd like that. Want me to show you to the dressing rooms?"

Rav does, very badly. He glances at Ana. She makes a scooting gesture, so Rav follows the manager to the dressing rooms. Mo stands at Jack's door, looking very Dwayne Johnson in a pale blue suit with matching arm sling. He knocks and sticks his head in, and then he tells Rav to go on in.

Jack is fresh out of the shower, hair wet and skin flushed, whether from hot water or the rush of the show, Rav can't tell. He suspects the latter, given the glassy look in Jack's eye. The room is small, and Jack prowls it like a restless animal. He doesn't say anything at first, and Rav wonders if he should be here. If maybe Jack needs a few more minutes to come down from this high, to shape-shift from supernatural being to ordinary man in faded jeans. He starts to ask whether he should come back—and then Jack crosses the room and kisses him. It's fierce and needy and everything Rav wants from him, and he gives it right back, drawing Jack's body against his. Then he does what he's been dying to do all night, sinking to his knees and ripping open the buttons of Jack's jeans. He doesn't care if he looks like a supplicant kneeling before a god. In fact, he kind of gets off on it—which is a little weird and something he'll maybe unpack later when he's capable of higher thought, but just now he commits himself wholly to the singular goal of getting Jack to breathe that beautiful little *fuck* he's been replaying in his head all night.

He gets something even better: his own name, spoken in a shivering whisper as Jack grips his shoulder. And when he kisses Rav after, there's a fierceness to it that makes Rav so hard it hurts. Jack's already tugging at his fly, backing him onto the tiny sofa, and he returns the favor with that same animal enthusiasm.

They slump there for a second, recovering. "Thanks," Jack manages eventually. "I needed that."

"My pleasure," Rav says, and *damn* does he mean it. Is dressing room sex always this intense? Further investigation is required. For science.

"Uh-oh." Jack snorts out a laugh. The knees of Rav's navy-blue trousers are smudged with dust from the floor. Jack starts brushing at it, both of them snickering like naughty schoolboys, and then they kiss for a bit. Jack asks if he liked the show, and Rav tells him, quite sincerely, that it was the most amazing thing he's ever seen. Then they tidy themselves up and head out to join the party.

They don't even make it to the bar before the fawning starts. Everyone wants a piece of Jack. Rav, meanwhile, might as well be invisible. No one is rude, exactly; they just forget he exists within moments of meeting him. Jack doesn't go out of his way to remind them, either. He's careful not to stand too close, and when he introduces Rav, it's always in neutral terms—*my friend*, or *my buddy*. Rav gets it, he really does, but it grows tiresome rather quickly. He peels off after a while, and he's fairly sure Jack doesn't even notice.

Ana finds him at the bar. "Get some?" she asks with a cheeky grin.

"Mind your own business. And yes."

She gives a sorority-girl squeal and orders two beers. "I think I might be on the right track myself," she says mysteriously before abandoning him to sidle up next to a cute platinum-haired girl with a crooked smile.

Rav lingers by the bar, taking it all in. His Instagram feed is a surreal echo of things he just witnessed in real life: Jack posing with Richard Rock, #Legends. Jack and Claudia with a couple of basketball stars, #Nicks&Knicks. It's a little overwhelming. These people are all just so achingly *cool*, with their tattoos and blue hair and ironic penny loafers, and here's Rav in Boss chinos and a striped button-down. (With trainers, but still.)

He's just about to order another drink when Jack turns up beside him. "There you are. You just vanished." His gaze falls to Rav's mouth, and he sighs. "It's torture."

"What?"

"You. Standing there, in the flesh for once, and I can't even touch you."

Rav smiles awkwardly. "You must be used to that. Having to be discreet in public."

"Used to it, yeah. And tired of it." He leans against the bar and looks out over the party. "To be honest, I don't much care what the internet says about me, but I wouldn't do that to you. The last thing you want is to be all over Instagram again."

"Ah, so you're keeping your hands off me for *my* sake." He's teasing, but Jack's expression is earnest.

"Mostly, yeah. There's no avoiding the spotlight for me, but you'd be crazy to put yourself through that if you didn't have to. Especially with Miller—"

"No." Rav gives his hand a discreet squeeze. "We are not talking about him tonight. We are drinking champagne and basking in the adoration of these glamorous people. And then . . ." He lowers his voice. "And then you're taking me home, and when I'm done with you, you won't remember your own name." He hits Jack with his best *come-hither* look—which, strictly speaking, is less *come-hither* than *I'm going to fuck you senseless*—and it's pretty safe to say Jack is not thinking about Joe Miller anymore. His pupils dilate, and he glances away with pink in his cheeks.

"That sounds . . . yeah." Jack's throat bobs through a hard swallow. Rav wants to nibble on it. "Give me an hour, and then we can, uh . . ." He pauses awkwardly while the bartender leans in to top up Rav's champagne. "We can do that thing you mentioned."

"I'll be here," Rav says airily, and takes a sip of his bubbles.

CHAPTER TWENTY-FOUR

N ot gonna lie, man," says a jacked twentysomething with a lantern jaw, "I straight-up cried in the middle of 'Soar.'"

Jack receives the compliment as graciously as he received the one before, and the one before that. He's been having versions of this conversation all night, and it must be exhausting, but he doesn't let on. He's smiling, seemingly enjoying himself. The music might be over, but for Jack, the show goes on. He poses for yet another selfie and accepts a pound hug from Mr. Universe.

"Nice guy," he remarks as he rejoins Rav and Ana at the bar.

"He looks familiar," Rav muses. "Did he play Superman once?"

Jack's eyebrows go up. "You don't recognize the quarterback of your hometown football team?"

Ana laughs. And laughs.

"I have no interest in what you Americans consider football," Rav says in his poshest Brit.

"So you're a soccer fan, then?"

Ana laughs harder.

"Anyway," Jack says, "what's this *you Americans* stuff? You're an American citizen, aren't you?"

"He's American when it suits him," Ana says, "and British when it doesn't."

"Unfair. I'm torn between two worlds. It's tragic, really."

"You should cut him off." Ana nods at the glass of champagne in Rav's hand. "One more ounce of liquid courage and he's gonna go full fanboy on Robert Pattinson over there."

"Oh yeah?" Jack glances over at Robert, who's chatting with Timothy whatshisname. "Do you want to meet him?"

Of course he does, but being introduced to your fourteen-year-old crush by your current crush would probably cause some sort of rupture in the space-time continuum and he doesn't need that on his conscience. "Actually, if you're almost done here . . ."

Jack gets the hint, signaling discreetly to his bodyguards. He's got two tonight: Mo and the new guy, Brad, who's been on roving backup while Mo is in recovery.

They radio for the car to come down to the loading area. Jack makes his farewells while Rav slips away—it's better if they're not seen leaving together—and when he shows up in the loading area five minutes later, he's got Ryan and Claudia in tow. "I hate to ask," Jack is saying. "I just don't want to let them down, you know?"

Claudia greets Rav with an awkward smile, and then she says, "You're not letting them down. They'll understand."

Nash, for his part, barely flicks Rav a glance. "She's right," he tells Jack. "They'll be disappointed to get the B list, but they'll understand. We'll head out in fifteen."

"I appreciate it. I know it's not your favorite thing."

"I got you, mate. Always." Nash claps his shoulder, and he and Claudia head back to the party.

"What was all that about?" Rav asks when they're alone again.

"Autographs. I usually sign some after a show, but Mo doesn't want me doing that tonight, for obvious reasons."

A sleek black car with tinted windows eases its way down the ramp. "You two crazy kids behave now," Mo says as he pops the door.

"You're not coming?" Jack asks.

"We're going in convoy. Me 'n Brad will be right behind you. That leaves a little more room for you two. Besides, something tells me the detective here is about to give new meaning to the words *close protection*."

Rav groans. "Why am I not surprised you're into dad jokes?"

"He's gonna show you why they call it a *body man*. Personal protection is about to get *really* personal . . ."

They close the car door before it gets any worse.

They make out in the back seat on the way to the hotel. And in the underground parking while they wait for Brad to do a sweep. And in the elevator on the way up to the room. (No cameras.) Mo is waiting for them in the hallway outside Jack's room, and Rav has just enough presence of mind to remind him about their meeting tomorrow.

"Sure," Mo says. "What time do you want to—"

Jack drags Rav inside and closes the door, and then they *really* start going at it. Rav's shirt is on the floor in seconds, and his belt, and Jack's shirt, a trail of clothing leading from the door to the bedroom. "Do you have a condom?" Jack whispers against Rav's mouth.

"I have everything we need," he says, emptying his pockets onto the nightstand. Which leaves just one question. "Top or bottom?"

"I'm vers."

"Me, too."

Jack looks him in the eye. "Your call. I just want to hear you say it."

Rav gives him a scorching once-over, letting him see how much he wants this. Then he puts his lips to Jack's ear. "I want to fuck you."

Jack unzips him. "Then fuck me."

Rav backs him bodily toward the bed, fingers hooked over the tab of Jack's jeans, as if he's going to tear them open. He pops a couple of buttons, but then he stops, taking Jack's face in both hands and kissing him deeply. He's fantasized about this for so long that part of him wants to go straight for the prize, to fuck Jack hard and fast, catch his breath, and then do it again, *properly*. But there will be no shortcuts tonight. He promised to blow Jack's mind, and he intends to deliver.

He slows the kiss, sliding his hands down Jack's bare shoulders, the small of his back, the curve of his arse. He pulls Jack's hips flush against his and grinds against him—just a little, mind, enough to tease but no more. Jack pushes back, seeking friction, tugging down on Rav's boxer briefs, so Rav backs off slightly.

"Fuck," Jack whispers. "So it's like that, is it?"

"I'm afraid so." He grabs the back of Jack's thigh, hitches his leg, and rides him down onto the bed.

He's biting Jack's neck, popping another button on his jeans; his fingertips tease just below the waistband, following the trail of silky hair below the navel. Those inked abs are covered in goose bumps, a tactile glory just begging to be explored, and Rav takes his time about it, kissing, nipping, hand diving the rest of the way down and taking Jack in a firm grip. Jack is losing his mind, both hands shoved in his hair, and by the time Rav finally pulls off his jeans, he's so worked up he tries to climb on top and take the lead. That's not going to happen. Rav flips him easily and pins him beneath his body, which drives Jack even more crazy.

He can't feel too smug about it, though: the look on Jack's face, raw and wanting, sets him on fire. He can't restrain himself any longer; he fumbles for the nightstand while Jack yanks off his trousers, and then he hikes Jack's leg over his hip and drags him close.

Even now, he'd like to take it slow, but there's no chance of that. Their bodies are done being patient. It doesn't help that the view beneath him is basically identical to the video for "Need": Jack's head tipped back, eyes closed, stirring with the rhythm of the tide. Only this is in vibrant color, a fantasy come to life, and it's fucking *beyond*. Jack's mouth parts, dark brows knitting fiercely, and when he turns his face away, arching just like he does at the climax of the song, Rav reaches a climax of his own.

He rides it out slowly, and then he collapses in a quivering heap beside Jack. "I've wanted to do that since I first laid eyes on you," he murmurs once he's caught his breath. "I shouldn't admit that, but . . ."

"I know the feeling."

"I'm guessing there was slightly less guilt on your side."

Jack makes a vague humming sound, as if he's not so sure about that. "It definitely didn't feel like my finest moment. A guy's been murdered, and here I am fantasizing about the detective looking into it. Like, am I seriously thinking about this right now? Am I picturing myself in this guy's handcuffs, when he might *actually* put me in handcuffs? It was . . . confusing."

"You pictured yourself in cuffs?"

Jack snorts softly, pushing damp curls off his forehead. "You don't even know. When you walked through my door looking like something out of *GQ*, oozing confidence and wit and the whole package . . ."

Rav props himself on his elbow. "Do continue."

"I thought the universe was messing with me. 'Hey, Jack, here's that gorgeous guy you ordered. Except you can't touch him. Or even really talk to him. Totally off-limits, unless you want to end up in jail. But be sure to check out his ass on the way out. It's our finest work to date.'"

Rav sighs and flops onto his back. "And here I thought this night couldn't get any better."

Jack laughs. "As though your ego needs stroking."

"Says the man who spent the entire evening being fawned over."

"Fair." He turns his head on the pillow and meets Rav's eye. "You should know, though, it wasn't just that."

"My arse?"

He rolls his eyes. "Shut up for a second? I'm trying to tell you something."

"Yes. Sorry."

"You weren't what I expected. You were respectful and compassionate, even when you thought I might be a killer. That blew me away. It still does."

Rav feels his skin warming. "For what it's worth, you weren't what I expected either. You have every reason to be an egocentric, entitled arsehole, and instead you're . . ." *Thoughtful. Kind. Complicated.*

Fucking amazing.

Jack smiles. "Swim?"

"You read my mind."

They shower and head for the pool, both of them wrapped in those luxurious terry cloth bathrobes one finds in the right kind of hotel. Jack leaves the terrace lights off in deference to Rav's paranoia about zoom lenses. There's enough light coming off the pool, and anyway, they can see the city lights better this way. They shuck their robes and glide into the water, admiring each other in the aquamarine glow.

"It's beautiful out here," Rav says.

"It's perfect. You're perfect." Jack's gaze drips like honey down the length of Rav's body. "I've got a feeling I'll be coming back to this memory a lot over the next few weeks."

Rav sighs. He'd almost managed to forget that the band will be leaving soon, heading out for the European leg of their tour. "When will you be back through?"

"Nothing planned, but I'll think of something, I promise."

"You'd better. I'd hate to have to confiscate your passport."

"I love it when you talk dirty, baby." He flashes a mischievous grin that has Rav's dick twitching even before their mouths meet. He tastes of chlorine and salt and pure dopamine, and Rav catches himself thinking he could die right now and be happy.

Later, they stand at the rail in their fluffy towel robes, gazing across the river at the twinkling lights of Manhattan. It's quiet out there at this hour. Jack is quiet, too, and Rav strokes the back of his neck. "Where have you gone?"

"I was just thinking about tonight, how relieved I am it went well. That show had a lot of baggage attached to it, but I didn't have any anxiety at all. Butterflies, of course, but the good kind. I think . . ." He looks at Rav, his face half obscured in shadow. "Would it freak you out if I said I think it has something to do with you?"

"Me?"

"This is the first time in forever that I've had a pocket of normal in my life. A little air bubble where I can just . . . *breathe*. Decompress, re-center. That's clutch." There must be something in Rav's expression, because Jack smiles and says, "Really, don't freak out. I'm not trying to overanalyze or pretend like all my problems are solved. I'm just saying I feel comfortable around you, and that's not something I get a lot of these days."

"Not even around your friends?"

"Friends." He looks out over the city lights. "Most of my real-life friends disappeared after *Alien Nation* came out. Stopped reaching out, stopped replying to my texts. It was the same for the rest of the band. We have each other, but that comes with its own stress. I feel responsible for them. Like I have to watch out for them. Our lives . . . as privileged as they are, they're also really intense. We've talked about it as a band, promised to speak up if we felt like we were starting to drown, but . . ."

Rav knows he's thinking about Tommy. About the signs he missed, or thinks he did. "That's a lot to put on yourself."

"It's worse here in New York. That's why we moved to LA. So I wouldn't have to see Tommy's ghost every time I turn around."

Rav strokes his neck again. "Whatever happened that night, it wasn't your fault."

"Objectively, I know that, but . . ." He sighs. "It doesn't help that we didn't leave things on the best foot. The night he died . . . it was during that period I told you about, where we had all this drama in the band. Tommy felt like we were going in the wrong direction. He wanted to make some drastic changes. He was butting heads with everyone, just really on a tear that night. We were at this party upstate, and he left in a huff, and . . ." He pauses. "Shit, I'm sorry. This is not a conversation I meant to have. We were having such a good time, and—"

Rav cradles his jaw and looks him right in the eye. "Never apologize. I'm your hotline, remember?"

"You're a fucking *lifeline*," Jack whispers, and kisses him.

For a moment it's all very tender and sweet—and then a hand finds its way inside Rav's bathrobe, checking to see if he's ready for an encore.

He is.

They make their way to the bedroom, untying each other as they go. It's a remix, this time with Jack on lead, and it's even better than the original.

"That's my fourth shower today," Jack remarks as he flops onto the bed.

"I hope you moisturized liberally." Rav picks up his phone to check the time.

"You're welcome to stay."

Rav meets his eye, trying to decide if he's just being polite. "It's easy enough to get a car."

"Stay. We'll sleep late and have fancy room service breakfast."

"Well, if there's breakfast involved . . ."

They shuffle under the blankets. Rav stares at the ceiling. Should he reach for Jack? Put an arm around him?

"If you're wondering," Jack says, "I'm a snuggler."

Rav slides over and gathers Jack into the curve of his body, trying not to notice how perfectly he fits there. He's still trying not to notice ten minutes later when Jack's breathing smooths out into sleep. He doesn't notice the scent of Jack's skin, or the soothing rhythm of his ribs rising and falling. He doesn't think about what it would be like to have this every night, to fall asleep with his arms around the most incredible person he's ever met.

He drifts off sometime after four, and whatever he dreams after that will be strenuously denied in the morning.

CHAPTER TWENTY-FIVE

Rav wakes with the sun in his eyes, naked and unaccountably chilly. Or perhaps not so unaccountably, the entirety of the duvet having been dragged into a pile on the other side of the bed. Somewhere within those downy depths is a rock star. At least, Rav assumes so; with only a single limb protruding from the heap, a positive ID is out of the question. It's ridiculous and adorable and he's tempted to snap a photo, but things are new enough between them that it would probably still qualify as creepy.

The bathroom is well kitted out, even for a hotel of this caliber. Toothbrushes, razors, luxury skin care products. He cleans up and slips back into bed, minty fresh and smelling faintly of bergamot. Not a moment too soon: Jack is stirring under his heap of blankets. Rav closes his eyes and pretends to be asleep. Let Jack think he wakes up smelling this good.

He hears the patter of bare feet on the floor, the soft hiss of the bathroom door sliding shut. He starts to reach for his phone but decides against it. Who cares what time it is? He's just starting to doze off again when the mattress shifts beside him, and he rolls over to find a pair of blue-green eyes watching him. "Hi," Jack says.

"Well, hello."

"Sleep okay?"

"I did, no thanks to you." When Jack raises an eyebrow, he adds, "You failed to disclose that you're a blanket thief."

Jack glances around, taking in the rather damning disposition of the duvet. "I am, aren't I? Sorry about that." He shifts closer but doesn't touch.

"If you're wondering," Rav says, deliberately echoing Jack's words from last night, "I'm a snuggler."

Jack smiles and scooches the rest of the way over. There's a glint in his eye that Rav's body is already becoming conditioned to, a Pavlovian response that has him hardening in anticipation even before the hand starts making its way up his thigh. At this rate, Jack will have his dick trained to sit up and beg by the end of the day.

Forty very satisfying minutes later, Rav is still lounging in bed while Jack orders room service. "Did you say you're meeting with Mo today?" he asks as he hangs up the phone.

"That's the plan. I'll have to head home first, though."

"Why?" Jack climbs back onto the bed and straddles him.

"Because I have some pride, and I refuse to meet your body-guard in the same clothes I was wearing last night."

"He knows you spent the night. We practically slammed the door in his face."

"*You* did. I take no responsibility for that."

Jack leans forward and pins Rav's wrists to the bed, a mischievous grin hitching his mouth. "You said it yourself, we have everything we need right here. Except handcuffs. Why didn't you bring those?"

That smile. It *kills* him. "Are you always this frisky after a show?"

"Seriously," Jack says. "Stay."

Honestly, Rav is surprised. It's not like he thought this was a one-time thing, but holiday weekend vibes is a whole other level. "Do you really want me hanging around all day?"

"Not if you don't want to. But we're hitting the road tomorrow, so . . ."

Get it while you can. Rav sighs. "When you put it like that."

"If you want, we can send someone to your apartment to pick up whatever you need."

Tempting, but that would be a bit decadent. "I'll be quick, I promise. And if I should return to find you lounging naked by the pool with frozen margaritas, I wouldn't take it amiss."

After breakfast, he nips home for a shower and a change of clothes. He packs an overnight bag, and within an hour, he's back in Brooklyn and ready for his meeting.

He finds Mo waiting on the sidewalk outside the hotel. The bodyguard hands Rav's bag over to a bellhop, and then he crooks his head in the direction of the river. "Let's take a walk. Jack doesn't need to hear this."

"Even if it concerns him?"

"I like to keep my clients on a need-to-stress basis."

"And he'll be all right by himself?"

"I made him promise not to leave the room, and I trust him to keep his word. He's not one of these dopes who pays me to protect them and then tries to give me the slip the first chance they get."

They head out along the waterfront. It's busy on a sunny Sunday, cyclists whizzing along the bike lanes and music drifting over from the park nearby. Mo pops into a coffee shop for a latte and one of those dense, overstuffed baked goods Americans insist on calling *scones*. "So," he says around a mouthful of ham and cheese. "Overwatch. Wanna tell me how you came across that name?"

Rav fills him in on the interview with Joe Miller's roommate. "He was adamant that this Overwatch person was in Miller's head, fanning the flames of his conspiracy theories."

"Yeah, from what I saw, Overwatch was laying it on pretty thick with the evil CIA thing for a while. And that was in his public posts. I can only imagine what he was saying in DMs."

Rav notes the use of past tense. "He's not posting anymore?"

"Not for the past week or so. I'm guessing he thought it was all shits and giggles until Miller actually took a shot at me, and then he got spooked."

"Why did you never mention him?"

Mo pauses, bending down to tie his shoelace. It's awkward with the sling, and he takes his time with it. "It's the nature of those forums. Didn't see the need to single him out specifically. That being said, I think Overwatch was the first to mention my intelligence background. I did wonder how he came across that information."

"You can see how that would do a number on a guy like Miller. As you said, the CIA is everyone's favorite bogeyman."

"Bottom line, he still did this." Mo gestures at his sling as he straightens. "Does it matter what was going through his head at the time?"

"Not really, but . . ."

"But what?" Mo's glance flicks over Rav's shoulder.

"The roommate claims Miller is being set up. He's a conspiracy theorist, so it's tempting to dismiss him, except the FBI reached a similar conclusion. They differ about who's behind it, but in both versions, someone takes advantage of Miller's history of stalking Jack and weaponizes it for their own purposes."

"Thought you didn't buy the FBI's theory?"

"They're wrong about Vanderford, I'm convinced. But what if they're not wrong about all of it?"

Mo's gaze goes over Rav's shoulder again, and then he resumes walking, faster this time. "Hustle up, Detective. I wanna get to Smorgasburg."

"The food market? Didn't you just eat?"

"We're being followed. Navy-blue windbreaker, ball cap."

It takes a second for that to sink in. When it does, Rav starts to—

"Turn around and I will punch you in the dick. Are you new at this?"

"New to being followed like I'm in a *spy movie*? Yes, Mo, I am new at this."

"Stay casual. Just two guys chatting on the street."

They're not chatting anymore, a tense silence settling between them as they head into the market. It's teeming with people, tourists and families and tipsy twentysomethings milling around dozens of vendors selling everything from oysters to artisanal pickles. Perfect for getting lost in a crowd. They join the densest pod of people they can find, letting themselves be carried along for a couple of minutes before ducking between a BBQ place and a taco stand.

"Here's the plan," Mo says. "I'm gonna stay here, out of sight. You're gonna head back out there and browse the market, nice and casual. Maybe join a line. Make sure you're visible, and keep within my line of sight."

"So I'm the bait? What if it's Miller?"

"We take him down."

"You can't draw your weapon in this crowd. It's too risky."

"Not my first rodeo, Detective," Mo says coolly. "I'll keep it low-key. Now get going."

Rav slips back out between the tents and rejoins the crowd. His mouth is dry, and he wishes he'd brought his handcuffs after all, not to mention his gun. He'd feel safer having it, even if he's not comfortable using it in a crowded place like this.

Hide, a voice inside him whispers. *Keep a lookout like Mo is doing.* But that's just the fear talking. Mo's play is smarter.

He chooses the busiest line he can find and joins it. His stomach is still full of decadent room service breakfast, and the food smells are making him queasy. Or, you know, maybe it's the stalker with the gun making him nauseous. He could be in a penthouse suite right now, having naked margaritas with a rock star, but *no*, he's standing in line for kimchi brisket subs with a bunch of college kids in oversized cargo pants, trying not to look over his shoulder in case someone is about to shoot him.

The back of his neck prickles. Someone is staring at him, he can feel it. *Don't look*, he tells himself.

He looks.

Standing a few feet away, immobile in a sea of moving people, is a guy in a navy-blue windbreaker and a ball cap.

First thought: it's not Miller.

Second thought: Rav has seen him before.

They make eye contact, and the guy reaches under his windbreaker. Something bulky shifts under the fabric; Rav gets a glimpse of black metal and—

—Mo is there, kicking the guy's knees out and wrenching his arm behind his back in a single smooth motion. He's about to plant the guy face-first into the pavement when they get a look at the metal object in his hand.

It's a camera.

Rav places him now: he was backstage at the concert last night. A tabloid journalist, obviously.

"Shit, man," the photographer gasps as he wriggles in Mo's grasp. People are staring now, cutting a wide berth around them. "Take it easy!"

"What the hell were you thinking?" Mo growls. "You know we're on high alert, and you're gonna pull this shady shit? You put everyone in this park at risk."

"I'm just doing my job." The photographer crooks his chin defiantly at Rav. "I saw the two of them eye-fucking each other backstage last night. Doesn't take a genius to see there's a story there."

Mo snatches the camera from his hands and starts pressing buttons. The guy tries to grab it back, but Mo has six inches and a hundred pounds on him; he holds the camera out of reach while he deletes a bunch of photos, and then he hands it back. "Now beat it," he says, and the paparazzo slinks off.

Rav's heart is still pounding. "Are you all right? How's the shoulder?"

"Don't think I pulled my stitches." He rolls it experimentally. "Guess we'll see."

"He must have followed me from my place. I'm sorry, Mo."

"Not your fault. These tabloid vermin are harder to shake than an FSB tail."

He's being nice. Rav fucked up and he knows it. "Does this mean you have to move Jack again?"

"He's safer staying put. It's only one more night, and then we're on a plane to Amsterdam. Let's sneak you in through the service entrance, though. Just in case any more of these assholes turn up." They start back, taking the long way this time. "So, where were we?"

"I think we've about covered it. It sounds like this Overwatch is worth looking into, and I have a friend who might be able to help." Assuming she's willing. He's pretty far in the red with Aisha already.

"I'll get Erika on it, too," Mo promises.

Jack is lounging by the pool when Rav gets back. He looks relaxed and happy, and Rav hates to ruin it, but Jack needs to know about the photographer. There could still be a story, and his publicist should be prepared. Rav skips the part where he thought he was about to be murdered, but even so, Jack's good mood vanishes in an instant.

"I'm so sorry," he says with a grim shake of his head. "You didn't sign up for this."

"Oh, but I did. *All* of this." Rav loops his arms around Jack's waist, trying to keep it light, but Jack isn't smiling.

"All of it, really? Stalkers and tabloids and panic attacks?"

"The whole package. We're in this together, love." The word is out of his mouth before he can stop it, and he freezes.

There's an awkward silence. Jack's expression is hard to read. "I appreciate that, but—"

"I mean it," Rav says breezily, as if he didn't just accidentally drop the L-bomb in the middle of a serious conversation. "But all that can fuck off right now, because it's a beautiful, sunny afternoon and we are egregiously overdue for naked margaritas."

"I might skip the tequila, but I'll take the naked. It's going to be a lonely few months on the road."

Lonely, but safe. He'll be out of Joe Miller's reach. That gives Rav time. He can't do much about tabloid photographers or panic attacks, but Miller? That he can do something about. He's got a fresh lead and a head full of ideas, and he's going to put every ounce of energy he has into seeing Miller behind bars.

Tomorrow.

Right now, he's going to take his own advice and hit pause on all that. Because these are their last few hours together before

Jack gets on a plane, and Rav doesn't really know what happens after that. So he takes Jack's hand and leads him to the bedroom, and if they don't see a drop of that beautiful sunshine all day long, that's fine by him.

CHAPTER TWENTY-SIX

Rav is on desk duty this week, getting ready to testify in the trial of a guy he arrested last year. That means his evenings are free, and he gets started at the stroke of 5 P.M. on Monday, calling up Aisha as he leaves the office. "You've been avoiding me."

"Hasn't deterred you from calling me every five minutes. You're pretty pushy for a guy begging favors."

"You know I have a good reason. Besides, this isn't just a favor. You're hoping to impress Jack's security team, remember?"

"Yeah, yeah." She cracks a can of something fizzy and gulps it noisily. "I hear he's in Europe these days. You must be bummed. Long-distance relationships suck."

Especially when you're not even sure it's a relationship. Aloud, he says, "At least he's out of Miller's reach. That's a pretty big upside."

"Unless Miller decides to come after you instead."

"You watch too many movies," he says, as if he didn't go full Jason Bourne at a food market yesterday.

"Uh, we're finding dead bodies and tracking down Russian hackers. Pretty sure this *is* a movie."

Bloody hell, he'd almost managed to forget the Russians.

"Which, by the way, there's more to that strange little tale. I got to thinking about what you said before. Why would Russian hackers fake a story about Jack Vale being harassed by the cops? Not just the usual bots spreading bullshit, either. They went to a lot of trouble. Deepfake video, phony blog, the works. So I took a closer look at their imaginary blogger and his deleted website, and now I'm thinking it's fishy."

"Fishy how?"

"There's clues in the metadata that point to Russians, but the baseline doesn't fit. As if someone deliberately left a trail of breadcrumbs so that if anyone came looking, they'd be led in a specific direction."

"Someone's covering their tracks?"

"Maybe. Either way, it's a dead end."

Disappointing, but Rav has more urgent matters on his mind. "Do you still have Miller's Fuse credentials?"

"Depends if he changed them. Even if he hasn't, there's probably not much to find. If he's smart, he's wiped that account clean. We still have the old stuff, but—"

"Hold on. What old stuff?"

"Everything in his cloud. I backed up his phone when we signed in that first time."

Rav does a full three-sixty pirouette on the sidewalk, pumping his fist in the air. "You are a national treasure." Also a criminal, but he's willing to overlook that part right now. "Why didn't you tell me this sooner?"

"I thought you already had what you needed. You told me they recovered his phone at the scene."

"The FBI has the device, but even if they managed to unlock it, they certainly didn't send copies to me."

"My bad, but I still don't see how it helps you. Like I said, it's old information. What are you hoping to find?"

Right now, he's more interested in what he *won't* find, at least if his hunch is right.

The link from Aisha is waiting in his inbox by the time he gets home. He's up until the wee hours going through Miller's emails, and first thing in the morning, he corners his partner. "You didn't fuck up."

Shepard arches an eyebrow. "Thanks?"

"Vanderford's emails."

"Um." Will glances at Howard's open door. "Should we be talking about this while we're on duty?"

Rav looks at his watch. 8:58. "We have two minutes. And you didn't fuck up."

"Yeah, you're gonna have to back up—"

"The FBI took over the Vanderford case because of emails he supposedly sent to Joe Miller, right?"

"Okay, yeah. You're talking about the messages they found on his laptop. Where he tells Miller how to bypass security at the Concord. Howard was pissed because I missed them."

"Except you didn't," Rav repeats patiently. "Those emails don't exist, at least not on Miller's end. Neither does the photo he supposedly posted—the selfie on the waterfront, with Vanderford in the background. Nothing on Miller's phone indicates he's ever met Dick Vanderford."

"How do you . . . ? Oh, right, your hacker."

"Vanderford and Miller never corresponded. Either the FBI lied about those emails, or they're phony, just like the roommate said."

"Or—and stop me if I'm being crazy here—Miller deleted them."

"Except I found plenty of other incriminating material on his phone. Photos, emails, texts, all proving he was stalking Jack for months. If he was trying to dispose of the evidence, why not delete all of it?"

"Maybe he used an email that doesn't push to his phone. A Hotmail, or—"

"His Hotmail did push to his phone, along with three other email addresses. Why is this so hard for you to believe?"

Will's eyebrows jump. "That the FBI or some shadowy third party is fabricating evidence? You saw the guy stab Morillo with your own eyes."

"I'm not suggesting Miller is innocent, but there's so much that doesn't add up. Did you know the bullet they dug out of Mo's shoulder was a .32 caliber? Vanderford and Greg Watson were shot with a .40 S&W. If all three shootings were Miller, why is he suddenly changing guns?"

"Rav . . ." Shepard sighs. "I wanna have your back, man, but are you listening to yourself? You're starting to sound like *them*. Like these crazy conspiracy theorists."

That stings. "Is that really what you think? That I've turned into a conspiracy theorist?"

"I just don't want you to get lost down some rabbit hole. You're on thin ice with Howard as it is."

It's true. And if he looks at it objectively, he can understand Will's skepticism. What he's suggesting does sound pretty far-fetched.

"I know you wanna help Jack," Will goes on, "but you've put your career on the line for him once already."

"It's not just about Jack. This was *my* case. I'm the one who let Miller get away at the Concord. I'd have skin in the game even if I'd never met Jack Vale."

Shepard drops his voice to a whisper. "You gave Howard your word."

He did. And he fully intends to keep it if he can, but he is not letting this go.

He hits a Staples on the way home to pick up a whiteboard and some dry-erase markers. Then he does something he's only seen in movies, mounting it on the wall in his apartment to make an evidence board. He starts with a timeline going back to the Concord. Then he writes down the evidence, categorized by the entity that brought it to light—the FBI, NYPD, and so on. It's all very orderly and neat, until he starts speculating about possible connections, drawing arrows in yellow marker. Is there a relationship between the Russian hackers and Overwatch? A connection between the deepfake video of Jack and the phony emails on Vanderford's laptop? Is the murdered private investigator part of the picture somehow?

He shoots Jack a quick text before he goes to bed, asking how he's doing. It's the middle of the night in Europe, so he doesn't expect a response, but when he wakes up, all he finds is: **All well thanks.**

No *how are you*. No *sorry it's been super busy*. Just three words.

Which . . . okay. Maybe Rav is being needy, but a text like that after a weekend of penthouse-suite sex does not feel great.

At least he doesn't have time to dwell on it, not when he's laser-focused on catching Miller. Tuesday night is devoted to a deep dive into the saved contents of Miller's phone, and it's a virtual shrine to the Nicks. Photos, MP3s, the works. What's strange, though, is that they're Jack's songs, Jack's photos. Not Tommy's, as Rav might have expected. Almost as if Miller's obsession with Tommy's death is for Jack's sake.

His contacts are in here, too, and it's *so tempting* to use them. If this were Rav's case, interviewing the suspect's friends and family would be standard procedure. But it's not, and if the FBI got wind of it, they'd have his arse. He can't do a thing with this information—but he knows someone who can. He grabs his phone.

"Carrie Campbell."

"Ms. Campbell. It's been a minute."

"Well, well, if it isn't Detective McDreamy. I hear you're back on the job."

"I am indeed, and I'm ready to give you that quote."

"Which quote is that?" she says, her tone all business now.

"Regarding the Vanderford case, and why the FBI took over. Strictly on background, Carrie. *Deep* background. I need your word."

"I can do that."

"Great. And one more thing."

He tells her.

"What the hell makes you think I'd let you dictate how I write a story?" she growls.

"That's not what I'm asking. But I think once you've heard what I have to say, you'll have a different opinion of Joe Miller."

"Suppose you're right. Say I end up feeling sorry for the guy, and I'm willing to brave the wrath of a million Nicks fans to put a sympathetic spin on things. What does that get you?"

"I'm hoping he'll reach out to you. I've got contact details for his family and friends, and I thought that if you put the word out that you'd like to give Miller the opportunity to tell his side of the story, one of them might know how to reach him."

A thoughtful pause on the line. "You think he'd go for that?"

"I think he might. Joe Miller is a conspiracy theorist. His whole thing is getting the truth out there, revealing the shadowy hand behind it all. Now he finds himself at the center of a murderous CIA conspiracy, or so he believes. I think he'll be dying to set the record straight."

"How do I know I'm not just offering a platform to some QAnon clown?"

"You'll have to make up your own mind on that score. All I can say is that *I'm* convinced he's being set up."

"Huh. Okay." Another pause. "Suppose he does get in touch, what then?"

"I'm hoping he'll agree to speak. I have a proposal for him."

"That's gonna be a tough sell."

No shit. Not only is Rav a cop, he's known to be friendly with Jack Vale. On paper, he's the last person Miller would trust. Except Rav remembers what he was like that day in the skate park, how he practically begged for Jack's help. Whatever the nature of his feelings toward Jack, they're a lot more complicated than his online persona suggests, and that means there's hope. "Nothing to lose by trying."

"I can't promise anything, all right? Except that I'll keep your name out of it, whatever happens. Deal?"

Rav glances up at the whiteboard on his wall, and his mouth goes dry. Howard is going to suspect he's the leak. Will is going to know it. If the FBI can prove it, they'll have his badge, or worse. But it's the only play he has.

"Deal," he says. And he tells her everything.

CHAPTER TWENTY-SEVEN

Trivedi! My office, *now*!"

Rav stands and slowly buttons his jacket. Then he walks the longest twenty steps of his life.

The newspaper lands on Howard's desk with a *slap*, headline splashed out in bold black ink.

"HE'S BEING FRAMED": SISTER OF SUSPECT IN SLAYING OF MUSIC EXECUTIVE SAYS THE EVIDENCE AGAINST HER BROTHER IS FABRICATED

"*Sit.*"

Rav sits.

Howard perches on the edge of her desk, looming over him with eyes blazing. "I just got off the phone with the Federal Bureau of Investigation," she says, slicing each word off with a razor. "Agent Rice is apoplectic. She thinks the unnamed source in this article is you. I assured her that was impossible. It is *impossible*, isn't it, Detective? Because I distinctly recall you giving me your word you would keep your nose out of the Vanderford file from now on, and I know you wouldn't risk being brought up on charges for interfering with a federal investigation."

"To be fair," Rav says slowly, "I gave you my word that I would confine my investigations to off-duty—"

"Do you really think being pedantic is going to help you here?"

"No, ma'am."

"I am at the end of my rope with you. I assigned you this case to give you a chance to shine. So that everyone could see what I saw: a talented detective with maturity beyond his years. Instead you've demonstrated poor judgment at every turn, and—"

"Have I, though?"

"Excuse me?"

He looks up, meeting her eye. "I realize I've made decisions that aren't in the best interests of my career, but with all due respect, that's not all there is. You're the one who reminded me of that. I understand the consequences of my actions, and I haven't taken them lightly. I'm doing what I believe is necessary—to protect someone I care about, and to get justice for Richard Vanderford. If it costs me my career . . ." He falters for a second. "If that's what happens, I'll live with it. Covering my own arse instead of doing the right thing—that I could *not* live with."

Howard stares at him, her mouth pressed into a thin line. "Is that what you're doing here? The right thing? Because for the life of me, I can't see how this"—she taps the paper—"helps anyone."

"I guess we'll find out," he says quietly.

"I guess we will. Dismissed."

* * *

Things go downhill from there.

Rav is assigned grunt work on Danny Jobs's latest case. If Howard wasn't benching him before, she definitely is now, and though he probably deserves it, it's humiliating having to eat shit like this. He spends his days sifting through grainy traffic cam footage and handling paperwork, pausing to check his phone every five seconds in case he somehow missed a call from Carrie Campbell informing him that his oh-so-clever plan actually worked. Then he goes home to his flat—once his perfect little oasis, now scarred by the presence of the evidence board. What was he thinking, putting that thing there? Nothing like having a constant reminder of your failure mounted on the fucking *wall*.

Then there's Jack, who is basically ghosting him.

Missed calls and voicemails, texts that go unanswered for days. They've spoken exactly once since the band left for Europe, and Jack was distant. Not cold, exactly, just . . . reserved. "The schedule's really crammed right now," he said when Rav hinted that it had been a while since they'd spoken. They were on a video call, and Jack was distracted, flashing past the screen while he changed his shirt, put his guitar away, and generally buzzed around his hotel room. Rav spent much of the call addressing a moving torso. "I might be hard to get a hold of for a bit. But we'll always have the pool, right? Listen, I gotta run . . ."

He's busy, Rav knows he is. But there's something else going on. Maybe Rav freaked him out with that "love" slipup. Maybe now that he's back on the road, Jack remembers that the world is full of interesting, attractive people, and he doesn't want to get too hung up on someone whose life makes no sense with his.

Or maybe it goes deeper. Maybe with the benefit of a little distance, Jack has realized it might be better to put the past couple of months in the rearview. New York has been the site of a *lot* of trauma for him. Maybe he just needs to get some space between himself and all that, even if it means putting space between him and Rav, too. If that's the case, Rav would understand, but he wishes Jack would just say so.

It's in the midst of this emotional nadir that his mother calls, naturally. Great white sharks have nothing on Eva. She can smell blood in the water from thousands of miles away, and she smells it now. Rav declines the call on his mobile, but Mummy Dearest isn't having it; thirty seconds later, his desk phone rings.

"Are you screening my calls now?"

"I've been screening your calls since I was fourteen."

"Then why did you pick up?"

"Because this is my work phone. I'm at work, Mum. Working." He pretends not to notice Will smirking beside him.

He knows why she's calling. The Nicks are in London this weekend, which means the skate park memes will be back in people's timelines. His Lordship won't like seeing his son's face all over social media. It's *undignified*. He'll be in a foul mood about it, which puts Eva in a foul mood, so she's calling to share the fun.

"Your boyfriend is making quite the splash over here," she says.

"I don't have one of those."

"What should I call him, then? Your latest fling?"

Hold on. He's never mentioned hooking up with Jack. Is this some weird maternal intuition? "I can't talk about this right now. I'll call you later."

"You've been ducking my calls for weeks. Enough is enough."

He sighs. "Fine. Give me five minutes." The office gossip about his scandalous relationship has finally lost steam, and he has no desire to revive it. He calls her back from the street.

"Your father is in quite a state," Eva informs him. She sounds wryly amused, as she often does when discussing His Lordship. For the life of him, Rav can't understand the dynamic between those two. They met at Columbia, and if he tries really hard he can sort of imagine how a starchy English boy and a hot American model get it on for a while. How they end up married after accidentally getting pregnant. He can *definitely* understand how they break up almost immediately, upon discovering that the world cannot, physically, revolve around each of them at the same time. The getting back together after more than twenty years . . . He just cannot. Especially because they still fight like cats and dogs. About the only thing Eva and His Lordship agree on is that their son is a huge disappointment.

"If he's worked up over a silly meme, that's on him," Rav says.

"I believe it's his son being in the tabloids that has his blood pressure up."

"You mean the TMZ thing? That was ages ago."

"I *mean* the torrid affair the two of you are allegedly carrying on. Your picture is in every checkout line in the country."

Rav's stomach drops. He'd dared to hope they were in the clear after Mo deleted those photos at the food market. "Is it a big story?"

"For a few days, but of course they've already moved on to the next thing. So has he, if the headlines are to be believed."

"What do you mean?" Rav asks, his stomach sinking even further.

"Apparently, he has a new love interest. Marcella something-or-other. A singer, I think?"

Marcella Marcus, presumably. Even Rav knows who she is. Extremely talented, and *extremely* beautiful. Rav experiences a sharp twist of jealousy before pushing it aside. The British tabloids are notorious muckrakers. They'll say anything to sell papers.

Also, you have no claim on him.

"So you're calling, why? To pass along a friendly *I-told-you-so? That's what you get for not being discreet?*" The words sound every bit as bitter as they taste.

"Oh, stop it. I've never said any such thing. Your father might have—"

"*Might* have?"

"—wanted you to be discreet, but I never asked that of you. Don't tar me with that brush, because it's not who I am and you know it."

Rav stares straight ahead, jaw twitching. The street is its usual mayhem: yellow cabs, trucks with shrieking brakes, irate honking. Sometimes, he wonders what the hell he's doing in this city. It's not as if coming here fixed anything. "Why did you go back to him?"

He's not sure why he's asking the question now, all these years later. It's not as if she can say anything that will change how he feels about it. Which is betrayed.

"I spent my entire childhood trying to please him, and when he couldn't cram me into his perfect little mold, he turned his back on me. I came to you to start a new life—"

"And I was there for you."

"For a *hot second* and then you went back to him! It makes me wonder if it was me you were trying to get away from all along!"

"Christ, Rav." A sigh on the line, and a silence. "Where is this coming from all of a sudden?"

"I don't know." He takes a moment, pacing back and forth in front of the station. "I'm just in a bit of a state. With work, and—"

"That's why I'm calling. I've been where you are right now, and I remember what it's like. How it eats away at your self-worth. And I don't just mean the tabloids. I've been celebrity arm candy too, more than once. It's not so bad if you enjoy it for what it is, but you don't want to lose your heart to someone like that. He'll break it."

"You don't know anything about him."

"Maybe not, but I've known men like him. Or at least, I knew one."

Rav takes a moment to digest that. "You're not talking about Dad."

"No. This was during one of our many breakups, before we were married. He was . . . Well. Never mind. What matters is that he was rich and famous and exciting, and trying to love him was like trying to catch a shooting star in a butterfly net. I was never the same after, and I don't want you to make the same mistake."

"Ah." Rav's voice feels like sandpaper. How is it your parents always know just where to hit you? With laser precision, they zero in on your worst fears, your deepest pools of self-doubt, and blast them open like fucking bunker busters. "In that case . . ." He clears his throat. "I'm sorry to say you're a bit late. Because I am very much in love with him."

It's the first time he's admitted it to himself, let alone someone else, and the fact that it's to his mother of all people makes him want to laugh. Or cry. Both, maybe.

She sighs. "Oh, Rav. My baby."

She hasn't called him that since he was ten years old, and he is *not* up for it. "Spare me the sympathy, Mum. It's not your style. Besides, it's not as if you're telling me anything I don't know.

There's every reason to think this ends badly, but I decided a long time ago that it was worth it. Cue clichés about gathering ye rosebuds, it's better to have loved and lost, et cetera."

His mother gives a humorless laugh. "I suppose I shouldn't be surprised. You're just like—"

"Yes, yes, I'm just like my father. Never could tell either of us a damned thing." He's heard it a thousand times.

"I was going to say you're just like me. A hopeless romantic."

"Please. You're the most cynical person I know."

"Who says you can't be both? A cynic is just a brokenhearted romantic. You've had your heart broken more than once, including by your parents. I have to live with that. I'd hoped to be there for you this time, at least. Apparently, it's too little too late, so I'll simply say this: if he truly is worth the risk, then take it. *Really* take it. No half measures. Because if things don't work out, what you'll regret most isn't the chances you took but the ones you didn't."

Another silence. Rav finds himself wondering where she is. In the garden, maybe, in the gazebo he nearly burned down. "What happened to him? Mr. Famous and Exciting?"

"He got married a couple of years later. Another model."

"Bastard."

She laughs. "It was partly my fault. I was famous myself, and very young, leading a fast and glamorous life. You get used to everything around you being profoundly superficial. I treated our relationship as casual because I fully expected him to do the same, and it became a self-fulfilling prophecy. I can't be sorry for how it turned out, because I have you, and your father. But I can't help wondering what would have happened if I'd let myself be vulnerable instead. If I'd shown him that I could be the true thing, the real thing, in his life. And he could be that for me, too."

"Bloody hell." Rav rubs his eyes harshly. "I was so not ready for this."

"What?"

"You. Parenting. It's completely foreign."

"Oh, fuck off."

"That's more like it." Against all odds, Rav finds himself smiling. "Go on, then, who was he? You have to tell me now."

"I really don't."

"I suppose I'll just have to find out on my own. I am a detective, you know."

"So I hear." A pause, and a sigh. "Should I buy tickets to this concert?"

Rav has a brief but vivid image of Eva elbowing her way backstage to go full Naomi Campbell on Jack. The tabloids would love it. "I'm sure they're sold out. But I appreciate the thought."

There's a beep in his ear. He glances at his phone—and his heart skips a beat.

"I have to go, Mum. I have another call."

There must be something in his voice, because she says, "Is it him?"

"It is, actually."

"No half measures," Eva says. "And Rav. Remember what I taught you about putting your chin up in photos. Let them see that perfect jawline." With that parting advice, she hangs up.

Rav draws a deep breath and hits the green icon. "Good afternoon." He hopes it sounds breezier than it feels. "I thought you'd be in sound check by now."

"Soon. Thought I'd get out and see the city for once, now that I don't have to worry so much about security. I'm taking a walk in Hyde Park, and I can't even tell you how good it feels."

"I bet."

There's a long pause. Then Jack says, "I can't stop thinking about you. Everything in this city reminds me of you, and I just had to hear your voice."

Rav melts onto a concrete bollard outside the station. "I've been missing you, too. How have you been?"

"Fine, thanks."

Bullshit. Rav can hear it in his voice. "You don't sound fine."

"It's been a tough couple of weeks. We had to postpone the Zurich show. But the last few days have been better, and—one sec." Jack covers the phone; he's talking to someone in the background. "Yeah, okay." Uncovering the phone, he sighs. "Listen . . ."

"You have to go."

"I'm sorry. It's just so intense right now."

Rav stands and turns a little circle on the sidewalk. "Jack, look, if this isn't . . . If you don't want to—"

"I do."

"I would understand, is all I'm saying. You can be honest with me."

"I am being honest with you." He sighs again. "I know I haven't been good at keeping in touch. It's not because I don't want to. Maybe we could try again later tonight? After the show?"

"Of course."

"Great. I'd better go. And listen, about this crap in the tabloids—"

"It's not your fault."

"Are there photographers following you again?"

Rav glances around instinctively, and . . . yes, there's a figure lurking nearby. He slips around a tree trunk when Rav looks his way, and a moment later he's gone. "Maybe," Rav hedges. "But don't you dare say sorry again. You don't owe me an apology and you don't owe me an explanation. It's not like we made any promises."

"Maybe not, but just so you know, that stuff about Marcella is bullshit. We're friends, that's it."

"Duly noted." A clamp releases on his chest, but his tone is airy as he adds, "Though for what it's worth, if you were so inclined, I wouldn't blame you. She's hot."

"Shut up," Jack says, laughing. "I gotta go."

Rav hangs up feeling better, but something tells him whatever is going on with Jack isn't going to be fixed by a couple of phone calls.

He's about to head back inside when his phone rings again.

Bloody hell, he's popular today. He checks the name. Unknown caller.

"Trivedi."

No response. Rav can hear traffic in the background.

"Hello? Who is this?"

Nervous breathing. And then: "This is Joe Miller."

CHAPTER TWENTY-EIGHT

J oe Miller," Rav echoes, his voice hollow with disbelief. Carrie must have given him this number. "I'm glad you called."

Which is not *quite* true. Part of him is celebrating, part of him is panicking, and part of him is thinking he and Carrie Campbell really need to have a talk about boundaries.

"That reporter at the *Times* said you wanted to talk to me. The question is, why would I wanna talk to you?"

It's him, all right. Rav recognizes his voice from the skate park.

This is a bad idea, he thinks. A crazy terrible idea and he's an idiot for putting himself in this position but he's come too far to back out now. Drawing a steadying breath, he says, "That's a fair question. But you've taken the first step already, and I appreciate the trust you're showing right now."

"I *don't* trust you. At all. I'm just curious to see how you'll play it." Confident words, but the tone doesn't match. He's nervous.

"Whatever your reasons, we're talking, and I'm grateful."

"Shit, man, you sound like a shrink. Look, you wanna talk, we're gonna do it my way. Highland Park, fifteen minutes."

"You want to meet in person?" Rav glances over his shoulder at the station behind him. "I don't know if I can do that."

"Then I guess you don't wanna talk to me that bad. Because that's how it goes, or it doesn't go at all. And no games. I got eyes on you right now. You're gonna toss your phone and your gun into that mailbox on the corner, and then you're gonna start walking. You try to go back inside the cop shop, or talk to anyone on the street, and we're done here. You'll never hear from me again."

He's bluffing, Rav thinks—and then he remembers the figure he saw ducking around a tree a minute ago. As if on cue, a delivery trunk honks somewhere just up the street, and Rav hears the echo on the other end of the line.

He's not just watching, he's close.

A trickle of sweat works its way down Rav's spine. "How do I know this isn't some kind of trap?"

"You don't. *You're* gonna have to trust *me*. How's it feel when the shoe's on the other foot, Detective?"

Rav licks his lower lip. "I want to trust you, but you're not making it easy. I can't leave a loaded weapon in a mailbox. You must know that."

"You think I'm gonna let you bring a gun to the meet?"

"I don't think anything, Joe," Rav says, trying to keep the frustration out of his voice. "This wasn't my idea. I'm just telling you what I can and cannot do. I'm willing to ditch the phone, but I can't endanger others."

A long pause. He's thinking. "What if it's not loaded? Take the clip out, then put the gun in the mailbox."

"Sorry, no. I can't leave my service weapon where some random postal worker could find it. But I could put the *clip* in the mailbox and keep the gun with me. That way it's secure but no danger to you."

"Okay, but I wanna see you eject the round in the chamber. And then drop it down a storm drain, so I know you didn't just stuff it in your pocket."

What am I, Quick Draw McGraw? Even if he did stash a round, how's he going to load it into his gun before Miller can react? This guy watches too many movies, but if that's what it takes . . . "Deal."

"Leave the call open when you dump the phone, so I know you're not calling somebody else."

Rav walks to the corner and waits until no one's looking

before ejecting the magazine and stashing it in the mailbox, along with his phone. Then, brandishing the loose round like a magician about to do a trick, he drops it through a grate in the gutter.

"Good," Miller says in his earbuds. "See you in fifteen. Don't be late." The line goes dead.

This is insane, Rav thinks as he starts toward the park. He half expects to be stuffed into some unmarked van and whisked away to his death. But Miller wouldn't go to all this trouble only to shoot him, right? If he wanted Rav dead, he'd just jump him outside his apartment or something, like he did with Mo. No, this spy routine appeals to the conspiracy theorist in Miller. It's part real life, part cosplay, and even though he's legitimately scared, he's getting off on it. That means he's unlikely to gun Rav down in cold blood, because he fancies himself the hero of this movie.

Probably?

Rav veers off the sidewalk and joins one of the paths winding its way through Highland Park. It's lush and green at this time of year, full of joggers and dog walkers and prams. Rav's shirt is clinging to him now, but it's not the June heat that's making him sweat. *Come on, Miller. Where—*

"What do you want?"

Rav nearly leaps out of his skin as a figure falls into step beside him. He starts to turn his head, but Miller hisses, "*Don't look at me.*"

"You're the one who wanted to do this in person," Rav growls.

"So you couldn't record the conversation on your phone. Catching you off guard like this was the only way."

Sure. Okay. Rav wonders what crank website he's taking this play from.

"You should know, I've got a gun." Miller drops his gaze meaningfully to where his hand is jammed in the pocket of his tracksuit trousers. "Try anything stupid, and you'll regret it. Now I asked you a question. What do you *want*?"

Rav tells himself this is an interview like any other. Except, you know, for the concealed weapon and the innocent bystanders and all that. "I want the same thing as you. For everyone to know the truth, so we can all get back to our lives. You. Me. Jack."

"Jack?" Miller snorts. "He's just fine. Living his best life, banging pop stars in Europe."

"You know better than to trust the headlines, Joe. Tabloids and social media—that's all bullshit. Airbrushed. The real Jack, the Jack I know, is scared. He thinks you want him dead, but I don't believe that. Should I?"

"Man, you must think I'm pretty stupid. You want me to say something incriminating."

"That's not true. Think about it: you caught me unprepared, as you said. I don't have a recording device on me." As soon as he says it, he realizes it's a lie: he's wearing his smartwatch. *Shit.* He didn't even think about it. If Miller spots it . . .

Rav forces himself to relax. The Marquesse is designed to look like a luxury analogue watch. Miller probably wouldn't recognize it as a wearable device even if he looked right at it. There's a panic function on it, and Rav briefly considers triggering it, but he dismisses the idea. Assuming anyone actually responds, it would just bring a cruiser to his location, and the last thing he wants is a shoot-out in a public park. "Besides," he goes on smoothly, "there would be no point in recording you. The FBI has all the evidence they need to put you away for life."

"*Fake evidence,*" Miller snarls, startling a woman pushing a pram. She swings out wide and quickens her step. "I'm being set up," he adds in a furious whisper.

"I believe you."

"Bullshit. This is a trap." His hand shifts in the pocket of his tracksuit.

"It's not. I want to fix this, Joe."

"How?"

"By proving you've been framed for the murders of Richard Vanderford and Greg Watson. I'm halfway there already. You saw the story in the *Times.* You know I'm the source. That's why you reached out, isn't it? You're hoping I can clear your name, and I can. But I need something in return."

Miller's eyes narrow sharply.

"I need your word that you'll leave Jack alone from now on. He's not behind this, and I'm going to prove it to you." *You want me to prove it to you.* Whatever Jack is to him—hero, archnemesis, some combination of the two—he's important to Miller, and part of him doesn't want to believe Jack is the villain of this story. "Ángel Morillo is not Jack's personal assassin. Someone wants very badly for you to believe that, just as they want Jack to believe you're out to kill him. You're being set against each other. By the same person, I believe, who tried to set me up."

"Yeah right," Miller says, but it lacks conviction. He half believes it already. "When did someone try to set *you* up?"

"A couple of months ago. Someone hacked Jack's social media—"

"Wait, yeah, I remember that. The deepfake." Miller slows down as the idea washes over him. "They *did* try to set you up. To make it look like you were harassing Jack."

"In order to discredit me. I was lead detective on the Vanderford murder, and—"

"And you were getting too close to the truth! *Holy shit, man!*" He crouches, hands on his head, mind blown. The conspiracy theorist is taking over, like the Incredible Hulk roaring out of Bruce Banner. It's in Rav's interest to let him run with this—and not, say, point out that he was actually nowhere near cracking the case at the time.

"I haven't figured out how it all fits together," Rav says as they start walking again. "But I will, and when I do, I'll share the evidence with the NYPD, the FBI, and anyone else who needs to know. Provided . . ." He lets that dangle.

"I leave Jack alone."

"That, and something else."

Miller scowls. "What?"

This is it; everything turns on this moment. Not just Rav's plan but very possibly his life. There's a gun in Joe Miller's pocket. If he takes this badly . . . "I'm going to need you to turn yourself in."

Miller stops, shoes scraping on the pathway.

"Not now," Rav adds hastily. "After I've shown you the evidence, so you know I've kept my side of the bargain."

"I knew it." Miller shakes his head. "This is a trap. All this bullshit about *I want everyone to know the truth—*"

"I do want that. The whole truth, not just the convenient bits. You're not a murderer, but you did shoot Ángel Morillo. There were mitigating circumstances. You feared for your life. With a good lawyer, you can probably plead down to—"

"I'm not going to prison, do you hear me?"

Heads swivel all around them, people freezing in their tracks and staring. Miller stiffens, and for a second Rav is sure he's going to bolt—or worse, draw his gun.

"I get it," Rav says soothingly. "But you have to ask yourself what the endgame is. Do you want to spend the rest of your life on the run? Or would you rather take your medicine and put it all behind you?"

"Why don't you just arrest me right now?" Miller challenges, eyes flashing.

"Because there's a gun in your pocket. I'd rather not die today, or see anyone else in this park get hurt. All I'm asking is that you think about it, okay?"

A muscle in Miller's jaw twitches. "No promises."

"One promise," Rav counters, and he's amazed how steady he sounds. "Or I drop my investigation here and now. You leave Jack Vale, and his bodyguard, alone. In real life and online, from this minute onward. It's not a lot to ask, Joe."

Miller looks away. "Yeah, okay."

"Good," Rav says, and the relief flooding his limbs is so intense he's feeling lightheaded. "Now, if I were you, I'd get moving."

"What?" Miller's eyes widen. "Why?"

"Because I'm a cop, and you're a wanted man. I'm obliged to call this in as soon as it's safe to do so."

"Are you kidding me?"

"You're the one who insisted on doing this in person. You must have realized the position that would put me in."

Miller licks his lips anxiously. "Give me a ten-minute head start?"

"I'll give you two."

"Aw, fuck you, man," Miller whines. And he bolts.

✳ ✳ ✳

"I'll say this for you, Trivedi, you certainly have a flair for drama." Lieutenant Howard rubs her temples. "Never in my thirty years on the force have I encountered the kind of Hollywood bullshit you keep getting mixed up in."

"To be fair, this wasn't my fault. I never expected Miller to pull something like this."

"Are you going to sit there and tell me you didn't engineer this encounter with that newspaper stunt?"

"I hoped he would reach out, but I certainly didn't expect to be threatened at gunpoint."

She sighs. "*He* contacted *you?*"

"Yes, ma'am."

"And you deemed it unsafe to attempt to take him into custody?"

"Yes, ma'am."

"Do you have any information on his whereabouts?"

And so on. She's ticking boxes, making sure their arses are covered. Not that it'll make her conversation with the FBI any easier. Rav feels guilty about that—about everything he's put her through. Maybe he should get her an apology gift. Something relaxing, like a day at the spa, or a high-end coloring book, or his letter of resignation.

"Tell me something." Howard leans back in her chair, studying him. "Do you really believe Miller is being set up? Or was that just a play to get him to trust you?"

"I honestly believe it, LT. Whoever murdered Vanderford

needed someone to take the fall, and Miller made a convenient scapegoat. The media were painting him as dangerous and unstable, and he had a connection to Vanderford via Jack Vale and the Nicks. It wouldn't take much to get the FBI to look his way, and someone knew just how to bait the hook."

She grunts thoughtfully. "And the dead roommate?"

"Collateral damage. Miller was a loose end that needed tying up. Greg Watson was just in the wrong place at the wrong time. I have a hunch the murdered private investigator comes into it too, but I haven't figured out how."

"Can you prove any of this?"

"I'm working on it. *On my own time,*" he's quick to add.

She grunts again, and unless he's mistaken, there's a hint of grudging approval in there. "Keep me informed, Detective."

Wait, she actually wants in on this? "Sure," Rav says. "Yeah, of course."

He makes it halfway to his desk before it really starts to sink in. *It actually worked.*

Not the way he thought, but it worked. Miller has paused his lethal vendetta, and Rav has his CO's blessing to keep digging on the Vanderford case. It's not over, but there's a path to fixing it, and that's more than he would have thought possible a few days ago. He sinks into his chair, dazed and a little overwhelmed.

"Hey, man, you okay?"

Rav glances at his partner, and the look of concern on Will's face is almost enough to tip him over the edge. His eyes burn, and he has to swallow a lump in his throat. "Yeah. Pretty chuffed, actually."

"Postal guys dropped off your gear." He slides Rav's phone and the magazine from his sidearm across the desk, and then he glances at his watch. "Hey, uh, it's almost five. You wanna grab a beer?"

They haven't done that since things went south between them, and it means a lot, especially right now. Rav feels himself choking up again. "You're a fucking awesome partner, you know that?"

"Damn right." Will grabs his keys. "Does this mean you're buying?"

"As long as you're driving. I miss that turd-brown Golf."

"Dude, how many times do I have to tell you? It's *chestnut*. It says so right in the owner's manual."

"Ah yes, chestnut. From the German *scheissenuss*."

"Yeah? Oh, wait. *Ha, ha,* aren't you hilarious . . ."

"But you're okay?" Jack asks again. "I mean, *really* okay?"

Rav puts his phone on speaker while he pours himself a drink. "I'm fine. It was intense, but I was confident he wasn't going to hurt me."

Pretty confident. Like, reasonably. With the benefit of hindsight, some of his logic actually looks a bit dodgy, but he's not going to share that with Jack.

"I can't promise Miller will keep his word. He's genuinely obsessed with you, and that can be an addiction. But I think he'll try, and if I can deliver my end of the bargain, hopefully he'll turn himself in."

"And if he doesn't? Would you really drop your investigation? Just leave him at the mercy of the FBI?" Jack sounds troubled by the idea. After everything Miller has put him through, he still feels compassion for his tormenter. As if Rav needed another reason to *adore* this man.

"Let's just hope he believes I would."

"Rav, I . . ." He trails off, as if he doesn't know what to say.

"It's late. You should try to get some rest. Sleep well."

"I will. For the first time in a really long time, thanks to you."

CHAPTER TWENTY-NINE

Two days later, Jack calls from France. Rav still gets butterflies every time he sees that name pop up on his phone, but he's at work, so he tries to look nonchalant as he jams his earbuds in. "How's Paris?"

"Pretty great. I love this town."

"Me, too." He pivots his chair toward the wall, grasping for what little privacy the squad room affords. "I had my first kiss there, actually."

"Oh yeah? How old were you?"

"Fourteen. It was a school trip. I met an Italian boy at the Louvre, and we agreed to sneak out after curfew and meet on the Pont des Arts. It all seemed terribly romantic."

"And?"

"He stuck his tongue down my throat and his hand down my trousers. Neither was especially revelatory."

Jack laughs. "Sounds like a great coming-of-age movie. So listen, what are you doing for the Fourth of July weekend?"

"The usual, I guess. Hit the gym, join some friends for drinks. Gently pine for you. Why?"

"It's a bit last minute, but can you get away? We have a few days off, and I've booked a beach house near Cannes. I'd love it if you could come."

"Cannes?" Rav swoons over the back of his chair.

"Down the coast a bit, where it's a little quieter. I'm not much into the celebrity/megayacht scene."

"Shocking. Whereas I think I could get into it."

"Does that mean you'll come?"

"I'll start looking into flights as soon as I'm off work."

"Eloise will take care of that. Just email her a PDF of your passport."

Rav's heart thrums. He knows this is probably just a thank-you after what he did with Miller, but it still feels pretty damned great.

He departs early on Thursday. He'll be flying via Paris—first class, bless the boy's heart, and private from there—and though he can't quite avoid the tug of guilt he feels about the carbon footprint, he rationalizes that it's a special occasion and he doesn't plan on making a habit of it. In the meantime, he orders a glass of Moët, just to get into the spirit of things.

It's late when they touch down at the private airport in Cannes. He's expecting to get into an Uber or something, and is a little bemused when they leave him standing on the tarmac outside the terminal building. Then he spies a slight figure in a hooded windbreaker, and his stomach does a little flip.

"Hi," Jack says, pulling his hood back. Even in the dark, those eyes are stunning. Literally: for a second, Rav freezes like a deer in the headlights. They haven't seen each other in weeks, and it feels a little like starting over again.

"I didn't expect you to come yourself," Rav says. "It's late."

"Of course I came." They embrace, and Rav feels something drain away, a tension he's been carrying for what seems like forever. "I'm so glad you're here," Jack murmurs into his neck. Then he takes Rav's hand. "Come on. You're going to love the car."

He leads Rav to a vintage convertible, sleek, sexy, and silver. "Is this an Aston Martin?"

"DB5. You know cars?"

"No, but I know James Bond."

"I bought her a couple of weeks ago. I'm not much for *stuff*, but I do have a bit of a weakness for classic cars."

If this is what he means by *classic cars*, maybe Rav has a

weakness for them, too. He's certainly feeling a little weak in the knees looking at this one. He hops in, and they pull out into the night.

The drive is magnificent. There's very little light pollution out here, so the stars are spectacular, and the breeze is scented with pine and the subtle tang of the sea. The road hugs the shoreline, winding dramatically along the rocky Mediterranean coast. To their right are towering ochre bluffs; to their left, the endless expanse of the sea, glittering silver-black under the moon. Jack rests a hand on Rav's thigh when it's not on the gear stick, and the smiles he flashes Rav's way are relaxed and beautiful. Rav is floating, drunk on this moment, and as impatient as he is to get his hands on the body next to him, he wishes this drive could go on forever. He tips his head back and closes his eyes, feeling the warmth of Jack's hand and the wind in his hair, and it's perfect.

They pass through a series of villages on the way, cruising along manicured boulevards lined with palm trees and olean-der and towering, cloud-shaped pines. The road rises and falls and rises again until Jack pulls up outside a wrought-iron gate. He brings up an app on his phone, and the gates part to reveal a long drive flanked with cypress, at the end of which sprawls an exquisite villa. Part of it looks to be at least a hundred years old, the rest glisteningly modern, stone and terra-cotta blending seamlessly into glass and hardwood. Jack is only too happy to defer the grand tour until after the welcoming festivities, and he leads Rav to a king-size bed looking out over the sea.

For a moment back there on the tarmac, it felt a bit like start-ing over, but it doesn't feel that way now. They might not have had much time together in New York, but they put it to good use, and already they're learning each other's bodies, how they respond and what they crave. Like the way Jack's skin tightens into tiny goose bumps in the heartbeat before Rav's lips brush it. Or how Rav melts when Jack kisses the soft hollow beneath his ear. Rav is obsessed with Jack's fingers, graceful and yet rough, callused from playing guitar. The feel of those calluses on his sensitive places—a nipple, his lower lip, the inside of his thigh—makes him thrum like a guitar string, and Jack knows it.

After, as Rav reclines contentedly against the overstuffed pillows, Jack picks up a remote from the bedside table. "Check this out." He presses a button, and the floor-to-ceiling windows glide apart, retracting until there's nothing between them and the sea but the cool night air.

"Stunning. Although . . ." Rav watches a mosquito drift in, drawn to their sweat-laced bodies. "I could do without mozzie bites on my tender bits."

"Yeah," Jack agrees, hitting the button again. "Beautiful, but maybe not that practical."

"Which, incidentally, is the working title of my obituary."

Jack laughs and tosses the remote away. "Wanna see the pool?"

"You know I do."

It's an infinity pool that seems to plunge into the glittering bay beyond. The sea laps gently against the rocks below, lifting salty breezes mingled with the spice of jasmine from the gardens. The temperature is divine, and they float contentedly with their elbows propped against the pool skirt, gazing out to sea. "*Beach house*," Rav snorts.

"Is it too much?" Jack looks adorably self-conscious. "I don't usually go for this kind of thing, but I thought it looked pretty romantic."

"*C'est pas mal*," Rav says, gathering him close and kissing salty pool water off his lips.

* * *

The ensuing forty-eight hours are quite simply paradise.

They get up late on Friday, but there's still plenty of day ahead. Rav would be content to lounge around the villa, but Jack has other ideas. Great ideas, as it turns out, involving more seaside drives, this time under the warm Mediterranean sun. He feels like he's in an episode of *Emily in Paris*, and it kills him—*kills him*—that he can't post a single picture of how amazing the two of them look in this car, with their sunglasses and wind-whipped hair. He settles for texting a few selfies to Ana and Mags. On Saturday, they go for a hike, which Rav quietly resents until they reach a summit overlooking the sea, and *wow*. More selfies. They spend the afternoon on the water, in a beautifully restored sailboat captained by a Greek woman with a delightfully bawdy sense of humor. Jack strums a ukulele he found at a flea market while Rav sips rosé and works on his tan. Later, they head belowdecks to escape the scorching sun and "have a nap."

It's so idyllic that Rav catches himself feeling a little melancholy while Jack dozes beside him. Because this can't last. This life . . . celebrities and villas and yachts . . . it's not his. The man sleeping next to him is not his, not really. He feels like he's rented a Ferrari, and sooner or later he's going to have to return it and get back in his turd-brown Golf.

"Hey." Jack is awake, watching him. "You okay? You look a little down all of a sudden."

"Already ruing the hangover I'm going to have." It's a version of the truth, anyway.

Jack props himself on his elbow. "What do you think about heading into town tonight? And before you answer, you should know that we might bump into Ryan."

They do bump into Ryan—along with every other celebrity in town, at a three-Michelin-star restaurant with a fabulous terrace overlooking the sea. The place positively oozes French elegance: crisp white linens, beautifully pruned boxwoods, sheer curtains that billow playfully through the open windows. Erika Strauss sits at the bar, wearing a slinky black dress and murderous heels, blond hair spilling down a plunging backline. She looks perfectly at ease, menu in hand, Cartier ring flashing as she toys with a glass of champagne. *Tough gig*, Rav thinks wryly. "Does Ryan always bring his bodyguard to fancy restaurants?"

"I don't think she gives him much of a choice."

"Mo gave you a choice, obviously." Rav glances around, but there's no sign of Jack's bodyguard.

"He's been great about giving me space over here, and he trusts me not to do anything stupid that'll put me in a tight spot. Ryan, though . . . I don't think Erika fully trusts his judgment, and I can't say I blame her. He can be a hothead."

"She's only been with him a couple of months. How much trouble can he have got into already?"

"She's been on tour with us before, though. And trust me, he put her through her paces."

"I'd say she's doing all right out of it. She fits right in on the Riviera. That dress is fantastic on her." He's not the only one who thinks so: there's a guy making eyes at her from down the bar. *Good luck to you, sir*, Rav thinks.

There's another familiar face here too, and Jack sighs as he spots Eloise making her way over. "Sorry to interrupt," she says, flashing Rav an awkward smile. "Ms. Reid said she needed your signature by close of business?" She hands over a document for Jack to sign and then scans it with her phone. "Great, thanks. I'm off."

"Why don't you stay and grab dinner?" Jack suggests. "There's room at the bar, and the food here is supposed to be amazing."

"Oh, I don't know . . ."

"My treat," Jack says. "Come on, El, you deserve it."

"Thanks." She gives Rav another tight smile and retreats.

"Does Eloise have a hang-up about cops?" Rav asks in an undertone. "She's always so nervous around me."

Jack shrugs. "She'll be fine once she gets to know you."

They chat briefly with Ryan and his date before making their way to their own table, Jack greeting his fellow glitterati as they pass. The Riviera is stuffed with celebs at this time of year, A-listers even Rav knows on sight. Bono is here, and Dame Helen, and . . . Is that Charlize? God, she's fabulous. Rav tries not to gawk, but it's hard, and even Jack gets a little fanboy when Bono raises a glass in greeting.

The server offers them some champagne to get started, followed by an amuse-bouche of dorado tartare with cucumber petals and delicately tweezed dill fronds. The whole thing looks like it's made of stained glass, but Rav resists the urge to take a photo. There are some things you just don't do, even for the 'gram.

A peal of feminine laughter sounds from a nearby table; Rav glances over to find Nash and his dinner companion practically sitting in each other's laps. Instinctively, he twists around to look at the bar and . . . yes, Eloise is watching.

Jack notices, too. "Maybe I shouldn't have encouraged her to stay."

So it's not Rav's imagination. "She's got a crush on Ryan?"

"Ever since she came over from Flashpoint. It's pretty awkward, honestly."

Rav's eyebrows go up. "Eloise used to work at Flashpoint?"

"For a couple of months, yeah. She was Vanderford's PA, but she quit after he started getting creepy with her."

"It wasn't listed on her employment history."

"I think she was afraid it would look flaky on her résumé, being there for such a short stint."

"Makes sense," Rav says, watching Eloise watching Ryan. "Wish you'd mentioned it before, though."

Jack looks startled. "You don't think . . . Rav, she *couldn't.* She can barely even look *you* in the eye."

"You'd be surprised what people are capable of. But no, I don't think your assistant killed Dick Vanderford. I *do* think I've just solved the mystery of how Ryan got the code to Vanderford's elevator." In all the fuss after the hoodie came to light, it hadn't seemed important. "Eloise probably had it saved in her phone, and he wheedled it out of her. Which means she probably knew about Ryan being there that night, or at least guessed, and she withheld it."

Jack sighs. "Does this mean she's in trouble?"

"That's up to the FBI, but if Ryan got off with misdemeanor obstruction, I doubt she has much to worry about."

Their soup arrives, the first of seven courses on tonight's tasting menu. Rav breathes in the heady aroma of truffles, but his brain is still snagged on something, a detail his subconscious isn't quite ready to surface.

Whatever it is, it'll have to wait. He's had too much wine and sunshine to think clearly; better to come back to it with fresh eyes tomorrow. For now, truffles.

Taking another deep draft of steam, Rav tucks into his soup.

CHAPTER THIRTY

After dinner, they head back to the villa to recline on the terrace with a couple of glasses of scotch. The walls of this main room retract as well, offering all the comforts of indoors in an outdoor space. These comforts include a piano, which Rav doesn't take much notice of until Jack settles in and starts playing. He's wearing that same look he had when Rav first set eyes on him, dark brows stitched as he runs through a haunting sequence of notes. The sight of him seated at that elegantly formal piano—this barefoot, tattooed rock star in swim shorts, gliding effortlessly through a beautiful string of music he's probably just composed on the fly—makes Rav a little lightheaded. "Are you writing?"

Jack nods and plays the sequence again. "I've been writing a lot lately. Guess you could say I'm feeling inspired." He glances over, and there's a glint in his eye Rav can't quite read. "I have a gift for you."

"More of a gift than this?"

"An early birthday present, since I won't be there to celebrate the real thing next week." He disappears into the bedroom, returning with a small lacquer box.

Rav takes it with halting hands. Whatever is in this box is going to *wreck* him, he just knows it.

"Are you going to open it?"

He does. And his breath stops.

It's an Indian Distinguished Service Medal. He recognizes it straightaway, with its profile of King George V and its blue-and-red ribbon. Gingerly, he lifts it out of the box and examines the engraving along the edge.

CAPTAIN PRAKASH TRIVEDI,
INDIAN MEDICAL DEPARTMENT

His great-great-grandfather's medal. The one he pawned all those years ago in a fit of adolescent spite. He's never been able to forgive himself, and now . . . "How?" he rasps.

"Luck, mostly, and the magic of crowdsourcing. Mo helped me. He knows a lot of ex-military types, and he pulled together a list of websites where collectors exchange information. I put the word out, offering a reward for information helping me track down the collector. It actually didn't take that long. He was cool about it, too. Once I explained the situation, he was happy to see it returned to the family."

Rav can't find his voice. Can't stop staring at the medal.

He can feel Jack's eyes on him. "I hope I'm not overstepping. It's just, I could see how much regret you were carrying, and I know what that's like. Most of the time, those big mistakes, you can't take them back. But this seemed like something it might actually be possible to fix. Like when we got our masters back. It healed this very deep wound that I'd been carrying around, and . . . I wanted that for you."

Rav's hands are shaking. He's thrilled to have his medal back, but that's not the overwhelming part. That Jack would do this for him, that it would even occur to him to try . . .

He looks up, meets Jack's eyes. *No half measures*, Eva's voice whispers in his head.

"I love you."

His stomach drops as soon as he says it. It's too much. Too soon. He's scrambling for a way to walk it back when he feels Jack's hand on his face, Jack's mouth on his. The kiss is soft and lingering, and when it's over, Jack sighs and rests his forehead against Rav's. "I don't think I realized it until this moment, but that's exactly the reaction I was hoping for."

"I . . ." Rav draws back and stares at him. "Really?"

Jack laughs, but his eyes are uneasy. "Are you that surprised?"

"Yes? Honestly, I wasn't sure if you were that serious about us."

"Bringing you here wasn't a clue?"

"I mean, I knew you were grateful about what happened with Miller . . ."

"Rav, grateful is a fruit basket. We're in France. On vacation together. I've spent the past month scouring the internet for your ancestor's war medal. I've told you every way I know how that I'm crazy about you. Why is it so hard for you to believe?"

"You must realize there have been mixed signals. You disappeared on me. For weeks."

"I know." He sighs. "I know I did, but it wasn't supposed to be mixed signals. I was trying to . . ." He shakes his head, as if he's not sure how to explain it. "My life is a train wreck right now. And maybe you think you're up for it, but however intense you think it's going to be, I promise you, it's going to be worse."

"So you're trying to . . . what, to shield me from your life?"

"Give you time away from it, at least. You've taken on so much of my shit already, and I wanted you to have a break from that. Some breathing space to think about things and decide if this is really what you—"

"It's what I want. *You're* what I want. I told you, we're in this together."

Jack rests his forehead against Rav's again. "Where did you *come* from?"

"Promise me you won't shut me out again. If this is real—"

"You might be the only real thing in my life right now."

"Then let me be here for you. No more keeping me at arm's length for my own good, or whatever it is you think you were doing. Promise me."

"Okay, if you promise me something." He sits back, meeting Rav's eye. "Stop waiting for the bottom to fall out. You've been doing it from the start, like it's inevitable. I know that's partly my fault. I can see how my backing off looked like maybe I wasn't feeling this. But it's more than that. It's like you think you're not enough, and that's just . . . it makes no sense to me, because you're such an amazing person. I'm blown away by you, Rav. Your compassion and your courage and your determination. What you're doing with Miller, what you did with Ryan and the security video . . ."

"I did that for you."

"In part, yeah, and that's . . ." He twines his fingers through Rav's and presses a kiss to his knuckles. "But we both know if I wasn't in the picture, you'd still be searching for the truth. Taking the hit if that's what it took to put things right. Because that's who you are, and it's beautiful. You're beautiful." He kisses Rav's hand again. "I've felt safe with you from day one. I want you to feel safe with me, too. This *is* real. You need to believe that."

It's going to take more than belief. Pretty much nothing about their lives makes sense together. Rav has no idea how they'll make it work.

But that's a question for later. Right now, it's enough to know they both want to try.

This is real. We're real.

"I love you," he says again, and this time, there's no chaser of fear.

Jack smiles. "I love you, too."

✳ ✳ ✳

It gets pretty crowded at the villa the next morning.

Ryan Nash shows up at a little after nine with his bass and a small amp. He's here to work out a few kinks in a song the Nicks have just added to their set. Erika is with him, and Eloise is due in a couple of hours to pick up the Aston Martin so it can be shipped back to the US. Rav isn't thrilled about sharing Jack for their last few hours together, but these guys are professionals and take pride in their work, and he understands that. He gives them space and heads out onto the terrace with his laptop.

He's just settling in when his phone buzzes. "Aisha. Shouldn't you be in bed?"

"Not much of a sleeper, especially when I'm working on something this juicy. What about you? I didn't really expect to reach you this early. Figured you'd be sleeping off a night of wild French sex or whatever."

He's about to tell her to mind her own business when he snags on something. "How did you know I was in France?"

"You told me."

He did? He doesn't recall doing so, but he's still super jet-lagged and can't really be sure of anything. "Anyway, you reached me. Does this mean you have something?"

"Those photos you asked me to dig up? I'm looking at them right now."

Rav sits up straighter, the cobwebs vanishing. "And?"

"I'm sending them to you now." There's a *swoosh* on the phone, and a moment later a message pops up in his inbox.

He double-clicks on the first photo. It's the selfie the FBI mentioned, the one supposedly taken outside Vanderford's apartment building. Joe Miller stands in the middle of the frame, the Manhattan skyline splashed out behind him; in the background, Dick Vanderford and a pretty redhead are walking along the waterfront. It's plausible enough. "What am I looking for?"

"Nothing. Absolutely nada. Every shadow, every glint of light—perfect. Same deal with the café photo."

"So they're legit?"

"I didn't say that."

"Aisha, please, I'm too jet-lagged for this. Have the photos been doctored or not?"

"They have. But it's beautifully done, and not just visually. Even the metadata checks out."

"Can that be manipulated?"

"Yes, but it's *very* hard to do well. Whoever doctored this photo did an amazing job. The tells are tiny."

"But you found them, because you're that awesome."

"I mean, yes, *obviously*, but you're not hearing me. This isn't just some rando tinkering with Photoshop. This guy is a pro. And that's not all. This Overwatch user you asked me to look into? His account is locked down *tight*. Which is weird. Most social media accounts are an easy hack. You could do it yourself with the right software. This one? Fucking Fort Knox. That means his password is regenerating on the regular. You know who does that?"

"Conspiracy theorists?"

"Professional hackers. The sort of people who know how to make a social media hack look like the work of Russians. Who could produce the most convincing deepfake video and doctored photos I've ever seen. My gut says all of it—the evidence against Miller, the phony blogger who tried to set you up, this Overwatch user—is the same person. Or *persons.*" She pauses dramatically. "So my question to you, Detective, is this: What if Miller isn't wrong, and the CIA really is behind this?"

"Come on. Why would the CIA want to kill Dick Vanderford?"

"No idea, but I am legit starting to feel nervous."

"Don't be. So there's a hacker involved. *You're* a hacker. New York is full of them, very few of whom work for the federal government."

She grunts, unconvinced.

"Is this solid enough to take to the FBI?"

"It's solid, but that doesn't mean there's no room for debate. It would take a very technical conversation with their digital forensics guys, and even then, there's no guarantee they'd agree."

He sighs. He's only going to get one shot at convincing the feds, so his case needs to be ironclad. He needs more.

"You should be careful, Rav. Whoever did this has already racked up at least two bodies. You don't want to be next."

"I appreciate your concern, but there's no need to worry. Thanks for this, and let's talk when I get back."

He slips his phone into his laptop bag so it's out of the sun, and then he studies the photo on his screen. He wonders who the redhead is. The photo is dated two days before the murder, so she might have useful information about Vanderford's final hours. Hell, she might even be the mystery date.

"Aren't you supposed to be on vacation?"

He looks up to find Erika coming through the sliding screen door, laptop in hand. He's not feeling very social, but he manages a bland smile. "Might as well make use of the time while Jack's busy, right?"

"Mind if I grab this seat? It's in the shade." She picks up Rav's stuff and shifts it to another chair. "Still on the Vanderford thing, huh?" She indicates his screen with a tilt of her chin. "I saw the article in the *Times*. Ballsy move, Detective. I'll bet the FBI was thrilled."

"Safe to say they were not."

"I'd be careful there. Those guys can really hold a grudge."

"Sounds like you speak from experience."

"Oh yes. We had our share of run-ins with them back in the day."

Rav starts to ask who *we* is, and then he remembers. "That's right, you and Mo were at Langley together, weren't you?"

She nods. "And like I said, we butted heads with the Bureau quite a bit. They're super territorial."

"I've noticed. But they'll get over it once I show them the proof."

"Figure you're closing in, do you?"

He shrugs, eyes back on his screen. "In my experience, it's largely a question of diligence. The evidence is out there. Finding it is about putting in the hours, doing the unglamorous stuff. Like looking through security footage." He's pulling it up now, double-clicking a saved file on his desktop.

"God, that sounds tedious. Surely you've gone through that a million times already?"

"A million and a half." But something's been bugging him since last night. Seeing that guy at the bar, working up the nerve to approach Erika—it made him think he's been going about this all wrong. He's been so caught up in the drama—hackers and CIA conspiracies and leaks to *The New York Times*—he's lost sight of the basics. Like the hole in the timeline the night of the murder, and the bottle of Petrus on Vanderford's coffee table. Dick Vanderford was expecting someone the night he was killed. Someone he picked up at a bar, maybe, or someone he already knew.

Like the redhead in the photo Aisha just sent. It's a long shot, but it can't hurt to go through the security footage one more time, on the off chance she appears.

The lads finish rehearsing at a little after eleven. Jack settles in beside Rav with an espresso while Ryan jumps in the pool. "Sorry about all this," Jack murmurs. "Did you manage to get some work done?"

"A little. I got a call from Aisha, and she's convinced those photos of Vanderford and Miller were faked."

Nash overhears from the pool, and he pauses, treading water. "There's photos of Vanderford and Miller? *Together?*"

"Supposedly," Jack says. "But I can't see Dick Vanderford hanging with a conspiracy theorist from small-town Georgia, can you?"

"Yeah, right. That guy was an elitist prick." Nash scrubs water off his face. "But why would someone bother to fake photos of them together?"

"Didn't you read the article in the *Times*? Rav thinks Miller is being framed."

Erika smirks at her laptop screen. "Guys. I'm pretty sure the FBI knows a manipulated photo when they see one."

"Rav's hacker friend has been on point so far," Jack says. "She's the one who helped him track Miller's phone, and told him about the fake Russians."

Erika's eyebrows go up. "Fake what now?"

"It's a long story," Rav says, cutting Jack a meaningful look.

"Sorry," he murmurs. "I'm the loose-lipped boyfriend in this movie, aren't I? I won't do it again, I promise."

Boyfriend. It still doesn't seem real, and for a second Rav just stares into those blue-green eyes like a sap.

Jack stands and stretches. "I've got a couple of quick calls to make, and then we should probably head to the airport." He pops his earbuds in and wanders off, and Rav goes back to his security footage.

It's not just tedious, it's bloody frustrating. Whoever installed the cameras in Vanderford's building did a shit job. The one in the elevator is mounted too high, so that if people have their heads down—which they nearly always do, looking at their phones—it doesn't get much of their faces. Even so, Rav goes through his spreadsheet diligently, checking each and every unidentified white female in the log. 8:44 P.M. 9:58 P.M. None of them resembles the girl in the photo. *This is a waste of time*, he thinks. *I'd be better off—*

He pauses. Jumps back. Hits play.

It's so fast you can barely see it: a hand comes out of a pocket, jabs a button, and goes back in the pocket.

Rewind.

Pause.

Rav zooms in. The woman is wearing a bulky windbreaker and a ball cap. She's looking down at the floor; between the hat and her chin-length black hair, her face is almost completely obscured. Rav hits play, watching in slow motion as she turns to punch the button for the twenty-third floor. Her hand comes out of her pocket, and—there it is.

A rose-gold ring in the shape of a panther.

He's seen that ring before. At a rock concert in Madison Square Garden, and again just last night.

On the finger of Erika Strauss.

CHAPTER THIRTY-ONE

Rav stares at his screen, mouth dry, heart pounding. He doesn't dare look up. Erika is sitting three feet away. He angles his laptop subtly away from her. The ring is barely visible through the glare on his screen, but there's no mistaking it. A Cartier panthère ring in rose gold.

Cartier is a massive brand. There are probably thousands of those rings out there. The woman's face is hidden, the color and cut of her hair all wrong. Nothing proves it's Erika Strauss on that screen.

Nothing except his gut.

She sneaks into the car park behind someone's vehicle. Waits for them to leave and then takes the elevator, but not to Vanderford's floor; she hits 23, just to throw us off. Then she bides her time for a while, waiting for Vanderford to show up. He's expecting her. She picked him up at a bar, probably wearing that same killer dress she had on last night. She's covered her tracks, paying in cash, using a burner phone, wearing a wig. Probably gave Vanderford some excuse why she needed to meet back at his place, so they wouldn't be seen together. He lets her in, thinking he's about to get lucky. One to the head, one to the chest, then she takes the stairs all the way down and goes out the way she came in.

Damn it, Trivedi, you were halfway there months ago.

He was right about the bodyguard, just wrong about which one. That's not his fault; Erika wasn't in the picture at the time. She joined the team after Vanderford was already dead and the investigation underway. But unbeknownst to him, she had a history with the band, and somehow that led to murder.

Okay, he thinks. Deep breaths. What's his play here? He doesn't dare confront her now. There's no telling what she'll do. Then there's Nash. Is he in on it?

God, this could get messy.

Rav reaches for his laptop bag, where his phone is stashed. How do you call 911 in France? Or maybe he should—

"Hey." Jack props himself against the table, breaking Rav's line of sight. "It's almost noon. We should really get going. Are you ready, Erika?"

She's supposed to be driving Rav to the airport. The last thing he wants is to get in a car with a murderer, but if that's what it takes to get her away from his boyfriend . . . "You should stay," he tells Jack. "No point in spending your last few hours of vacation in a car."

"He's right," Erika says as she tucks her laptop away. "After I drop him off, I've gotta pick up Mo, then back here for you guys, then straight back to the airport. It's a milk run."

Jack glances at his watch. "Maybe we should all go now."

"And spend three hours cooling your heels at that little airport when you could be drinking rosé by the pool? Don't be silly." Rav musters a smile, still rooting around in his bag.

"What are you looking for?"

"My phone. It's in here somewhere."

"Let me just get my shoes and we can go." He turns away, but Rav grabs his wrist.

"Jack." He forces another smile. "Stay. I'd feel better about it."

"What's with you?" Jack laughs. "Sick of me already? Hey, Ryan, when Eloise shows up, can you give her the keys to the Aston Martin? She's driving it to Marseille for me."

Rav casts about for some way to convince Jack to *stay the fuck here*, but Erika is watching, and the most dangerous thing he can do right now is give himself away. She doesn't know he's on to her. His best bet is to play it cool until it's safe to alert the authorities.

Jack is calling Rav's phone now. "It's going straight to voicemail. Is your battery dead?"

"It's on silent. Never mind, it'll turn up."

Rav collects his luggage and moves like a zombie toward the car. It's a half-hour drive to the airport. Thirty minutes to work out how to get Erika Strauss in handcuffs without putting Jack at risk. Is there a way to reach Mo without tipping her off? But wait, what if Mo is in on it? No, that doesn't make sense . . .

He's spinning out so much that he barely registers Eloise showing up in a rideshare. Jack gives her a few last-minute instructions about the Aston Martin, and then they're off, Jack and Rav stuffed in the middle seat of a van being driven by a murderer.

"You okay?" Jack threads his fingers through Rav's. "You seem distracted."

"Just a bit worried about my phone." Also, the cold-blooded killer sitting three feet away. He squeezes the hand in his, silently pleading with the universe to keep Jack safe.

Jack chats away as they drive, oblivious. Rav barely hears him, his eyes drilling holes in the back of Erika's head. The *things* this woman has done. Executing a man in cold blood, and for what? Because her client hated the guy? Then there's what came after. Greg Watson, gunned down in his own home. Joe Miller, on the run, so shit scared that he tried to kill the CIA bodyguard out to get him. Mo, still recovering from his gunshot wound. Most of all, Jack, terrified, looking over his shoulder night and day.

Anger chases fear in Rav's stomach, a swirling yin and yang that's making him nauseous. If Jack wasn't in this car . . .

What? You'd take out the trained killer with your bare hands?

They're coming into a village now, a line of traffic stacking up in front of them. "Uh-oh," Jack says. "Hope this doesn't make us late."

Rav glances instinctively at his watch, and his heart skips a beat. *The Marquesse.* His smartwatch has a panic function on it. He presses it discreetly—and then he remembers. His watch isn't set up for international SOS. He's just sent a beacon out into the void, where no one will hear.

Jack's phone rings. "Oops, that's Charlie. I'd better take this." He puts his earbuds in and glances out the window. "Hey, Charlie, what's up?"

Rav starts rooting around in his laptop bag again. He *knows* he put his phone in here . . .

"Looking for this?"

He glances up and meets Erika's eyes in the rearview. She's holding his phone—what's left of it. The screen is smashed. "Gotta hand it to you, Detective, you've got a great poker face. But you tried a little too hard to keep Jack out of the car."

Before the words can even sink in, she whips around; the last thing Rav sees is the butt of her .40 caliber pistol swinging at his face.

* * *

Reality creeps back in fragments: sore head, blurred vision, the smell of rubber and motor oil. He's in an old office chair, hands bound behind his back, a foul-smelling rag stuffed in his mouth and tied at the back of his head. There's a faint electric buzz overhead, but otherwise, all is quiet. Where is he? He remembers being in the car with Erika and . . .

Jack.

"*Jack!*" It comes out a muffled groan. Rav struggles to get his arms free, but his wrists are bound with some kind of strap, and there's no give to the knot.

A grunt sounds from a few feet away. Jack is sitting on the concrete floor, back against the wall, bound at ankle and wrist. There's an oil-stained rag in his mouth and a trickle of dried blood at his temple, but his eyes are clear. Rav tries to talk, but the words are swallowed by the rag. He manages to wriggle down in his seat, using the back of the chair to slide the rag up to the crown of his head until it's loose. He spits it out and shakes it free. "Are you all right?" he rasps.

Jack nods once.

"How's your breathing?" If he has a panic attack with that

rag in his mouth . . . But he nods again, and grunts something that sounds like "okay."

Rav scans their surroundings. It's dark except for a single fluorescent light overhead; by its flickering glow, he can just make out the outlines of Peugeots and Renaults in various states of repair. An auto garage. "Where's Erika?"

Jack nods toward the back of the garage. Rav can't twist around very far, but it looks like there's an office back there. *Dealing with the witnesses, most likely.* There'll be at least one mechanic tied up in that office, assuming Erika hasn't killed them already.

It's a messy play, bringing them here. She's improvising. "It's going to be all right," Rav says. "We'll get through this, I promise."

Jack nods resignedly.

"I don't think he believes you."

Erika Strauss steps into the light, and if Rav wasn't scared enough already, he bloody well is now. The woman before him bears little resemblance to the cool, take-charge personality he observed at the hospital that day. Sweat gleams on her brow as she paces under the flickering light, tapping the trigger guard of her Glock. She's a cornered animal, which makes her incredibly dangerous. If she feels trapped, she might decide killing them is her best option. Rav needs to give her a better one.

"A boat," he says.

"Shut up."

"The nearest harbor can't be more than a couple of miles away. Find a boat that'll get you across the Mediterranean, and you're home free."

"Shut up or I'll stuff that rag back in your mouth."

"Morocco, Tunisia, Algeria—none of them have extradition treaties with the US."

"Spending the rest of my life on the run in North Africa? No, thanks."

"Think this through, Erika. Charlie Banks was on the phone

with Jack when you attacked us. He'll have called the police by now."

"Charlie Banks heard a shout and then the line went dead. He'll probably assume we were in a car wreck. Maybe we drove over a cliff, just like Tommy Esposito."

"And no one saw? On the French Riviera? You're not thinking clearly. But there's a way out of this—"

"You can quit with the hostage negotiator shit. No one's coming for you, all right? I smashed our phones. We're on our own. So shut up and let me think."

Rav tests his bonds again, but it's a waste of time. That strap isn't going anywhere, at least not without some leverage. There's a knob at the small of his back, the sort used for raising or lowering the back of the chair. If he can hook the strap over it, maybe he can work it loose. He leans back as far as the chair will allow, straining to reach.

"Why couldn't you just leave well enough alone?" She's not looking at him, stalking back and forth with her eyes on the floor. "Dick Vanderford was a piece of shit. Christ, it wasn't even your case anymore. And you." She waves her gun vaguely in Jack's direction. "Of all the strays for you to bring home. A fucking *homicide detective*. Thanks for that, Jack, really." She shakes her head. "It wasn't supposed to go like this. For what it's worth, I'm sorry. You're a good guy, Jack. I never meant to put you in harm's way."

Jack stares up at her, his expression a mixture of anger and disbelief.

"Miller was supposed to be out of the equation right after Vanderford. But he turned out to be a slippery little shit. I couldn't track him down—"

"So you pointed him at Mo." The realization washes over Rav even as he says it. "Overwatch. It's you, isn't it? You created an online persona for the express purpose of whipping Miller into a paranoid frenzy. You hoped he'd get himself shot."

"*And he should have!*" She throws her hands up in impotent

fury. "Ángel Morillo is a beast. A fucking *legend*. And he gets taken down by some crackpot hillbilly? How does that happen?"

Because Mo isn't a cold-blooded killer like you. Aloud, Rav says, "I guess you did your job a little too well. You made Miller desperate, and desperate people are unpredictable."

"Yeah." Erika stops, looking thoughtful. "Yeah, you're right. Never underestimate a desperate man, right? Who knows what they're capable of?" She looks down at Jack and tilts her head. "Murdering their heroes, even."

It takes Rav a moment to grasp her meaning, and when he does, his blood runs cold. "Miller is on the other side of the Atlantic."

"Is he? Who's to say? If the authorities had any idea where he was, he'd be in custody by now."

Jack glances sharply at Rav. He understands now, too.

"Deep breaths, there, Jackie boy," Erika says. "I don't need you having a panic attack while I'm trying to think."

Rav arches his back, straining to reach the knob, the chair digging painfully into his arms. *Just an inch*, he thinks desperately. *Please, just give me one bloody inch . . .*

Erika crouches in front of Jack, her expression almost pitying. "You'll be immortal," she tells him. "Like John Lennon. And your poor boyfriend, gunned down trying to save you . . ."

"No one will believe it," Rav says hoarsely.

"It's not about what they believe. It's about what they can prove."

"Guess you'd know that better than anyone," says a new voice.

Fluorescent light glints off the muzzle of a gun, and out of the shadows steps Ryan Nash.

CHAPTER THIRTY-TWO

Erika stares at her client for several long seconds. Then she snorts and rubs her eyes. "Of course. If there's a way to fuck things up even more, you'll find it."

"Not sure things can get any more fucked up than this," Nash says grimly.

"And whose fault is that?"

Rav has no idea what's going on. Are they working together? If so, why is Nash eying her down the barrel of a 9mm?

"So," she says, rising from her crouch. "You followed me here, is that it? In the Aston Martin?"

"Fake photos." Nash dares a glance at Rav. "As soon as I heard you talking about fake photos and setting Miller up, I knew. It's straight out of her playbook. She used to be counterintelligence, did you know that?" He tilts his chin at Erika. "I made Eloise tell me the truth. About how you tricked her into giving you Vanderford's elevator code, telling her it was for me."

"At least I didn't seduce it out of her," Erika says sourly.

"I should have known it was you. Execution-style killing. Clean murder scene. Of *course* it was you." Nash starts toward Jack.

"Leave him," she snaps.

"Or what? Are you going to shoot me?" He crouches to untie Jack.

Jack spits out the gag and draws a ragged breath. "What the *fuck*, Erika?"

She ignores him. "So what now, Ryan, huh? If I go down, you go down."

"I never asked you to do any of this."

"No? *You've gotta help me, Erika. It was an accident. Please, Erika . . .*"

A muscle in Ryan's jaw twitches. "That's in the past."

"It *was* in the past, until you got it into that hot head of yours to take out Dick Vanderford."

"Ryan." Jack flicks a wary glance at his bandmate. "What is she talking about?"

A grim look settles over Nash. "Yes, I asked for your help back then. But that was different. It was an accident. I never meant for him to get hurt."

Oh, Rav thinks, his glance cutting instinctively to Jack. *Oh no . . .*

The wretched look on Nash's face seals it. Rav knows what's coming, and his heart aches for Jack.

"It was an accident."

"Shut up," Erika snaps. "For once in your life!"

Nash ignores her. He's looking at Jack now, his eyes pleading. "I was drunk. Pissed off. He was being *such* an arse that night. You know how he could get."

"No," Jack whispers, the blood draining from his face.

"He wanted me out of the band!"

Jack moans softly and folds over himself, as if he's been kicked in the gut.

"He was going to make you choose. Him or me. We both knew how that would go." Tears brim in Nash's eyes. "I tried to corner him at the party, but he wouldn't talk to me. He ripped out of there on his bike. I got in my car and followed him."

Jack curls into a ball, hands clamped over his ears, but Nash keeps talking. Erika looks on in disgust, and even though Rav's heart is breaking right along with Jack's, he takes advantage of her distraction to keep working at the strap. He's hooked part of it over the knob. If he can just get some leverage . . .

"He managed to lose me. I thought he'd decided to head back to the city. I just kept driving. I was out of it, crying and talking to myself. And I guess instinct kicked in, 'cause I started driving on the left, like I would back home. Next thing I know he's coming the other way on that tight corner, and—"

"And I get a phone call," Erika interrupts coldly, "from my fuckup client, begging for my help. Because he's already left the scene of the accident, and Tommy Esposito is lying dead at the bottom of a ravine, and Ryan here knows that best-case scenario, he's looking at vehicular manslaughter. But mostly, he just can't face Jack."

The scorn in her voice is too much for Rav. "You could have said *no*, Erika. You didn't have to help him cover it up. Stage the accident or pay off witnesses or whatever it is you did."

"You're right, I didn't. I felt sorry for him, and Tommy was past help, and I'm in the business of solving problems. That's on me, and I've been paying for it ever since."

Poor you. Rav keeps working at the strap.

"She did a shit job of it anyway," Nash says with a bitter smile. "The conspiracy theories started popping up straightaway. Miller was the worst. Posting all over the internet about the phantom car chasing Tommy on his motorcycle."

"He was right," Jack murmurs dazedly. "This whole time."

"Even a stopped watch is right twice a day," Erika says. "He wasn't a problem, not after I was done with him. Guys like Miller are easy to discredit. Hack his account, post a couple of threats, maybe a paranoid rant or two, and voilà. Certified crackpot."

"Yeah, you're so clever," Nash says. "Bit harder with a detective, though, innit? I should've seen your fingerprints all over that deepfake video of Jack. I suppose you got his social passwords from Eloise, too? Only that was a huge flop, wasn't it? Because you're not as smart as you think you are. Vanderford found out about Tommy, too, did you know that? He was trying to blackmail me. Told me if I didn't get Jack to drop the lawsuit—"

"Of course I knew, you dumb shit! He was trying to blackmail me, too! I was dealing with it. *Quietly.*"

That's when the last piece slots into place. *Did you hear about*

the private investigator? They found him in a shallow grave upstate . . .
Vanderford *did* hire Chris Novak, and he dug up the truth about
Tommy Esposito.

Poor bastard. He never would have seen it coming.

"It was under control," Erika goes on. "Then I asked Eloise for
Vanderford's elevator code, and she told me she'd already given
it to you. Wasn't hard to guess what for. Did you seriously think
you could pull something like that off? All you were gonna do
was get yourself arrested, and then what? You'd spill your guts,
like you're doing now. I wasn't about to let you take us both
down, so I did it right."

"*This* is doing it right?" Nash shakes his head. "No, enough.
This has gone way too far. We're out of here. Come on, Jack."

Erika racks the slide of her Glock. "*Sit. Down.*"

Nash raises his own gun and moves toward Rav.

"Uh-uh," Erika warns. "You untie that cop, I'll shoot him in
the head."

"No, you won't. I've got a gun too, remember?"

"Yeah, I see that. Digging around in my luggage, were we?
Do you even know how to . . ." She trails off, eyes narrowed, and
a moment later, Rav hears it too: police sirens, and they're definitely coming this way. He's so surprised he fumbles the strap he's
just worked free from his wrists; it hits the floor with a loud *slap*.

Erika looks at it, and then she looks up at Rav.

It all goes down in a heartbeat.

She raises her gun. Nash tries to shoot first, but the safety
is on; Erika whirls on him and fires—missing by a hair as Jack
shoves him out of the way. Now her weapon is pointed at Jack,
and Rav does the only thing he can.

He lunges.

Erika pivots; the gun goes off. Pain blazes across Rav's shoulder, but before she can get a second shot off, he tackles her. He
drives a fist into her face, then makes a grab for the Glock, bash-
ing her hand against the floor over and over. But he's hurting

from being pistol-whipped earlier, and she takes full advantage, throwing an elbow into his temple. White light flashes through his vision. He's so dizzy he tumbles off her, and she scrambles to her feet.

Rav hears a gun click—but not Erika's.

"Drop it." Jack has the 9mm, and he holds it as convincingly as any cop.

Erika wipes blood from her mouth. "Come on, Jack. Who are you kidding?"

"You don't know me, Erika." His face is pale but composed, his voice steady. "You think because I get panic attacks that I'm weak, or fragile, but you're wrong. Now drop it."

The moment stretches, thin as a razor blade.

Erika's arm jerks up—and Jack fires, putting a round in her chest. He puts another in her thigh, and she goes down with a cry. Rav scrambles over and kicks her gun away, but she's in no condition to reach for it anyway, gasping and writhing on the floor. Jack stands frozen, lips pressed into a thin, bloodless line. Gingerly, Rav lifts the gun from his boyfriend's shaking hands. "You're all right, love," he murmurs. "You did it."

The gendarmes burst through the door a second later, guns raised and shouting, and Rav has never been so grateful that he speaks fluent French. There's a few moments of confusion, and then he's got his arms around Jack, and Erika is being put in restraints, and Rav is vaguely aware of Ryan Nash slumped on the floor and a trio of terrified auto mechanics being escorted out of the building, but it's all happening on the other side of some invisible, watery barrier. In here, there's only Rav and Jack, clinging to each other.

He's not sure how much time passes, but when the world starts to sink in again, he sees Mo threading his way through the tangle of law enforcement. "You okay, boss?" the bodyguard asks, not quite able to meet his client's eye.

Jack nods vaguely, still lost in a haze of shock.

"How 'bout you?" Mo's glance falls to Rav's bloodied shoulder. "I'll get some EMTs over here. They're looking after Erika, but they can let her bleed out as far as I'm concerned."

He doesn't mean it. He's just heartsick, like the rest of them. Mo and Erika go way back. Today's revelations will be as painful for him as they are for Jack.

"How are you here?" Rav asks him. "Did Ryan call you?"

"That can wait. Take a load off, both of you."

They do as they're told, sinking to the floor and huddling together while the chaos carries on around them. Rav's ears are still ringing from the gunshots, and his mouth tastes like blood and adrenaline. Questions are buzzing in his head like flies. But right now, the only thing that matters is the person nestled against him. Rav rests his head against Jack's and closes his eyes, and everything else can wait.

✳ ✳ ✳

"Spyware. You installed *spyware* on my smartwatch?"

Aisha is unapologetic. "If I hadn't, you'd probably be dead."

He can't deny it, but still. How long has she been keeping tabs on him? "That day you asked to look at my watch—is that why you wanted to see it?"

"It wasn't the *only* reason. But look, you must realize that having you around is a risk for me. Not everything I do is strictly legal, so I figured it couldn't hurt to keep an eye on you in case you got any funny ideas about burning me."

"I wouldn't do that, Aisha."

"I didn't think you would, but if these past couple of days have proved anything, it's that nobody really knows anybody."

He can't argue with that, either.

He glances down at his watch. "So, when I hit the panic button . . ."

"An alarm came through on my phone. I cued up the camera and mic, and when I realized what was going on, I called the police in Cannes and passed on the GPS coordinates."

"Does that mean you recorded the conversation in the garage?"

"Every word. Figured you might need the evidence later, but man." The voice on the phone grows subdued. "It was tough to listen to. Poor Jack."

Rav's glance strays to the far side of the hotel suite, where Jack and what's left of the New Knickerbockers are crashed out on the sofa, just . . . dealing. Jack's got his arm around Sarah. Claudia is knitting quietly, sniffling every now and then as she swipes a tear from her cheek. They've got some tough decisions ahead, but for now, they're just here for each other.

"What about you?" Aisha asks. "How are you holding up?"

He rolls his stitched-up shoulder, but he knows that's not what she means. "Okay. My friend Mags is coming down from London tomorrow. It'll be nice to see a friendly face. As much as I'd like to go home, Jack needs me right now."

"The press must be all over him."

"Yeah." Rav pushes the curtain aside and looks down at the gaggle of reporters on the street below. It gets bigger every day as journalists fly into Paris to cover the story—and they don't even know the half of it yet. Ryan Nash is working with his lawyers, preparing to come forward about his role in the death of Tommy Esposito. That's when the shit will *really* hit the fan. For now, the Nicks' publicist is working overtime to keep the lurid details out of the headlines. All the public knows is that Jack Vale was involved in a police incident near Cannes, and someone affiliated with the Nicks is in custody for the murder of Richard Vanderford. Rav's name has been kept out of it, much to his relief.

"Well, you got your proverbial man, at least," Aisha says. "That's gotta be some consolation."

"Does it? She was right under my nose the entire time."

"Cut yourself some slack, Rav. The woman is a professional counterintelligence agent." Wryly, she adds, "And can I just say, it's very on-brand that you caught her because you noticed her *outfit*."

He laughs ruefully. "Her jewelry, to be precise. Let's hope that little detail doesn't get out. My colleagues would never let me live it down." He pauses, his smile fading. "I never would have caught her without your help. You're the only one who was willing to keep pulling the thread with me. I owe you one, Aisha."

"You owe me a lot more than one, Detective. And I fully intend to cash that check one day."

Rav doesn't doubt it for a second.

CHAPTER THIRTY-THREE

It's another five days before the truth about Ryan Nash hits the headlines, and it sets the internet on fire. The band puts out a statement asking for privacy in this difficult time—which of course the media ignore, multiplying outside the hotel until the police order them to disperse. Jack and Rav stay holed up in their suite, waiting for the storm to blow over. The rest of the *Background* tour has been postponed indefinitely, and after a great deal of agonizing, Jack and his bandmates have come to a decision. The New Knickerbockers are no more.

"It's fitting, don't you think?" Jack murmurs against Rav's shoulder. They're curled up on the sofa, watching old seasons of *Top Chef* and diligently avoiding their new phones. "The Nicks were born in an auto garage, and they died in an auto garage. There's a nice symmetry to it."

Rav kisses the top of his head. "The Nicks will never really die. They're immortal, like the song says."

"Do you think Ryan will be okay?"

"I expect he'll serve time. How much will depend on the lawyers."

"I was thinking more about his state of mind. He's been carrying that secret a long time. Maybe now he can start to heal."

Rav looks down at him. "You have an amazing heart, you know that? To be able to forgive him after everything he's done."

"I'm not saying I forgive him. I'm not ready for that, but that doesn't mean I want to see him suffer."

"He let you believe Tommy took his own life. He saw what

that guilt was doing to you, and he just let it happen." All those showy gestures of loyalty, his *Jack is my brother*s and *I got you, mate*s. It makes Rav sick.

"That's the hardest part," Jack says. "The accident . . . it came out of nowhere, and he panicked. But it's hard to understand the choices he made after that."

"I hope *you* can start to heal, now that you know the truth."

"It'll be a process. Tommy's death might have been an accident, but that doesn't change the fact that I wasn't there for him when he needed me. We were all struggling with this huge upheaval in our lives, but Tommy was drowning and we didn't see it. *I* didn't see it. That's why I believed the story about him taking his own life. Self-care is important, but it can't come at the expense of showing up for the people who need you, and that's something I'll always regret."

Rav sighs. "Death and regret go hand in hand, don't they? I don't think you can lose someone close to you without feeling guilty about *something*."

"Maybe, but I need to own my mistakes before I can move past them." He shifts, looking up at Rav. "I will, though. Move past them. For the first time since Tommy died, I feel like I can get there."

"Of course you can. You're the strongest person I know."

Jack's mouth quirks. He thinks Rav is bullshitting him.

"I mean it. Do you know what was going through my head when you had that gun pointed at Erika? That of all the people she'd underestimated so far, this was her biggest mistake. I thought, this man was prepared to go to prison to protect a friend. He risked his life pushing that same friend out of the path of a bullet. He's absolutely fearless when it comes to protecting the people he cares about. If she thinks he's not going to pull that trigger, she's a fool." He cups Jack's chin and looks him in the eye. "You saved my life. You are a *total* badass."

"Right back at you," Jack says, and kisses him.

Rav spends his thirtieth birthday in the most romantic city

in the world—cooped up in a hotel room. Mags has come and gone, and Claudia and Sarah, too, so it's just the two of them. Jack already gave Rav his present back in Cannes, but he buys another: a record player and fifty "essential" albums going back to the 1930s. The history of rock and roll, as curated by Jack Vale. They sip thirty-year-old Macallan and listen to music until the wee hours, Jack narrating his favorites with a passion and depth of knowledge that takes Rav's breath away. It's so sexy he can hardly keep his hands to himself, and by the seventies he gives up trying, tugging at the buttons of Jack's jeans and backing him toward the bed as Mick Jagger croons about wild horses.

At some point, the needle hits the edge of the grooves, and the arm swings quietly back to its cradle. The record spins on, silent and unattended.

It's the best birthday he's ever had.

✳ ✳ ✳

Rav deposits his suitcase by the door. "Rav goes to the airport, take two."

"Let's hope it goes better than last time," Jack says, looking up from his guitar with a rueful smile.

"Are you sure I can't convince you to come with me? I don't like the idea of you being alone." He would stay, but the department's patience has run out. Family emergency or no, they want their detective back on the job.

Jack shakes his head. "The circus travels with me, remember? You don't need that. Besides, I really need to see my family. I'm thinking of renting a cabin in the woods somewhere. Montana, maybe, or Wyoming. Someplace my folks can visit without being mobbed." He sighs and peers out the window at the journalists gathered below.

"How many today?"

"Not many." Bitterly, he adds, "Too busy hounding Tommy's dad."

It's been that way since the news about Ryan broke. Nobody

cares about the police incident in Cannes anymore, or the murder of Dick Vanderford. The story is Ryan and Tommy, and the "deadly rivalry" that claimed Tommy Esposito's life. "Informed sources" are coming out of the woodwork to claim the two couldn't stand each other; that Ryan Nash is an alcoholic; that Jack Vale had his suspicions about what happened that night but never told the cops. Reporters have been gathered outside the Esposito residence in Bushwick for days.

"I wish there was something I could do to take the heat off," Jack says. "Tommy's family has been through so much already, and now it's being dredged up all over again. I just want to wave my arms and go, *Over here! Come and get me!*"

"Well, if you really want to distract the T-Rex, it's easily done."

"How's that?"

"Your publicist did a great job of keeping the details about Cannes out of the papers, but is there any point anymore? The Nicks are through. Ryan's story is out there. Why not tell the rest? What happened in that auto garage is far more sensational than a three-year-old motorcycle accident. And you're the star of the show, the badass who took Erika down. If you want to shift the focus to you, all you have to do is tell your story."

Jack mulls that over. "But how do we do that without bringing you into it?"

"We don't," Rav says, ignoring the nervous flutter in his belly. "Every good story has a romance, right?"

"No way." Jack shakes his head. "I won't ask that of you. You've taken enough bullets for me."

"It's hardly a bullet. I'll have some photographers following me around for a while, like last time. No big deal."

"It won't be like last time." Jack sets his guitar aside and fixes Rav with a serious look. "Before, you were just a rumor. Twenty-four-hour clickbait. This would be a whole other level. They'll dredge up everything. Every photo, every tweet, everything you ever wanted kept private. Your entire life in the public domain."

"People are going to find out about us eventually."

"Not like this. If we tell this story—the *whole* story—it'll be front-page news."

"That's the idea. If we do it right, Tommy's accident will be a footnote. With a little luck, they'll leave his family in peace."

Jack stares at him for a long time, visibly conflicted. "You understand, once that genie is out of the bottle, there's no putting it back. Your life will never be the same."

"I know."

"I mean it, Rav. Everything will change. Forever." There's an edge to his voice, a hint of mounting anxiety. They're in the fall-out zone here, dangerously close to the source, but Rav steers them away with a confident smile.

"We've had this conversation, remember? You don't need to shield me from your life. At least this way, it'll be on our terms."

Jack nods slowly. "So how do you want to do it?"

"I've got a friend at the *Times*. She'll do the story right, but in the meantime . . ." Rav glances at his watch. Still a few minutes before he needs to leave. "Shall we give them a preview?"

They take the elevator down together. Jack's got his windbreaker on, hood pulled up to hide his face as he walks through the lobby. Mo is waiting for them by the front desk. "You guys sure about this?"

Jack looks at Rav.

Rav looks through the glass doors at the journalists waiting on the sidewalk, and his stomach knots. For all his brave words, this is fucking *terrifying*.

"You don't have to do this," Jack says.

Rav threads his fingers through Jack's. "No half measures."

Mo heads out first, followed by the bellhop with Rav's suitcase. The photographers recognize Jack Vale's bodyguard, and by the time Jack and Rav join him on the sidewalk, they're clustered in close.

Jack's eyes are wet as he tugs his hood back. "I love you," he whispers. "So fucking much."

He reaches for Rav, and the shutters start snapping.

* * *

The kiss is all over Rav's timeline by the time he lands at JFK.

NICKS' FRONT MAN JACK VALE IN HOT AND HEAVY PARIS ROMANCE

IS IT LOVE? INSIDER SOURCE CONFIRMS JACK VALE COP AFFAIR "SERIOUS"

He's got about a zillion messages, too. There's Ana: **So can i call him your boyfriend now?** And Mags: **You little scandal! call me ASAP.** Various college friends he hasn't heard from in ages. And, of course, Eva.

> **Don't worry, darling, your father is
> on new blood pressure medication
> and I'm told it's very effective.**

Rav laughs darkly. Wait until His Lordship hears the rest of it. His head might actually explode.

He wonders who the "insider source" is. Mo, maybe, or Charlie Banks? Whoever it was knew just how to reel them in, using words like *fairytale* and *storybook* and *love at first sight*. It's done the job: Rav scans the major tabloids, and there's almost nothing about Tommy's accident. It's been pushed out of the headlines, at least for now. The only thing sexier than death is sex, especially when it involves a media-shy celebrity like Jack Vale. This is the first time he's gone public with a romance, and the fact that it's with a guy makes it that much juicier. It won't distract the T-Rex for long, but this was just an appetizer; the main course is yet to come. Rav calls Carrie Campbell at the *Times* and sets her up with Jack's publicist. "Thanks for this," he tells her. "I know it'll be a rush."

"Are you kidding? If even half of what you just told me is printable, you've made my year."

It's on the front page the next morning. Below the fold, but still. Rav braces himself for the tsunami of media attention he's about to get—not to mention the ball-busting at work.

As usual, the squad doesn't pull any punches.

"Bro, could you be any more of an attention whore?"

"Damsel in distress is a good look on you."

"Snooped on by your own CI. That's some top-notch police work."

And so on. Rav lets them have their fun. There's only one voice in this peanut gallery he cares about, and he's coming in for a hug. "Good to have you back, man," Shepard says, slapping his back warmly. "Sounds like it was a close call in that garage."

"As close as they come. She had us dead to rights. For a second there, I was sure . . ."

The whole squad room goes quiet. There are a few knowing nods from guys who've been there. Then Ayalew thumps him on the shoulder. "Yeah, but she didn't know who she was messing with."

"*Detective McDreamy*," Jiménez says in Movie Trailer Voice, and everyone busts up. Jobs digs out a half-empty bottle of rye, and Ayalew fetches a bunch of crusty coffee cups from the sink, and while Rav does not love this idea, he reasons that the booze will probably kill whatever's growing in there. Jobs metes out a splash into each cup, and they drink a toast to Detective McDreamy, which Rav supposes he's stuck with for life.

A little later, Lieutenant Howard summons him to her office. "Interesting article."

"I cleared it with the spokesman's office—"

"That's not why I called you in here. I just got off the phone with the Bureau. They're doing their usual follow-up, dotting their i's and crossing their t's before they close the file. They mentioned you'd be hearing from them soon. There's an opening coming up in CID. You're encouraged to apply."

Rav stares. "They're offering me a *job*?"

"It's the closest they'll come to admitting they were wrong.

You're the only one who saw through the smoke screen Erika Strauss was throwing up. They're impressed."

"I should have worked it out sooner."

"There was a hell of a lot of noise drowning out that signal. What counts is that you stuck with it, even when it wasn't yours to stick with."

"Maybe, but I—"

"Take the win, Detective," she says, gently but firmly. "You earned it."

It's high praise from Howard, and he feels himself smiling. "Does this mean I'm forgiven?"

"Get out of my office."

He settles back into his usual routine pretty quickly, and by the end of the week, it's starting to feel like life has almost returned to normal, plus or minus a tabloid photographer or two. There's just one more piece that needs slotting into place, and luckily, he doesn't have to wait long.

Joe Miller turns himself in to the NYPD on the first of August. In keeping with his penchant for drama, he insists on doing it in a public place, on the waterfront in South Williamsburg, with Dick Vanderford's building looming in the background. Carrie Campbell is there for the *Times*, along with a handful of other journalists. It's Rav who takes him into custody, again at Miller's insistence. Detective Trivedi is the only cop he trusts, or so he says; Rav reckons it has at least as much to do with wanting to be arrested by Jack Vale's boyfriend.

"I told you," Miller says triumphantly as Rav puts the restraints on him. "I told *everyone* that Tommy was murdered, but nobody listened."

"It wasn't murder," Rav points out. "Ryan Nash was responsible, but it was an accident."

"You keep telling yourself that, man."

Rav lets it go. "You're doing the right thing. It'll go a long way with the DA, trust me."

Miller swallows, his bravado fading. "You'll speak for me at the hearing?"

"I'll speak to the facts."

"That's all I ask." Raising his voice for the benefit of the assembled journalists, he adds, "All I've ever wanted was the truth!"

You keep telling yourself that. He's probably already pitching his memoir to publishing houses and fantasy-casting his Netflix movie. Whatever. As long as he's out of Jack's life, that's what counts.

The uniforms start to escort him away, but Miller pauses and looks back over his shoulder. "Tell Jack . . ." His gaze falls. "Tell him I'm sorry."

Rav nods. Then they put Joe Miller in a cruiser and drive away.

∗ ∗ ∗

"It's over. All of it."

Jack is quiet for so long that Rav wonders if the Wi-Fi has frozen. "Some part of me didn't think it ever would be. For a while there, it felt like Miller was some kind of cosmic punishment." He gives himself a little shake, and then he smiles. "Feels like I can breathe again."

"The fresh air obviously agrees with you." His hair is longer, and the dark stubble on his jaw brings out the startling hue of his eyes. "I'm not usually into the feral mountain man look, but it works on you."

"When in Rome, right?" He pivots his phone, showing Rav the incredible view of the Rocky Mountains behind him.

"Stunning. I'm envious."

"You could come out for the weekend."

"I wish. A new case just landed in my lap. I'll be burning the midnight oil for a while."

"Well, break a leg, or whatever it is you supercops say."

"Thanks. What about you? Any plans?"

"I'll probably stay out here for a few more weeks. It's been good for me. After that . . . Sarah and Claudia and I are talking about starting a new project, but I'm thinking of touring on my own first. Nothing big, just some smaller US venues. I've been doing a lot of writing here, and I think it might be my best stuff yet. There's just one problem." He brings the phone close, his face filling the screen. "I miss you like crazy. I need to see you soon, or these will all turn into sappy love songs."

Rav laughs. "We can't have that."

"When do you think we can manage it?"

"I don't know. It's a bit hard to make plans at the moment." It feels bigger than he meant it to, that statement. Jack is on the other side of the country, and neither of them knows what comes next, and—

"That's okay." Jack smiles. "We'll figure it out."

"Yeah," Rav says, smiling back at him. "Yeah, I think we will."

ENCORE

The last notes of "Pretty Parachute" have long since faded away, but the crowd is still singing, the triumphant *oh-oh-OHs* of the fade-out chorus rising and falling under the gilt ceiling of the Concord Theater. Rav wouldn't have thought anything could match the atmosphere of the MSG show last year, but there's something about the intimacy of this smaller space that makes the experience incredibly special.

"Wow," Jack says when the chorus finally dies away. "Y'all are spoiling me tonight." He waits for the cheers and whistling to pass. "I mean it, truly. I've been all over the place these past twelve months, but New York"—he pauses for another swell of cheers—"New York, you still feel like home."

Someone in the crowd calls something out to him. Rav can't hear what they're saying, but Jack nods. "That's true," he says into the mic. "And yeah, it was a rough ride there for a while. But New York gave me something, too. Something amazing." His gaze sweeps the VIP area and finds Rav, and he points. "That guy right there." The spotlight hits Rav full in the face, and it's *blinding*.

"Oh shit," Ana says, and starts laughing. Will is laughing too, throwing his arm up against the glare.

Jack's grin turns mischievous. "Y'all wanna meet him?"

"Don't you *dare*, Vale," Rav hisses. Jack can't hear him, but he can bloody well see the look on Rav's face.

"They wanna meet you, Rav. Come up and say hi."

"No," Rav growls, but Ana is pushing him, and Will too,

shoving him toward the stage, and the crowd is parting to make way and then Mo is there, reaching for him from the no-man's-land between event security and the stage. Rav gives the bodyguard a pleading look, but Mo just winks and says, "Sorry, man, the people have spoken," before boosting him up onto the stage.

Rav spends thirty *very long* seconds giving his boyfriend the stink eye while the crowd whistles and cheers. Jack grins, perfectly aware of how mortified Rav is and enjoying it altogether too much. There's nothing to do but play it up, so Rav jams his hands in his pockets and strikes a playfully irritated stance, and when Jack finally walks over and tips the mic toward him, Rav says, "You're a bastard."

The crowd loves it. They cheer and laugh and call out all sorts of nonsense, and by rights Rav should be proper annoyed, but Jack's smile in that moment could light up the world and it's impossible to be anything but squishy looking into those eyes, so he just shakes his head and pulls Jack's head into a kiss. The crowd goes crazy again, and Rav sweeps into a mocking bow and walks off stage.

"Detective Rav Trivedi, ladies and gentlemen," Jack says, still grinning. Then he signals to the drummer and they kick into "Tornado."

Rav spends the last couple of songs backstage, nursing his dignity over a scotch, and by the time he makes his way back to the mixing desk, it's time for the encore. Jack takes the stage alone, perching on a stool with his guitar. The crowd goes quiet as he plucks out the first few notes, and Rav's breath catches as he recognizes the tune.

> *All those little moments I recall / Hang like pictures on my wall / The truth just out of frame / Gallery of my shame . . .*

He's never performed this song before, and Rav can hear the trepidation in those first notes. But somehow that only makes it more poignant, and as Jack loses himself in it, the audience is swept along with him, holding up their phones and bathing the auditorium in a cool blue glow. *"In the blinding storm / I couldn't see / I see you now / I hope you're free . . ."* He sings so beautifully it hurts, and when he reaches for the high note—sad and sweet, his voice scattering like smoke—Rav feels the prick of tears behind his eyes. He knows what this moment means to Jack, how long he's waited to sing what was in his heart. *I hope you're free too, love,* he thinks.

After the show, the usual VIPs gather backstage. There's talk of decamping elsewhere for an after-party, but Jack has other ideas. He does his rounds with lightning speed, and then he's herding Rav to the car. Rav assumes they're going back to the hotel, but instead they turn east toward Gramercy Park. "Where are we going?"

"There's something I want to show you."

The car deposits them at the curb on East Seventeenth. A few passersby do double takes as Jack Vale mounts the steps of a brownstone with magnificent bay windows. Rav follows him inside, and his jaw goes slack as he takes in the gorgeous interior. Parquet floors and nineteenth-century moldings, sumptuously patterned wallpaper and bold velvet furnishings. To the left, a walnut staircase curves gracefully to the second floor; at the foot of the hall, an elegant archway hints at the sprawling square footage beyond. "I didn't realize there was a boutique hotel on this street," Rav says.

"There isn't. It's a private residence."

Rav looks at him. "You're renting it?"

"For six months. I figured since I'm going to be in town more often, it would be nice not to have to stay in a hotel all the time. After that, who knows." He shrugs self-consciously. "Maybe it makes sense for me to buy a place."

"Here? In New York?"

"Yeah. I mean, no pressure or anything, I just—"

Whatever else he was planning to say is lost in the sort of kiss that really ought to come with its own dramatic swell of music. Rav has half a mind to scoop him off his feet and carry him straight up to bed, but a troubling thought holds him back. "Are you sure you want to do this? After everything that's happened to you here?"

Jack shrugs. "Like I said earlier, there have been a lot of lows in this town, but a lot of highs, too. I never really loved LA, and I haven't lived in Atlanta since I was a kid. I'm not sure where home is anymore, except . . ." He puts a hand on Rav's chest. "This is home."

Rav doesn't know what to say. He's no poet like Jack; he can't put into words what's in his heart. He rests his forehead against Jack's, and he doesn't say anything at all.

There's a fireplace in the main room, and a pair of comfortable-looking sofas. Jack builds a fire while Rav acquaints himself with the contents of the bar, and then they settle in, whiskeys in hand, watching the fire rustle and snap. Or at least, Rav is watching it; Jack is watching him. Rav meets his eye, and they stare at each other for so long that Rav finds himself contemplating the precise curve of Jack's eyelashes.

"Your eyes are the color of amber," Jack muses.

"What?"

"Your eyes. They're the color of amber."

"The color of amber is amber. You don't actually have to say the *color* part."

"Has anyone ever told you you're pedantic?"

"It's come up once or twice."

"Or honey. Dark honey."

Rav narrows his amber/dark-honey eyes. "Are you writing a song? Right now, in your head?"

"No." He laughs. "Maybe."

"We've talked about this. No sentimental love songs. Your rep as an edgy rock star would be ruined."

"Maybe I should reboot my brand. I could pull off an Ed Sheeran vibe, don't you think?"

"Dear god."

"Hey, if you can change up your life, I can, too."

"Who says I'm changing up my life? I'm thinking about it, that's all."

"You're more than thinking about it, if those law school applications I saw in your kitchen are anything to go by."

Rav gives him a wry look. "A blanket thief *and* a snoop. Anything else you'd like to disclose?"

"Does that mean you decided to pass on the FBI job?"

"For now. There'll be other opportunities, if I decide to go that route."

Jack sets his empty glass aside. "So what now? A new master plan?"

"Let's call it a strategic review for now." Rav sips his whiskey while Jack nestles into the curve of his shoulder. His eyes are just starting to close when Rav says, "Are you sure it doesn't bother you?"

"What?"

"You're talking about uprooting your life, moving across the country for me, and here I am being wishy-washy about my future."

"I think it's great you're considering your options. Besides, you've spent the past year being there for me. It's my turn." He yawns expansively. "You'll figure it out, and in the meantime, that's what this place is for. We can nest here for a while. Get a dog or something."

Rav snorts into his whiskey. "Do I strike you as a dog person?"

"That's the cool thing about relationships, though. You never know where you'll end up. If I think back to how this all started, with a couple of cops interrogating me in my hotel room . . . Who could have imagined we'd end up here?"

Who indeed? Some days, Rav still has trouble imagining it.

"We've got options, and we've got each other," Jack says sleepily. "That's enough."

Rav has never been *enough* before. Not for his parents. Not for himself. But he believes Jack when he says Rav is enough for him. This, he reckons, must be what it is to feel safe.

You're reminding me what that feels like, Jack told him once, but it's the other way around. Jack is the one reminding him.

Outside, dawn is breaking. Rav watches the sun come up, a new day spreading its orange wings over the city. If New York is anything, it's possibilities. Possibilities and people, just like Jack says. Rav doesn't know how they fit into that yet, but it doesn't matter.

This, right here, is enough.

ACKNOWLEDGMENTS

The journey this story took to reach the shelves was long and complicated, with plenty of plot twists and heartache along the way. There were times when I wasn't sure we would ever get here, with a reader holding this book in their hands. But here we are, and there are so many people to thank. Don, for never letting me waver, even when I wanted to. Jaleigh Johnson, who provided such insightful feedback and steadfast moral support. My amazing agent, Amanda Jain, who knew just how to pitch this quirky, cross-genre tale. Vanessa Aguirre, whose thoroughness and sharp eye for detail would impress even Rav. Kelley Ragland and Anne Marie Tallberg, who were willing to take a chance on something different. Sandro Carrà, who patiently answered my oddly specific questions about the NYPD. The BookEnds squad, who are always ready to workshop titles and taglines. And everyone at Minotaur who had a hand in getting this book out into the world: Catherine Richards, Alisa Trager, Ginny Perrin, Amy Carbo, Meryl Levavi, David Rotstein, Peyton Stark, Rowen Davis, Janna Dokos, Sara Eslami, Allison Ziegler, Paul Hochman, Angela Tabor, Esther de Araujo, Emma Paige West, and Drew Kilman. And finally, Anvita Patwari for the thoughtful authenticity read.

Heartfelt thanks to each and every one of you. We did it.

ABOUT THE AUTHOR

Erin Dunn loves twisty mysteries and swoony rom-coms, so she decided to combine the two. A native of Calgary, Canada, Erin has lived in Brooklyn long enough to officially call herself a New Yorker, or so she is informed. When she's not writing, you can find her playing music, cooking, or sampling other people's cooking.